THE RESURRECTION
of Dylan McAthie

a pine bluff *novel*

NANCEE CAIN

Serrated Edge Publishing

Serrated Edge Publishing
PO Box 969
Jasper, AL 35502
www.nanceecain.com

First published June 2017

ISBN: 978-0-9976139-3-3

10 9 8 7 6 5 4 3 2 1

Editor: Jessica Royer Ocken
Cover Design by Shannon Lumetta
Interior Book Design by Coreen Montagna

Printed in the United States of America

For Carrie and Vickie.
You were Dylan's first fans.

Chapter One

Paparazzi. The fucking bane of his existence, and the price he paid for fame. Escaping them used to be fun, and over the years he'd become a pro at avoiding the scumbags. *But this? This* was the most complicated escape plan to date.

To pass the time and keep his mind off the discomfort of being unable to move, Dylan McAthie—lead guitarist of the now-defunct rock band Crucified, Dead and Buried—ticked off his best avoidance tactics in his head:

1. Hide in a nasty bathroom and wait out the bastards.

2. Pull a coat over my face to thwart their money shot.

3. Utilize a decoy.

And his personal favorite:

4. Smash the cameras.

Unfortunately, he knew from experience that last one was costly.

Dylan clenched his teeth, fighting the urge to shift and relieve his aching side. Somewhere he'd read it was impossible to hurt in more than one place at the same time. That was a load of bullshit. Right now, it seemed a two-way duel between his side, where the chest tube had been removed, and his leg, which was still healing. And his inability to see unnerved him more than the pain. And even if the tight, itchy gauze were removed from his healing eyes, he still wouldn't be able to see a damn thing. A sheet covered him from head to faux toe-tag.

Sweat dripped down his neck, and his nose itched, but he remained still. The irony of leaving the hospital under *literal* cover as a dead man didn't escape him. If things had happened just a little differently six weeks ago when he'd hydroplaned off the side of the road, it might have made him just that. And his career was also on life support, considering that his band, Crucified, Dead and Buried, had fallen apart three months ago. The trouble had started before that, but he didn't want to think about it now.

He'd wanted to fake his own death—a way to escape not just the hospital but his entire miserable existence—but Jimmy Vaughan, his manager, had nixed that idea for legal reasons. Instead, they'd compromised with this elaborate escape plan. He needed time alone to think. This wreck had been a wake-up call. He had to fucking get his shit together.

The stretcher moved down the hall as slowly as a funeral march. After several turns, his sense of direction was gone, and he felt claustrophobic. He'd also give his right nut for a cigarette right about now. The stretcher stopped, and his heart rate escalated with his rising panic. *What's going on?* The elevator's ding and opening doors reassured him. Surely that meant this nightmarish ride was almost over. With a painful bump, the stretcher moved. He contemplated sitting straight up and yelling, "Boo!" However, with his luck, someone would probably have a heart attack, not to mention he'd be blowing his cover. The resulting tabloid backlash wouldn't be worth it. Although he felt dead on the inside, he was still, painfully, very much alive.

The elevator stopped. Once again the stretcher hit a bump, and he winced. *For my next goddamned career, I'll design a fuckin' stretcher with shock absorbers.* A strange *whoosh*—which he determined to be an automatic door opening—was followed by the loud, static clamor of sirens and traffic. After six weeks of the rhythmic beeps and whirs of hospital equipment, the chaotic noise unsettled him.

The stretcher lowered, then lifted. Doors slammed, once again making his heart pound. Two men behind him spoke in low, respectful tones. Finally, the vehicle started moving.

He shoved the sheet off his face. Jimmy had promised the hearse would have no windows for nosy paparazzi. Digging in his pocket, he found the cigarettes and lighter the janitor had snuck him. Thanks to Jimmy, he had cartons stuffed in his duffle, wherever the hell it was. After two attempts, he managed to get one lit. Sucking in his first draw of nicotine since the accident, more than a month and a half ago, he exhaled with a contented sigh. Forget the patch and those ridiculous, fake-ass vaping e-cigarettes; he didn't want to quit smoking.

A male voice from the front seat interrupted his enjoyment. "Sir, you can't smoke in here. It stinks up the hearse."

Dylan smirked. "Had complaints from your customers, have you?"

Another guy laughed. "He has a point. Leave him alone."

Dylan took another draw off the cigarette, wishing he were truly dead. No doubt he'd bust the gates of hell wide open and give the Prince of Darkness a run for his money.

Seven hours later, Dylan wished he'd been more specific about his desired time of death.

"Welcome to Alabama!" The flight attendant's perpetual cheerfulness had driven him to drink nonstop for the last six hours. "It's been a pleasure *serving* you, sir."

He shrugged. The blowjob had been okay, but he'd had better.

"I, um, really love your music! Crucified, Dead and Buried is, er, was my favorite band," she continued. "Could I—I mean, do you mind…Um, I'd love an autograph." Her nervous, high-pitched giggle made his jaw clench.

Jesus, I'm fuckin' blind! "Call my publicist."

As if he'd sign anything without knowing what the hell it was. If nothing else, he was a savvy businessman. It was a fucking shame he hadn't been as on top of things in his personal life.

"Oh, okay." Disappointment laced her voice.

Guilt ate at his conscience. She was a fan. And even a crappy blowjob was better than no blowjob. "Give me your address. I'll make sure you get an autograph."

"Thank you!" She tucked a napkin into his hand. "I included my number."

Of course she did. They always do.

"Give me a call any time, *night* or day." Another annoying giggle almost made him rescind his offer.

Alafuckin'bama. The last damn place he ever wanted to return to after escaping thirteen years ago. Karma was a real bitch at times. Dylan grimaced as the giggler weaved his wheelchair, hitting several bumps. Once again cursing his inability to see and overwhelmed by the dissonance of unfamiliar noises, he wished he had another drink.

Is the press here? Will I be recognized?

When the giggler failed to volunteer information about what was happening, he drummed his fingers with annoyance. He expected people to anticipate his needs.

"Is the airport crowded?" he snapped.

"No, sir. We're in a private area per the instructions from your manager. Our airline takes pride in our service and confidentiality."

Considering the nature of the *service* she'd just provided, he hoped so. He nodded and exhaled the breath he'd been holding. After another *whoosh* from some sort of electronic door, he found himself engulfed in muggy heat. He'd forgotten how miserable summers were in Alabama.

The flight attendant locked the wheelchair with a jolt. "Here we are, and your nurse is here. It's been a real pleasure meeting you. I hope you enjoyed your flight," she purred.

But Dylan was already on to the next challenge. *I bet my douchebag brother hired some old, crabby nurse.*

A car door opened, and the scent of citrus greeted him. For some reason, it seemed familiar. It certainly beat the antiseptic smell of the hospital.

"Good afternoon, Mr. McAthie. I'm Jennifer Adams, your nurse. May I help you into the car?"

He hated being called *Mr.* McAthie. It made him feel old, and he wasn't even thirty, goddammit. There had only been *one* Mr. McAthie, and thankfully, his asshole father was dead.

"I'm not feeble," he snarled. The throbbing in his injured leg intensified as he stood. He threw the duffel bag in what he presumed was the vicinity of the floorboard. Someone took his guitar from him, and he managed to maneuver himself into the passenger seat of the car. Pain hissed between his teeth as he situated himself. The nice, numbing effect of the alcohol was rapidly dissipating. The car door slammed, and he jumped like a kid in a spook house.

Why can't people tell me what the hell is going on? I can't see, dammit.
Another car door opened and closed. The nurse reached across him and buckled his seat belt. He froze, hating feeling so goddamned vulnerable. She adjusted the belt so it wasn't choking him, her soft fingers grazing his neck.

"I'm sorry; I know you're tired. Hang in there. Unfortunately, we've got quite a drive. Even though Pine Bluff is only seventy-five miles away from Birmingham, I've been instructed to take a long, convoluted route. Seems crazy to me."

He nodded, unable to speak for a moment. Aside from the technically correct but uninspiring blowjob earlier, this was the first non-clinical touch he could remember since…well, a long time. Before the hospital for sure. He hadn't realized how much he missed normal human contact. At last, the nurse started the car and headed toward his grandmother's.

The house wasn't going to be the same without Gran, but Dylan shoved that thought aside. He'd deal with his grief later. Instead, he focused his attention on the here and now as a bubble of panic once again rose in his chest as the car started moving. *I'm going to die.*

"You're checking to make sure no one is following, right?" *What did she say her name was?* He white-knuckled the seat as flashbacks from the wreck threatened.

"Yes, sir. Just take a few deep breaths and try to relax," she cooed, as if talking to a child.

The deep breaths helped. Irritated and exhausted, Dylan settled into the lulling motion of the car. Maybe he could just sleep his life away…

"How long has it been since you've been home? Oh, gosh. I didn't think to ask—are you in pain? Thirsty? Or hungry? Dr. McAthie said the house is on the lake. I can't wait to see it. I bet it's beautiful."

Please God, not a chatterer. The giggler on the plane was bad enough.
"Thirteen years. No. No. And no. And why would I care if the lake is beautiful? It isn't like I'll be able to *see* it." He reached into his shirt pocket and pulled out a smoke.

Cigarette poised in his mouth, he flicked the lighter, anticipating that first heavenly draw. Abruptly, the cigarette disappeared.

"What are you doing?" the nurse screeched. "You can't smoke in my car. You *have* heard those things will kill you, right? Not to mention your lungs are still healing. And the doctors expect you to make a full recovery, including your vision. You're very lucky."

What the hell? The sound of the car window rolling down and back up sparked his anger. *Lucky?* He'd been betrayed, damn near died, and his career was on the verge of extinction. How could any of that be considered "lucky"? His brother had obviously hired a lunatic.

"Motherfuckin' sonofabitch." Dylan shoved the lighter back in his pocket. "Did you really just throw an unlit cigarette out the window?"

"Yes."

"Do you know how much those damn things cost?"

"Another good reason to quit."

Judging by her smug tone, he bet she was smirking.

"I may be *lucky*, but I need to save my money because I don't have a band anymore. And since I can't see at present, I hope you're keeping your eyes on the goddamned road. I don't relish the thought of *another* accident."

"I'm s-sorry."

The tremble in her soft voice made him wonder how old she was. He heard her suck in a deep breath.

"There's no need to be so hateful. I didn't mean to be insensitive, but you can't smoke in my car."

"Litterbug," he muttered.

His eyes burned, the bandage itched, his leg hurt, and he needed a drink, a painkiller, or both. What he didn't need was some know-it-all, bossy nurse telling him what he could and couldn't do. He'd had his fill of that in the hospital.

"Would you *please* pull over and let me smoke a goddamned cigarette?"

Silence.

"Now what? I said please, dammit."

Another drawn-out sigh confirmed she hadn't been snatched from the car by aliens nor disappeared into thin air.

"Oh, for heaven's sake."

This time he was certain an eye roll was involved.

She sighed. "Wouldn't stopping for your nasty addiction be counterproductive to this ridiculous, covert escape plan so no one knows where you'll be recuperating?"

Dammit, she's right. He hated being wrong.

"Fine. Could you at least step on the gas a little and quit driving like an old lady?" *Shit. What if she is an old lady?* He didn't think she was, but still…

The car jolted and picked up speed, and he swore she'd just called him a jerk under her breath.

"Jerk," Jennifer muttered.

She dashed away a tear, thankful he couldn't see her acting like a fool. This was *not* how she'd pictured their reunion. She'd grown up next door to Dylan McAthie's family, and as a little girl, she'd watched his comings and goings with great interest, always wishing the blond-haired teen would notice her. The night her world fell apart, her wish came true.

At age six, the word *cancer* hadn't had much of an impact on her, but seeing her parents cry did. Upset and confused, she'd snuck out of the house to say goodnight to the moon. Hearing a car door slam, she'd peeked through the fence and watched Dylan stumble and laugh. He'd collapsed on his steps and lit a cigarette. Curious, she climbed the fence.

Tiptoeing toward him she'd asked, "What's so funny?"

He'd jumped, and she'd giggled.

"Shit. Where did you come from?"

Tongue-tied, she'd pointed toward her house.

"It's late. You better go home before you get in trouble."

She'd refused, not wanting to leave his presence.

Putting out his cigarette, he'd hoisted her in his arms. She'd snuggled into his neck, enchanted by his smile and feeling safe as he carried her home.

"You look like a prince," she'd blurted.

He'd laughed, and his chest rumbled beneath her ear. "*Ribbit.* I'm more of a frog." To her dismay, he'd gently placed her on her feet. "Now scoot, and don't sneak out at night. The bogeyman might get you."

The moon had appeared above him like a spotlight.

"There's no such thing as a bogeyman."

"Yes, there is, and he gets bad girls who wander at night. Goodnight, angel." He'd opened her door and given her a gentle shove inside.

He'd waved as she closed the back door. That night she'd dreamed of a blond-haired prince who rescued her. A week later, she'd overheard her father say Dylan was troubled and had run away from home.

That had been the last time she saw him in person until today.

But she'd never forgotten him.

However, in less than thirty minutes, Dylan had managed to crush her dreams. His lank, dirty hair hung to his shoulders, and a full scruffy beard covered his face, leaving him looking like anything *but* the Sexiest Man in Music he'd once been dubbed. White gauze bandages hid the silver-blue eyes known to make women cry and scream with delight. A distinct smell of alcohol permeated his being, not to mention the stench of a cigarette he must have snuck somewhere. He was, in a word, *disappointing*.

In addition, so far, the press reports she'd read about his attitude and paranoia did not seem exaggerated. Of course, he'd been through a lot. The breakup of his band, followed by the overdose death of the band's lead singer and then his car accident, would leave anyone bitter. Maybe her father was right. Perhaps she *was* too young and inexperienced to handle someone like him.

The car in front of her hit the brakes, and she swerved to avoid hitting it. On instinct, she threw her arm across his chest.

"Shit, what's happening?" Fear laced his voice, and he held her arm in a death grip.

"Sorry! The guy in front of me braked suddenly. We're okay."

Feeling guilty, she eased her arm from his grasp and gave his hand a squeeze. Was he suffering post-traumatic stress, too? It wouldn't be uncommon after his accident. She glanced at him again. He was a pale imitation of the vibrant man she'd seen all over magazines and entertainment television. She needed to utilize her psych nursing and not take things personally.

He pulled his hand from hers. "I suggest you keep both hands on the wheel and pay attention to what you're doing."

Okay, he's still a jerk.

"When the hell are we going to get there? Are you sure we're not being followed?"

Yep, her dream job was rapidly disintegrating into a nightmare. Looking at the cars around them, she rolled her eyes. In all probability, the eighty-year-old man to her right, the family in a van to her left, and even the trucker behind her didn't know, nor care, who her passenger was.

"Nobody around but that news truck behind us." She bit her lip to keep from laughing.

"What?" He slunk lower in the seat. "Fuck, fuck, fuck."

"I'm kidding."

He crossed his arms in front of his chest. "Great. My brother hired Nurse Ratched."

"Careful, I might actually be Annie Wilkes from *Misery*." She smiled when his face paled.

Chapter
TWO

At the sound of crunching gravel, Dylan sat up, relieved. *Made it to Gran's.* What's-her-name hadn't said a word since her quip about *Misery.* He'd never admit it, but the reference had been funny as hell.

The driver's door opened, and excited chatter greeted him.

"It's him! It's him. Mama, he's here! Hiya, Jennifer!"

Ah, Jennifer, that's the nurse's name. Who the heck is the kid?

"Hi, Robbie. I swear you've grown three inches in the past month." Jennifer laughed.

It was a pleasant sound, as was her voice when she wasn't fussing.

His nephew. *Great.* How did the nurse know Robbie, and how many other McAthies would he have to endure today? Maybe electing to recuperate just an hour away from them was a mistake. Jimmy had neglected to mention that his arrival was going to be a goddamned family reunion.

"Tell Mama I'm gonna go get Grandma."

Dylan assumed Robbie took off running up the path to Mrs. Jordan's. The trail had been worn in when he was a kid. He and his brother, Rob, had traipsed daily through those woods to see Cathy Jordan whenever they were visiting their grandmother.

"I'll get your things," the nurse informed him, crisply.

Keys jingled, and the car door slammed. Why did all noise seem exaggerated when you couldn't see? Mentally, physically, and emotionally exhausted, he unbuckled his seatbelt and searched for the door handle. Someone yanked it open, and he damn near fell out. Wincing, he eased from the car, fumbling with the damn crutches. Pain jolted through his leg.

"Dammit."

Then female arms and the scent he associated with betrayal embraced him. He stood frozen, unprepared for this encounter. Over the years, he'd refused to have anything to do with any woman wearing that brand of perfume.

Dammit, dammit, dammit. "Hello, Cat. Long time, no see." He covered his unease with nonchalance and a fake smile.

"Welcome home. It's been way too long."

His gut clenched at her familiar voice. Soft lips brushed his cheek, and he pulled away as if burned. His feelings where Cat was concerned were convoluted at best.

"What are you doing here?" he asked. "Is Rob here, too?" *Please, God, no.* He needed to be on top of his game to deal with his know-it-all brother.

"No, Robert couldn't rearrange his schedule. The children and I came up to help Mom get your grandmother's house ready for you."

Fumbling in his pocket, he pulled out a cigarette. This was now his home, and he intended to smoke. Leaning against the car, he lit it and inhaled, enjoying the first glorious puff. He exhaled with slow satisfaction. The collective female *harumphs* made him grin.

"Smoking? Really, Dylan? I wish you wouldn't in front of the kids."

"It isn't like I'm snorting a line of coke. This is perfectly legal. And let me remind you, Gran left this house to *me,* so this is *my* home. If it bothers you, leave."

Cat huffed again, and he sucked in another deep draw.

It felt good to be in control, at least for the moment. For weeks, he'd been at the mercy of nurses and doctors. Thanks to Jimmy's finagling while he was under the influence of hospital medications, he was now dependent on the people he hated most: his family. He wondered what had happened to the nurse.

The familiar screech and *thwack* of the wooden screen door brought a lump to his throat. For once he was thankful for the bandage covering his eyes, shielding his emotions. It didn't seem right not having Gran here. She would've raised holy hell about the smoking and told him he needed a haircut.

A soft hand took his, startling him. "Hi, it's Mary."

His niece. How old were Robbie and Mary? He knew next to nothing about them; his assistant usually kept up with this sort of thing. He vaguely remembered hearing talk about various gifts being sent for birthdays, Christmas, and from his tours. Just because he wasn't on speaking terms with Robert and Cathy wasn't any reason to be a total dick to their kids.

He squeezed her hand. Should he hug her? "Nice to meet you. I'm Dylan."

"*Uncle* Dylan," Cat corrected.

He grimaced. *Uncle Dylan* made him sound old.

"Come, Jennifer, I'll show you to your room," Cat continued. "Mary, will you help your uncle up the steps after he's finished with his cancer stick?"

Her jab didn't bother him one bit. He'd chain smoke if it would get rid of everyone.

"Yes, ma'am," Mary answered.

The nurse didn't say a word, but the screen door screeched open and banged shut again.

Dylan finished his cigarette and threw it on the ground. "Stomp that for me, would ya? So, what do you know about this Jennifer?"

"She lives next door to us. She used to be our babysitter." Mary took his left elbow and jerked him forward. "You shouldn't litter."

True, but it was annoying to be called out by a kid.

"It's biodegradable, and at least I got to smoke this one," he muttered. *Babysitter? What the hell?* Of course, it could be worse. At least the nurse didn't *sound* old. As he wondered what she looked like, his stomach flipped from the combination of hot sun, no food, nicotine, and pain.

"I'm really excited to finally meet you, Uncle Dylan. I've got all your music. My favorite song is…"

Dylan tuned her out as he concentrated on his footing. Darkness and pain — his constant companions of late — surrounded him, sucking him in like quicksand. He clenched his teeth to keep from tossing his cookies. Uncontrollable shaking overtook him, and he broke out in a cold sweat.

Stepping wrong, he tripped and fell, hitting the stone step. Pain shot through his injured leg. With a groan, he rolled to his side, bile stinging the back of his throat. Clutching his stomach, he vomited as his niece screamed with preteen hysteria.

God knew he'd thought about dying, but this wasn't how he wanted to go. The unflattering photo that would accompany the headline, "Dylan McAthie Dead in His Own Vomit," in *The National Intruder* motivated him to attempt to get up off his ass.

The screen door squeaked.

Efficient hands scooped his hair back and ran down his body, checking for injuries. "I'm so sorry! Are you okay? This is my fault; I should have stayed to help you."

Truthfully, he was glad the nurse had come. But this could be his out. He'd fire her for incompetence.

"I agree." Instead of sounding authoritative, he sounded weak and winded. Fuck, he had the energy of a limp, ninety-year-old dick. He shrugged out of her helping hand.

Wiping his mouth, he steadied himself. After three failed attempts to get up, he finally accepted help from Jennifer and Cat and made it into the house. Collapsing on Gran's old couch, he wondered if it was humanly possible to be any more miserable than he was at this moment. The cacophony of Cat's fussing, his niece's sobbing, and the nurse's apologizing irritated him further.

He leaned his head back. "You can quit crying, kid. Cat, I need something for pain, and I want to brush my teeth. As for you, Jenny, you're fired."

"I g-go by Jennifer not Jenny, and I'm not leaving. Quit being a jerk." Hesitancy tinged her words, but she did seem to have some backbone.

"What? Don't listen to him, Jennifer. He isn't paying you; Robert is. You can't fire her, Dylan. Now quit acting like a two-year-old having a temper tantrum."

Damn, Cat was bossy. Maybe he'd dodged a bullet when she dumped him for Saint Robert.

"Mary, would you please get your uncle a wet washcloth and a toothbrush? I'll get his medicine from the kitchen."

"I'm just going to check your bandage."

Jennifer's all-business hands carefully checked his injured leg, which throbbed like a motherfucker. He wished for the millionth time that everyone would leave him the hell alone.

The hands moved away, and Dylan stretched out on the couch. *They'll leave.* It would just be a matter of time. Right now, he was too damn tired to fight. The hum of the window air conditioner and ticking clock on the mantle soothed him. After a few minutes, the nausea eased, and he relaxed. This was why he was here. The peace and quiet...

Bam! He sat up, his heart racing until he realized it was just the front door.

"Grandma's here! Grandma's here! She's got new kittens, Mama. Can we take one home?" Robbie's skittering footsteps sounded through the house.

Dylan groaned. All thoughts of peace and quiet fizzled like a spent firecracker. What the hell had possessed him to want to leave the hospital? Something nudged his arm.

Please, God, let it be a toothbrush, a painkiller, or a gun.

"Strachan Dylan McAthie."

Jesus H. Christ. He hated being called by his full name. Nine times out of ten it meant trouble. It should have been labeled child abuse, saddling him with his mother's unpronounceable maiden name. He couldn't count the times he'd had to spell it and pronounce it for people. *S-T-R-A-C-H-A-N, Stra-khan.*

And yet, he couldn't help but smile at the familiar voice. At least Eloise Jordan, Cat's mother, pronounced it correctly. Along with his maternal grandmother, Mrs. J and her late husband had provided him with a sense of family he'd never felt from his own cold father.

"Why are you here, Mrs. J?" He yawned and stretched, trying to work some of the kinks out.

"I've brought you some supper." She fussed, opening things, and the smell of food made his stomach lurch.

"I'm not hungry—"

A cold, wet washcloth hit his face. He sincerely hoped Mary didn't aspire to be a nurse. And speaking of nurses, where the hell was his with that damn pain pill? Working around the bandage, he did his best to wash his hands and face, and he brushed his teeth. He grimaced and swallowed the toothpaste, since no water had been provided.

"Robbie's really excited about those new kittens, Mom. He's trying to convince me we need the black one with white paws." Cat chattered while tucking a napkin around his neck. "Dylan, do you have any pets?"

Terrific, am I to be spoon-fed next? "I said I'm not hungry," he protested. "And I hate animals. Almost as much as I hate people."

"You need to eat something so you can take your medicine," the nurse encouraged.

"I brought you a plate of fried chicken, a biscuit, fried okra, and some fried potatoes. I knew you'd want some home cookin'." Mrs. Jordan stuffed a bite of dry biscuit in his mouth. "If you're a good boy and eat everything on your plate, you can have one of my fried apple pies for dessert. Look at you. Why, you're nothing but skin and bones; didn't they feed you in that hospital?"

Before he could reply, someone shoved a chicken leg in his mouth. He spit it out. He hated fried food. His tastes had changed considerably since he was a boy. The gulp of ice tea that followed damn near drowned him. Pushing the hand away, he attempted to stop the forced feeding. He didn't want to hurt Mrs. J's feelings, but he had no appetite whatsoever. Mary and Robbie argued in the kitchen, adding to the sense of pandemonium.

"Mrs. J, I really appreciate this…"

"Oh, Dylan, just try to eat a little," Cat coaxed.

"You have to eat to keep the medication from making you sick," Jennifer added.

"Mama, Mary hit me!"

"I did not; he's a big fat liar!"

"She did too. Look at my arm."

"You can't turn your nose up at *my* fried chicken. You've always *loved* my fried chicken…" The deafening racket rose as everyone talked at once.

He'd had enough. "Shut the fuck up and leave me the hell alone!" The room went silent. He brushed at the aggravating bandage over his eyes in frustration. "*Please,* just go away."

"We're trying to help. There's no need to be so cranky. And I don't appreciate the profanity in front of my kids," Cat admonished.

"Excuse me." The nurse's authoritative voice rose above the melee. "I'm going to have to insist everyone leave. Mr. McAthie is exhausted from the trip and needs his rest. I'll make sure he eats something."

For the first time today, Dylan was thankful for the private-duty nurse.

"Jennifer's right," Mrs. Jordan agreed. "Come, Cathy, children. Say goodbye and let's go."

He endured hugs from the kids, a kiss on the forehead from Cat, and a pat on the arm from Mrs. J. Then the front door opened and closed, leaving blessed silence.

"If you'll eat at least a few bites of something, I can give you the pain pill. It will ease your discomfort when I help you to your room."

His grandmother used to tell him to choose his battles. Exhausted, Dylan ate the biscuit without protest. He'd lost the battle, but the war was yet to be won.

Jennifer ate the delicious food Mrs. Jordan had provided for her, along with her patient. She worried about Mr. McAthie not eating as she quietly put his plate in the refrigerator and washed the dishes. The kitchen was like a time capsule from the seventies with its avocado green appliances and Formica countertops. A table with a flowered tablecloth and four chairs sat in the center. And like the kitchen, the rest of the house was small and unassuming, not anything you'd think a famous musician would own. She loved its cozy hominess.

She stood at the doorway to the living area. Beautiful hardwood floors shone in the waning sunlight through the Venetian blinds. The room had mismatched, but comfortable-looking furniture, along with a small, older television. The white walls were covered with family photos and over the fireplace mantle hung a gun.

The quiet was interrupted by Mr. McAthie's snoring. Taking a knit afghan, she tucked him in and left him alone. It wasn't worth the argument to get him to move to the bedroom. If he wanted to wake up stiff and uncomfortable, that was his choice.

Jennifer collapsed on her bed, emotionally spent. She'd been woefully unprepared for her patient's belligerence. Tempted to quit, the thought of listening to her father's *I told you so* shored up her courage to stay. Tomorrow she'd stand firm and let Mr. McAthie know she was in charge. Taking out her phone, she tried to call home to let her dad know she was here, but there were no bars for service. Hopefully, Mrs. McAthie would tell him. She wasn't sure about using the house phone. And anyway, she didn't want to wake her grouchy patient.

Gathering her things to take a bath, she paused at the doorway to read two framed essays on the wall above the light switch. Each essay was titled "What I want to be when I grow up."

Robert's was a page long, written in a precise, neat hand, and listed ten reasons why he wanted to be a doctor. A large red A+ topped the page. Dylan's essay was hard to decipher, with several smudges and erasures. Musical notes, stick people, and planes dropping bombs on dinosaurs had been drawn haphazardly in the margins. A red D graced his paper, which held just one misspelled sentence:

> When I grow up I want to be
> a rich famus sitarist and kick a$$.

Jennifer smiled as she left the room. She could do this. Her surly patient had been through a lot. She remembered reading the breakup of his band had been related to personality clashes and drugs. And the media had speculated Dylan's car accident was either a suicide attempt or related to drugs. She knew the latter wasn't true. But the depression? Perhaps. Surely somewhere, underneath all his antagonism, the sweet, carefree boy she remembered still lived. She had to believe it.

Or cry.

Chapter
Three

Dylan awoke with a start, his heart pounding like a jackhammer. *Where the hell am I?* He could hear no squealing tires or metal crashing, no screaming. Nope, that had just been his recurring nightmare about the wreck.

As he worked to control his breathing, he realized he also heard no beeps and sounds of machinery or nurses in the hall. After a moment, he focused on the hum of his grandmother's window air conditioner and the ticking mantle clock, which eased his anxiety and reminded him of his location. He stretched his stiff muscles, wondering what time it was.

The nurse must be asleep. *Good.* Nurses were like sleeping dogs: best left alone.

Finding his crutches, he stood, painfully, and went toward the bathroom. Stumbling into the doorjamb, Dylan rubbed his arm and swore under his breath. Would he ever master crutch walking? Leaving the bathroom, he ran into the coffee table and whisper-cursed as he struggled to maintain his balance. At last he found his way to the kitchen. Reaching up to the top shelf of the pantry, he knocked over cans and other stuff in a blind search for the hidden treasure.

"Yes!"

Finding the jar of Leroy Tyler's infamous moonshine he knew his grandmother kept, Dylan gave an air pump of happiness and slugged down a gulp. Gran had claimed she used it for "medicinal purposes." Right now, it was an answer to prayer. The smooth heat burned into his system, and he sighed happily. Capping the jar, he shoved it in the waistband of his loose jeans.

"What are you doing? Do you need something? It's two o'clock in the morning."

"Shit!" He jumped.

If that nurse continued to sneak up on him, he'd have to insist she wear a collar with a bell on it, like a cat.

"Nothing."

"What's that in your pants?"

What? Is there morning wood? *Shit, she means the moonshine.* He hoped.

"Interested in what's in my pants, Jenny? You naughty girl, you."

He heard her walking toward him and smelled the citrus scent of her hair.

"What? No! Why do you have a mason jar stuck in your pants?"

"Why are you so nosy?" *Why am I acting like a six-year-old caught with his hand in the cookie jar?*

He crutched past her, accidentally brushing against a soft, full breast covered in silky material. Her outraged gasp made him smile. It was her own damn fault. After all, he was the one who couldn't see. He snickered as she stomped down the hallway. Making his way toward the front porch, he stubbed his toe twice.

He stepped out onto the screened-in porch and pulled the front door closed behind him. Using his crutches like a blind man with a cane, he found the metal glider, pulled out the moonshine, and sank with a loud grunt. Shit, he felt like an old man. Another large gulp of the moonshine helped. He searched his shirt pocket for a smoke and his lighter.

A sense of peace enveloped him. Crickets and frogs trilled their evening song in a welcoming crescendo, and in the distance, an owl hooted. The water from the lake lapped the shore, and the rhythmic sound soothed his battered soul. There wasn't a hint of a breeze, and honeysuckle hung heavy in the humid night air. This was home; it always had been—even though he'd only spent summers here. He'd never felt this way about his mansion in California and certainly not about his childhood home in Birmingham where Rob's family now lived.

How many nights had he, Rob, and Cat sat on this very porch, shelling peas and shucking corn with his grandmother? He remembered playing hide and seek in the dark and catching fireflies before collapsing in their sleeping bags. Those had been good times. Before Rob and Cat had gone behind his back...

That deceit had been mild compared to the breakup of Crucified, Dead and Buried. Sara was dead...*Stop. Don't go there. Not now.* Betrayal. *It should fuckin' be the name of my next band.* He shoved the painful memories aside. Now was not the time to dwell on it.

Stubbing the cigarette out, he pushed the glider with his good leg and hummed a song his grandmother used to sing. He stopped, unable to go on. What felt like liquid acid burned his eyes behind the itchy, annoying bandage as he struggled to suppress the memories. Sucking in a deep breath, he leaned back, listening to the creak of the glider.

Sara, Sara, Sara...Why?

The front door opened, and the nurse sat beside him.

"Are you saying goodnight to the moon?" she asked in her soft, melodic voice.

Her odd question niggled, but the memory seemed out of reach. "What time did you say it was?"

"A little after two in the morning. Can I get you anything? Are you in pain?"

"Nah. This is pretty much taking care of anything I need." He held up the jar of liquor. Maybe it would loosen her up. "Want some?"

"I don't drink."

Figures. "Want a cigarette? I didn't mean to wake you up," he offered as a semi-apology. *She's not so bad.*

"I don't smoke either. You're not supposed to drink with your medications. Or smoke."

Okay, maybe she's a tad annoying.

"Go back to bed, Jenny."

"Jennifer," she replied with a yawn.

"Whatever. Leave. I don't want you here."

"Are you always this insufferably rude?" She stood and attempted to take the moonshine. He clamped a hand around her tiny wrist.

"Yes. Now go back to bed like a good little girl." It was a shot in the dark. He had no idea how old she was.

Her soft laughter filled the air. "That's not the first time you've told me that. Fine. Pickle your liver and pollute your lungs. Don't complain if you trip because you can't see to get back inside. It's your life. Goodnight." The front door slammed.

Not the first time I've told her that? What the hell did she mean?

Shrugging out of his shirt, Dylan lit another cigarette and opened the jar of moonshine. *Over the lips and past the gums...*

Jennifer checked her reflection in the mirror and frowned as she tucked an errant dark curl into her bun. The dark circles under her eyes matched her violet-colored scrubs. Determined to take charge, she raised her chin and straightened her shoulders. *I am the nurse.* For emphasis, she slapped her chest with her closed fist. *I can do this!*

Her job depended on her ability to take control. She didn't want to let Dr. McAthie down. He demanded quality care for his patients, and she suspected even more so when the patient was his younger brother. He wasn't the type to cut her any slack simply because they were neighbors.

Besides, going home wasn't an option. She'd taken this job to escape the fishbowl existence of being Pastor Glen Adams's only child. She was tired of having every aspect of her life examined through the magnifying lens of his vocal, ultra-conservative congregation. At almost twenty, she wanted to live her own life on her own terms.

Jennifer peeked in Mr. McAthie's room, where the bed remained unmade. Where was he? Surely he hadn't left. Hurrying to the front door, she threw it open and found her patient sprawled on the old, green, metal glider. Clutched in one hand was the now-empty jar of liquor. Below him, cigarette butts littered the porch. Her nurse's training went down the drain as panic surged through her.

Oh my God! Who do I call to report a death out here? Will they think I killed him? Will I go to jail? Does Alabama still use the electric chair? She tentatively approached him to check his vital signs. A loud snore made her jump, but reassured her he wasn't dead. She resisted the urge to smack him for scaring her half to death.

Now that she could breathe again, she allowed herself the luxury of staring at the half-naked object of her dreams. To her surprise, he had a Bible verse tattooed on his ribcage. The famous tattoo of a cross with a snake wrapped around it adorned his well-defined bicep. Though a little thin, his chest was still sculpted, and one of his hands rested on positively drool-worthy abs. She tore her eyes away from the happy trail dipping below his low-riding jeans. Her heart rate escalated and heat traveled to places it had no business going.

Movement from the woods caught her eye, and she looked up to see Mrs. Jordan carrying a casserole dish. Jennifer waved and smiled at the plump woman.

"Good morning," Mrs. Jordan called when within earshot, a wide, easy smile on her face. She mopped her brow with the dishtowel tucked at her waist, and her tight gray curls bobbed as she scurried up the steps. "How is the poor dear this morning?"

As Mrs. Jordan opened the porch door, the "poor dear" turned over and fell to the floor with a loud thud.

"Goddamn motherfuckin' sonofabitch!"

Mrs. Jordan raised an eyebrow, and a knowing look crossed her face. "My, my, isn't this a lovely sight to behold. I'm sure your dear, departed grandmother is rolling in her grave. Why in heaven's name are you out here, Dylan? You look like one of Leroy Tyler's derelict customers."

Kicking the cigarette butts aside, she took the empty jar from Dylan's hand and sniffed, giving a look of revulsion. Jennifer bit her lip to keep from giggling.

"I dunno. Reliving my youth, I guess," Dylan muttered, sitting up and ripping the dirty bandage from his eyes. He rubbed his forehead and groaned.

With Mrs. Jordan's assistance, Jennifer helped him to his feet. Handing him his crutches, she wrinkled her nose. He smelled of sweat, stale cigarette smoke, and liquor. Dylan squinted and looked around, digging in his jeans pocket.

"Now what? Do you plan on standing here all day holding court, or are you going to get your sorry butt in the house?" Mrs. Jordan asked.

"I want a cigarette."

"And I want a million dollars. It looks to me like you smoked the entire pack last night. Now march yourself inside and behave."

Jennifer's eyes widened as she watched the battle of wills. Mrs. Jordan spoke to him like he was a naughty little boy. And the scowl on Dylan's face made him look just that. With one hand on her hip, Mrs. Jordan held the door open, her foot tapping.

"I want a goddamn cigarette *now*."

Mrs. Jordan's eyes narrowed. "Come along, my dear. Obviously Dylan doesn't require our help. Do you have any coffee made? Have you had breakfast?" She motioned for Jennifer to enter the house.

"No, ma'am. We slept in and just got up." *Oh my God, you fool, this is Dr. McAthie's mother-in-law! Don't make it sound like you fell into his bed, dummy!* "I mean, he slept out here, and I slept in my room…" Heat flooded her cheeks.

Despite his swollen eyes, Dylan squinted and stared at her, adding to her anxiety. Flustered, she fled inside to start coffee. Mrs. Jordan followed, and like a short-order cook, the older woman quickly took over the breakfast preparations.

The front door opened and slammed shut. Muttered expletives punctuated the irritable man's journey to the bathroom.

"Do you mind if I give you some advice?" Without waiting for an answer, Mrs. Jordan continued. "I've known Dylan most of his life, and this obnoxious behavior isn't like him. He's always been headstrong but never this ill-tempered. He's usually very charming."

Jennifer kept her skepticism to herself, having been raised to respect her elders.

Dylan lumbered into the living area, still swearing like a drunken sailor.

Ugh. Did he just fart? Jennifer grimaced. *Yeah, real charming.* She dug deep to access her training. "Yes, ma'am. I'm sure everything he's been through is impacting his behavior."

"Make no mistake; he's still being difficult." Mrs. Jordan winked and called, "How nice of you to grant us an audience, *your majesty*. Breakfast will be ready in about fifteen minutes." In a softer voice and with a reassuring nod toward the other room, she added, "Go check on him; I'll finish his lordship's breakfast. I know exactly what to make."

Though she'd rather poke a rattlesnake, Jennifer walked toward the living area. It was her job, after all.

Dylan couldn't remember the last time he'd been this hung over. After the first few years of excessive partying and life on the road with the band, he'd settled down, realizing he was too much of a control freak to overindulge so often. Sure, he might have reverted to drinking too much after the demolition of his band—and his whole life along with it—but just prior to the accident, he'd stopped. Stupid shit was sure to follow when drunk or strung out—like getting shitfaced and passing out on your own front porch. He wondered if Robert had had the nurse sign a non-disclosure agreement. *I sure as shit don't need pictures of this leaked to the tabloids.*

He attempted to focus his stinging eyes. He didn't need breakfast; he needed a painkiller and a bath. Fumbling around, he searched for a cigarette. He turned to see what looked like the blasted nurse standing in the doorway like a timid mouse. Throwing the crutches down, he sank onto the couch, fuming.

"Find me a cigarette," he barked.

He heard her sharp intake of breath. For a fraction of a second, he regretted taking out his frustration on her. Dammit, he wished his vision wasn't so blurry so he could make out her features. She rummaged through his duffle bag and handed him a new pack. Lighting the long-awaited cigarette, he enjoyed that first magnificent puff and exhaled. She fanned the smoke away.

"Where did you get five cartons of cigarettes? Your brother's a cardiologist!"

Right. Nonsmoker. "My manager brought them to me before I left the hospital. So how'd you get the job, sweetheart? You work with my brother? I'm sure Saint Robert the Divine has painted a picture of me as the very Devil incarnate." He sneered as he waited for Miss Prim and Proper to lie and tell him what she thought he wanted to hear.

She coughed. "I am *not* your sweetheart. I babysat your niece and nephew. And yes, your brother said you could be difficult. I believe the actual term he used was 'an ass.'"

Dylan raised an eyebrow and chuckled. "Call me Dylan. Mr. McAthie was my old man."

"Fine. Is there anything I can do for you before breakfast?"

Ah, there it was…the hint of sex offered freely. The eagerness in her voice reminded him of thousands of sycophant band followers. *Oh well, I knew it was too good to last. Strike one.*

"The hair of the dog?"

"You have a dog? What kind? I can ask Mrs. Jordan for a lint brush—"

Dylan burst out laughing, holding his sore ribs when the painful hiccupping started.

"What's so funny?" Annoyance laced her voice, and although everything looked blurry, he could tell she was frowning.

"Are you really that naïve? I need something for this damn hangover."

A sharp intake of breath let him know she was pissed. Good. At this rate, he'd be rid of her soon.

"Once again, you need to eat before you take anything, or you'll be sick. You also need to drink water because you're dehydrated from your binge drinking. Now, raise your arms and take deep breaths. It will raise your diaphragm and stop those annoying hiccups."

She whirled and disappeared into the kitchen.

Strike two for her uppity attitude, even if she is right.

"Behave, Dylan. Come and get your breakfast," Mrs. Jordan scolded from the doorway.

Dylan hiccupped again. "Just bring it to me out here, Mrs. J."

"Do I look like someone who's going to wait on you hand and foot? Get your lazy rear end to the table right now." With a loud huff, she was gone.

Jesus, everyone is so touchy. Despite the pain, he raised his arms and inhaled deeply several times. The hiccupping stopped.

Dylan found his crutches and with slow, careful steps crept to the kitchen. He had to squint continuously to see. *Shit, I don't need frown lines before my thirtieth birthday.* He found the nurse and Mrs. J seated at the kitchen table. The smell of hot coffee hung in the air, almost but not quite negating the disgusting smell of bacon.

Collapsing in the chair, he accepted a glass of water. Taking a bite of toast, he wondered why everyone was so quiet, and stopped chewing. *Now what?*

"Would you like to ask the blessing, Dylan? Jennifer's father is a *minister*." The disapproval in Mrs. J's voice registered at least a seven on the Richter scale.

Fucking great—instead of a cranky old lady, my asshole brother hired a preacher's kid?

Swallowing the dry toast, he wiped his mouth. "No, ma'am, you go ahead."

Mrs. Jordan asked a quick blessing over the food, and both women added a quiet *Amen.*

After a brief pause, Dylan added his own exuberant *Amen* and flashed the shit-eating smirk that had served him so well in the past.

Mrs. Jordan shook her head. "Charming me with that sweet smile doesn't make up for your poor manners, Strachan Dylan McAthie."

Dylan broadened his grin. He hoped his dimples would soften the lecture he knew was coming. She'd used his full name, after all.

"Yes, ma'am," he replied with exaggerated politeness. He winked at the nurse, whose eyes widened.

She's kind of cute. I wish I could make out the details of her face.

Shoving the bacon aside, he took a big bite of eggs, and his stomach lurched painfully. *Oh no, she didn't.* With the help of his crutches, he hobbled to the garbage can and barely made it before retching for the second time in twenty-four hours. Too miserable to be angry, he maneuvered to the sink and rinsed his mouth with a handful of water. He leaned his forehead on his arm, too embarrassed and weak to move.

"Why, Dylan, whatever is the matter?" Mrs. Jordan's feigned innocence didn't fool him. She was a sly old fox. The undercooked-breakfast stunt had long been a favorite retribution for drunken behavior. His grandmother had used it as well. It was his own dumb fault for not remembering.

Jennifer came to assist him back to his chair. In no condition to move on his own or even put up an argument, he allowed it and accepted the glass of water. *Damn, she smells good.*

Dylan strained his eyes to focus, and what he discovered shocked him. Whispery dark tendrils trailed tantalizingly down the back of her neck. He fought the urge to wrap one around his finger. He scanned her face, starting with her full pink lips—a mouth that begged to be kissed. Color spotted her pale cheeks, but her eyes were by far her prettiest feature. They were an intriguing blue-violet color and framed by dark lashes. One eyebrow arched slightly, and he looked away, embarrassed he'd been caught gawking like a love-struck teenager.

"Take a few sips and eat some toast," she coaxed, brushing his hair out of his face.

Her gentle touch sent an electrical current shooting through him. *What the hell is wrong with me?* Must be the pain making him act like a dumbass. He gratefully swallowed the pills she handed him. If nothing else, they should kill his hard cock. Covering his eyes with both hands, he rubbed his aching head, his elbows resting on the table.

Mrs. Jordan sniffed. "Get your elbows off the table. For heaven's sake, you weren't raised in a barn, although at present you smell like it. You stink like someone who actually works for a living. When did you last have a bath?"

What the fuck? Why don't people ever think I work? I didn't get to the top sitting on my ass.

"I dunno. Yesterday, I guess," he mumbled, removing his elbows from the table. He glared at the greasy, runny plate of food in front of him, so unlike the other plates of fluffy eggs and crisp bacon. Payback was hell. A bath *might* help...*Holy shit, it's the answer to my prayers!*

He turned his attention to Jennifer and smiled. "I guess Miss, uh, Nurse will help me with my bath." He drummed his fingers in anticipation of her outrage.

She paled.

He could practically smell her fear and struggled to keep from laughing. *She'll be out of here by dusk.*

"Y-Yes, I'll be happy to assist you with your bath, Mr. McAthie." She twisted her napkin and jumped to her feet, overturning her chair. To tip her over the edge, he flashed a roguish grin and gave what he hoped was a convincing leer.

Mrs. Jordan stood up as well. "Nonsense. Jennifer has only just arrived. I'm sure she still needs to get settled in. Go finish unpacking, my dear, or you could take a walk down to the dock. The lake is beautiful this time of morning. I'll assist his lordship with his bath."

Jennifer fled to her bedroom as if the Devil himself was after her.

Dylan grinned. *And I haven't even moved from my seat yet.*

Mrs. J's words sunk in, and his smile faded. He spun in his chair, horrified.

"What? Wait. You're gonna give me a bath? She's a nurse, for Christ's sake. It's *her* job. Y-You can't help me."

"Don't be ridiculous. I've bathed you more times than I can remember." She yanked him out of his chair.

For a second he was half afraid she was going to smack him as if he was still the child she remembered.

"While we're at it, how about a haircut and a shave?" She marched toward the bathroom ahead of him.

Grabbing his crutches, he followed as fast as he could. "I like my hair fine just the way it is, thank you very much. And I want to keep my damn beard." He would've loved a shave, but was afraid she'd slit his throat.

He hit an end table with his sore leg. "Ouch! Fuck!" At this rate, he'd get his mouth washed out with soap, too.

When he finally reached the bathroom, Mrs. Jordan had a hot, steamy bath running in the old-fashioned, claw-foot tub.

"Why can't the nurse bathe me?" *Shit, did that whine just come from me?* "I mean, she has to change the bandage anyways."

Mrs. Jordan frowned, hands on her ample hips. "You're baiting her on purpose, and we both know it. Quit acting like a spoiled brat. I'll ask her about the dressings. Now undress and wait on us." She handed him a towel as she bristled past, slamming the door and leaving no room for discussion.

Grumbling under his breath, he used the sink to balance as he kicked off his shoes and socks. When he managed to pull off his jeans and underwear, he looked at the towel. For a moment, he debated whether to shock the hell out of the innocent and greet her in all his glory.

The thought of what Mrs. J might do in retaliation led him to wrap the towel around his waist. He wasn't that brave.

Chapter Four

Jennifer paced back and forth like a caged animal. Glaring at her image in the mirror, she silently berated herself. *Pull yourself together, nitwit.* Dylan McAthie had to be the most infuriating, arrogant, selfish man she'd ever met. To her dismay, he'd managed to surpass all the horrible stories she'd read in the tabloids. And yet when he smiled, her body reacted in a way she couldn't deny. That smile could melt ice cream in January.

She re-pinned her hair into a tight knot, daring the curls to pop loose. A soft tap at the bedroom door stopped her inward rant.

"Yes?" *Please, God, don't let it be him. Show me some mercy.*

Mrs. Jordan poked her head in the door. "I'm sorry to bother you, but I'm not sure what to do about that rascal's injured leg. He says there's a bandage on it. Could you take a quick look and tell me if it's okay for him to soak in a bath? Lord knows he needs it."

Jennifer's confidence inched upward. Bandages. *I can handle bandages. I'm a trained nurse, whether I have experience or not.* With one final pat to her hair, she squared her shoulders and held her head high.

"Of course. I can give him his bath, too. He's right; it's my job." She grimaced, annoyed with herself for sounding like a squeaky mouse.

"Nonsense. He's being obnoxious, and we both know it. Trust me, if I help him bathe it'll knock some of that hot wind out if his sail, if you know what I mean. Now, let's go get him cleaned up and presentable, shall we? He's really quite a handsome devil when he has a haircut and a shave. However, I don't know what possessed him to get a tattoo and pierce his ear like a little girl. Kids these days…"

Jennifer followed on her heels as Mrs. Jordan continued fussing. They found Dylan leaning against the bathtub. Jennifer forced herself not to stare, though the towel left little to her imagination. The deep ripples of abs and his hip bones showed he was fit, if a bit thin. She approached him in a clinical, non-personal manner. After all, he was a patient—like any other handsome, arrogant patient.

Balancing on the balls of her feet, she removed the bandage with a swift yank.

"Ouch!"

A bit of hair tore loose. Jennifer bit her lip to keep from snickering. It served him right.

The leg was swollen, but the incision didn't look infected, and the staples had been removed. She didn't remember any prohibitions against bathing in the doctor's orders.

"I don't think a bath will hurt him at all—"

She lost her balance, and Dylan grabbed her arm to steady her. In the process, his towel fluttered to the floor.

Dylan McAthie stood before her, gloriously naked and proud.

Very proud. Eye-level with the last place she needed to be looking, she closed her eyes. *Please, God, kill me now.* Her face flushed, and tears threatened.

Dylan helped her to her feet.

"Are you always this clumsy, or are you just eager to see me naked?" His husky voice held promises…Chill bumps of desire skittered across her skin as she stared at the object of her school-girl fantasies.

She averted her eyes, wishing the floor would open and swallow her whole. She picked up the towel and handed it back to him, refusing to meet his gaze.

"I'm terribly sorry, Mr. McAthie." Her cheeks burned as she turned to flee the scene.

Dylan caught her by the hand and pulled her back against his bare chest. "Dylan. Please call me Dylan," he whispered in her ear, his hot breath tickling her neck. Her tongue seemed frozen to the roof of her mouth. She nodded. In her hurry to get away, she almost ran into Mrs. Jordan.

As Jennifer fled the room, he covered himself with the towel, sighing as it tented over his obvious reaction.

What the hell is wrong with me? I'm not usually this much of an ass. He turned to call her back and apologize, but Mrs. Jordan appeared in the doorway, arms crossed, eyes narrowed. Her disapproving look served as a bucket of ice water on his erection.

Offense being the best defense, he decided to play the innocent card as she assisted him into the bathtub.

"What?"

Once she'd averted her eyes, he pulled the towel off and sank into the tub of bubbles. *This is beyond embarrassing.*

She smacked the back of his head.

"Oww. What'd you do that for?"

"You know perfectly well why. You ought to be ashamed of yourself. I've a good mind to tan your hide. You better start acting like the gentleman you were brought up to be, *or else.*" Throwing the washcloth at him, she stormed out of the room, muttering about ingrates.

As he bathed, he contemplated Jennifer's startled reaction. *Most women don't have a problem with me being naked. As a matter of fact, most women want me naked.* He stopped bathing and rubbed his aching head. *Sonofabitch.* Just how old was she? If he were on speaking terms with his asshole brother, he'd give him a piece of his mind.

Grabbing her phone, Jennifer ran down the driveway, but didn't get a cell signal until she'd reached the mailbox at the top of the hill. She hadn't realized there were still places that didn't have cellular service. Gasping for air, she dialed the phone and waited until a familiar, comforting male voice answered.

"Hey, Jennifer."

"David," she panted, still out of breath from her run.

"Are you okay?"

Biting her lip at the concern in his voice, she paced, kicking at rocks. "Yes, I, uh, just went for a jog to let off some steam." *Why did I call David?*

"Uh, oh…" He chuckled. "Is it that bad already? You hate jogging."

"I, um…oh, David." The words tumbled out despite her effort to hold herself together. "I don't know if I can do this. I'm a terrible nurse. I let him intimidate me, and he knows I'm inexperienced. He's an arrogant jerk, just like everyone says. What if I do something really bad and injure him even more? What if I never gain control of the situation? I don't know what to do; it's quite possible I'll be fired by the end of the day. How will that look on my résumé?"

She sniffed and wiped away a tear making its way down her cheek. "Maybe Daddy was right. I'm not cut out for this job. Mr. McAthie smokes, drinks, and cusses. He's horrible." *And drop-dead gorgeous.* She stomped her foot, furious with herself.

"Hey now, this doesn't sound like my girl. You're the child prodigy who graduated top of her nursing class. Give yourself a chance. From what I've read, this guy is a real prima donna. Just be firm and let him know you're there to do your job. After all, you said he couldn't fire you since his brother's paying your salary. Don't forget everything he's been through, too. He probably isn't himself and just needs to rest. Everything will be fine. You're not a quitter."

David's encouragement made her feel better, but he didn't know about the mortifying towel incident. He wouldn't understand anyway. Their romance was safe and boring.

Safe and boring? Where did that thought come from?

"I know. You're right. I need to keep reminding myself that nurses can't take patient behavior personally. Thanks for talking me off the ledge. You're always so level-headed. I miss you."

"I miss you, too. I've gotta run though. Class starts in two minutes, and I'm late. Call me tomorrow. Now go face down your Goliath."

"Will do." She smiled and hung up.

Hitting speed dial, she called her father to check in. When asked, she fibbed and told him she loved the job. Thankfully, there was no lightning strike.

Returning to the house, she busied herself with sweeping the front porch.

Mrs. Jordan joined her. "Feel better?"

Jennifer nodded, smiling at her lifesaver. "Yes, ma'am. I'm sorry. I promise I can do this job, and I *will* take good care of him."

"I have no doubts, dear. Dylan's behavior has been that of an unpleasant child. I'm happy to report he's now clean and smells one-hundred-percent better, although he refused to let me cut his hair or shave that awful beard." Mrs. Jordan sniffed her disapproval. "There's sandwich makings for lunch, and I brought a casserole for your dinner. His majesty is thankfully asleep, so you should be able to have a break from his unpleasant company."

She framed Jennifer's cheeks with her hands. "You're a bright girl and a wonderful nurse. My son-in-law and daughter love you and trust you. You'll be fine. My phone number is on the refrigerator. Don't hesitate to call me if he gets to be too much to handle. I can be over in ten minutes to tear his butt up."

Jennifer laughed and hugged Mrs. Jordan goodbye. Once inside, she followed the sound of snoring and peeked in Dylan's room. She found him on top of the covers with one arm thrown over his eyes. The light from the window accented the carved contours of his naked chest and abdomen. It was easy to see why he'd been voted one of the sexiest musicians of the decade.

Tiptoeing out of the room, she closed his door. The dressings could wait. No need to poke a sleeping bear. Jennifer ran a bath for herself after her impromptu run. A nice, relaxing soak would give her time to collect her thoughts and soothe her battered ego. She was determined to be ready when Goliath awoke.

Jennifer put her book down when she heard the familiar flick of a lighter followed by a crash and a string of profanity. Running to Dylan's doorway, she paused to stare at him as her mouth went dry. He stood, running a hand through his mussed shoulder-length hair. It was a sandy color with California beach blond highlights and too true to have come from a bottle. His muscles flexed as he bent to rub his sore shin.

"Are you okay? I need to reapply your dressings."

He sighed. "I'm fine. How long did I sleep?"

"A couple of hours."

He stretched with a loud yawn, causing his abdominal muscles to dance invitingly.

"How long have you been a nurse?" He took a draw off his cigarette as she gathered the bandaging materials.

"I graduated in May." She applied the clean bandage, trying to ignore the expanse of his stomach. In truth, she wanted to explore the dips and valleys and wander down that happy trail... *What's wrong with me?*

"Am I, like, your guinea pig or something?" For once his voice sounded teasing rather than snarky.

"Yes, it's a requirement that all new nurses take care of at least one non-compliant, irritable patient."

"Irritable? Me?" He grinned, acting shocked. "I'm not irritable. You signed all the paperwork barring you from revealing anything to the press, right?"

"Yes, sir. Not that it was necessary. I wouldn't do that." She stood and prepared to bandage his eyes.

"Uh-huh." He snorted. "Anybody will do anything for the right amount of money."

She frowned, feeling sorry for him. "It must be hard not trusting people. These drops will sting, but try to hold still."

His eyes were a haunting shade of blue, with silver glints in them. The intensity with which he stared at her was unsettling. An image of him naked flitted through her mind.

"Sonofabitch, that stings!"

With care, she wiped his tears, praying he didn't notice her hand shaking. Spinning around, she hid her burning cheeks under the pretext of capping his eye drops.

"So how did you get this job? Did Rob send out a casting call or something?"

With a nervous laugh, Jennifer turned to face him again. "Or something. Casting call? Are we filming a reality show? Was that what all the fine print was about?"

Dylan laughed, and the transformation made her uneasy. When relaxed and unguarded, a trace of the boy she remembered reappeared. Some feminine instinct warned her that this man with the two perfect dimples and seductive voice was dangerous. It would be far too easy to fall for his charm.

"Sure, *Beauty and the Beast*. I'm Beauty, of course," he quipped, stubbing out his annoying cigarette. "Didn't you read what you were signing?"

"I skimmed it, and Dr. McAthie went over the fine points. I'm not going to talk to the press or take pictures. I'm not like that. Like I told you, I grew up next door to your family's house in Birmingham. Dr. McAthie told me this was your grandmother's house and that you two spent your summers here, and it's where he met his wife. I'm grateful he offered me the job. It pays well, and it was nice to get away, even if I'm just an hour from home."

"Get away? What do you have to get away from? A romance gone bad?"

"No. I wanted out of the spotlight of being the daughter of a well-known pastor. You have no idea what it's like. His congregation seems to think he walks on water, and the well-meaning people in the pews pick apart every detail of my life. If I dress too well, Daddy is overpaid. But if I don't dress nicely enough, I'm a poor reflection on him. I can't dress too provocatively, but I can't be dowdy, either. If I don't volunteer enough at the church, I'm lazy and backsliding. If I volunteer too much, I'm holier than thou."

He snorted and shook his head. "No idea, huh? You haven't got a fuckin' clue, angel. Did you know the paparazzi snuck into the hospital the night of the wreck? They posed as hospital personnel and took pictures of me on death's door. I had to sneak out of the hospital on a stretcher, covered like a stiff, and I left in the back of a hearse to escape another media blitz. I can't go out to eat without someone recognizing me and interrupting my meal for an autograph. I have a goddamned PhD in living life in the limelight. That's why I'm here."

"Okay. You win. At least I can eat a burger in peace." She wrapped the bandage around his eyes. When he placed a hand on her hip, her skin tingled beneath her scrubs.

Dylan grinned. "I always win. So what are your plans for your newfound freedom? Wanna sow some wild oats?"

A yearning for something she didn't understand shot through her body. Removing his hand, she stepped away, her heart racing. "Want a sexual harassment suit?" she quipped back.

He scowled. "That's not funny."

She gentled her voice but spoke firmly. "Your comment was inappropriate, Mr. McAthie."

Dylan cocked his head to the side and smiled. "Duly noted. Miss Adams, is it?"

"Just Jennifer is fine." She put the bandaging materials away, grateful his eyes were covered so he couldn't see her red face and trembling hands.

Chapter Five

Jennifer rocked in the old bentwood rocker by Dylan's bedside as he napped. The last couple of weeks had been difficult, but she no longer felt like David facing Goliath. She'd moved on to feeling more like Job. Physically, her patient was better, but his depression wasn't improving, and he refused antidepressant medication.

Withdrawn, he spent his days smoking, sleeping, and working out with the free weights on the back porch. Nightmares plagued his sleep, but he refused to talk about them. As a matter of fact, he rarely spoke to her at all—unless it was to bark orders or fire her. She lost count after the first fifty times he told her to pack her bags and leave. He picked at his food, and even Mrs. Jordan's famous fried pies remained untouched and thrown away.

After that first eventful bath, Dylan had insisted on bathing himself, much to her relief. He still refused to shave and adamantly declined her offer to do it for him, claiming he lived in mortal fear she'd slit his throat. In truth, she did contemplate his demise, in a variety of creative ways, at least six times a day.

Yesterday, when he'd demanded yet another tomato sandwich, she thought about stuffing it in his face to shut him up. And his paranoia over the media bordered on being worthy of a DSM-V diagnosis for mental illness. One of Mrs. Jordan's kittens had wandered over, and he'd heard her taking a picture with her cell phone. Livid, he'd torn off his fresh eye bandage and insisted on scrolling through her phone to make sure there were no pictures of him. *As if.*

But she hated the boredom more than the quarrelling. She'd found she kind of enjoyed their verbal sparring. She and David never argued, and her father was loving but old-fashioned. She'd been brought up to understand that children were to be seen, not heard.

She picked up the framed photo on the bedside table. Three children stood with their arms wrapped around each other. The tallest was Dr. McAthie, smiling straight into the camera. Mrs. McAthie stood in the middle, giggling, as Dylan pulled her pigtail and stuck out his tongue. *Typical.* She replaced the photo and gazed at him.

It wasn't hard to see the young boy in him right now. She wrinkled her nose as she peered at the snake tattoo. It was a bit creepy. Her father would likely go so far as to say sacrilegious. Around his neck he wore a gold religious necklace of some sort. Without thinking, she reached out to pick it up, to study it more closely. Her knuckles grazed his chest, causing Dylan to stir. She froze when he grasped her hand.

Dylan lay still for a moment, not wanting to surface from the peaceful sleep. Still not fully awake, he brushed her hand with his lips.

"Sara, come back to bed," he whispered. The hand he held to his lips jerked away.

"N-No, Mr. McAthie, it's me, Jennifer."

Memories flooded his grief-stricken mind, and he crashed into full consciousness. Sara was dead. So was Greg. And his grandmother. Not to mention his career.

Sleep was the only damn bit of relief he had from this nightmare, and his annoying nurse had just robbed him of even that.

Pain swept through him. His heart raced, and he couldn't catch his breath. The room spun like a Tilt-a-Whirl.

"Get out!" he screamed, whether at Jennifer or the memories, he couldn't say.

He gulped air like a drowning victim.

Jennifer sprang to his side and eased his head between his legs. Stroking his back, she encouraged him to breathe in and out, counting with each torturous breath. As the memories receded to a dark corner of his mind, his terror lessened.

Embarrassed, he kept his head bowed and mumbled, "Thanks."

He didn't want to admit it, but her silent company helped. It was unsettling to realize he both needed and wanted her here. He didn't like the thought of needing anyone. *Never again.*

"It's time for me to redo your dressings," she told him. "Oh, and Mr. Vaughan called for the umpteenth time. He said it was urgent he speak with you."

He clenched his fists. *Jimmy.* He'd eventually have to deal with his manager. With a nod, he signaled he was ready for her to proceed with the dressings.

Although still light-sensitive, his eyesight was improving, and he took the opportunity to gaze at his angel of mercy. Her exotic blue-violet eyes, framed by those impossibly long black lashes, entranced him. His cock twitched in appreciation. He shifted, hoping she didn't notice.

Concentrating on her task, she seemed unaware of his frank perusal. As he continued to stare, her cheeks blushed, and the pulse in her neck pounded. Maybe he was wrong. It had happened on occasion. *Did she feel this kinetic energy between them?* He swallowed, unnerved.

Not only was Jennifer beautiful—she was *young.* Now that he thought about it, he hadn't had much conversation with her since that first day. She was quiet, efficient, professional, and full of piss and vinegar when riled. He liked that about her. *A lot.* Too many people in his employ gave him the answers they thought he wanted, not what he needed.

"Just how old are you?" he asked abruptly.

She tucked a stray black curl behind her ear. His fingers itched to release that ridiculous bun and see just how long her hair was.

"Almost twenty. Why?"

She's only nineteen? His body reacted as if cold water had been thrown on him. He hadn't been with teenaged band broads in years, especially after he got involved with Sara. Grabbing a cigarette off the nightstand, he changed his mind and put it down. *What the hell is wrong with me?*

"Nineteen and already a nurse?" He grasped for conversation as he pulled himself together.

"I was in the gifted program. I skipped two grades and exempted some of my college classes."

Young, smart, and innocent. I'm fucked. "Do the dressings and get out."

Jennifer knelt and bandaged his leg, wondering what she'd done to make him mad this time. His cut-off jeans hung low on his lean hips. While it made the dressing change easier, the expanse of well-toned skin made it difficult to concentrate on the task before her. She dropped the tape three times and found herself having to do the same deep-breathing exercises she'd just instructed him in.

"How old are you, Mr. McAthie?" Perhaps attempting conversation would help.

"Not old enough to be called *mister*. I've told you a hundred times to call me Dylan. I'm twenty-nine, why?" His acerbic response spoke volumes.

Glancing up, she caught the look of interest in his eyes. Finished, she stood and placed one hand on her hip. "That explains it then. I was brought up to address my elders with the appropriate title."

His mouth dropped open, and then air hissed between his teeth.

She smirked as she placed the eye drops in his eyes. He stared at her with a smoldering look. The silver glints reminded her of light reflections on water.

"Damn, those sting," he complained, blinking. Grabbing his hand, she stopped him from rubbing his eyes. She jumped when his hand clamped her wrist as she unwrapped the gauze.

"Can't we leave it off, please? I hate not being able to see." He paused and grinned. "That is, unless you want to do naughty things to me while I'm blindfolded, *Miss Adams.*"

Images of handcuffs and feathers ran through her mind. He winked, and she wanted to squirm. "I can't, *Mr. McAthie.* Doctor's orders," she managed to croak.

"I wish to hell I could fire you," he muttered.

She finished bandaging his eyes. "No more than I wish I could quit."

Scowling, he shrugged into the shirt she held for him, but didn't bother to button it. Taking the crutches from her, he bolted from the bedroom, slamming the door behind him.

Two steps forward, three steps back. This was the nature of their relationship. But his flirting had caught her off guard. Checking her reflection in the mirror, she gave up on the flyaway curls escaping her bun.

Squaring her shoulders, she left the bedroom to face the next battle. She found him sitting on the couch, tapping a cigarette with a frown on his face.

"I know you don't care if you get cancer, but haven't you heard of the dangers of secondhand smoke?"

"Misery loves company, angel. You can join me in an early grave," he snarled, lighting up and snapping the lighter closed. "If you're lucky, we'll head in opposite directions."

"Look, I know you're not angry with me. You're frustrated with your situation. Would you like to talk about it?" She sat and wrinkled her nose as she waved the smoke away. Her clothes and hair stunk of tobacco, and she was sick of it.

Dylan whipped around to glare at her. "*Oh, really?*" His whispered question sent a shiver up her spine. "And just who the *hell* else would I be angry at?" His voice rose as his temper flared. "Trust me, darling. I don't need some kid trying to play shrink on me. I've had the best damn therapy money can buy. I've attended plenty of twelve-step meetings. What makes you think *you* can do any better?"

"Why don't you play your guitar?"

"What?" He reeled back as if he'd been struck.

"You're supposedly the world's sex — uh, I mean, talented lead guitarist. But I've yet to hear you play." She could feel herself blushing.

"I'm a sex-talented lead guitarist? Do you think I play with my damn dick?"

"Don't most men?" She slapped a hand over her mouth.

Dylan howled with laughter.

Trying to cover her mistake, she shrugged. "You know what I meant. You were voted one of the sexiest musicians of the decade. Obviously, no one has seen you *lately.*" She grinned when his laughter stopped. "You're also supposedly one of the top lead guitarists in the business, and yet you never pick up your guitar and play."

"There's no *supposedly* about it. I *am* one of the best, but the music died after…" He paused and hung his head. "After the band broke up," he muttered.

"I think that's a pretty flimsy excuse, Mr. McAthie. You're alive. You could form a new band."

"Get the hell out. Better yet, you're fired!" Punctuating each word with his cigarette, he added through clenched teeth, "And quit calling me *Mr. McAthie. My. Name. Is. Dylan!*"

The cigarette grazed her arm, and she yelped.

"What? What happened? Are you okay?" Dylan snuffed the offending weapon out in the ashtray and tore the new bandage from his eyes. He grabbed her burned arm, peering at it closely. "Oh shit. I'm sorry. I didn't mean to hurt you."

"I-I don't think it will need a skin graft," she moaned, melodramatically.

He blanched. "Shit, call an ambulance!" He began searching for the phone.

Jennifer giggled. "I'm kidding. I'll get an ice cube, and it will be fine. But I'd appreciate a little more consideration when you smoke."

"You're really okay?"

"I'll live."

Dylan pulled at his beard, his face registering true remorse.

Jennifer smiled. "Do you need anything while I'm up?"

He shook his head, refusing to look at her. Jennifer ran a hand down the back of his hair, wanting to comfort him. "I'm fine, Dylan. I promise."

She returned from the kitchen rubbing an ice cube on her arm. The phone rang, and she answered, "McAthie residence."

"Hey, Jennifer. It's Jimmy again. I really need to speak to Dylan, and please don't take no for an answer."

Tired of fielding his calls, she handed the phone to Dylan. "Guess who, and the first three guesses don't count."

Dylan shook his head and motioned her away. "Tell him I'm sleeping," he whispered.

"No. Mr. Vaughan says he'll just keep calling, and I'm tired of lying for you." Slapping the phone in his hand, she perched on the arm of the sofa and didn't budge.

Chapter
Six

"**W**hat the hell do you want?" Dylan barked. He glared at Jennifer as Jimmy raised hell. Wincing, he held the phone away from his ear.

"Well, for starters, return my calls, motherfucker. Is that all you can say to me? *What the hell do I want?* What happened to *I'll call you when I get to Pine Bluff?* I'm your manager, Dylan, not to mention your *best friend.* Why won't you take my calls or get in touch with me? Are you dead set on tanking your career?

"I finally tracked you down through your sister-in-law. I suggest you hire Cathy McAthie as your chief of security. I almost had to provide her with proof of citizenship along with a pay stub before she would even talk to me."

Dylan closed his eyes. Jimmy was livid and loud. There was no doubt, judging by the grin on her face, that Jennifer could hear every damn word.

"Jesus H. Christ, you're every manager's nightmare, do you hear me?" he continued. "Wendy—remember her? Let me refresh your memory: tall, frizzy hair, pit-bull mentality, and your damn publicist for the past three years. When you refused to see her in the hospital, or answer her calls, she quit! So thanks a lot, old buddy, old pal. Now I get to do the work of at least five people." Jimmy finally stopped to catch a breath.

"I'm fine, thanks, and you?" Dylan replied. Turning to Jennifer, he motioned her to leave. "This is a private call. Do you mind?"

"Oh no, I don't mind at all. Go right ahead." Jennifer didn't move.

He squinted. Was that a smirk? *She's kind of hot when she's snippety.* Shooting her another half-hearted glare, he returned his focus to the phone and Jimmy's laughter. "I'm so glad I amuse you."

Jimmy laughed harder, and Jennifer giggled. Dylan smiled. He might not be the smartest guy in the world, but he knew when he was being an ass.

"What's the matter? You haven't got your nurse properly terrified of the world-renowned McAthie temper, yet? Why, I read in *The National Intruder* that you were such a royal pain in the ass they had to pay the nurses at the hospital extra just to take care of you," Jimmy goaded.

"Very funny. Do you always believe everything you read?" Dylan huffed, unsure whether to believe Jimmy or not. *Is crap being published about me again? Am I a pain-in-the-ass patient?* He glanced up at Jennifer and decided not to pursue that last thought. Instead, he asked her, "Do I terrify you?"

"I'm quaking with fear," she replied, examining her fingernails.

Dylan grinned. A brief vision of her quaking from something other than fear flashed through his head.

"Talk to me," Jimmy demanded. "Why are you still in the backwoods of *Deliverance* country? You have a beautiful home in Corona del Mar, and I'm sure we could bribe *someone* to take care of you. There are probably at least fifteen of your so-called friends at the house now. And what do you want me to do about the media? They're hounding me night and day wanting to know where you are, how you are, and your plans for the future. Throw me a fuckin' bone."

Dylan sighed. "Okay, calm down. I'm here in *Deliverance* country to avoid the media circus. You know I don't talk to the press, particularly those sleazebag tabloids. Dealing with them is your damn job and why I overpay you, Wendy, and multitudes of others. Tell them I'm recuperating in Switzerland, or I've joined a monastery, or was eaten by locusts. Hell, tell them I died and descended in to the seventh level of hell — they'd believe that. Or I'm hiding out with Elvis. I don't care what you tell them; just keep them the fuck *away* from *me*. And clear my damn house of those scumbag leeches, too." Dylan shook his head, disgusted. He didn't need this.

Jimmy sighed. "Okay. I'll handle it for now, but you know they'll track you down eventually. Lemme give you my new cell number; I've had to change it yet again. I've tried calling yours, but you either don't have it on or you're ignoring me."

"I turned it off. Plus, there's no reception here. That's why I like it. Give the number to my nurse. I'm done. And call Wendy and increase her salary if she'll come back." Tossing the phone to Jennifer, he eased to his feet, stuffing the cigarettes and lighter in his shirt pocket.

Limping without his crutches, Dylan slammed the front door behind him.

"I'm here, Mr. Vaughan," Jennifer said.

"Damn, I heard that all the way out here. Tell me something: is he okay? Regardless of what he thinks, he *does* have a career to come back to." The concern in Jimmy's voice sounded genuine.

But she wasn't about to break patient confidentiality or that stupid nondisclosure agreement. "I'm not at liberty to discuss his condition…"

"I know. I know. You signed the NDA. I'm just worried about him. He was a fucked-up mess when the band fell apart. And then Greg's overdose, and then…" He sighed. "It's been a tough few months on all of us, especially losing Sara."

Curiosity got the best of her. It wasn't *exactly* breaking patient confidentiality, she told herself.

"Sara?"

"Sara, my sister. She died about a month before his accident. She and Dyl were together for over six years. He hasn't mentioned her?" Jimmy's voice dropped off. "Oh wow, look at the time. I gotta run. I'll call tomorrow."

"Bye."

Jennifer hung up and pondered this new information. No wonder Dylan was so sad and bitter. She'd forgotten he'd been in a relationship because he never talked about it in the media, and they had rarely been photographed together. Six years? Why had they never married? She vowed to Google the circumstances of Sara's death next time she had a signal.

Her heart swelled with sympathy, and she promised herself to be more cognizant of his grief. Composing herself, she went to check on her patient, ashamed of her flash of jealousy over a dead woman.

Dylan sat on the porch swing, smoking. No matter how hard he tried to keep them at bay, the memories kept resurfacing.

Jennifer sat beside him.

"How's your arm?" he asked gruffly, shifting away from her. Why did the loose curl at her neck beckon him? She was off limits. For too many reasons to list.

"Fine. The cigarette barely touched me."

He nodded, his guilt compounded by her easy forgiveness. Burning her arm was the least of his many reprehensible crimes, but made him feel no less terrible. They sat for a few minutes in an uneasy silence, rocking. *It's all my fault, it's all my fault, it's all my fault*—his daily mantra repeated itself relentlessly.

With a faint catch in her voice, she offered, "I'm sorry."

"For?" He frowned and looked at her. *What did she have to be sorry about?*

"*Sara,*" she whispered, gazing at her clasped hands.

"Ah, Sara." He sighed and shook his head. "I don't want or need your pity." Grinding the cigarette out in the ashtray, he kept his voice devoid of emotion. "How much do you know?"

"Jimmy told me Sara died a few months ago, and that she was his sister."

Silence loomed for another painful moment. "Tell me something. Have you ever lost someone you loved?" His voice cracked, and he clenched his jaw, embarrassed by his show of emotion.

"Yes, I lost my mother to cancer when I was six." Sorrow etched her eyes.

Dylan gave her hand a squeeze. "I'm sorry. I never knew my mom. She died having me..."

Her voice was soft when she responded. "I didn't think I could bear it when Mama died. But I had my dad, and he needed me as much as I needed him. Your family loves you. I know you haven't spoken to him the two times they've been up to visit, but Dr. McAthie is worried about you. Could you try talking to him? He's a wonderful man—"

"Drop it. I don't want to talk about me, or the past, and certainly not about Saint Robert. Go find something to do or think of something we can do to pass the time. I'm fuckin' bored out of my mind."

He knew from experience that boredom led to trouble. He needed to stay busy.

To keep from thinking.

To keep from remembering.

And most certainly to keep from feeling.

"Do you want to watch television?" she asked.

"Without cable? Hell, no. Besides everything is still a little blurry, and I know you'll slap that damn bandage back over my eyes." Various ways to pass the time came to mind, most of them not possible with his naïve nurse. "Tell you what, let's play a game." He patted her thigh.

"A game? But I need to re-bandage your eyes."

"Not that type of game. Truth or Dare."

"What?" she squeaked.

"Yup. You first. Truth or Dare?"

An obvious battle raged within her for a moment as she chewed on the side of her mouth. He hoped she never played poker; she'd lose her shirt. Which, now that he thought of it, might not be so bad...

Taking a deep breath, she said, "Truth."

Dylan grinned. "Let's see. I bet you've never been properly kissed."

Her mouth dropped open. "I have a boyfriend," she huffed. "This is very inappropriate."

"Will you relax? Answer the question."

"I, uh, I've been kissed," she admitted.

Her cheeks were the color of Gran's roses, and her leg bounced. He wanted to pull that delectable lower lip from her teeth with his own.

"But have you been *properly* kissed?"

"Not that it's any of your business, but yes. Besides, it's my turn." Her chin rose, and those amazing eyes sparkled before narrowing. "Truth or Dare?"

"Truth, by all means." He lit a cigarette and waited, not bothering to hide his smug smile. *This ought to be good.*

"Have you properly grieved your lead singer's dying? I know the band was broken up, but you had to have been friends, at least at one time. Or how about Sara's death? What have you done since the band broke up? I don't think you have honestly dealt with any of it. You suppress it behind your snarky attitude. You act like you don't care about anything, but you do care. A lot. You won't let your family in because you're scared to let go of the pain—you don't know how you'll deal with it. You're afraid it will break you. You're thirty. Why won't you talk to your brother?"

Dylan stared at her, dumbfounded. He was pretty damn sure his balls were now at waist level after that hit below the belt. "You don't know a damn thing about me. And I'm not fuckin' thirty."

Dammit, most of what she said was true.

She shrugged. "You're twenty-nine. Close enough."

Is that a smirk on her never-been-properly-kissed mouth?

"Do you know how many times I've dreamed about *firing* you?" he countered. He took a draw off his cigarette and exhaled. "I envision you crying, begging me to kiss you. Er, I mean, begging to keep your job, but I refuse. As a matter of fact, I turn you out into the driving rain," he added.

"Me? Kiss you? I suppose you think you could *properly* kiss me. In your dreams, mister. And that's funny, because I've dreamed about *quitting*. My favorite dream is of you chained to the pier with various creatures pecking at your rotting flesh. You rant and rave, threatening to fire them all for not killing you in a manner worthy of the great and mighty Dylan McAthie."

He raised his eyebrows, amused. "Bloodthirsty little thing, aren't you?" *Okay, missy, let's take this up a notch.* "Are you one of creatures staring at my pecker?" He flashed her a leering grin.

Her eyes dropped to his crotch for a brief second. Her color heightened and she gasped, "W-What?"

"Oops, sorry. I mean, pecking at my rotting flesh?"

"No. I'm sitting there watching you die a slow, painful death as I shred your cigarettes, one by one, into the lake."

"Shit, now that's cold." He laughed.

She giggled. "What did you expect? I'm a nurse."

Dylan put out his cigarette and noticed an open book on the glider. "Whatcha reading?"

"Nothing you'd be interested in. It's a classic."

He smiled at her unintended insult. "I'm a musician, not illiterate. I've read classics."

"But it's probably nothing you'd like." She blushed and picked up the book, clutching it to her chest.

Dylan tore his gaze from her mouth before he did something he'd regret.

"Yuck. Jane Austen with the ever-suffering heroines and sensitive heroes? Mr. Darcy was a wimp."

"You've read Jane Austen?" Her disbelief was priceless.

He laughed and confessed, "No, but I endured the movie."

She raised a skeptical eyebrow.

Throwing his hands up he admitted, "Okay, I slept through most of it."

"I'm re-reading *Wuthering Heights*."

"Fine." He shrugged. "*The Odyssey* would be better, but go ahead; read me the classic chick lit and educate me."

He stretched out and placed his head in her soft lap, smiling at her gasp of surprise. Closing his eyes, he remembered sitting on this very porch as a boy, listening to Robert read about King Arthur and the knights of Camelot.

Chapter Seven

The aroma of fresh-brewed coffee drifted into his room. Rolling over, he tore the bandage from his eyes and squinted at the clock. Seven? *Who gets up at this ungodly hour?* He turned over, covering his head with his pillow. Last night they'd stayed up late, reading a good portion of *Wuthering Heights*. He'd been surprised the story had held his interest. After an unappetizing supper of disgusting fried food, he'd asked her to read more. When he'd pointed out that Heathcliff was a pompous ass, Jennifer had laughed so hard she'd snorted cola up her nose.

He was going to miss her when she was gone. The past few days, when he'd threatened to fire her, he'd realized he didn't really mean it. He enjoyed her sense of humor, and he had to admit, her patience was immeasurable. Teasing her and watching her blush had become his favorite hobby. She might say she'd been kissed, but he still doubted she'd truly been *kissed*.

Lifting the pillow, he listened, perplexed. *What the hell is that infernal racket?* It sounded like a cat in heat.

Dylan made his way to the kitchen. He'd just about mastered the crutches, and his eyesight was improving. Maybe if he was lucky, he could talk her into leaving off the bandage today.

He stopped dead in the doorway to the kitchen. Oh, hell yes, his eyesight was better.

Shit, look at that girl.

Oblivious to his presence, Jennifer continued singing her loud, off-key rendition of "I'll Fly Away." The angels in heaven had to be praying for God to strike her mute. He winced; he certainly was.

As she stood in front of the open refrigerator door, the light shone straight through her demure cotton gown. He leaned against the doorjamb, taking the time to admire the silhouette of her lush figure. Her shiny black hair cascaded down her back in a wild array of curls. He felt an almost uncontrollable, crazy urge to nibble her bare, pink-polished toes. *She's fuckin' sexy as hell.*

Jennifer shut the refrigerator door with her hip and turned around, humming as off key as she sang. When she saw him, she shrieked, and the butter dish clattered to the floor.

"Good morning, angel," he purred.

"Holy hotcakes, you scared the daylights out of me!" Her pulse pounded just above the collarbone he wanted to lick. "Y-You don't have your bandage on your eyes."

Her eyes widened in direct correlation to the blush infusing her cheeks. Her thin, gossamer cotton gown hid little, and she clutched it tight in an unsuccessful attempt to shield her body. Dylan smiled, enjoying the view. Head down, she moved toward the door but skidded to a stop when he blocked her exit.

"Please, Mr. McAthie, I-I need to get dressed." She refused to meet his eyes, and her adorable polished toes curled.

Cupping her face, he forced her to look at him. With his thumb, he stroked her soft, red cheek. For a split second, he entertained the thought of throwing caution to the wind and burying his face in her neck. She always smelled so good.

"Dylan. Call me Dylan." He grazed her jaw with the back of his fingers.

Jennifer nodded and returned her gaze to the floor. A lock of her silky hair fell over his hand, and he watched it wrap itself around his finger. She jerked away as if burned.

He wanted to pull her closer and kiss her with everything in him. Kiss her until she moaned his name and begged for more. Kiss her until all thoughts of why that would be wrong disappeared.

Instead, he moved just enough so she could squeeze by him. Her shoulder brushed his bare chest, and he sucked in a ragged breath. The joke was on him. This innocent girl fascinated him.

She scampered to her room, slamming the door so hard the sound echoed down the hallway. He chuckled when he heard the lock click. Humming "I'll Fly Away," he poured himself a cup of coffee, looking forward to the day.

Jennifer collapsed on her neatly made bed. *Why is he up so early? Why didn't I get dressed before starting breakfast? What would Daddy say?* The thought of her father spurred her to dress quickly and conservatively. Yanking the brush through her unruly hair, she wrenched it into a ponytail.

Placing her ice cold hands on her hot cheeks, she stared at the mirror. Her eyes remained bright, and she certainly didn't need any blush. The phone rang. To her surprise, it didn't ring again. Dylan must have answered it. Glaring once more at the mirror, she threw her shoulders back, determined not to let Mr. Sex God know how much he had affected her.

Returning to the kitchen, she found Dylan leaning against the counter with the phone tucked against his ear. He grinned as she entered the room.

"And you know her how?" He paused and took a puff off one of his infernal cigarettes. "I see. Well, she just walked in the door. She had to get dressed." Smirking, he handed the phone to her. "It's *David.*"

"David?" *David who?* She grabbed the phone. *Your boyfriend, idiot.* "Hey."

"Uh, hi. Everything okay there? I tried to reach you by cell and then text, but it didn't go through. I forget you don't have service there. Mrs. McAthie gave me this number."

"Everything's fine. We just woke up."

Dylan snickered, and heat flushed her cheeks.

"I mean—it's early. I can only get a signal at the end of the driveway, so I don't bother checking my phone. What's wrong?"

"Now don't panic. I didn't want to alarm you until I had all the facts. Your dad's fine, but he had a little chest pain yesterday. He didn't want to worry you while you're working out of town, but I thought you should know."

"Daddy? Chest pain? Is he in the hospital? Does he need me?" Fear gripped her heart. Her knees buckled, and she gratefully sank into the chair Dylan pulled out for her. He stroked her shoulder, and without thinking, she reached for his hand. He squeezed it.

"No, no, he's fine. I was there when it happened. He assured me he's keeping his appointment with Dr. McAthie next week. The chest pain went away when he sat down and rested. I just thought you should know. How's the job going? I know it's still early, but has Dylan tried to fire you today?"

"Not yet, but it's only seven thirty, still plenty of time for that."

Dylan limped to the other side of the kitchen. She looked out the window, attempting to ignore the cut of his bicep as he poured more coffee. Instead, she found herself watching him in the glass reflection. Talking to her boyfriend in front of her handsome employer was beyond awkward. Dylan scratched his toned abs, stretching and yawning.

Doesn't the man ever wear a shirt? It's awfully hot in here. Is the air conditioner working?

"I miss you, Jennifer. When will you get a day off?"

"Huh? Oh, hold on, David." Holding her hand over the mouthpiece, she spoke to Dylan. "Do you mind? I'll bring you some breakfast to the front porch in a moment."

He hitched himself up to sit on the counter. "Oh, I wouldn't miss this for the world. Payback can be such a bitch," he added with that annoying, lopsided grin.

She turned around. "Not any time soon, David. I'll let you know when I do. You're sure Daddy's okay?"

"He's fine, I promise. Don't mention it when you call; he'd be furious with me. I really need his letter of recommendation for school…" David's voice trailed off, and he sighed. "Are we okay, Jennifer?"

Guilt made her want to cross her fingers like a child. In truth, she hadn't thought much about David over the past week or so. "Yes, of course."

"Okay, I gotta run. Love you."

"Thanks for calling. Keep me posted on my dad." Hanging up, she realized she hadn't told him she missed him and loved him in return.

"Is David the guy who's kissed you properly?"

She sighed. Dylan's persistence was downright annoying. She dropped to wipe the butter off the floor, refusing to meet his eyes. "Yes."

Dylan grinned. "And?"

She huffed with annoyance. "And nothing. We've been friends since we were kids, and we've dated the past two years. He's going to be a teacher and then apply for the seminary."

"Is Deacon David a good kisser?" He hopped off the counter and sat across the table from her.

"Why do you want to know? Are you interested in him? Sorry, he's taken." Jennifer stood, placing a hand on her hip, and frowned. "My personal affairs are none of your business, Mr. McAthie."

"Affairs? *For shame,* Miss Adams." Dylan reached for the pack of cigarettes.

"Stop it! You know what I meant!" Jennifer snapped, grabbing his cigarettes away from him. "You smoke entirely too much, and I'm *sick* of it."

"Give me my cigarettes." His tone was low and lethal.

"No."

Dylan shot out of the chair, grabbing her hand. "I said give me my damn cigarettes, *now!*"

"No. You're a condescending bully. I'm tired of you taking your ill temper out on me. And your cigarette smoke makes my hair and clothes *stink*. It's disgusting."

She was so angry, she wrenched her arm out of his grasp and shoved against his chest. Her unmanageable hair had loosened from the ponytail, and she blew a strand off her face. Dylan's eyes darkened to the color of tempered steel. He yanked her close, his fingers tangling in her hair, and slanted his mouth across hers.

It was the kiss to end all kisses. It was the kiss she'd imagined alone at night. It was the kiss that ruined any kiss she'd had before. His lips were softer than she'd imagined, the coarse beard tickled, and she gasped when his tongue slipped into her mouth. Resisting for all of five seconds, she closed her eyes and surrendered to his persistence, thrilling at the tender exploration of his mouth on hers. He deepened the kiss, and she moaned. Gripping his shoulders to keep from sliding to the floor, she reveled in the hard body pressed against hers.

She was positive time stood still, the heavens opened, and a current of electricity zipped straight through her body. Light-headed and breathless, parts of her body she knew shouldn't be tingling and aching longed for more. Pulling away, she touched her trembling lips with shaky fingers. Her face burned from his rough beard and embarrassment over her desire.

"Damn," he whispered, looking just as confused as she felt.

His warm hand held her burning face. She lowered her gaze to his seductive smile. Her heart raced as if she'd run a marathon.

"Strachan Dylan McAthie."

They jumped at the sound of Mrs. Jordan's voice.

Jennifer covered her mouth in horror. Humiliated, she glanced at Dylan, beseeching him with her eyes to say something, anything. He winked in reply.

Flashing his dimples, he turned and smiled at the nosy neighbor. There was no way Jennifer could speak. Her tongue seemed glued to the roof of her mouth.

"Morning, ma'am. Would you like a cup of coffee?" he asked with exaggerated politeness.

Mrs. Jordan raised an eyebrow, but a tiny smile touched the corners of her mouth. "I knocked, but *obviously* no one heard me."

Jennifer glanced at Dylan, who shrugged and grinned.

"It's nice to see you two getting along so well. I just stopped by to bring you this casserole and tell you Cathy and Robert will be here tomorrow." Mrs. Jordan placed the dish on the table. As she turned to leave, she offered a sly smile. "Dylan, you really need to shave. You look like a caveman. Jennifer's face is red enough without the abrasion." The door closed behind her.

They stood in silence, eyeing each other.

"Uh, well, that was all kinds of awkward." Dylan smirked like the Cheshire cat.

"I feel like I did in high school when Daddy caught David and me kissing."

"That was, like, a year ago, right?"

She smacked his arm, and they both burst out laughing.

"I don't know about you, but I need a cigarette." His blue eyes sparkled like sunlight flickering across the lake.

Jennifer rolled her eyes and handed him the pack.

Peeking at the casserole, she sighed, unable to hide her disappointment. "Ham and tater tot again."

"Oh, hell to the no." Dylan grimaced and lit the long-awaited cigarette. "Let's go do something. If I have to stare at these four walls one more day, I'm going to go stark, raving mad."

Jennifer quirked an eyebrow.

"Okay, so I'm already stark, raving mad. Let's just go get a pizza or something." He flashed her a devastating smile. "Pretty please?"

"Is there some place around here that will deliver?"

"I doubt it. But I don't want anyone knowing I'm here. That's why Mrs. J has done all the grocery shopping for us." His shoulders sagged for a moment, but then a grin spread across his face. "I know exactly what we'll do. Do you have any clothes besides those damn uniforms?"

"I have a skirt and blouse." She'd packed them thinking she might go to church somewhere, but she'd yet to make it.

"No jeans? I guess it'll work. I need clothes, though. Do you think the bandage could be compressed enough so I could wear a normal pair of jeans without a slit up to my ass?"

Jennifer laughed and nodded. His leg was almost healed. As a matter of fact, he probably wouldn't need her nursing skills after Dr. McAthie assessed him tomorrow. The thought made her heart sink a little.

"Great! I have an errand for you."

Before leaving the parking lot of the store, Jennifer took advantage of cell service and phoned her father to make sure everything was okay.

"Hi, Daddy."

"Jennifer, what a pleasant surprise." The warmth of her father's voice made her homesick.

"How are you? Are you eating? Taking your medicine?" She fussed, knowing full well he wasn't going to mention the chest pain.

"I know how to cook; I don't remember you starving as a child," he replied with a chuckle. "Besides, the Ladies Auxiliary has kept me inundated with fried chicken. I actually snuck out to grab a hamburger the other night on the way home from church."

"Oh, Daddy. You're not supposed to eat red meat or fried food."

"If the good Lord chooses to bring me home eating a hamburger, at least I'll die a happy man."

Jennifer shook her head. He was as stubborn as ever.

"How are things with you?"

"Fine. Dyl—er, Mr. McAthie is almost fully recovered. I should be home soon." Although she missed her father, the thought of never seeing Dylan again made her sad. She chatted for a few more minutes before hanging up. As David had predicted, her father hadn't mentioned the chest pain, but seemed fine.

Next she phoned Dr. McAthie to give him an update on Dylan, glad he couldn't see her red face when she reported Dylan's improved vision. Dr. McAthie listened to her report and agreed she could leave off the eye bandage. He'd arranged Dylan's follow up with the ophthalmologist next week and gave her the date and time.

As she hung up, Jennifer resolved to try once again to talk to Dylan about his brother and convince him to repair their relationship.

Then she headed toward home. How weird that the lake house felt like "home" now. It wouldn't for long, she reminded herself.

She hoped everything she'd bought would fit. Dylan had refused to go with her, saying he didn't want to be relegated to the "dead pecker bench" while she shopped. She hadn't understood what he meant until she passed all the elderly gentlemen sitting on the benches throughout the store. After their kiss this morning, she didn't think Dylan needed to worry about being there anytime soon.

Her skin tingled every time she thought about it, which was pretty much all the time. It had left her aching and wanting something more. If Mrs. Jordan hadn't arrived when she did…Jennifer didn't want to think about what might have happened.

This wouldn't do. She was here to do a job and needed to be professional. Kissing the patient was not only inappropriate, it was unethical. And deliciously mind-blowing and toe-curling…

Chapter
Eight

Dylan considered shaving, but thought better of it. A beard would help hide his identity when he and Jennifer went out. He'd scratched the annoying beard and smiled as he recalled her red cheek after their kiss. *Fuck the workouts. That nurse is my anti-depressant.*

His attraction to her confused him. Sweet and innocent wasn't at all his type. Sara had been nothing like Jennifer...*And how well did that work out for you, dumbass?*

A morbid longing led him to plug in his phone for the first time in weeks. No signal meant he could go straight to his photos. Thumbing through them was like having his life flash before him. His band had been more than co-workers; they were his chosen family. They'd laughed together, played together, fought and worked hard together—until Greg's addiction had started affecting the music.

Then it had affected everything. The fights in the final months of their last tour had been horrific, and rather than admit his problem, Greg had sabotaged everything, pushing everyone away. The bastard had even planted a story in the press that his wife, Loree, was having an affair with Dylan, when really the opposite was true. Greg and Sara, first brought together by their addiction, had crossed over into something more. Jeff, their drummer and Greg's brother, had of course sided with him in the ensuing arguments, though he knew

Greg's version was all a lie. He'd used the excuse that Greg was family. *Fuck family.* Family meant nothing.

After the band was done Greg's problem had only gotten worse. His death a month later had been devastating, but he hadn't really known pain until Sara followed him a few weeks after that. They'd all once been so close…Such a waste.

Against his better judgment, he stopped on his favorite picture of Sara. Her long red hair was mussed, and she wore no makeup. She'd always hated her freckles, but he'd loved them. The next picture hit him like a sledgehammer. Her hands cradled her pregnant stomach, but pain etched her glassy eyes. Waves of emotion washed over him. Grief, regret, and longing for something lost forever consumed him with a mighty vengeance. The tears started. God knew he and Sara had had their problems, but he'd loved her. And he'd wanted that baby.

McAthie men do not cry. The adage oft repeated by his asshole father ran though his head.

He sighed, taking stock of his life for the first time, well…ever. He had so many damn regrets. *Sara.* He should've done more…And if he was honest, he knew his family didn't deserve the way he treated them. Rob and Cat were happy. His teenaged crush on her had never been reciprocated; it had been all in his mind. Cat belonged with Rob. Was it a gene he'd inherited from his father that made him hold on to unreasonable grudges?

So many questions plagued him. How could Greg have thrown away everything—their friendship, their success? They'd been on top, dammit. The pain of his betrayal hurt the most, and he couldn't get past it. Not yet. If ever. Burying his face in his knees, the tears flowed, despite his efforts to stop them. *Sara. The baby.* All were gone. He was alone.

Where was Jennifer? He needed her…She'd be leaving soon. Everyone always left.

The harder he tried to repress the memories, the harder he sobbed. A knock at his door startled him, then sent him into a blinding rage. He froze, feeling trapped and vulnerable.

"Dylan? Are you okay?"

McAthie men don't cry.

"Get the hell away from that door or you'll be sorry," he bellowed as he scrambled to get up, rubbing his burning eyes with the heels of his hands.

"Dylan, let me in. What's wrong?"

The concern in her voice pushed him over the edge. Reaching the door in one step, he threw it open. The picture on the nightstand tumbled to the floor as the door slammed against the wall. "What part of *get the hell away from my door* didn't you understand?" He clenched his teeth so hard his jaw ached.

Jennifer lifted her chin and looked directly into his eyes. "I'm not leaving you."

Dylan took another breath to yell again, but instead turned and limped to the window. *Fucking stubborn woman.* Why wouldn't she leave him the hell alone? *Please don't leave me...*

Taking a smoke from the dresser, he lit it and leaned against the window. The sunlight burned his sensitive eyes, but he welcomed the sensation. He could tolerate physical pain. It was tangible.

He closed his eyes and with everything in him suppressed the agonizing memories, and boxed his emotions, tucking them away as he clawed his way out of his despair. The pain in his chest receded, leaving him empty and bereft.

Still unsteady, he at least felt strong enough to deal with Jennifer. He stubbed out the cigarette and faced her. A tear slipped down her cheek, and his tenuous hold on his sorrow slipped. Freefalling, he sank to the floor, wrapped his arms around his legs and hid his face in his knees. His ragged breathing filled the air as he choked on his sobs.

McAthie men do not cry. He heard it again as clearly as if his father stood over him with his folded belt in hand.

Jennifer knelt beside him and placed a hand on his shoulder. "Let me help you."

"Don't," he choked out. Her kindness after the way he'd treated her the past few weeks only added to his guilt. He didn't deserve her.

Jennifer framed his face, and reluctantly, he raised his head. He saw no condemnation, no hatred, just understanding and acceptance.

"It's okay. Let it go," she whispered.

He pulled her into his lap and wrapped his arms around her, burying his face in her neck. She held him tight, and with a primordial groan, he clung to her like a life raft. His body shook as his anguish shattered into a million pieces. For the first time, he truly grieved for everything he'd loved and lost.

Filtered sunlight slanted through the blinds, making him blink. He was surprised to see it was five in the afternoon. Rolling over, he found a sandwich and a sweating glass of tea on his nightstand. He sat up, picked up the sandwich, and threw it down. Turkey. *Blah.*

Still, he felt lighter, less tense. Rummaging through the shopping bags Jennifer had left on his dresser, he found a new pair of jeans. They weren't tailored to fit, but were still a hell of a lot better than what he'd been wearing. He patted his washboard abdomen. If nothing else, his relentless workouts had put him back to being camera ready—he'd have to remember to ask Jimmy when the hell that photoshoot was.

Hesitant to leave the room, he sat on the bed. He was in no hurry to face Jennifer after his meltdown. He scratched his irritating beard. Maybe tomorrow he'd ask her to help him shave. He didn't want to rub her face raw when he kissed her again. *Jesus—stop, asshole. She's an employee.* Not technically, his dick argued. After all, he wasn't paying her salary.

Chucking the crutches, he limped to the bathroom. After washing his face and brushing his teeth, he found one of her ponytail elastics on the sink and used it to pull his hair back. Feeling human again, he went to face the music.

He found her on the porch, sound asleep. Soft curls danced across her face, escaping the ridiculous ponytail. Asleep, Jennifer looked every bit the sweet young girl she tried so hard to hide under her professional nurse persona. Yet the full breasts moving up and down with each breath were not those of a mere girl. Dylan sat and watched her, strangely content just being in her presence.

Their kiss this morning had left him wanting more. But pursuing those feelings was a disaster waiting to happen.

Jennifer opened her eyes and stretched, arching her back. Her cheeks were rosy from sleep, and it wasn't hard to imagine how she might look flushed with desire. She yawned and gave him a soft, drowsy smile.

"You okay?" she asked.

"Yeah." Without thinking, Dylan leaned over and wrapped one of her loose curls around his finger. She reached out and caught hold of the medal around his neck, looking at it intently.

"What is it?" she asked, her voice husky.

The brief touch made his breath catch, and he grasped her hand. Sexual tension shot between them.

"It's a saint medallion. St. Jude, the patron saint of lost causes. Gran gave it to me on my sixteenth birthday. Appropriate, don't ya think?"

A curl blew over her eyes. Jennifer smiled and shook her head. "I don't think you're a lost cause. I have high hopes for you."

Her bright smile further diminished his dark mood. He stared at her mouth.

To his surprise, the shy little nurse cupped his cheek, pulling him toward her. It started as a tender, hesitant kiss and stirred him to his very soul. Using his tongue to part her lips, he delved deeper. Her soft moan sparked the flame of his desire into a roaring fire. *Mine.* His control slipped under the power of her innocence. *I'm hers.*

When her breathing became as erratic as his own, he knew he had to stop. Pulling away, he kissed her forehead and rested his cheek against her hair. He closed his eyes, just enjoying the moment. Everything felt so *right* for a change.

The book tumbled out of her lap, bringing him crashing back to reality. He picked it up and handed it to her.

"Did I miss anything in the story?"

"Cathy just died." Her hand shook as she pushed a strand of hair behind her ear and looked away from him. Embarrassment flushed her pale cheeks.

In seconds, she'd transformed from sexy seductress back to in-experienced teen. His lust-filled body begged for the return of the bold temptress.

Clearing his throat, he shifted away from her. "Died? Wow, that sucks. What kind of romance is that? Does it get all supernatural and she becomes a vampire or something?"

"No, but there *are* ghosts." She laughed but refused to look him in the face. "I'm sorry. That was uh, totally i-inappropriate on my part..."

"It's okay." Dylan had mercy on her. If she was half as confused as he was, they needed the change of scenery they'd discussed this morning. "I'm starving. Go get dressed in something besides those damn scrubs. We're going out."

"I left you a sandwich by your bed—"

Dylan grimaced. "It was *turkey*. Ten bucks says I can be ready before you. And remember, I'm crippled. Better yet, I promise *not* to fire you today if you beat me to the car."

Jennifer laughed, her shoulders relaxing. "Now that's an offer I can't refuse."

She raced into the house and threw the book down on the couch as the phone rang.

"Hello?" She shrugged at Dylan's inquiring look and hung up. "No one there. Must've been a wrong number or robo-call. You really need caller ID."

Jennifer grinned, watching Dylan as he studied the menu.

"Oh my God, this all looks good." Wearing dark sunglasses with his hair pulled back under a ball cap, he hummed as he read over the menu. He remained in desperate need of a shave—he'd said the beard would help him remain *incognito*.

"What do you want to eat?" Nodding his head to the music playing in the restaurant, he began to make rap noises.

She couldn't help but laugh. "How about a loaded pizza, thick crust?"

Looking up from the menu, he pulled his sunglasses down and peered over them. "You're kidding, right?"

"No, why? You don't like all the toppings? How about ham and pineapple?"

Dylan shook his head and pushed his sunglasses back up on his nose. "For a nurse, *Miss Adams*, your diet is atrocious. And is there a particular reason you want me to eat pineapple?" His brow jumped, and his grin widened.

"My diet? Are you kidding me? You eat Frosted Flakes every morning for breakfast, *Mr. McAthie*. And what's wrong with pineapple?"

"Well, I've developed an aversion to *eggs*, thanks to Mrs. J, and no one ever asked me what kind of cereal I wanted. As for the pineapple, you can look on the internet to see why men should eat that."

Jennifer frowned. "The Frosted Flakes were in your cupboard. I just assumed you liked them…"

Still perusing the menu, he said, "Mrs. J shops for the groceries, and in case you haven't noticed, she thinks I'm five years old."

Jennifer laughed. "True. What kind of pizza do you want?"

"Veggie, extra mushroom, hold the onion—in case you want to kiss me again—thin crust." Smiling, his dimples deepened when she wrinkled her nose.

"I'm *not* eating fungus on my pizza. Yuck." She gulped. *Wait, did he just say in case you want to kiss me?* "Why don't we order pepperoni? Everybody loves pepperoni pizza."

He shook his head.

She bit her lip, at a loss. "No?"

"Sweetheart, I'm vegetarian. Well, ovo-lacto vegetarian to be precise." He paused and chuckled. "Though like I said, not so much on the ovo lately, thanks to Mrs. J."

"*You're* a vegetarian?" Jennifer asked, stunned. "Is this why you pick at your food? Why on Earth didn't you say something?"

Dylan looked up from the menu. "I don't like to complain."

Jennifer's mouth popped open. "*You* don't like to complain?" She rolled her eyes when he didn't respond. *He truly believes he doesn't complain?* Shaking her head, she looked up when the waitress brought their water.

"What would you like, darlin'?" The server's attention focused on Dylan.

"Salad, Italian dressing. Jen? You want a salad?" When she shook her head, he continued, "And a large pizza, half loaded with every greasy, disgusting topping you have and half veggie, hold the onion. I'll concede to the lady's wishes: thick crust. She likes her meat, and she likes it thick."

The waitress snickered.

"Anything to drink?"

Jennifer shook her head again, and Dylan flashed the waitress his dazzling smile as he handed her the menus. "Just water, thanks."

The waitress nodded, winked at Dylan, and left to turn in the order.

"That was totally inappropriate. And does that happen often?" Jennifer crossed her arms, annoyed. By what, she couldn't be sure.

"What?" Dylan clasped his hands and leaned forward, beaming.

"Do strange women succumb to your charm and fall all over themselves trying to please you?" She bit her lip when she realized she sounded jealous. Maybe he wouldn't notice.

Dylan stirred his water with his straw for a moment, his brow furrowed. "Succumb? Is that one of your forty-dollar literature words? Lemme think. One particular incident comes to mind…A few weeks ago, there was this beautiful young woman who fell all over herself trying to get my clothes off. She couldn't wait to see me *nekkid*."

She gasped her outrage.

His brow furrowed. "Jennifer, there's something I've wondered for a while; have we met before?"

Jennifer swallowed, feeling her face flush at the reminder of the towel incident. She nodded. "Once."

He frowned. "Did we, uh, I mean, you know. Was it when I was touring?"

"What?"

"Did we, you know, *do it?*" He waggled his eyebrows and stared at her.

"Do it? Have you lost your mind? As if! No!" She kicked him hard under the table.

"Shit," he howled, rubbing his shin. "That hurt. What if you'd kicked my bad leg?"

"It would have served you right." Unnerved, she grabbed her purse and dashed to the restroom, nearly running into the waitress bringing Dylan his salad.

As if, indeed. The thought of *it* had plagued her dreams for the past week.

Chapter
Nine

Jennifer returned from the restroom and plopped back into the booth, promptly knocking her fork to the floor. Diving under the table to pick it up, she heard Dylan ask the waitress for another. For the next twenty minutes, the server smiled and flirted with Dylan, returning to the table numerous times to see if he needed anything. Despite her best efforts, Jennifer couldn't seem to get a grip on her nerves. She spilled her water down her chest, and her nipples hardened instantly. Although she couldn't see behind his dark glasses, she knew Dylan's eyes were riveted. When she dropped her napkin, Dylan began to laugh.

"Jen, honey, you're going to give these customers the wrong idea if you keep ducking under the table."

Retrieving the napkin, she asked, "What do you mean?"

When he gave her a wicked grin, understanding permeated her dumbstruck brain.

"Please stop," she whispered. While in the restroom, she'd of course Googled the reason men should eat pineapple.

The food arrived, but anxiety twisted her stomach. She picked at her pizza, not wanting to risk throwing up. That would be the cherry topping her humiliation.

Dylan, on the other hand, seemed oblivious to her discomfort and ate with gusto. This sort of thing was probably an everyday occurrence for him.

Just how many girls has he "you knowed" with? His devastating smile, easy conversation, and teasing didn't help the butterflies in her stomach. She longed to be back home in her scrubs, safe in their usual roles of surly patient and frustrated nurse.

That's precisely my problem: frustration.

Startled by the thought, Jennifer refocused her attention on her meal. She picked up the pizza. A glob of sauce plopped onto her white skirt. With a sigh, she dipped her napkin in her water and dabbed at the stain. *Great, now it looks like I peed on myself.* She gave up on eating and waited for Dylan to finish his meal, smiling as he talked. For all she knew, he could be reciting the Pledge of Allegiance. The pounding in her chest and her over-heightened awareness of *him* made concentration impossible.

Furious with herself, when they left the restaurant she slammed the car in reverse before racing out of the parking lot.

"Hey, slow it down. I don't need whiplash added to my injuries," Dylan complained.

Without replying, Jennifer slowed down, realizing he was right. Plus, she didn't need a speeding ticket. Only the contemporary Christian music on the radio broke their strained silence.

"I don't think that guy ever had a music lesson in his life," Dylan mumbled.

Jennifer snapped the radio off.

"Look, I'm sorry for what I said. I've just had the feeling we've met before. And turns out I was right. When? Tell me when we met. Plus, I can't help but tease you. You're kind of an easy mark. Sorry."

Jennifer glanced at him. Why wasn't he as confused as she was? Her mixed-up feelings for him had her on the verge of a mental breakdown. She bit her lip, pulling up every ounce of professionalism she could muster to keep a semblance of patient-nurse boundaries.

"Besides, you're cute when you blush." He winked. "Come on, tell me. Did we kanoodle after a show or something?"

"Of course not. It was a long time ago."

Flatterer. I bet that charm works on every woman he meets...including me. I'm falling for him. Wait. Whoa, him? He's the most conceited, arrogant, condescending man I've ever met. So why do I want to rip his clothes off and explore every inch of his perfect body? Surely it's lust, not love.

"Too bad. I bet we would've had fun. But you've piqued my curiosity. Come on, tell me. When did we meet?"

"It was a long time ago. I was just a little girl."

"Last year, huh?" He laughed, and his eyes roamed the passing landscape. "Seriously, I'm sorry. I didn't realize it had been that long ago. Look, I don't wanna go home." Whether he did it on purpose or not, his lower lip slipped into a pout, and he hung his head like a kid in trouble.

Jennifer bit her lip to keep from smiling. It was rare she had the upper hand in their strange, convoluted relationship. And truthfully, she was almost afraid to go home and be alone with him.

"Okay. What do you want to do?"

He flashed his brilliant smile. *Look at those dimples.*

"Turn up here!" Excited, he motioned with his hand. "We'll go to the movies, if it's still open."

Movies, lots of people, safe, dark theater, kissing...Stop!

"What do you want to see?"

He shrugged. "I don't care; you pick. It's a drive-in theater, double feature."

Sure enough, cars lined the highway where they'd stopped to enter. Jennifer cast Dylan a dubious look.

"A drive-in?" Scenes from corny, old B-movies with teens making out in the backseat of a car played through her head. Uneasy, she slowed down, hoping he'd change his mind when he saw the number of cars waiting to get in.

"Hey, it's cheaper than a movie theater. You get two movies for the price of one. It'll be fun. You'll see." Dylan gave her a wide, easy grin.

Playing on one screen was an action film and a suspense thriller. On the second screen was a Disney movie and a chick flick.

"I'm surprised Mr. Rock God doesn't have a movie theater in his home. I can't imagine you going to a drive-in," Jennifer said.

Actually, the problem was she *could* see him in the backseat of a car. She squirmed and turned up the A/C.

Dylan laughed. "Ah, yes. But Mr. Rock God has money *because* he knows a bargain when he sees one. And I believe you should address me by my full title, *Miss Adams*. 'Your Supreme Royal Pain in the Ass Rock God' will suffice. I used to work here when I was a kid."

Jennifer laughed. It was hard to stay upset with him. Dylan dug in his pocket.

"Aw, shit."

Glancing over, she saw precisely seven dollars in his hand. Not enough to pay for admission.

"I never carry cash, and I can't use a credit card here. I'm sorry, angel." His disappointment was clear.

"I got it." She drove up to the box office.

Slumping in the seat and pulling his hat low, Dylan suddenly seemed inordinately interested in the grass outside his window.

"Which movies?" she asked again.

He shrugged without looking at her. Choosing the Disney/chick flick combo for spite, she pulled ahead and looked for a place to park.

Dylan sat up and turned to face her. "Sorry about that. I didn't want old man Wade to know it was me."

"Who?"

"The guy collecting money."

"Would he care enough to alert the media that the great Dylan McAthie was here?"

"I wasn't thinking about that," Dylan said. With a sheepish grin, he added, "I worked here when I was a teenager. I made an order mistake, kind of, er, sort of, on purpose. Instead of ordering *Bambi,* I took a dare and ordered a porn flick starring a girl named Bambi."

"What happened?" She giggled.

"Well, for starters, old man Wade refused to give me a letter of recommendation for my next job."

"No!" She pretended to be shocked, and he laughed.

"And then Mr. Jordan put my ass to work doing hard labor as a favor for Gran." He chuckled, pulling at his beard.

Jennifer parked the car and relaxed when she realized most of the vehicles around them held families with small children, all having a good time. A beautiful full moon shone overhead, and there wasn't a cloud in the sky. Children ran after fireflies, laughing, as the adults sat in lawn chairs, visiting with friends. The radio station used as the movie sound system played songs from the fifties and sixties, giving the night a nostalgic ambience.

Dylan pushed his seat back and removed his sunglasses and hat. He closed his eyes, and Jennifer wondered if he was falling asleep. She caught her breath when he began to softly sing along with The Troggs about love being everywhere.

Dylan opened his eyes when the song was over, and a rare peacefulness settled across his features. "I haven't sung in weeks. I guess I've missed music, even corny music."

"You have a beautiful voice." *Was that me sounding all breathy and star-struck? Yeesh, I'm pathetic.*

"Thanks. I prefer just playing guitar and singing backup. Greg was always the lead singer. His brother, Jeff, was our drummer." He sighed and looked out the window, seeming incredibly sad until he turned his full attention back to her.

She squirmed and glanced away. Her strange new awareness of Dylan made her even more shy and awkward than usual.

"Did I tell you how pretty you look tonight?"

"N-No." Heat enveloped her body. "You look nice, too."

"I like your hair down. And that skirt and blouse you're wearing are a huge improvement over those asexual scrubs. You know, you don't have to be so damn formal when we're at home. You can wear jeans and T-shirts, if you want to. There's no dress code."

Naked comes to mind. Jennifer looked out her window in horror. *What's wrong with me? I bet he uses lines like this all the time to get girls. Why can't he go back to being a jerk?*

Not knowing how to respond, she kept quiet, staring out at the blank movie screen.

He reached over and brushed his fingers along her jaw. Again, the electricity between them crackled, and Jennifer froze. She held her breath until physiology kicked in. Her heart pounded so hard she wondered if he could hear it. Dylan dropped his hand and picked up a cigarette.

"Thank you," he said, tapping it.

"F-For what?"

"For being you." He lit the cigarette, inhaled, and blew the smoke out the window.

Jennifer pinched herself. *Nope, not dreaming.* The previews started, and she sighed, relieved.

Four hours later, she punched the snoring man beside her. "Dylan. Wake up!"

"Hmm?" he mumbled, swatting her away.

She shook his shoulder. Grumbling, he moved to rub his eyes, but she stopped him.

"What time is it?" He yawned and shielded his eyes as bright headlights pulled past them.

"After midnight. You slept through both movies. I don't know how to get home from here, and of course there's no signal on my phone. You'd think if they can hack embassies around the world, they'd be able to provide cell service in Alabama." She cranked the car. "And you snore. Loudly."

Dylan yawned again and let the seat back up, buckling his seat belt. He loosened his hair from the ponytail. "Snore? I don't snore. I'm sure all the little animals ended up living happily ever after. As for the chick flick, let's see. Boy met girl, they fell in love, happy ending. Or one of them died, sad ending. I might have stayed awake if we'd gone to the other movie."

Jennifer laughed. "Perfect summarization. Maybe you didn't sleep through them."

"Nah, I did. But of course, I'm Dylan McAthie, Supreme Rock God and Know It All."

Jennifer snorted.

As she drove home, Dylan pointed out various familiar places from his youth: the woods where Robert had taken him snipe hunting when he was eleven, the field where the annual fireworks show would be held on the Fourth of July.

"Hey, down this road is where everyone used to go parking. Wanna check it out?"

He laughed when she declined with a horrified gasp.

When they rounded a bend on a back road, lights revealed an old concrete building. Once painted white, the siding was now dirt gray, the tin roof rusted. A neon Budweiser sign flashed in the window. The parking lot was packed with pickup trucks and cars. From inside the building came the muffled strains of loud music. The half burned-out sign in front said:

RO DSIDE TAV RN, COV R $2

Dylan whistled low. "I'll be damned. Pull over, Jen. Let's go check it out."

"Here?" Jennifer pulled over and frowned, looking at the rundown building. "It's a bar, Dylan."

"No kidding, really?" he asked in mock horror.

"A *seedy* bar," she stressed.

He nodded, smirking. "Worse than that, it's a *dive*."

"But, Dylan, I'm underage. And it's…it's a bar."

"Angel, trust me; Bobby Joe Armdale isn't gonna turn down two dollars by carding you. Let's go. I want a beer." The parking lot was full, and he directed her to park behind the building.

"A beer? You *can't* drink a beer." It took her two tries to get the keys out of the ignition.

"Why the hell not? You're driving, and I'm *old*, remember? I won't take any pain meds, promise." Opening the door, he grabbed his crutches and made his way to her side of the car. He didn't really need them, but didn't want to risk busting his ass on the gravel.

"But you're broke," she argued. Part of her wanted to experience a seedy bar, but the rational side of her brain slammed on the brakes.

"Spot me a twenty. I'll pay you back. I know where you live, remember?"

*If he only knew—or rather, remembered…*She sighed, knowing he'd won. He was hard to resist when he poured on the charm. "Okay."

Dylan gave an air pump of victory. "Live on the edge. It's the only way. Life is too damn short not to. It'll be fine. You can have a soda, and I'll have one beer. If you promise not to grab my ass, I'll even slow dance with you as best I can." He flashed his most devastating smile, and the last of her resolve melted like ice cream in a hot fudge sundae. He held out a hand to her as she stepped out of the car.

"I'm more worried about *you* grabbing *my* ass."

Dylan roared with laughter. "Why, *Miss Adams*, I'm shocked at your language."

"It must be the company I keep. My father better not *ever* find out I was here. What if I get arrested?" She stopped dead in her tracks. Despite the Ten Commandments, her father would kill her.

Dylan held up a hand like a Boy Scout. "I solemnly swear to explain to Pastor Adams—*after I post your bail*—that you were here to rescue my immortal soul from the very pits of hell. Furthermore, because you were at the Roadside Tavern preaching on the sins of debauchery, the entire clientele of said establishment was converted. From henceforth and so on, the Roadside Tavern will be known as the Holy Watering Hole with services led by Brother Bobby Joe."

"You're so silly. Okay, okay, lead me into this den of iniquity."

His laughter made her smile. She liked him like this, carefree and easy going. *A lot.*

Chapter Ten

Dylan grinned as they entered the bar. It hadn't changed much at all since he was a teenager. Bobby Joe Armdale stood at the door, drinking a beer and looking bored. He ran his hand over what was left of his sweat-drenched, greasy hair. Still scrappy, he looked a little more jaundiced than Dylan remembered, but he stood up straighter when they approached.

"Four dollars," he said curtly, not looking at them as he took the money. He did a literal double take when he finally looked up.

"Dylan?" Bobby Joe shouted above the noise in the bar.

Dylan shook his hand, regretting his impulsive decision to stop here. There was no chance of staying unidentified. But no matter, he'd be leaving town soon. He'd call Jimmy and get Tyrone here tomorrow. He gave a curt nod as they walked past. Looking around, Dylan noted that only stage lights and low-watt bulbs over the bar and pool table lit the cavernous room. Not that light would have improved its appearance. Hazy cigarette smoke hung suspended in the air like an early morning fog. Clanking glasses, the crack of pool balls, and people talking over the music added to the cacophony.

Dylan pulled out a chair for Jennifer and sat facing her. He leaned back and lit a cigarette. It was kind of like being in a time warp to smoke in a bar. So far, only Bobby Joe had recognized him. On stage, his old friend Alan Mitchell rolled his eyes at a drunken request and launched into a cover of Lynyrd Skynyrd's "Freebird." Dylan chuckled. It was a standard in any backwoods bar in the South.

He turned just in time for a blousy, overly perfumed woman to lean in and plant a long, hard kiss on his mouth. After disengaging himself from the arms wrapped around his neck, he discreetly wiped his mouth before smiling at her. The look of disgust on Jennifer's face was *almost* worth the kiss.

The years had not been kind to Lucy Hargrove. At one time, she'd been a voluptuous knockout, but too many years of hard living had left her skin lined and leathery. She wore her standard red lipstick and heavy eyeliner, and tonight her hair was platinum. He'd seen it all colors over the years. Lucy was brash and unapologetic about her lifestyle, and Dylan had a soft spot for her. It was rumored she'd initiated more than half of the males in the county into manhood. She'd certainly been patient with him many years ago.

Lucy didn't care that he was rich and famous. She still treated him the way she always had. On the rare occasions when he'd visited his grandmother, he'd always snuck in a visit with her—strictly for conversation and his favorite chocolate cake. Although she'd let it be known that if he ever wanted more, she was game.

Lucy smiled at Dylan, straightening his shirt in an overly familiar manner. "What can I get y'all?"

"I'll have a beer, on tap. And please don't draw attention to me, okay? Jen?"

"A diet cola, please."

Ignoring Jennifer, Lucy gave a lusty laugh and winked. "My lips are sealed. Unless you want them otherwise engaged." She waggled her penciled brows and then turned to the other side of the table. "Just a diet cola? You sure? We don't card unless the law is around."

Jennifer nodded, wide-eyed as she surveyed her surroundings.

Lucy shrugged and leaned over to comment in his ear. "If you get bored with innocence, you know where I live. Or if you just wanna catch up on the gossip, I'll make ya a cake." With a wink, she left to fill their order.

Jennifer leaned toward him, frowning. "What did she say to you?"

Her proximity made him want to kiss her again.

"She made me an offer that's hard to refuse," he shouted back as the music got louder. After all, he loved her double fudge chocolate cake. Jennifer frowned, and he chuckled.

Lucy brought their drinks and thanked him for the generous tip with another kiss. It might be worth not tipping next time.

After the set, Alan called for a break, and canned music played as he leaped off the stage, headed toward them. Dylan's heart sank. As happy as he was to see his old friend, his cover was now officially blown. He'd definitely have to contact Jimmy to get some security ASAP.

"Damn, I didn't believe it when they said you were in the house! What's up, Dylan?" Alan pounded his back, and Dylan stood and shook his hand. Laugh lines now creased Alan's face, but other than that, he hadn't changed.

"What are you doing in my neck of the woods? Come play a set with us, man. It will be like old times." Turning, he noticed Jennifer for the first time and whistled in appreciation. "Dylan, you sorry dog. Who is this gorgeous girl, and why the hell is she with your ugly ass?"

Jennifer blushed and smiled. Alan gave her a quick kiss on the cheek. Dylan threw his head back and laughed.

"Jennifer, let me introduce you to Alan Mitchell, the guy who gave me my first job playing guitar. He got top billing in the band because his mom let us practice in their basement."

Alan smiled. "Jennifer, nice to meet you." He turned back to Dylan and slapped him on the shoulder. "Come on, what do you say? Just one set."

Dylan hesitated. "I don't know. I shouldn't leave Jen." He grasped for excuses as his stomach took a familiar lurch at the thought of performing.

Alan walked back to the stage, motioning for Dylan to follow.

"Go on; I'd love to hear you play." Jennifer smiled wider than she had all evening and flicked her hand, motioning him to go.

I'd walk through fire for one of her smiles. Damn, that was sappy. What was in that beer?

"Okay, one song." Why the hell not? His time here was ending. Maybe a bit more rapidly than anticipated, but it was his own damn fault. Why not relax and have fun? He knew most of the people in the bar. Even if they posted shit on social media, he'd have security by tomorrow, anyway.

Dylan took a deep breath, and followed Alan to the stage. He shook hands with the other band members, some of whom he knew. Someone handed him another beer, which he threw back to bolster his confidence. This was more than his usual pre-performance jitters in his stomach. He put on his sunglasses to shield his eyes from the lights and hide some of his nervousness. It had been months since he'd performed. He took the guitar handed to him. The fluttering, sick feeling in his stomach subsided as he settled down and plucked a few strings, getting a feel for the instrument. He grinned. Holding the guitar felt like home.

Alan conferred with Dylan and the other band members on what to play. The audience erupted with cheers and applause when Alan stepped up to the microphone and shouted, "Dylan McAthie!"

The drummer tapped his drumsticks, yelling, "One, two, three!" and the opening riff to "Lust for Loree" flew from Dylan's fingers automatically. It was the first of Crucified, Dead and Buried's songs to go platinum. Alan sang lead vocals, and when Dylan joined in with backup, the cheering patrons stood and sang along.

Forgetting where he was and who he was playing with, he relaxed and embraced the rush he always got from a crowd. The feel of the guitar in his hands and the pulse of the music began a catharsis of the pain he'd harbored for far too long.

Jennifer watched wide-eyed as Dylan played. She'd seen him play on television, but watching him perform live was a hundred times more exciting. A commotion stirred to her left, diverting her attention. She frowned as Bobby Joe strode toward her, shoving several patrons aside. He slithered in next to her and stared at her chest. She wished she were wearing a burqa. He wrapped his arm around her shoulder, pulling her into his sweaty, wiry body. Her crawling skin and inherent warning signals had her immediately pushing back.

"Wanna dance, doll?" he slurred into her ear, licking her earlobe.

"Ew, no! I don't dance." Disgusted, she wiped her ear and wrinkled her nose at the smell of his beer breath and sweaty clothes.

She looked nervously at the throng of people laughing as she once again shrugged away, spurning his advances. With a curse, he stormed back to the bar. He continued to glare, leaving her uneasy.

A few minutes later, Lucy came by and handed her another glass of diet cola.

"I didn't order this," Jennifer protested.

"Dylan must've ordered it for you," Lucy shouted over the screaming crowd.

Hot and thirsty, Jennifer nodded her thanks and smiled. Taking a sip, she cheered as the song came to an end.

Around her, the crowd shouted, "One more! One more!"

Dylan broke out in a wide grin. Seeing him enjoying himself made her happy, yet a feeling of sadness overcame her. She was going to miss him, much more than a nurse should miss a patient.

Watching his fingers strum the guitar, she imagined what it would feel like to have those same hands running across her skin. Heat rose in her cheeks, and she glanced around as if she'd spoken the thought out loud. She needed to get a grip. There was no way someone like Dylan McAthie would ever be interested in a serious relationship with her. And casual sex wasn't an option. She just wasn't wired that way.

Halfway through the song, a wave of nausea swept over her, and the room seemed to spin out of kilter. She sipped on the diet cola, hoping it would settle her stomach. When it ended, the man next to her began cheering and jumping around. In his excitement, he knocked her drink out of her hand. Apologizing over and over, he tried to help her clean up the cola stain now highlighting the pizza smudge on her skirt.

Jennifer motioned his help away, too ill to care about her ruined clothes. The longer the band played, the more uncomfortable she felt. Sweat soaked her blouse, and her heart raced. A panicky need to get away from the crowd and the noise overtook her. Wondering if she had a touch of food poisoning, she looked around for the ladies room. With her heart pounding and the room spinning, she staggered off, hoping some cold water on her face would help. Stumbling into people, she was pushed and steadied by strangers as she made her way to the back of the bar.

Relief in sight, she groaned when the bathroom door didn't budge. Slumping against the wall, she waited, praying she wouldn't embarrass herself by throwing up in front of everyone. At last, two giggling girls exited, and she staggered in, gripping the side of the sink for support. Splashing cold water on her face didn't help. Terrified and sick, she knew she had to get out. She refused to pass out on the nasty floor. Un-tucking her blouse, she used it to wipe her face, as there were no towels to be found in the disgusting bathroom. After a moment, her nausea subsided enough for her to leave. Opening the door, she tripped, falling right into Bobby Joe's arms.

"What's the matter, doll?"

The creepy smile on his face unnerved her, and bile once again threatened the back of her throat.

Swallowing, she began to cry. "I, I don't feel well. I need some fresh air…Where's Dylan? I want to go home. Please, will you find him for me?" Her vision swam, and she closed her eyes. Surely there weren't two Bobby Joes. The thought was horrifying.

"Sure, baby doll. Let me help you to your car, and then I'll get Dylan."

"Thank you." Grateful for the arm holding her up — even if he was a sleazy worm — she clung to him, afraid of blacking out at any minute. She stumbled out into the fresh air, but the world continued to slip away as she fought to remain in control.

As the door to the bar slammed behind them, Bobby Joe pulled her against his sweat-soaked body. She froze, her heart pounding in her ears as his mouth forced hers open. His tongue scraped against her teeth, and his foul, stale breath nauseated her further. His hands squeezed and pinched her breasts, and she whimpered in pain and terror. She pushed against him and hit him.

Frantic, she broke free and ran around the building toward her car. Bobby Joe caught her, shoving her back against another car and slapping her, hard.

"Why, you little bitch! You want it rough? I'll give you rough!" he screamed.

Grabbing her by the neck, he forced her face down onto the hood of the car. Dizzy and nauseous, her efforts to fight him were futile.

Jennifer sobbed as his grimy hand pushed her skirt up and ripped her underwear. But then, a primitive urge for survival overrode her altered state. She managed to twist around and scream. Clawing and fighting with everything in her, she prayed the looming darkness would stay at bay until someone rescued her.

Dylan finished the last song and waved, thanking the band and the enthusiastic patrons. He accepted another beer, thoroughly enjoying the release as it slipped down his parched throat. Flying high on the adrenaline rush from playing again, he limped off the stage to return to Jen, anxious to know if she'd liked the music. Lighting a cigarette, he hobbled through the well-wishers, trying not to appear rude. He found her purse on the table, but she was nowhere in sight. He looked around. Something didn't feel right.

Shouting over the din, he asked Lucy if she'd seen her. She pointed toward the ladies room. Feeling ridiculous holding the purse, he grabbed his crutches and slowly made his way through the regulars wanting to talk to him, as well as get autographs and selfies. Dammit, he missed Tyrone and the secure bubble he provided. Finally reaching the bathroom, he knocked on the door.

"Jen?"

The door opened and a tipsy woman exited, giggling. "Wish I was. Nice purse."

Twisting to avoid her attempt to cop a feel of his junk, he ignored the dirty look from her boyfriend. *Dammit, where is she?* He elbowed his way back through the fans, scanning the crowd for the only person whose opinion mattered. Maybe she'd gotten fed up with the bar scene and gone to the car. He opened the door, shrugging out of the cloying grasp of a drunk girl, and limped toward the car.

The sound of her screams snapped everything into focus. Rounding the corner, cold fury surged through Dylan, and he roared like an animal in pain. His only rational thought: *she's mine.* He swung one crutch like a bat, hitting Jen's attacker.

Bobby Joe spun around and charged, hitting him squarely in his recently mended ribs. Dylan doubled over in pain and attempted to duck the next blow. Bobby's fist grazed his lower jaw, and he felt his lip swell as his head snapped back. He struggled to remain on his feet.

Bobby Joe came at him again. This time, Dylan smashed his crutch across the asshole's face. Blood spurted from his nose. Fueled by rage, Dylan continued to pummel him.

"Whoa, Dylan. Stop!" Footsteps came running, and Alan intervened. "He's passed out. He's down, man."

"You goddamned sonofabitch! You ever so much as look at her again, I swear to God, I'll kill you!" Dylan roared, struggling to be free from Alan and the two other men who held him.

"It's over. Calm the fuck down. You're gonna end up on social media. You don't want that."

Alan's voice finally permeated his rage. The other band members worked to disperse the crowd. Dylan braced his tender ribs with his bloody hand as he struggled to catch his breath. Wiping the sweat off his face, he looked for Jen. The adrenaline subsiding, he slowly comprehended the enormity of the situation. Glancing around, he estimated a minimum of ten cell phones documenting the entire fuckin' ordeal. He ducked his head, still searching for her.

Shit.

He found her curled in a fetal position, quietly sobbing on Lucy's lap. Bruises covered her arms where that fucker had manhandled her. He should've killed that sonofabitch.

"You're okay, hun. Boys will be boys," Lucy crooned, awkwardly patting Jen's back. She flashed him a weak smile, looking uncomfortable in the role of caregiver.

Some of Bobby Joe's cronies dragged the barely conscious man back into the bar.

"What happened, Lucy?" Dylan asked, kneeling beside the trembling girl.

Lucy shrugged. "I don't know. Bobby Joe was flirting with her, and she pretty much shot him down. He slunk back to the bar. I got busy, and the next thing I know, you were out here beating the hell out of him." She sighed and added, "I know I'll pay for it later, but I'm glad you did it."

"Do you want the cops?" Alan asked.

"No! No cops," Jennifer choked as she sat up, her face still covered by her hands.

Dylan sighed and stroked his sore jaw. "I don't know. I don't know what the fuck to do."

He helped Jen to her feet, and she buried her face in his shirt.

Before going back inside, Lucy paused. "Hey, Dylan? Bobby Joe sent your girlfriend a diet cola after she rejected him. He said you ordered it for her. I didn't think anything about it at the time. But now…" She sighed, and her shoulders slumped.

Dylan nodded, feeling sorry for her. Lucy not only worked with the asshole, she sporadically dated him. She disappeared into the bar.

Dylan wrapped his arms a little tighter around his traumatized nurse. *This is all my fault.* "Shh, angel. I'm here. You're safe now. I'm so sorry." Dylan held her and gently rocked until her sobs subsided. Brushing her hair from her wet face, he looked for bruises and signs of injury. She pushed away and looked up at him. Her tear-filled eyes shone like amethysts in the dim lights from the building.

"You need a shave," she murmured as her eyes rolled back. He caught her just before she fell.

"Jen! Jennifer! Don't pass out on me, baby. Are you okay? I need to take you to the hospital. We need to call the police." He looked around and motioned to Alan. She peeked at him from under heavy lids and gave him a silly, crooked smile as she ran a finger across his aching jaw and swollen lip.

"I'm a nurse. I can help you," she slurred. Clumsily she tugged at his hair.

"Yeow—" His surprised yowl was cut short when she kissed him. Hard. *What the hell? Is she drunk?* He didn't taste alcohol on her breath. Reluctantly, he broke the kiss and held her at arm's length. Her hair fell in a riot of unruly curls. A red mark on her cheek and bruises on her arms infuriated him, but he thought she looked okay, considering what had nearly happened.

"Jen, stay with me now and think carefully. Did someone spike your drink? We need to call the cops."

"No! No cops. I'm underage. Daddy will kill me. Maybe the pizza was bad, and I have food poisoning. I, I don't feel well…" She raised a shaky hand to her temple and closed her eyes, giggling. "You make my head spin 'round and 'round." She leaned precariously against the car.

"Yeah? Well, just make sure it doesn't spin like a possessed girl. No pea soup vomit, promise?" he teased, searching through her purse for the car keys. "I'm going to drive us home."

"I can drive," she murmured.

He assisted her into the backseat. "Uh-huh, we're better off with me driving, and I'm almost blind."

"Neither one of you is driving. I'll take you home. My buddy will follow." Alan held up his hand. "No arguments."

Dylan took a deep breath, but nodded. "Thanks. Let's go and end this nightmare."

Alan grabbed his arm before he got in the car. "Is she okay? We can swing by the hospital or the police station if needed."

Dylan sighed. "Give us just a minute, okay?"

Every bone in his body ached as he eased into the backseat. Fuck safety, he pulled her into his lap and wrapped his arms tight around her, never wanting to let her go.

"Jennifer, we need to get you checked out at the hospital and make a report."

A whimper made his heart clench. "No. Please just take me home. I'm okay, just extremely embarrassed." Her head rolled, and she gazed up at him with a lopsided grin. "I must look a mesh."

He chuckled. "A mesh?" He pinched her nose. "Yep, you're a mess, my angel."

Alan opened the door and slipped behind the wheel. "Where to?" His worried gaze met Dylan's in the rearview mirror.

Jen answered, "Home. My father can't find out I was in a *bar*."

"You heard the lady. Home." Dylan closed his eyes and held her tight.

Chapter
Eleven

With the help of Alan and his friend, Dylan got Jennifer into the house. The men left, offering assurances that they'd say nothing to the press and would squelch the story as much as possible. An improbable feat, as Dylan knew from experience. First he'd make sure Jen was tucked safely in bed; then he'd call Jimmy to start damage control and send for Tyrone.

His leg hurt like hell, especially without his crutches, but he managed to help her to the bathroom. He left her alone to clean up and lit a much-needed cigarette. The more he thought about it, the angrier he became. If he weren't so damn exhausted, he'd pace off his nervous energy. Instead, he inhaled the cigarette like a dope fiend.

He was fairly certain someone had slipped something in her drink, and he didn't know what to do. Calling his brother was one option. Rob was a doctor, after all. But the thought of the resulting lecture nixed that idea. He felt guilty enough as it was. Maybe he should call the police? Or take her to the hospital? His stomach twisted at the thought of the publicity.

Cracking the door to check on her, he watched as she moved like a zombie, her movements uncoordinated and slow. Three times she attempted to put toothpaste on her toothbrush. Exasperated, he dropped his cigarette in the toilet and did it for her. She needed to get cleaned up and sleep it off.

He left her brushing her teeth with instructions to get a bath and dragged himself to the kitchen to find a painkiller—screw what he'd said before. His eyes burned, his leg throbbed, his chest hurt like hell, and the beer was long gone. Holding his side, he winced. His ribs were probably broken again. After four tries, he managed to get the eye drops in his eyes and not on his face.

Jennifer's laughter echoed down the hallway. Curious, he limped back to check on her.

"What's so funny?"

"Look." She pointed at her image in the mirror. "Who's that ugly clown?"

Dylan laughed. "That's you, angel. You need to wash your face."

"That's me?" She closed her eyes and held on to the sink, swaying. "Why is the room spinning? Make it stop."

With great care, Dylan eased her to the side of the bathtub and started the bath water. He poured in half a bottle of her citrus soap, praying for loads of bubbles. Tenderly, he washed her face, wishing she wouldn't look at him with those innocent, trusting eyes. The red mark on her cheek might be fading, but his guilt escalated at an alarming rate.

"Jen?"

"Yes?" Her eyes glazed over, and she looked up at him with a dopey grin.

"I want you to take your clothes off and get a bath. You'll feel better, okay?" he croaked, his mouth going dry at the thought. When she didn't make a move to undress, he took a deep steadying breath before pulling off her blouse. No surprise her bra was white, but it was also lacey and sexy as hell. *Damn, she's beautiful.*

She half-heartedly batted at his hand. "Noooo, my daddy warned me about men like you. You can't see me *naked*; it wouldn't be right." She rubbed her eyes like a sleepy little girl.

Dylan snapped out of it. *She's under the influence. I need to think and act as an adult, not some horny asshole.*

"Don't be such a prude. You're going to take a bath and go to bed. I won't take no for an answer." Deciding this task would best be done like removing a Band-Aid, he exhaled and swallowed his nervousness.

I've removed women's clothes plenty of times. Nothing to it; I can do this.

Ignoring her weak protests, he began undressing her. *Shit, bra hooks always trip me up, stupid motherfuckers. My next career, I'm designing a man-friendly, easy-to-remove bra.* Fumbling with the hook, he hesitated and chuckled when she slapped his hand away.

"It isn't rocket science; let me do it, Dylan." In one easy motion, she reached behind and had the bra unclasped and off before he could blink. "Magic!" She swayed, and her eyes rolled back.

Catching her, he quickly removed the rest of her clothes and helped her into the bathtub, averting his eyes as much as possible. *Dammit, she's even more beautiful than I realized.* He thanked God for the tub full of bubbles. A man could only withstand so much.

As he scrubbed her scalp with shampoo, she purred like a kitten. He wished circumstances were different as his jeans tightened uncomfortably.

"Time to rinse," he warned, pouring a cup of water over her head.

She sputtered her protest and splashed him, sloshing water all over the floor.

Wiping the water from his face with a laugh, he tossed her a washcloth. "You can finish on your own, okay?"

Like a coward, he fled the room before he dove in with her. When she began "singing," he rolled his eyes heavenward, sincerely hoping she wasn't in her church's choir.

Dylan stumbled to her bedroom to find her nightclothes. Turning on the bedside lamp, he pulled open a dresser drawer and found a soft, pink cotton gown. Then he paused. Did she sleep in panties? *How the hell should I know what virgins wear to bed?* Sara had always slept nude, as did he prior to the accident. After a moment of indecision, he decided on just the nightgown to make things easier. The caterwauling had stopped, and no noise whatsoever came from the bathroom now.

He raced back in a panic, tabloid headlines screaming through his head. *Teenage girl found drowned in Dylan McAthie's bathtub.*

"Are you okay?" He threw open the door and sagged with relief. Head thrown back, her mouth open like a guppy, Jennifer was sound asleep. Gently, he shook her awake.

She opened one eye and gave him a crooked grin. "Hullooo, Dylan."

He chuckled and pinched her nose. "Hello, Jennifer. Ready to get out? If you stay in there much longer you're going to look like a prune." Pulling the bathtub plug, he grabbed a towel. She stood, swaying until he steadied her with a hand on her warm, wet hip. He froze, unable to do anything but stare at the sight before him. The water and soap bubbles dripped in tantalizing rivulets down her lush body. One wet, black curl circled a dusky-colored nipple. She looked like Venus rising from the sea.

"Prune? I thought you said I was a prude."

"I may have been wrong about that," he muttered, wrapping a towel around her and providing a flimsy barrier between his hands and her flesh. She stepped out of the tub, wrapping her arms around his neck. Holding her for a moment, he closed his eyes, resting his chin on top of her head.

God, it feels like home having her in my arms.

Mentally shaking himself, he stepped away, tugging the nightgown over her head. Jennifer placed her hand in his as he guided her to her bedroom. With great care, he brushed her unruly, wet curls. Finished, he eased her into bed, pulling the covers to her chin. He needed to get out of here.

Jennifer closed her eyes and a dreamy smile crossed her lips. "My prince rescued me again," she whispered before drifting off to sleep.

Dylan kissed her forehead before turning out the light.

"I'm no prince. Goodnight, angel. I'm so sorry." Guilt pushed him from her room, and he returned to the bathroom to clean up.

The mirror revealed that he looked as bad as he felt. He scratched his annoying beard and inspected his aching jaw and swollen lip. His shirt was stained with blood; whether it was his or Bobby Joe's, he had no idea.

I should have killed that sonofabitch.

Angrily, he tore his clothes off, throwing them on the floor. His upbringing pricked at his conscience, but picking up clothes required too much effort. Gran could just raise hell in heaven over the mess; he'd clean it up tomorrow.

As he sank into the tub, he offered a few well-chosen profanities. His body ached as if he'd been beat to hell and back. It'd been years since he'd been involved in a barroom brawl, and he didn't remember it hurting this badly. *Damn, I'm getting old.* He flexed his hand, knowing he was lucky he hadn't broken it beating the shit out of that asshole. He turned to find Jennifer's torn pink panties on the floor and closed his eyes as regret washed over him. Her terrified scream and look of panic would join his other haunting memories. He leaned his head back against the tub, physically and emotionally spent.

Dylan sat straight up, his chest aching and pounding. He squinted at the clock and groaned. The muffled sobs coming down the hall must've awakened him. Feeling like death warmed over, he slipped on some underwear, splinted his throbbing side with his hand, and limped to Jennifer's room.

Remorse tore through him as she tossed and turned in the throes of a nightmare. Tenderly, he brushed the hair from her face.

"Hey, wake up, angel."

"No, stop," she screamed, scratching and hitting him as he tried to contain her flailing arms.

"Wake up, Jennifer! It's me, Dylan."

She stilled and wrapped her arms around his neck, sobbing. Dylan scooped her into his arms and held her tight.

"You're okay. It was just a bad dream. You're safe now." Not knowing how to comfort her, he softly sang an old lullaby his grandmother used to sing as he stroked her back.

Jennifer pulled away, her lower lip trembling. "Why are you going to buy me a diamond ring?" The moonlight through the window caught the tears in her eyes, making them glimmer.

He gave a soft chuckle and kissed the top of her head. "I'll buy you anything you want. Just don't cry. Please, baby, you're breaking my heart."

"I…I'm sorry." She covered her face with her hands and shuddered. "It was an awful dream. His hands…I thought…" The crying began again, and she pulled away, curling up in a ball with her back to him. "I should have listened to you. The boogeyman *is* real."

He didn't know what the hell she was talking about, but his heart slammed against his ribcage and shattered with guilt. He curled up behind her, spoon fashion, nestling his cheek in her soft hair.

Wrapping an arm around her waist, he closed his eyes, feeling helpless as she cried.

Jennifer's tears gradually subsided, but Dylan still held her, not wanting to leave. He didn't think about the impropriety of her lying in his arms; he simply needed to hold her, wanting to make her feel safe, wanting to lessen his guilt.

A few minutes later, she rolled over and faced him. She cupped his bearded cheek and rubbed her thumb over his bruised jaw.

"You look so tired. What happened?" She pushed his hair out of his face.

"Nothing." His voice sounded hoarse, and he remained still, every nerve in his body on fire with liquid heat. It had been way too long since he'd held a woman, and these gentle caresses were pushing him over the edge of reason. He grabbed her hand.

"Stop, Jen. You don't know what you're doing to me."

"Kiss me," she whispered, kissing his palm.

He rolled on top of her, caging her face with his arms. He kissed her forehead, running the back of his fingers across her soft cheek.

"Really kiss me, Dylan. I want to be kissed properly."

He wanted to, but hesitated. It was so many kinds of wrong. Attempting some semblance of control, he took a deep breath and shook his head. The pain from the cracked rib hurt like a motherfucker, and he exhaled slowly through gritted teeth. That wasn't the only thing that hurt. Looking deep into her pleading eyes, his heart ached. Her pain was his.

"Jennifer, no…this could go too far, and quite frankly, I'm almost to the point of no return." His conscience screamed for him to stop while his body pushed him forward.

"Don't you want me?"

Her eyes reflected the same longing and attraction he felt. *Fuck, I'm a goner.*

Dylan stroked her cheek and rasped, "Want you? My God, I want you and need you more than anything else right now. This isn't about want. This is about what's right. This is about caring for you, respecting you—"

Smiling, she tangled her fingers in his hair, pulling him closer, and pressed her lips to his. She didn't close her eyes and neither did he. Her soft hand stroked his cheek, and his resolve shattered like a broken mirror. He closed his eyes and accepted what she offered. She parted her mouth to allow his tongue access. Brushing his lips over her eyelids, he trailed kisses down her cheek and up her jaw to behind her ear. Her eyes fluttered closed, and a soft moan whispered across his cheek. Against his chest, through her thin gown, her nipples hardened, and she arched her body into his. With one fluid motion, he removed her nightgown, and it sailed through the air.

He nibbled down her throat and breast before capturing one hard nipple in his mouth. She moaned again, and he murmured her name in response. Her fingers ran through his hair, and her gasp of surprise when he tickled her belly button with his tongue made him smile. Her warm, inviting body was like a smorgasbord after near starvation.

Dylan worshipped her with his lips until he felt her go limp, overpowered by the last of the drug in her system. Rolling beside her with a frustrated groan, he threw an arm over his closed eyes as war raged between his need for release and his need to protect her. He had to be the biggest douchebag in history for coming so close to taking advantage of an innocent girl.

Although painful to take deep breaths, he did so, slowing his heart rate to normal. He needed to think with something other than his dick. Hands behind his head, he stared at the ceiling, planning damage control. In the morning, he'd call Jimmy. It was time to go home to California and stop this insanity before it got out of hand. He'd give Jennifer a good severance package and recommendation. She should have no problem finding another job as a nurse. He'd fly Tyrone in tomorrow and provide her with security, if needed.

Jennifer rolled on her side, resting her head on his shoulder. One arm snaked around his waist, and her leg came to rest on top of his. She snuggled in with a contented sigh.

Her soft body felt right next to his. Too exhausted to think, much less move, Dylan closed his eyes. Maybe he'd just rest for a moment and make sure she was good and asleep before returning to his own bed. An unladylike snore blew across his chest as he too drifted off to sleep.

Chapter Twelve

Donald Rowe glanced at his watch. Camped out at the edge of the woods with the McAthie house in sight, he sighed with frustration. Dammit, it was mid-morning. He'd arrived four hours ago, and still there were no signs of life in the house. His camera with the zoom lens lay ready beside him, his phone in his pocket. Swatting a mosquito, he again cursed Dylan McAthie for living in this hellhole. Why couldn't the almighty McAthie have convalesced at the beach? Already drenched in sweat, he wished he'd used more deodorant this morning.

Taking a swallow of water, he paused, movement from the other end of the property catching his attention. A small boy ran through the woods directly toward the house. He picked up his camera and zoomed in but didn't see anyone else. This was an opportunity he couldn't resist. Stupid kids could provide a wealth of valuable information. Leaving the camera behind, he sprinted toward the house, meeting up with the kid at the front door.

"Hello!" He plastered a fake smile on his face and pointed to the squirming kitten in the boy's hands. "What have you there?" *I should fuckin' get an Oscar for this performance.*

"It's my new kitten. I'm going to show him to Jennifer and Uncle Dylan."

Donald gave a sly smile. "That's awesome, kid. I'm here to see your Uncle Dylan, too. We have some business to discuss. Mind if I go in with you?"

The boy shrugged. "Sure, c'mon." They stepped inside the screened-in front porch, and the kid knocked on the door. When there was no answer, he retrieved a key from a nail by a window.

"Shhh," he stage-whispered. "Mama says it's Saturday, and if Uncle Dylan's still sleeping, we have to be quiet. She says Uncle Dylan is mean as a rattlesnake but still needs to rest. Daddy says he's an ass and that Miss Jennifer must have the patience of a saint for putting up with him. Don't wake him, or my Mama will tear my butt up."

Donald grinned at the informative chatter and signaled his compliance with his index finger to his lips. This was better than anything he'd anticipated. Tiptoeing through the living area toward a hallway, the boy motioned for Donald to follow him.

Glancing around, Donald was surprised by the modest house. It wasn't at all what he expected of the pompous Dylan McAthie. Passing the bathroom, Donald damn near shouted with excitement. He couldn't have staged an incriminating picture any better himself. He motioned to the kid that he was ducking into the bathroom for a moment and closed the door.

The clothes Dylan and his woman had worn last night were strewn all over the wet bathroom floor. Using his phone camera, he made sure to capture the torn, pink satin panties and bloodied shirt. When he stepped back into the hall, the boy motioned him toward the kitchen.

"What's the matter, kid?" Donald asked in a hushed voice.

The kid screwed up his face and replied in a loud, disgusted whisper, "My name is Robbie, *not kid*. They're still sleeping." The kitten meowed.

"Really? Together?"

Robbie scrunched his nose and nodded. "They're naked." He opened the refrigerator, taking out a carton of milk for the squirming kitten.

"Hey, Robbie, I left my wallet in the bathroom. I'll be right back." Donald sprinted down the hall like a track star. It was now or never; the money shot was within his grasp. Tiptoeing down the hall, he passed one bedroom with an empty, rumpled bed. He peered in the next one and bit his tongue. *Cha-ching.*

He found Dylan McAsshole lying on his back, the girl curled into him. His hand rested on her waist and the covers were pushed down low on their stomachs. The light filtering through the blinds exposed the woman's breasts in the best possible light. Damn, no wonder Dylan was screwing her. With tits like that, it wouldn't take long for this to go viral. He added a little video for good measure. After snapping several shots, he shoved the phone in his pocket and returned to the kitchen. Now to pump the stupid kid for more information...

Not awake, yet not asleep, Dylan surfaced from his dreams with a jerk. He had the uncomfortable sensation of being watched. Squinting, he damn near jumped out of his skin when he saw someone standing in the doorway.

"Who are you and what the hell are you doing in my house?" he hissed, sitting up. Jen stretched, and he hastily covered her naked breasts.

"That happens to be my daughter!" the man roared. Flushed with anger, a vein popped out on his forehead.

Dylan groaned. *What the fuck did I do in a past life to reap this kind of karma?*

A stampede sounded down the hall toward Jen's room. With a sinking feeling in the pit of his stomach, he remembered it was fuckin' family Saturday.

The sound of her father's angry voice pulled Jennifer out of a deep sleep. Disoriented for a moment, she wondered why he sounded so irate. *Did I oversleep for church again?* Opening her eyes, she squeaked and dove under the covers. She placed her trembling hands over her eyes, not wanting to see the expanse of naked flesh next to her. This was a living nightmare.

"What the hell, Dylan?"

She groaned at the sound of Dr. McAthie's voice. On top of being humiliated, she was about to lose her job.

"Robert, calm down. The children will hear."

Mrs. McAthie is here, too?

Lowering the sheet, she stole a peek at the doorway. Dr. and Mrs. McAthie stood with her father. The dumbstruck looks on their faces would have been comical, if she hadn't been the one in bed, naked... *with Dylan.* She pulled the covers back over her pounding head. From her hiding spot, she heard Dylan clear his throat.

"Good morning, everyone. If we'd known we were having company, we would've been up and dressed. Now, if you'll just give us a moment, we'll join you in the living area."

How he could sound so nonchalant? *Is this an everyday occurrence for him?*

Peeking through the hands covering her eyes, she couldn't help but admire the expanse of cut muscles above his boxer briefs. Blushing, she closed her eyes, and then peeked again before squeezing them shut. *Why is he halfway dressed and I'm naked?*

"I'm not going anywhere until I get some answers," her father retorted.

Jennifer shuddered at the disappointment in her father's voice. Her all-too-brief life flashed through her memories. Would her father preach a nice funeral after he murdered her?

"Well, not meaning any disrespect, sir, but we need to get dressed."

Jennifer gasped at Dylan's audacity.

"You better have some answers," Dr. McAthie warned.

"Glen, Robert, come to the kitchen. Let's all have some coffee," Mrs. McAthie coaxed through the chaos. "I'm sure there's a reasonable explanation for all of this."

The door slammed shut. Jennifer peered from under the sheet as Dylan limped to the door and locked it, holding on to his side.

"Asshole," he muttered.

"Don't call my daddy that!" She pulled the covers back over her head, unable to face him. *Why can't I remember what happened? How did Dylan end up in my bed?*

The bed dipped as Dylan sat back down.

"Shit, I need a cigarette. And I was referring to my brother, not your father. You can come out now, Chicken Little. The sky hasn't fallen — yet." He poked her under the cover.

"Hilarious. You better keep your day job. I don't think the Comedy Club will be calling anytime soon. My father's going to kill both of us."

She sat up, keeping the covers pulled to her chin. Movement made the pounding in her head almost unbearable. "Why were you in *my* bed?" She glared at him. Dylan's betrayal confused her. *Or is this somehow my fault? Did I invite him?* She'd been having feelings and thoughts...

Dylan interrupted her internal debate. "Jennifer, uh, what do you remember about last night?"

"I, I don't remember anything much after the movie. We stopped at that sleazy bar, and you played a song with a friend..." Her voice trailed off as she realized she truly couldn't remember anything else. "What happened to me? What did we *do?*" Tears tracked down her hot cheeks as she struggled to recall the events from last night.

"Nothing happened, I swear. Look, I'm not even naked."

"You're only wearing underwear, and I *am* naked," she wailed, louder than intended.

"Shhh. Calm down! Your old man's ready to castrate me as it is. I don't relish the thought of singing soprano," Dylan whispered. "Now get dressed. I'm going to go try to explain this mess to your father and my brother, who seems to think he's *my* father."

"What's going on in there? So, help me, if you hurt one hair on her head, I'll have you arrested!" Her father's pounding on the locked door jarred her already aching head.

"Goddammit, give us a minute!" Dylan swore, limping toward the door.

"Dylan! Watch your language. Daddy doesn't like cursing," Jennifer whispered, terrified that her father had heard him.

"Seriously? You're lecturing me about cursing when we've been caught in bed together?" Shaking his head, he left, slamming the door in his wake.

Jennifer sank back on the pillow and tried to assemble her scattered thoughts. Her head felt like a ticking bomb, ready to detonate at any minute. She wondered if she had an aneurysm or a brain tumor. Recalling her father's angry face, she rather hoped she did. Maybe he'd take pity on her if she were dying.

Is this my punishment for wanting more excitement? She'd never been a rebellious child, but she'd longed for adventure—to see the world outside her father's loving, but narrow view on life. *What happened last night?* But no matter how hard she tried, all she could remember were hazy, disconnected images. With a sense of foreboding, she rolled out of bed and dressed, dreading what awaited beyond the bedroom door.

Dylan grimaced as he slipped on a pair of jeans under the watchful eye of the good reverend. Not bothering with a shirt, he limped past Jennifer's irate father into the living room. *This must be what it's like to walk the green mile.* He needed a goddamned cigarette and a painkiller. A loaded gun to blow his brains out would be nice, too. Jennifer's father seethed, and Dylan couldn't blame him. He imagined he'd feel the same way if she were his daughter.

As he attempted to swagger nonchalantly into the room, advice his father had given him years ago came to mind—not that he'd ever been in the habit of taking his father's advice, but it seemed strangely useful, given the circumstances. *Never let your enemies know what you're thinking.* Ignoring the stony looks that greeted him, he yawned and stretched, acting like getting caught in bed with a young woman was an everyday occurrence. He lit a smoke, squinted, and surveyed the room.

Jennifer's father—a trim, middle-aged man with gray hair—stood with his arms crossed. The look of disgust and fury on his face was a little unsettling. Still looking like an all-American girl with her shoulder-length blond hair and blue eyes, Cat stood by the fireplace in jeans and a blue blouse. She was even more beautiful than he remembered. Time had been kind to her, and motherhood had softened her features and rounded her figure into appealing curves. Mrs. Jordan stood next to a sweaty, sleazy-looking man he vaguely recognized. *Who the hell is he?*

And then there was his brother. Leaning against the front door—probably to bar him from escaping—Rob stood with his hands on his slim hips, glaring. It was eerie how much Junior resembled their old man with his dark hair and those glacial blue eyes.

"Now, what seems to be the problem?" Dylan plunked down on the couch and propped his hurt leg on the coffee table. His side was killing him, but he'd be damned if he'd ask Junior to check it out. Shit, he never had called Jimmy. If he had, Tyrone would be here, and none of this would be happening. No telling what was plastered across social media. He swallowed nervously. *Is that why everyone's here?*

"Why, you insolent—" Pastor Adams shouted, pointing at him.

"Just a minute," Mrs. Jordan interrupted. "Before anyone says anything else, I'd like to introduce you to Donald Rowe. He's a reporter for that trashy tabloid *The National Intruder.*"

What the fuck?

Only the hum of the air conditioner and ticking of the clock on the mantle broke the stunned silence. Dylan leaned his head back and closed his eyes. His worst nightmare was now a reality. As he tried to think, pandemonium erupted as his brother and Pastor Adams argued with the reporter. Mrs. J and Cat quarreled with the children to go outside to play.

Dylan picked up the phone and dialed Jimmy as the chaos heightened into bedlam. He took a drag off the cigarette, thankful when Jimmy answered on the first ring.

"What?" he asked sleepily in greeting.

"Catch the first available flight out here, and bring Tyrone," Dylan commanded. "No, wait…Hire a jet. Hell, if you can get it, a stealth bomber. The shit just hit the fan, and I need you here *now*," he barked.

"Damnation, Dylan, what have you done?" Jimmy sounded more awake now.

"I don't have time to explain, but Donald Rowe from *The National Intruder* is currently in my living room and will be waiting for you at Mrs. John Jordan's home. You can find it on GPS."

"Fanfuckintastic. I can't wait to hear this story. I'll be there as soon as I can, and I'll get in touch with Wendy. And for God's sake, *hold your temper and don't say one goddamned word!*" Jimmy disconnected.

The attention in the room remained focused on the douchebag reporter. It took a couple of tries, but Dylan managed to stand and limped to the fireplace. Removing the twelve-gauge shotgun hanging over the mantle, he opened a box, took out a shell, loaded it, and pumped the gun. The room went silent, and everyone stared dumbfounded as he pointed the gun at the place where Donald Rowe's heart should've been.

Cat gasped with horror as her hand flew to her mouth. "Dylan! Think of the children!"

Pastor Adams bowed his head. Dylan wasn't sure if the good reverend was praying for him, or damning him to hell for all eternity.

"Oh, for Pete's sake, put the damn gun down, you idiot." Robert rubbed his eyes and pressed his fingers to the bridge of his nose.

Sweat dotted Donald's brow. "H-Hey now, listen, we can talk about this." The asswipe's voice cracked as he eyed the gun.

For the first time this morning, Dylan felt in control. He smiled. "I don't talk to the press. I never have; I never will. My manager, however, is paid to keep bastards like you away from me, and he's on his way from California. Now, give me your phone," he said.

Donald hesitated until the barrel of the gun butted up against his chest. Dylan took his phone and threw it against the bricks on the fireplace, watching it shatter. Turning to Mrs. Jordan, he handed her the gun.

"Mrs. J, will you please take this asshole to your house and keep him there until my manager, Jimmy Vaughan, arrives? Treat him with all the respect he *deserves*." Dylan forced himself to smile again.

Mrs. Jordan broke into wide grin. "Why, not at all, dear. But I'll be sending *you* the bill for fumigating my house after this varmint leaves, or *is killed*." She poked the gun against Donald's back. "Hands up in the air. And don't try anything; I'm a good shot."

The startled look on Donald's face was the highlight of the morning thus far. Dylan chuckled as the man marched out with his hands held high.

"That's just great, Dylan. Now you've gone and involved Cathy's mom in your lunacy." Rob scrubbed his hands over his face. "What if this guy presses charges for kidnapping? Please tell me you're strung out on drugs and not this damn stupid; there's help for an addiction problem. Stupidity? Not so much. Did you suffer oxygen deprivation during the accident? Do you ever think about anyone besides yourself?" Stopping in front of Dylan, he shoved him.

Dylan shook with rage. This was too much. Facing his older brother, he clenched his fists. "I'm warning you, Junior. Don't you *ever* put your hands on me again. You're not my *father*. I took his goddamned abuse, but I refuse to take yours."

"Please, everyone just calm down," Cat pleaded. "Now that we don't have an audience, let Dylan explain. Only he and Jennifer know what really happened. I guess you know by now this is Glen Adams, Jennifer's father."

Jennifer appeared in the doorway, her eyes huge in her pale, pinched face. "I'm sorry to disagree with you, Mrs. McAthie. I actually don't know what went on last night." Her voice wavered and her lower lip trembled.

The fear written on her red face pricked Dylan's conscience. Her words made him panic. This shit was getting real. He sucked in a painful breath.

"Nothing happened, Jennifer." He met her gaze straight on, trying to reassure her.

"Nothing? *I just found you and my daughter naked in bed!*" Pastor Adams roared.

"Everyone, please calm down. Let's sit and discuss this rationally. Now start at the beginning, Dylan," Cat encouraged.

No one sat except Jennifer, who sank in a chair and rubbed her forehead.

"Hold on now. Technically, I wasn't naked. We went out to eat. We went to a movie, and on the way home, we stopped at the Roadside Tavern. I don't know what happened. I guess someone slipped something in her drink while I was onstage with Alan and his band. When I went looking for her…"

He stopped, not wanting to reveal the horrid details and further embarrass her. "I got to her before she was hurt, I promise." He nervously ground out his cigarette. To his surprise, the minister lunged for him. Easily sidestepping the punch, he still managed to trip, falling against the corner of the coffee table. Sharp pain radiated through his chest, and he found himself unable to take a deep breath.

"You took my underage daughter to a bar, someone spiked her drink, and *then you had the audacity to come home and take advantage of her?* What kind of man are you? Rapist!" Ryan shouted.

Rob intervened before he could throw another punch.

Dylan laboriously pulled himself to his feet, holding his side. *Fuck, it hurts to breathe.* Shaking, he tried to explain. "No! Look, Reverend Adams, it isn't how it appeared. I was comforting her after a nightmare."

"No, Daddy! D-Dylan wouldn't do t-that," Jennifer stammered, red faced. "But I still don't understand why you were in bed with me. Why was I n-naked?"

Dylan tried to think, but it was like a fog had settled over his brain. Things were escalating way out of control. Sure, he'd kissed her, but nothing more had happened. An overpowering sense of doom consumed him. His grasp on the entire situation slipped away as the darkness crept in, hovering over him. His vision tunneled, and he panted as fear took over all rational thoughts. He had to get out of there.

Reverend Adams continued his tirade. "How do I know *you* didn't drug her? What if she's pregnant after this disgusting one-night stand?"

Dylan broke out in a cold sweat, coughing. "I have to get out of here. I told you, nothing happened…" His heart raced, and he felt like he was drowning. He needed air. Clutching his chest, he limped toward the front door. Fatigue made his limbs feel like lead. The room swam before his eyes, and his knees buckled.

"Dylan?" Jennifer rushed over and placed her fingers on his neck. "Pulse one hundred and thready. Respirations thirty and shallow."

His angel. He attempted to smile and reassure her.

"Cathy, call an ambulance *now*," Rob shouted, kneeling beside her. "Dylan, relax and breathe slowly. You're going to be fine."

"Calm down. Take nice, slow, deep breaths," Jennifer encouraged. "You're going to be okay." The tears coursing down her face said otherwise. She gripped his hand.

He held tight, terrified.

He was dying.

Who knew violet-eyed angels resided in hell…

Chapter
Thirteen

Dr. McAthie entered Dylan's room. Jennifer put down her book and smiled as she tucked a loose curl behind her ear. Assessing her appearance, he scowled, and she looked away. She knew what she looked like. The mirror this morning hadn't lied. No amount of makeup could hide the dark circles under her eyes. She'd been at the hospital for five days, only leaving late at night to go home. She wasn't proud of her cowardly behavior, but she didn't want to listen to her father's lecture either. He'd said plenty as they followed the ambulance seventy-five miles to Birmingham.

"Good morning, Jennifer. You need to go home and rest," Dr. McAthie encouraged, slipping on his reading glasses as he perused the computer at Dylan's bedside.

"Good morning, Dr. McAthie. You don't look much better than I do," she chided in return.

"I think after everything we've been through you can call me Robert. And the same with Cathy." He continued clicking through the chart, his composure intact after years of experience as a physician. He pocketed his glasses in his starched lab coat. "Dr. Owens says Dylan's recovering nicely from the pneumothorax. We're watching him closely; we don't want that lung collapsing again. The fight and fall were too much, especially since he won't quit smoking. Is he responding much to verbal commands this morning? Has the dressing been changed since the chest tube was removed?"

"Yes, sir. The site's clean, no infection. He kind of slips in and out of consciousness, probably from all the pain medication."

"Hard to say with Dylan. For all we know, he could be playing possum on us. He was a master at faking sleep as a kid. It got him out of any number of chores." Dr. McAthie chuckled.

"I could see that." She straightened Dylan's cover as an excuse to look away, still mortified at her part in all of this.

"He'll be fine. Now I'm worried about you. You need to go home and get some rest before you end up down the hall hospitalized from sheer exhaustion. Everyone, especially your father, is worried about you. Cathy or Jimmy will stay with Dylan. Tyrone is just outside the door."

"I'm okay. I want to stay. Unless, of course, you think it best…I know I'm not doing more than just sitting…" She wrung her hands. She'd actually been surprised and relieved no one had fired her. The shame of being caught in a compromising position made her physically sick.

"Dylan insisted you stay." He pushed the computer to the wall and focused his attention on her. "I just don't want you staying out of any false sense of obligation. You're not to blame for any of this. If anyone needs to make any sort of restitution, it's Dylan. I still have a lot of questions about that night, as I'm sure you do. But hear me, I'm not blaming you, okay? We're cutting back on his pain medication, so he should be more with it and ready to be released in a day or so."

He waited until she nodded.

"Now, if for no other reason, have mercy on *me* and go home and get some rest. It will spare me the lecture from Cathy. She's worried about you. She and Jimmy plan to rotate shifts today. I'm staying this evening for a while, and he'll be fine on his own tonight. Doctor's orders, *go home*." He stood for one last moment by Dylan's bed and squeezed his arm. "Wake up, dumbass."

After Dr. McAthie—*Robert*, she told herself—left, Jennifer smoothed the hair out of Dylan's face. Now that he was recovering, she had a lot of questions, too. But not all of them were for him. When had he become more than a patient? Or had he always been more? She pulled the chair closer to the bed, needing him in a way she couldn't explain.

Swimming deep underwater, Dylan tried to surface toward the light with slow, careful strokes. He hadn't swum competitively since high school. Maybe he wasn't swimming. His mouth was dry, and he felt like shit. Wanting to open his eyes, he struggled, but it required too much effort. *Am I dead? What a shame. I still have so much music left to share.*

Now closer to consciousness, he heard beeps and a whirring noise. *Not underwater, not dead, thank God.* His eyes fluttered open, and he frowned at the IV and medical equipment. He tore the mask off his face, and the heart monitor beeped faster as his anxiety level rose. *Dammit.* He kept forgetting he was back in the hospital. His eyelids felt like lead and closed of their own accord. *Jennifer…*He forced his eyes open. *Where is she?*

Relief washed over him when he found her asleep in a chair, a book clutched in her hand. Her head rested on the side of his bed, near his left hand. He reached out and stroked her soft, dark hair. A loose curl from her ponytail wrapped around his finger. As long as she was here, he was okay—though pride prevented him from telling her he'd begged Rob to keep her on as his private-duty nurse.

He tickled her face with her hair, and she stirred, wrinkling her nose. Sitting up, she yawned.

"Hey, you. Welcome back to the living." She smiled and squeezed his hand.

"How long have I been here, what time is it? *Wuthering Heights?*" He nodded toward the book.

"Five days, and they should be bringing you some lunch soon. I'm reading *Jane Eyre*. I seem to have a penchant for stories about women who fall for arrogant men. Go figure." She bit her lip, and for one unguarded moment, Dylan saw deep emotion in her jewel-colored eyes.

"You look like hell," he replied with a weary smile. *Damn, that didn't come out right.*

Her lips curved. "You don't look so great yourself."

"Probably not," he conceded, scratching the irritating beard. His brain felt fuzzy from the narcotics. "Your old man still want to kill me?"

"Yes, but he's waiting for you to recover," she quipped, standing.

"Please don't leave me." Dammit, he sounded like a whiny four-year-old. "We need to talk." He held onto her hand, searching her eyes for the accusations she had every right to cast his way.

"I know, but we'll have time for that. The nurse wanted me to let her know when you woke up so she could get your vital signs."

"But you're coming back, right?"

Jennifer nodded as she replaced his oxygen mask.

He smiled with relief. "Get me a cigarette, while you're up." He closed his eyes and nodded off to the sound of her fussing.

Dylan stirred when he heard the door and opened his eyes, hoping it was Jennifer. Instead Jimmy threw himself in the chair, his ear to his cell phone. Occasionally he responded with a terse "yes" or "no." He hung up and grinned.

"Damn, Dyl, you wanting to take over for ZZ Top when you get out of here, or are you applying for some redneck reality show?"

Dylan shot him a bird. Jimmy laughed.

He tore off the annoying oxygen mask. "Where's Jen?"

"I just passed her in the hall. I told her to go home, but she said she was going to go get some coffee and a bite to eat. She's dedicated; I'll say that. She's been here every time I've checked on you. Aren't you glad to see me? I'm not as pretty as she is, but you know, in a pinch I can get you a glass of water, or at the very least, ring for someone to wipe your ass."

Dylan laughed and winced, holding his side. Only Jimmy talked to him like this. The losers who clung to his coattail of fame would never dare. They were too busy sucking up. He'd grown sick of them a long time ago. Jimmy's genuine concern since the accident—and Jennifer's care—had made him realize the fake sincerity of others in his life.

Jimmy looked a lot like his sister, Sara. Except where her red hair had been dark and her features exotic, Jimmy's hair was more the color of burnt copper, and behind his easygoing demeanor was a legal shark.

"I'm glad you're here. Get me out of this prison, okay?"

Jimmy shook his head and paused as a nurse came in to check Dylan's IV.

Dylan flashed her a smile. "Got a cigarette?"

She replaced the oxygen mask over his face. "This is a smoke-free environment. Not to mention you're on oxygen. Do you really want to blow yourself to kingdom come?"

He pulled the mask off. "You can cut the oxygen, and I'll sneak a smoke in the bathroom. Please?" He tried using the smile that accented his dimples this time.

"I'll get Dr. Owens to order a nicotine patch," she replied, firmly replacing the oxygen mask. Checking her beeper, she pulled the privacy curtain and left.

Jimmy laughed. "You're losing your touch, bro."

"Shut up," Dylan muttered as he once again tore the annoying mask off his face. "Get me out of here."

"No can do. I know you rarely adhere to my wise counsel, but I'd mind my Ps and Qs for a while if I were you. You're in deep enough shit as it is."

"How deep, and how much is it going to cost me?"

"Well, you sure as hell won't be retiring any time soon. For fuck's sake, Dylan. What the hell were you thinking? No piece of ass is worth—"

"That's enough," Dylan cut him off. "Nothing happened. I believe I've mentioned this *ad nauseum* to anyone and everyone." Flicking on the television, he began punching the buttons, channel surfing.

"Don't cop an attitude with me. You employ me to take care of you, and that's exactly what I'm trying to do. Your career is in jeopardy, and you damn well better pay attention to what I say. The photos and video Donald shot paint a different story."

Dylan bit back a nasty retort. Jimmy looked entirely too serious for comfort. "I threw his phone against the fireplace. There are no pictures. Pay the fucker off and be done with it. I should have shot the damn idiot when I had the chance."

"*I've seen the pictures*, Dylan. Jennifer is naked, in your arms, in her bed. Luckily, the video's a little blurry, but still." He paused, waiting for the statement to process. "He outwitted you. He'd already saved them. Not to mention, other people have posted pics of the barroom brawl all over social media. Wendy has a plausible statement to make for you. But…"

"But?" Uneasy, he lowered the volume on the television.

"This one isn't going to be easy to skirt. Jennifer was underage and in a bar. Her drink was probably spiked with a date-rape drug. There's no police report, and now there are photos. It's the perfect storm. If we play this right, you can survive the publicity. You're in an industry where this kind of scandal is considered par for the course—but if it gets as ugly as I fear, it's going to be a battle, and there will be casualties. Regardless, you're going to have to pay top dollar and pray it keeps Donald silent—"

Dylan interrupted, "But there's no guarantee he won't double cross, right?"

Jimmy sighed. "It's a helluva crapshoot."

"Pay it. Whatever the amount, I don't care. Everybody has a price. Give Mrs. J a generous check, too. She deserves it."

Done with the conversation, he went back to perusing the inane crap on daytime television.

"You know, Dylan, you could take this a little more seriously. This is a huge problem, and I'm working my ass off for you. I convinced Wendy to come back, and her team is working nonstop on damage control to put as positive a spin on this as possible. You aren't grasping the depth of this mess. You're in this shit so deep, you may never resurface. As I've told you, this doesn't just affect you. You employ hundreds of people. Think about it, if you go down, so do your employees.

"Sure, you can attempt to buy the pictures, but I don't trust Donald, and you better not underestimate him either. Even if you pay what he's demanding, there are other threads of this nasty business surfacing. Bobby Joe Armdale says he never touched Jennifer's drink and is pointing the finger at *you*."

Dylan blinked and frowned. "What?"

"You didn't call the police. You didn't take Jennifer to the hospital. You know how fickle the public is. People *want* to believe the worst in celebrities, and you know how damn fast bad publicity goes viral. For once in your goddamned life, would you think about someone besides yourself? Jennifer's father is a prominent minister not just here, but nationally. What if his church fires him because of the scandal?

My take is, he doesn't give a rat's ass what his congregation thinks. He's rightfully more concerned about his daughter. As a matter of fact, from what I hear, he wants to nail your hide to the wall.

"The only thing people love more than celebrity scandal is a church scandal. Did you know Jennifer's a Sunday school teacher, for Christ's sake? What if she decides to press charges? Or if she doesn't, who's going to hire a nurse with this kind of media baggage? This situation must be handled fast and handled with finesse. Think, will ya? She could very well get fed up, or money hungry, and turn into a loose cannon. She could hire a lawyer and accuse you of any number of things.

"Now option one—and the easiest to accomplish—would be to paint Jennifer as a conniving bitch who worked her way into your bed as a setup for blackmail—" Jimmy paused and shot a worried look toward the privacy curtain.

Sighing, he shrugged before turning his attention back to Dylan. "I'm not saying she'd go rogue, but we have to be prepared, get her and keep her on your side—like a team."

"Absolutely not. That option is off the table. Look, even if something happened, she's old enough to be a consenting adult, and she signed the nondisclosure agreement before she was hired," Dylan snapped.

Jimmy pounded his fist with exasperation. "Would you *listen* to me? Jennifer has the face of a damn angel. If she, or her father, press charges just for the underage drinking—or worse, for attempted rape—do you really think the press will side with the hedonistic musician or the innocent Sunday school teacher?

"Furthermore, I don't think an NDA counts when someone spikes her drink. She's the victim, her life was at risk. That negates any legal mumbo jumbo she signed, you moron. Regardless, any good lawyer worth his salt will work in a damaging statement during the trial and let it be thrown out, just so public opinion can crucify you. It won't matter if you're found not guilty; the public will convict you regardless. Dammit, don't you see? This has the potential to escalate so damn fast and skew so far from the truth that no one, *including you,* will know what really happened." Jimmy rested his elbows on his knees and rubbed his face.

"What's the worst-case scenario, and how are you going to handle it?" Dylan tried pulling his scrambled thoughts together, but the pain medication made it difficult. *Why would Jen sue me? I rescued her.*

"My biggest fear is that this goes to court. There, the story gets twisted and they establish probable cause that you spiked her drink to take advantage of her. You come across as a creeper, or worse, a potential rapist. But don't worry. I have the solution to all of this: marry her."

"*Rapist?*" Dylan couldn't begin to wrap his mind around the disgusting thought. "Nothing happened...Wait, *what the hell did you just say?*"

"Marry her. Wendy and I can then spin anything that comes out into a lovers-caught-in-the-throes-of-passion situation. Even if the pictures surface, it won't matter. We'll have you so in love, the god-damned birds in the trees will be singing your praises. It's a win-win for everyone involved, with minimal bad publicity for you. I'll even have Wendy help Pastor Adams with a story to satisfy his congregation. He can't very well sue his future son-in-law, and when you divorce, you'll provide Jennifer enough money to keep any woman happy. I'll make sure everything is spelled out in the prenup she signs. Look at the fringe benefits—I mean, damn, she's beautiful."

"Have you lost your fuckin' mind? I am *not* going to marry her. I'm not a marrying man. For crissakes, I didn't marry your sister."

"Yeah, well, you and Sara would have ended up divorced anyway. Everyone knew that. So, okay, dumbass, what's *your* plan?"

Tired and confused, Dylan felt railroaded. He just wanted to talk to Jennifer. He wanted to explain to her that nothing had happened. He didn't want a scandal. And he certainly wanted to avoid her experiencing the relentless scrutiny of social media.

He scrubbed at his face, exhausted. He cared about Jennifer, and the sexual chemistry between them sizzled for sure. Maybe Jimmy was right. A quick marriage could solve everything, and it might even be fun, not to mention giving him time to see if a true relationship would form. *It could work—stranger things have happened.* Hell, some cultures still had arranged marriages.

Maybe this wasn't really such a big deal anyway. Hollywood had several on-paper and for-photos-only marriages already underway. He knew of one prominent couple that didn't even share a wing of their mansion, much less a bed. He and Jennifer could always divorce later if things didn't work out.

Shit, these drugs were messing with his head. He couldn't think. He paid Jimmy to think for him, but this sounded like a viable plan...

"Fine. Whatever. Just handle the problem."

As if in a trance, Jennifer stumbled her way to the visitor's sitting area and collapsed in a chair. Obviously, Jimmy and Dylan weren't aware she'd been standing behind the curtain for the better part of their conversation—a conversation that planned her life without any input from her. Feeling sick to her stomach, she'd left when she heard Jimmy saying she could blackmail Dylan. Surely he didn't believe that of her? Or maybe he did...Staring at the wall, she tried to make sense of the awful things she'd overheard. Her hand shook as she took the last sip of the now-cold coffee, trying to steady her nerves.

Photos? There are photos of me naked in bed with Dylan? And video? She still didn't have any firm recollections of that night. Apparently, her not remembering wasn't an issue. After all, Jimmy Vaughan seemed to be on top of things, ready to do damage control and put a positive spin on the *situation.*

I'm nothing to Dylan.

Simply an inconvenience.

A situation to be handled.

A conniving bitch.

They might even use their *people* to make it seem like she was some sort of money-hungry whore. Devastated, her heart slammed in her chest, and she couldn't stop shaking. All her life she'd been the obedient, smart girl—the one who never fit in. Gifted, she'd been promoted in school to classes with children older and more mature than she was. Add shyness to the mix and consequently, she'd had very few friends. In nursing school, she'd finally developed a true friendship with Vickie, one of her classmates. She considered calling and talking to her, but Vickie had a young daughter. If there was a scandal, she didn't want Vickie involved. Or her father...

Daddy. His disappointment in her gnawed her conscience. As the daughter of a minister, she'd lived by what her church and father expected. And she hadn't dared step out of bounds, for fear of disappointing those who held such high expectations for her. This job had been her chance to explore her freedom and pursue her dreams of being on her own, at least for a little while. Now it was her nightmare, and others were still planning her future for her.

Crushing the empty coffee cup, she threw it across the room, missing the garbage can. She slumped and covered her face with her hands. The day Dylan collapsed had been the worst day of her life—and not because of how her father found her that morning. Hers wasn't the normal concern a nurse felt at the prospect of losing a patient. It had been the heart-wrenching, personal fear of losing *him*.

"Jennifer."

Looking up, she attempted a weak smile for her father. He seemed to have aged ten years since she left home. She stood and met him halfway, hugging him for a minute, taking in the familiar scent of his aftershave. How she wished she could go back in time to when one of his hugs could make her problems go away. She tightened her hold.

"Have you eaten today?" He held her at arm's length, worry crossing his face. "You need to come home and get some rest. The McAthies will stay with that man." It was amusing—in a weird kind of way—that her father couldn't, or wouldn't, call Dylan by his name.

"I'm fine, Daddy. I drank some coffee."

"You need to eat," another voice chimed in. "You look as if you'd blow over in a strong wind." David stood leaning against the doorframe, looking more like a quarterback than a future seminarian.

Tall with dark, chestnut brown hair, he wore his jeans and white shirt with grace and ease. More than one nurse walked by and turned around to stare. His warm, kind brown eyes were filled with concern. David Patterson was handsome, no doubt about it, but he was no Dylan McAthie. Jennifer gave herself a swift kick back to reality. *Idiot, you're nothing to Dylan but a legal difficulty.*

She gave David a hug, deflecting the kiss he leaned over to give her. Guilt flooded her when he paused, looking confused, but she couldn't kiss him with her father watching. Her father already regarded David as his future son-in-law, and right now, she didn't know what her future held for her. She shoved a curl behind her ear and turned away to look out the window.

"Let's go home. I'll make my famous pancakes for supper, *after* you've had a long nap," her father coaxed.

Jennifer nodded, wanting the safety of home to sort through her feelings. She needed time to think. "I need to get my purse and tell them I'm leaving."

"Want me to go with you?" David's brows knit together.

"No, I won't be but a moment."

Before entering Dylan's room, she took a deep breath and composed herself. Stepping around the privacy curtain, she found Dylan asleep, but Jimmy Vaughan looked up and smiled.

"I'm going home." Thankfully, her voice held cool and steady, unlike the tumultuous flipping of her stomach.

"Good idea. You need the rest. We'll need to talk soon," Jimmy replied.

If she hadn't just overheard his remarks to Dylan, she might've thought he was concerned about her.

She knew better.

Chapter
Fourteen

Why won't people leave me the fuck alone?

The rhythmic jiggling of the bedrail annoyed Dylan to no end. He opened one eye and glared at his nephew, who obliviously tapped out a rhythm while plugged into his phone.

"Robbie."

No response.

"Robbie! Stop!"

Still no response. Dylan reached over and grabbed the earbud out of Robbie's ear. He couldn't stay mad when he saw the look of sheer happiness cross the kid's face.

"Hiya, Uncle Dylan!"

"What are you listening to?"

"Hip hop."

"Oh. Not one of mine, huh?" Dylan asked.

"You haven't done anything *new*. You've been sick."

The kid had a point. Dylan glared and shook his head *no* when Robbie reached to push the up and down button on the bed.

"True enough. Where's your mother?"

"She and Mary went to get snacks. It's boring watching you sleep."

I need to put Robbie on the payroll. He definitely isn't a yes man.

"Hey, Uncle Dylan, what's it like being on stage and having all those people watching you?"

"It's like Christmas and your birthday all rolled into one. The adrenaline rush is so damn exciting you feel like you could fly." He smiled at his nephew. "But I have a deep, dark, nasty secret."

Robbie leaned forward, his eyes huge. "What?"

"I get so nervous before going on stage, I get sick, every damn time," he whispered.

"Like, throw-up sick?" Robbie's look of disgust was priceless.

Dylan nodded.

"That's gross." Robbie pretended to gag.

"Yep, it is."

Laughing, they looked up when the door opened. Cat handed her son a cola and a bag of chips. Mary threw herself into the other chair, never missing a beat as she texted on her phone.

"Cat, really. Chips and a cola? Wouldn't fruit or juice be better for the kid?"

She glared at him, hands on her hips.

Damn if she doesn't look like Mrs. J.

"Perhaps you're right. Maybe I should go get him an apple and a pack of *cigarettes.*"

"Okay, okay, don't get your panties in a wad." Dylan shook his head and grinned.

He shoved the sheets aside and, with great care, sat up on the side of the bed, bracing his ribs where the chest tube had recently been removed.

"Where do you think you're going?"

"Hell, I dunno, Cat. What do you say we go out dancing? I'm trying to get out of this damn bed to take a piss."

"Stop. You can't get up. You're supposed to be wearing that oxygen thingie, and you have an IV. Plus, with that hospital gown, you might expose yourself to my kids. And quit cussing, dammit." Eyes wide, she slapped a hand over her mouth.

Dylan laughed so hard tears tracked down his face and his ribs hurt. "I'm sure they watch television, Cat, and have seen plenty of bare butts. I wish to hell you'd quit treating me like one of your *kids*," he grumbled as he made sure everything stayed covered. "Look, I need you to send them out of the room and help me to the bathroom."

Cat gasped. "Me? I can't help you—I mean, really, Dylan." Her mouth set firmly in a line of disapproval, and she crossed her arms.

"Oh, for crying out loud. Don't get all hoity-toity on me. I remember having pissing contests with you until you wised up to the fact that your plumbing put you at a disadvantage."

"We were five and six years old!" But she threw her hands up and shooed Robbie and Mary into the hall as they squealed with laughter.

Dylan stood, grabbing the IV pole with one hand and holding his gown closed with the other. With Cat's help, he made it into the bathroom.

He wiggled his eyebrows and leered. "Wanna hold it for me, darlin'?"

"Oh, for heaven's sake, I'm not one of your band bimbos." She closed the door, waiting outside.

Looking in the mirror, Dylan sighed. In desperate need of a shave and a haircut, he looked like a homeless derelict. When he finished, Cat assisted him back to bed.

Damn, he was weak. He didn't even have it in him to fuss when she pulled the covers up, tucking him in like he was indeed one of her kids. He gave her a weak smile.

"There you go, safe and sound," she cooed. She patted his hand and moved to leave, but Dylan didn't let go.

"Cat? Wait a minute."

"Yes?" Frowning, she tried placing the oxygen mask back on his face.

He brushed it away and asked, "Do you ever think about the night of my high school graduation?"

He remembered like it was yesterday: coming home drunk and finding the girl he loved making out with his brother.

"What about it?" She gave him a slight frown of worry.

"Why didn't you tell me about Rob? I did love you, you know." He couldn't quite keep the old bitterness from creeping into the question.

"We were young. I made mistakes," she said. "I've always loved you, but not the way I love Robert. You were more interested in your music than me."

"Ever regret your decision?" His gaze held hers as she squeezed his hand.

Brushing his hair out of his eyes, she shook her head. "My only regret is that we parted in such anger. You were my best friend, and oh, how I've missed you these past thirteen years," she whispered, her eyes filling with tears.

Dylan nodded and kissed her hand. "I've missed you, too. You were my first love, but I was stubborn, and so full of anger. My damn pride kept me away, and you're right. My music was everything. I focused on my career…" He sighed, his voice hoarse. "I've wasted a lot of damn time, Cat. I have so many regrets…"

"You have a lifetime ahead of you, Dylan." She leaned over and kissed him on the forehead as she replaced the oxygen mask.

Lifting the mask, he caught her before she opened the door. "Hey, Cat? We would've killed each other in the first year of marriage, wouldn't we?"

"Damn straight, we would've!" She opened the door and jumped back with surprise when her husband walked through, followed by Mary and Robbie. He gave her a quick kiss on the mouth.

"The kids say they're bored and ready to go home. I'm done for the day, so I'll stay with Dylan." Rob shrugged out of his lab coat and handed it to his wife.

"Are you sure? We can stay. You need to relax a bit." Cat straightened Rob's collar.

"*Hello?* I'm not comatose, and I don't need a damn babysitter," Dylan complained as he once again tore off the oxygen mask. He wanted Jennifer. He didn't feel like dealing with his condescending older brother.

Rob glared at him. "Given your recent actions, I differ with your assessment. What you need is a damn keeper." He turned his attention to his children, giving them each a kiss goodbye.

"Language," Cat cautioned.

Dylan rolled his eyes and rang for the nurse to bring him a pain pill. Maybe it would knock him out.

Cat paused before leaving, her eyes tracking from Rob back to Dylan. "Try to get along; it's just one evening." She blew a kiss to both men, closing the door.

"Damn, she's starting to sound more and more like her mother, Rob."

He smirked and nodded. "I, uh, tend *not* to point that out to her. Self-preservation." He stood with his hands clasped behind his back. "I'm glad to see you're feeling better. You had us worried for a few days."

"Stop doing that!"

"Doing what?" Rob moved his hands to his hips and glared.

"You look like the old man when you stand that way. It's creepy as hell. Sit down or leave." Dylan shuddered at the memory of his father. "I don't know why you think you have to stay. Go home to your family, Junior."

Rob collapsed in the chair, propping his long legs on the side of the bed. He looked at Dylan for a long moment and shook his head. "I know you've tried to sever the ties, but the fact remains, you *are* my brother. That makes you family, dumbass."

"Right, you're my *brother*, not my keeper. Go home. I don't need you." *Dammit, that didn't come out right.*

Rob's feet slammed to the floor. "Well, you sure as hell needed me the other day. Just who do you think saved your miserable life? God, you're such an ungrateful ass. Have you ever considered that maybe *I* need *you?* Where were you when Dad died? I know he was an abusive bastard, but dammit, he was still our father. Cathy and I left our honeymoon to come home and plan his funeral." He ran a hand through his short, dark hair. He leaned forward, pointing his finger at Dylan.

"Do you know how hard it was to track you down? Gran finally got in touch with you, but did you come home? Hell, no! And don't even get me started on when Gran died, because that was the last goddamned straw..." He sagged in the chair, crossing his arms.

They sat in a stony silence for several uncomfortable minutes, the air thick with years of animosity. A knock at the door broke the quiet as the nurse brought a pain pill for Dylan.

"Where's Jennifer?" Dylan asked when he realized he hadn't seen her in hours. He swallowed the narcotic with a sip of water. The nurse replaced his oxygen mask, which he removed as soon as she left.

"Home. She's exhausted." Rob rubbed his face, looking dog-tired himself.

Dylan nodded absently as he wrestled with his convoluted feelings toward his brother. "I hated Dad, and he hated me. If he'd been on fire, I wouldn't have crossed the street to piss on him. But Gran..."

Years of hard-held anger warred with the need to comfort his brother and be comforted in return. He had to acknowledge that while Rob might look like their old man, he was nothing like him. Rob loved his family, was a good father, and—if he was honest with himself—had been a good brother. Dylan had never had a claim on Cat. He'd loved her, but never had the gumption to tell her so. Not that it would've mattered.

"I wanted to be there for Gran's funeral."

Rob looked up, his stormy blue eyes questioning.

Dylan took a deep breath. "I couldn't be there; I was burying Sara the same day. She was pregnant…I just couldn't deal. I used to talk to Gran every damn Sunday. She'd tell me about you and Cat and the kids, about the gossip in Pine Bluff." He looked away and swallowed the lump in his throat. "I'd go see her when I could, but not often enough…"

"Damnation." Rob leaned forward, placing a hand on Dylan's arm. "Why didn't you call us? Cathy and I would've been there for you. We had no idea. If we'd known, we could've delayed Gran's funeral—"

"It happened so fast. After the band broke up Sara and I…we weren't in a good place. She was strung out on heroin, and I'd only stayed with her because of the baby. I thought she had her shit together since she'd entered treatment. I thought it was working…" He paused and hit the bed with his fist. "I hate her for what she did. She OD'd on fuckin' heroin and coke, killing herself…and yet…" He shook his head and looked down, unable to speak.

"I'm sorry." Rob touched his arm.

Dylan nodded and rubbed the heels of his hands against his eyes.

There was nothing more to be said, and they sat in silence.

It felt good to have Rob here. Life was too short to live with regrets. It was time to let go.

"I miss Gran," Dylan offered. He gave Rob a sad smile. It wasn't an apology for the past, but it was the start of a new beginning.

His brother smiled in return. "Me too. She was a grand old lady. Remember when you snuck pot in the house and convinced her it was oregano?"

Dylan laughed. "Best damn spaghetti she ever made."

Years of strife slipped away as they reminisced about their childhood summers at the lake.

Chapter
Fifteen

Jennifer admired her freshly painted pink toenails as she waited on the coffee to finish percolating in her father's kitchen. A knock at the back door startled her. Carefully walking on her heels with her toes spread, she answered the door.

"Good morning!" David gave her a quick peck on the cheek as he entered.

Jennifer ran her fingers through her uncombed hair with dismay. She wondered, irritably, how David managed to look so put together at only eight in the morning. He gazed at her with a critical, but not unkind eye.

"You still look tired," he noted as he poured himself a cup of coffee.

Unable to look him in the face, she lied. "I'm fine. Really, I am."

Truth be told, she hadn't slept much at all. For the past two nights, the snippet of conversation she'd heard between Dylan and Jimmy had replayed over and over in her mind. And when she did fall asleep, disconcerting dreams of lying in bed naked with Dylan plagued her. Dr. McAthie and her father had insisted she stay home, rather than be at the hospital, and she hadn't argued. She needed to figure out how *she* was going to deal with *the situation*.

"Look, Jennifer, your father told me what happened." The kindness in David's voice heated her face with embarrassment.

She poured a cup of coffee, still avoiding eye contact with David. Although they'd never formally discussed it, there was an unstated sort of understanding that they would marry after David finished school. Before meeting Dylan, Jennifer had been happy with the prospect of becoming Mrs. David Patterson.

"I'm not blaming you. You were drugged. But I *am* worried about you." He reached over, stopping her as she went to put a fifth teaspoon of sugar in her cup.

"Dylan says nothing happened…I don't know. I can't really remember, but I believe him."

"Come here. You're okay. That's all that matters." David pulled her into his arms and held her, stroking her back as tears ran down her face. How could there be any left? And how could he forgive her? *Would he be saying this if he knew about the pictures and video?*

The doorbell rang, and Jennifer wiped her face. She relaxed when she heard her father plodding down the stairs to get the door and remained in David's strong arms, taking the comfort he offered. After a moment, she heard the front door slam.

Without looking, she sensed it was Dylan. She attempted to disengage from David's arms, but he held her tighter. Using the napkin David offered, she dabbed at her eyes.

"Young man, I told you to wait at the door. My daughter has nothing to say to you." Her father's brusqueness surprised her. He wasn't typically a rude person. But then, this wasn't a typical situation.

"Are you, okay, Jennifer?" her father asked in a much warmer voice.

Will Daddy ever call Dylan by his name?

Nodding, she pulled away from David and kissed her father on the cheek. He walked past her toward the coffee pot. Taking a deep breath, she turned to face Dylan, and her heart gave a painful lurch. Standing in the doorway, unlit cigarette and lighter in one hand, and a cane in the other, was a man much different than the one she'd grown used to seeing.

He looked so much younger, so much more like the pictures and posters hanging on his nephew Robbie's walls. She liked the way his trimmed, sun-kissed hair looked as if he'd just run his fingers through it as it fell above his broad shoulders. The beard was now a designer stubble. He was, in a word, *breathtaking*, even in plain jeans and a white oxford shirt with the sleeves rolled up. Reminding herself to breathe, she stood frozen, facing him. His brow furrowed as his gaze drifted from her to David.

"I need to talk to Jennifer," Dylan told her father before turning to her. "Aren't you going to introduce us?" He attempted to put the cigarette back in the pack and missed. He finally stuck it behind his ear and stuffed the lighter in his pocket.

"Dylan, this is David Patterson. David, this is Dylan McAthie." Shaking hands with nods of acknowledgment, they seemed to be sizing each other up. The testosterone-laden air added to the awkwardness of the situation.

A slight clenching of Dylan's jaw betrayed his nerves, or annoyance; she wasn't sure which. "I need to talk to Jennifer," he said again.

Looking tired and wary, her father sat at the table. "Be my guest." His tone was a bit too cold to be considered polite. He motioned for Dylan to have a seat.

"Alone, please."

David's face reddened, and she felt his grasp on her arm tighten. Her father tipped over the chair in his haste to stand.

"Stop!" Jennifer shrugged out of David's grasp.

Grabbing Dylan by the hand, she tromped into the living room and turned to face him. To her surprise, Dylan kept walking, dragging her behind him out the front door. She attempted to wriggle out of his grip, but he held on tight.

"What are you doing? Where are we going?"

He pointed with his cane to a red, shiny convertible with a California license plate parked in the McAthies' driveway. Perplexed, she followed him next door. He opened the driver's side door and motioned for her to get in.

"What? Wait…I'm barefoot. I haven't even brushed my hair, and I don't have my driver's license. Where're we going?"

"Get in."

Curious, she sat down in the car. Dylan walked around to the passenger's side.

Slipping on his sunglasses, he grinned for the first time that morning. "Buckle up, and let's get the hell outta Dodge."

Any thoughts of tabloid photos, nondisclosure agreements, David, her father, or being in a *situation* left as she gazed at his perfect dimples and sunlit hair. Maybe Dylan had disagreed with Jimmy's assessment of her after all. Returning his smile, she threw the car in reverse and drove, never giving a backward glance to the men she left standing on her father's front porch.

Dylan leaned his head back and closed his eyes. The wind and sun on his face felt so damn good. He had a new appreciation for life, thanks to the girl sitting next to him. Jennifer's absence at the hospital the past two days had made the time seem endless and downright boring. He'd missed her. Now he just had to get her on board with Jimmy's master plan. And then he had plans for her…

But worry ate at his conscience as he watched her drive. The dark circles under her eyes alarmed him. She looked delicate and very young in her bare feet, shorts, and oversized football jersey with PATTERSON on the back. He scowled. David hadn't looked at all like the skinny nerd with a pocket protector he'd pictured.

"Where did you get the car?" she asked above the wind. "I thought you wrecked it."

"Thank God, I totaled the Benz. Not the NSX. This is my pride and joy. I had Jimmy send for it. Like it?"

"Are you freaking kidding me?" The sound of her laugh made him smile. Beaming like a kid with a new toy, her hair blew behind her in a wild, carefree mess. She stepped on the gas, and the speedometer shot up to ninety and then a hundred as they flew down the highway with Beethoven's Fifth blaring through the speakers. With a squeal of delight, she looked over at Dylan and hit the gas a little more.

"Slow down, angel. I'm not paying for your ticket," he shouted, laughing at her pout as she let up on the gas.

God, what I'd like to do to that lip…

"This car is a dream machine!" she shouted before turning down the volume on the music. "Where are we going?"

Her question brought him back from a place he had no right to go. Today was about taking care of her.

"I don't care. Someplace where we can be alone." At Jennifer's pensive look he added, "To talk. We need to talk."

She nodded, and in a few minutes, she pointed to a roadway sign indicating a state park ahead. He nodded with a thumbs up. He flipped the satellite radio to another favorite station and closed his eyes as the strains of Puccini's "*O Mio Babbino Caro*" surrounded them. The irony of the piece amused him.

Jennifer turned into the park, bringing the car to a stop in front of a deserted picnic table as the last note of the melancholy aria lingered. The wind whispered in the stately pines as birds chirped. She turned to face him, and he frowned at the unshed tears in her eyes.

"What's wrong, angel?" He brushed his fingers along her jaw.

"That was the most beautiful song I've ever heard. The emotion was incredible."

"You've never heard it before?" He resisted the urge to kiss her tears away.

She shook her head. "What was she singing about?"

Dylan smiled. "Lauretta is trying to convince her father she loves Rinuccio. If her father doesn't allow their marriage, she threatens to kill herself by jumping into the River Arno."

Jennifer's eyes widened. "Oh," she whispered. "I, uh…oh." She sighed and looked down at her lap. Her brow furrowed. "I didn't know you liked opera."

"What? Did you think I'm so vain I only listen to my own stuff?" He laughed when she nodded. "I should be insulted by that. I happen to have very eclectic tastes in music. Even opera." He opened the car door and stood, bracing his side and wincing as he straightened his aching leg.

Jennifer followed him toward the picnic table. "Thanks for letting me drive your car. That was fun." She ran her fingers through her hair, attempting to bring order to the windblown tangles.

An urge to bury his face in her neck washed over him. *How can she be so damn sexy and so totally unaware of it?* Although still early in the morning, the summer sun and humidity had raised the heat index to an uncomfortable level. But Dylan knew it wasn't the temperature alone causing him to sweat.

He motioned to the bench as he lit a cigarette. "Sit."

Her eyebrow shot up. "Am I supposed to pant and fall at your feet?"

"Only if you insist." Dylan laughed. "God, you're so cute. Please have a seat?"

"You're not supposed to be smoking." She remained standing as he sat on the table, his feet on the bench.

Looking her in the eyes, he took a draw off his cigarette. "We have a lot to talk about." Her unwavering gaze gave him pause. "I know I've said it before, but I want you to truly understand, *nothing happened between us that night*. You believe me, don't you?"

A myriad of emotions crossed her pale face. "*Then why was I naked?*" Her eyes narrowed and smoldered as she waited for his answer. With her hair all over the place, she looked a little dangerous, like a dark warrior goddess.

"Uh, well…" Thrown off guard, he fumbled for an explanation.

A resounding slap across his face was her answer. He jumped off the table and grabbed her wrist, his fury sparked by the unexpected attack.

"Don't you *ever* hit me again," he said through clenched teeth. He dropped her arm and paced for a moment to diffuse his anger. "My old man used to slap me around. I didn't like it then, and I sure as hell don't like it now."

"Sorry," she whispered. "I'm just so confused…"

Coming to stand in front of her, he rubbed his eyes in frustration, and Jennifer caught hold of his hand, stopping him. An instant sexual current flashed between them. Staring wide eyed, she gasped, attempting to move away. He threw the cigarette to the ground and yanked her close. His fingers threaded through her hair as he ground his mouth into hers. She froze for a split second before giving in, returning his kiss with a passion that surprised him. Her lips parted, and he deepened the kiss. When he nipped her lower lip with his teeth, she moaned and pressed against him, gripping his biceps with her nails.

He pulled away before he lost himself. She was a siren in disguise, her innocence dangerously enticing. Her lips whispered across the notch between his collarbones. His pulse hammered at a frenetic pace. He groaned, struggling to maintain control. A primal need for this woman roared through his body. *Mine.*

Dylan grabbed her by the shoulders and rasped, "That…angel… is why you were naked."

She swallowed and reached up, touching her swollen lip with a trembling hand. "Sorry?" she whispered. Her eyes searched his.

Taken aback, he asked, "For what? You did nothing wrong. *We* did nothing wrong. Can't you feel the chemistry between us? That night we just got a little carried away. The drug lowered your inhibitions, and I'd had a few beers…Look, you were a mess. I helped you with your bath, and I put you to bed. You had a nightmare, and I came in to comfort you. We kissed, and it got a little heavy, but, angel, I would never take advantage of you. Surely you know me well enough to know that. I know you're inexperienced."

Jennifer spun away from him. When she turned around, her eyes flashed with fury. "And what makes you think I'm a virgin? Why did you stop? Am I not attractive enough for you? And you need to quit smoking if you're going to kiss me!" Glaring, she tossed her hair and lifted her chin.

"Huh?" Dylan stepped away, his mind not quite grasping her words for a moment. "Of course I find you attractive. You're goddamned beautiful! That's not the point. Despite what you and your father might think, I don't take advantage of women." His mind reeling from her questions, he busied himself with pulling out a small cooler and a folder from the trunk. He placed them on the picnic table. "Please sit. We need to talk about the repercussions of that night."

Not a virgin?

He offered her a bottle of water, which she declined. Still standing, she peeked in the cooler and took out a diet cola and a pastry.

"Your diet is as atrocious as ever." Shaking his head with a grin, he took a bite of an apple and uncapped a bottle of water. She stuck out her tongue.

Not a virgin…

Licking the icing off her lips, her luminous eyes bore straight through his sunglasses. Her smile suggested mystery and promises as she sucked in her lower lip.

Not a virgin? Dylan shifted uncomfortably, hardening at the thoughts of what he wanted that beautiful mouth to do to him. With difficulty, he pulled his mind back to the task at hand. He shoved the folder in front of her and flipped it open.

Lighting another smoke, he again sat on top of the picnic table, his feet on the bench. "I'm not sure how much you remember of the events prior to being caught *in flagrante delicto*."

"In what?" She sank onto the bench and pushed a curl behind her ear. Her skin flushed and eyes widened when she saw the incriminating pictures.

"In bed, Jennifer. It goes without saying, your father is unhappy, my team is unhappy, and now that we know there are photos and a video, we're in a shitload of trouble. Now, for starters, do you plan on pressing charges against me?"

Jennifer peeked at Dylan from underneath her lashes. His stupid sunglasses prevented her from seeing his eyes. His kiss, and the shock of actually seeing photos of her naked in his arms, had twisted her stomach in knots.

"...fortunately the video is blurry, so we're not concerned..." Dylan talked as if discussing something as mundane as the weather.

Numb, she stared at the incriminating prints while Dylan talked about "ramifications and possible solutions." For all she comprehended, he might as well have been speaking Greek. Her mind felt encased in a thick fog. Sucking in a deep breath, she could smell *him*—a unique blend of light aftershave, tobacco, warm skin, and just...him, *sex and sin*.

She squeezed her thighs together. Truthfully, she wasn't sure if she'd been relieved or disappointed to learn things hadn't gone as far as everyone thought. However, the photos appeared to tell a different story. Seeing them, she could well understand Jimmy's concern. She was horrified, but she wasn't the one at fault!

"...the *situation* demands we act quickly..." Dylan was saying.

Ah yes, *the situation*. That brought reality crashing back and reminded her what she'd heard he and Jimmy discussing—deciding, really. Without her. How dare they come up with a plan without even consulting her? But if that's how Dylan felt about her, why was he even here?

And what was that kiss about?

Dylan's voice droned on, as if from a distance, as her mind continued to wander. Did he have any feelings at all for her? Or was he still mourning Sara? He spoke of their sexual chemistry, but what about her as a person? Although true, his *inexperienced* comment had wounded her feminine pride.

Is it tattooed on my forehead or something? Here she is, folks, innocent and ripe for the picking! Come and get it!

She was neither proud nor ashamed of the fact that she was a virgin. David was her one and only serious boyfriend, and they hadn't been ready to take things to a deeper level.

Whoa, wait...hadn't been? Am I now ready to move forward? David. What about David?

These photos would ruin her reputation. She didn't want that to happen, but she knew she'd survive. However, the potential backlash on her father's career concerned her.

"Jennifer! Are you paying attention to me?"

She snapped out of it. "Uh, yes, of course," she lied.

"What did I just say?"

She sighed, feeling like a kid caught lying. "That 'asshole' Donald Rowe has photos that could ruin your reputation of being the world's greatest lover of all time — you know...being caught in bed with a stupid *virgin*. And this *situation* has to be *handled* because of *your* precious career."

His lips twitched, and he raised an eyebrow. "That's *not* exactly what I said. You need to pay attention. This concerns both of us."

"Then what, Dylan? What did you say?" She slapped the folder of pictures. "What am I supposed to do to help *you* get out of this *situation?* What do you and your legal sharks want me to do? Sign some stupid piece of paper relinquishing you of all responsibility? Do I need to go on every sleazy talk show and proclaim your innocence? How about I release my medical records to *The National Intruder* to show I'm still a dim-witted *virgin*. Will that work?"

She snapped her fingers. "Oh wait, no! I have the answer! You and your *team* can paint me to be the *whore* who crawled into your bed to blackmail you. That's it! The perfect solution! *You* can be the *innocent victim*." Heat rose in her cheeks in direct correlation to her rising voice. She looked around, relieved to see they were still alone.

Dylan's mouth settled into a straight line. "You can start by checking your attitude. I'm trying to do what's best for *everyone* involved. What the hell is wrong with you?" he roared back.

Fed up, she crossed her arms and glared. "I'm tired of everyone planning my life for me. It's *my* life, *my* mistakes."

Dylan lit another blasted cigarette off the one in his mouth.

"You're killing yourself with those things." She sighed, looking away, hating the fact that she cared.

Dylan rubbed his brow with his thumb. "Yeah? Well, marry me, and you'll be a rich widow."

The thought of Dylan dying caused her heart to catch, but she refused to be swept away by her emotions. Was he being serious? Marry him? She snorted her disbelief.

"*Jennifer.*" He smiled. "It isn't just me I'm concerned about. Your father will be pulled into this mess simply because he's a well-known minister. Your reputation matters to me; I want to protect you as much as possible. There's no way I would *ever* let anyone say you were a whore, or that you attempted to blackmail me. What kind of man do you think I am?"

At that, her mouth opened and then closed. She had no idea what to think about Dylan McAthie in this moment, let alone anything to say.

"I admit I'm concerned about my career," he continued after a moment. "I don't want whatever may be left of it to go down the toilet if the press twists this into something truly nasty. I don't want my niece, nephew, and goddaughter to see me on the cover of a tabloid labeled as some sort of lecherous pervert — or worse, a rapist. I don't want *anyone* to get hurt. I want to protect you, our families, and my career. If that makes me a selfish bastard, fine."

She forced herself to take a deep breath. Despite her anger, he had a valid point. She knew in her heart he wasn't a bad person. It was a bad situation, and he was trying to help. But the question remained, did he care even a little about her?

"My people in risk management have worked out a solution. This is to protect both of us. If we get married, then even if the photos are published, which we hope won't happen, or people talk, which is inevitable, we can sail through this situation without any significant ramifications. We marry, the press dies down, and everything will be okay. In a few months, we can part on irreconcilable differences. I promise, you'll be well compensated for all of this. You can think of it as a job. Of course, we'll have to deal with the necessary legal documents. You'll have to sign a prenup and another non-disclosure agreement, but you can have your lawyer look over them."

He waited for her response.

No ramifications? What about my broken heart? No talk of feelings, no talk of regrets. Just getting the situation handled and finances. No romance. No true love.

"I don't want your money," she told him.

"Money isn't bad. I quite enjoy it myself." He rubbed his brow, looking tired and resigned.

"And if I don't marry you?" Her voice trailed off to a hoarse whisper, and she stared at the ground, unwilling to let him see her pain. Her childish dreams of a fairy-tale romance and wedding were exactly that. A stupid, unrealistic fairy tale.

"Then we play the cards as they land and hope no one's life falls apart. It's a huge gamble, and *someone* will lose. *I don't like to lose,*" he added in a low voice. His meaning wasn't lost on her. He had "people in risk management" after all.

"I need to think about this." Jennifer stood and threw their trash in the garbage can. Maybe she could think of another way out...

He nodded, putting the cooler and folder back in the trunk of the car.

Dylan opened the car door for her and kissed the top of her head. "Thank you. What if I sweeten the pot and say I'll try to quit smoking?"

When she didn't reply, he added, "I hate to pressure you, but I need an answer by tonight. We can't keep a lid on this much longer. I'll pick you up at six for dinner, and we can talk more about it." He walked around to his side of the car and eased into the seat. "And, Jen? Don't overthink it. We can do this and maybe even have fun with it."

Have fun with it? What did he mean? Sex? Her breathing hitched. "I can't give you an answer right now." She sighed, her mind whirling. "I don't feel like driving back." *Don't overthink this?* How could she not? Her life was no longer her life; it was a situation being handled by a risk-management team. Her heart had been removed from the equation.

"On this, you have no choice."

She straightened her back, ready to argue once again.

"I can't see well enough to drive, angel, especially as light-sensitive as my eyes are. My glasses won't be ready until later today, and I'm not allowed to wear contacts yet."

Nodding, she returned to the driver's seat. They buckled their seatbelts as she started the car and revved the motor.

"Try to keep it below eighty," Dylan teased.

She drove home going fifteen miles below the speed limit just to annoy him.

Chapter Sixteen

Despite her protests, Dylan walked her to the front door. As they arrived, it opened, and neither her father nor David looked pleased.

Before this thought had fully registered in her brain, Dylan dragged her close, kissing her with finesse. This time his breath was minty fresh. His silver-blue eyes danced with mischief when he finally broke the kiss, leaving her breathless. His hand remained on her cheek, and his thumb brushed over her tingling lips.

"In case you decide to marry me, I thought I'd better show your old man how much I care about you," he whispered.

She stared, mute. Did he care about her? Or was this part of the plan?

"Cat's taking me to pick up my glasses, so text me. Regardless, I'll see you at six."

Did he say sex? No six. Dazed, she simply nodded.

"Jennifer Adams, if you're through making a spectacle of yourself, I'd like to speak to you. Now!"

Her father's voice snapped her out of her kiss-induced reverie, and she scampered through the door, dreading the lecture. Her mind raced in a vicious circle. Photos, marriage, Dylan, seductive kisses, legal teams...

"David, if you'll excuse us—"

The doorbell rang, and her father answered it. Jennifer panicked for a moment; surely Dylan wasn't back to stir up more trouble. Still, the momentary reprieve from the inevitable *I'm so disappointed in you* lecture was welcome.

Unfortunately, the door opened to something far worse. Mrs. Baxter, renowned church gossip and Jennifer's least favorite member of their congregation, stood before them, a gleam in her beady eyes.

"Hello, Mrs. Baxter, how are you?...Yes, that was Jennifer and her, uh, friend..."

The sound of her father's voice became muffled as he escorted the busybody into his study. She sighed; Mrs. Baxter made the tabloids look like rank amateurs when it came to spreading rumors and innuendos.

"So where did you and Dylan go?" David asked from behind her.

David! She'd forgotten about him. Jennifer bit her lip and looked away, flushing with guilt when she saw the concern and hurt on his face.

"Just to the park. He let me drive his car. It's a dream machine and really fast." *What an inane, stupid comment.*

"I see," he said as they sat at the kitchen table, awkward for the first time ever in each other's presence.

"Jennifer..." He paused, running a hand over the table, as if pondering what to say.

"Yes?" Her heart sank at the resigned look in his beautiful eyes.

"I have a lot of years of schooling left, and I wanted to be out and settled before I spoke—"

Tears filled her eyes, and before he could continue, she put her fingers to his lips, shaking her head. She didn't want to hurt him. But even if she refused Dylan's so-called proposal, she knew it was over with David.

"He doesn't deserve you." David sighed, looking away.

She was spared having to respond by the reappearance of her father. He slipped his heart medication under his tongue, looking very tired and old.

"Sit down. Are you okay?" Jennifer sprang from her chair, checking his pulse.

Her father smiled. "I'm fine—just a twinge from dealing with Mrs. Baxter and her wagging tongue. She thinks she means well, but everyone knows otherwise. She stopped by to ask about the church picnic, so she could bring to my attention a matter of 'urgency.'" He threw a copy of *The National Intruder* on the table.

"Oh, Daddy, I'm so sorry!" Jennifer gave a small prayer of thanks it wasn't *the picture*. A blurry picture of Dylan taking a swing at Bobby Joe appeared on page three. She could be seen huddling on the ground in the background.

"I assured her all children test the waters in some way or another, and you were fine. Of course, your public display a moment ago on the front porch didn't help things." He shook his head.

Her father continued as she checked his blood pressure. "I don't understand what's going on here. This man isn't your type at all. I would think his actions from that night would speak volumes about his character. He's older, your employer, and he took advantage of you. As I've told you, if you want to pursue this legally, I'll support you."

Jennifer smiled, relieved to find his pulse normal and blood pressure only slightly elevated. Her father rubbed a hand across the well-worn Bible he'd left on the kitchen table. Guilt overwhelmed her at the thought of him or David being dragged into a scandal due to her foolish choices. It was bad enough breaking David's heart, but what if this prevented him from pursuing his dreams of seminary? And her father lived to serve his congregation—one of those men truly called to be a pastor.

"Daddy, I'm sorry." Her decision became clear; she'd do anything to spare them embarrassment or pain. "Dylan didn't do anything wrong. And, uh, I love him. I can't help it."

David winced and stared out the window but remained silent.

"I see." Her father's voice sounded strained. "I would ask you to truly search your heart before you make a decision. Has he expressed the same feelings for you?"

She nodded, unable to verbalize the lie.

Her father sighed and rubbed his brow. "You're young, and I know you have stars in your eyes. It takes more than love to make a relationship work. You and this man have nothing in common; you barely know each other—"

Jennifer interrupted her father by hugging his neck and kissing his cheek. "He's not bad, Daddy. He even has a Bible verse tattooed on his ribcage. I know what I'm doing; it'll be okay. I love you."

He raised a brow. "I hardly think that makes him a Bible scholar, Jennifer." He patted her hand as he stood. "I love you, too. I just wish I could protect you from the heartache I'm afraid is inevitable." As he walked past David, he paused and gave him a fatherly squeeze on the shoulder. David stood and headed toward the door.

Jennifer grabbed his hand. "David? I, I'm so sorry..."

He didn't look at her, but his throat bobbled. He nodded and left without saying a word.

Jennifer followed her father to his study and stood in the doorway. He sat with his face buried in his hands. *Oh, Daddy, if you only knew how much worse this could get...* The photo of Dylan beating Bobby Joe would be a mere blip on the radar compared to the other photos that existed out there.

"Daddy?"

"Yes?"

"I do love him." Her heart fluttered, and she pondered the truth in her statement.

"I was afraid of that," her father answered.

Walking upstairs she texted Dylan:

OK. Marriage it is.

He replied immediately:

Good. cya at 6.

Aggravated, Dylan yanked the tie off as he stalked up to the front door and leaned on the bell.

"Hi, Uncle Dylan. Cool glasses." Mary smiled up at him. *Damn if she doesn't look like Cat at that age.*

"Flattery will get you nowhere, kid." He scowled and shrugged past her. "Cat! Cat, where are you? I need you! *Now!*"

"Good heavens, Dylan, what's the matter?" Cat stepped out of the kitchen, wiping her hands on a dishtowel.

"I can't get this godda—" He stopped at her sharp look and amended. "This stupid tie. I can't get the knot right. Help me!" He shook the offending fabric in frustration, slamming his cane down for good measure. *Goddamned noose.*

Cat giggled and walked around him, giving him the onceover and adding to his irritation. "My, my, look at you. You clean up well."

He looked down at his tailored gray pants and crisp white shirt. "I'd rather be in jeans and a T-shirt." He waved the crumpled maroon-and-gray-striped tie.

"I love your new glasses. You look very Madison Avenue," she teased.

He grimaced. "Thanks a lot. You do realize that statement could potentially ruin my reputation as a debauched musician who never bathes."

She grinned as she fixed his tie. "Why are you so dressed up?" she asked with a smirk.

"I, uh, have a date." He mumbled the last word and turned to his niece. "So, Mary, how's summer vacation going?"

Mary shrugged, never looking up from the cell phone that seemed permanently attached to her hand.

No lifeline there. Thanks for nothing, kid. Thankfully, his phone rang before Cat could start with the twenty questions. He gave her a quick kiss and mouthed, "Thank you."

He walked out the door, listening to Jimmy yammer in detail about the upcoming evening.

Dylan glanced at his watch and grabbed his jacket out of the car, shrugging into it. "Look, I'll text you when we leave the house."

He hung up and ran his fingers through his hair and around the tight neck of his shirt. How the hell was he supposed to eat? The very thing he hated most about his success and fame was the invasiveness of the tabloid press. And in a few hours, he'd be handing them fuel for the fire. He paced, smoking like a fiend, trying to calm his nerves.

This is for the best. You can do this. You care for Jen, and you want to protect her.

Crushing the cigarette with his shoe, he exhaled deeply, rolled his shoulders, and marched to Jennifer's father's front door. He slipped a mint in his mouth. *Why the hell didn't I have a stiff drink or three before leaving the hotel?* After ringing the doorbell, he tried shaking the nervousness out of his trembling hand.

Please don't let her old man answer the door. Please don't let her old man answer...

Flashing a smile, he offered his hand to Pastor Adams, inwardly cursing his luck.

Glen Adams paused for a moment before shaking it and motioned him into the foyer.

"Jennifer, *he's* here," he called toward the staircase.

"My name is *Dylan*," Dylan stage-whispered with a wink.

A rustling noise drew his eyes toward the staircase, and his mouth dropped open. Jennifer gracefully descended the stairs in a floral halter dress that hugged her curves in all the right places.

Breathtaking. He wrote lyrics, but in his awestruck state, it was the only word he could think of. The lavender color accented her eyes, and a riot of soft curls framed her face and cascaded down her back. He wanted to bury his hands in those curls and kiss her senseless. Only the purple smudges of exhaustion under her blue-violet eyes flawed her beauty.

"Hiya, Jen." He grinned and took her hand, brushing his lips across her knuckles.

"Hello, Dylan." She returned his smile before lowering her gaze. Her long lashes swept her pink cheeks.

He loved making her blush and would have whispered something suggestive, but her old man stood glaring. Instead, he whispered in her ear, "Wish me luck, Lauretta."

Nervous, he pulled at the tie that seemed much too tight. "Father, er, I mean Mr. Reverend, uh, pastor, sir. I was wondering if I might have a word with you in your study before Jennifer and I go to dinner."

Glen Adams pressed his lips into a tight, straight line. Dylan shot Jennifer a worried look. Then, with a heavy sigh of resignation, her father motioned Dylan to follow him into his study and closed the door.

Stunned, Jennifer watched Dylan and her father disappear into the study. His compliment had been unexpected and sweet. And what did he mean about Lauretta? She'd never seen Dylan so nervous... She blinked and bit her lip. Was he asking for her father's blessing on their marriage?

For thirty minutes, Jennifer sat on the stairs picking her cuticles, straining to hear their conversation. Fearing one or the other of them might be dead, she eventually gave in to her curiosity and crept to the door to eavesdrop. Their voices were low and hushed. She wished she had her stethoscope.

The door flew open, catching her unaware, and she fell into Dylan's arms. A faint sheen of perspiration glistened on his brow. The top two buttons of his shirt were unbuttoned, his tie loose. He smirked as he steadied her.

Sneaking a peek at her father, she bit her lip. Pain lined his tired face. She shoved her guilt away, justifying her decision. Her father appeared to have aged overnight, and those photos would tax his already stressed heart; he must never see them. He kissed her cheek and held her tight before trudging upstairs without saying a word.

"Now what?" she whispered, biting her lip to keep her tears at bay.

"I need a smoke and a stiff drink." Dylan tugged at his loose tie, making it worse.

Jennifer buttoned his shirt and straightened the knot in his tie. "You don't *need* either. Besides, you said you'd try to quit."

Dylan fished his phone out of his pocket.

"Who are you texting?"

"Jimmy. I'm telling him to add no nagging to the prenup."

She crossed her arms and snorted. "Very funny. What just happened between you and my dad?"

"I asked for your hand in marriage. He pretty much told me — in reverend terminology — that I was a dick and not worthy of his daughter. I agreed with him, and told him I understood his reservations regarding me as suitable husband material. I then did my best to assure him I would do everything in my power to make you happy. He refused, but finally consented when I said we could be married with his blessing, or we could elope without it. It was the longest goddamned hour of my life." He shoved his new glasses up his nose and stared at her with an intensity that made her squirm.

"How *romantic*. Thank you. And it was only thirty minutes." *What did I expect — flowers, candy, and a proposal on bended knee? This was merely a business proposition. Wasn't it?*

"You're fuckin' kidding me. C'mon, Jen. Cut me some slack. I thought your old man was going to pull out a gun and shoot me. I'm not exactly what he had in mind for you. Now let's go."

"Where are we going?"

"To dinner, silly. Or we can go back to my hotel."

Jennifer stared at him. "Y-Your hotel?" Visions of Dylan naked in a huge bed made her flush and go tingly all over.

"I'm kidding. Just dinner." He waggled his brow. "Unless you want to get an early start on the honeymoon."

"W-What?" *Why have I suddenly developed a speech impediment?* She gave herself a mental kick. "In your dreams."

He laughed as he escorted her to his car. His hand on her bare lower back made her knees feel weak.

"You look stunning tonight, angel."

She stopped dead in her tracks. "Who are you, and what have you done with Dylan?" Was he teasing?

He laughed. "I'm right here. I mean it. This is the first time I've really, truly seen you." He pointed at his new glasses. "You're a beautiful woman, Jennifer. If I was the type to recite poetry, I would."

His smile made her heart skip a beat. "You look beautiful, too."

And he did. She'd never seen him in anything but jeans or cutoffs, and she couldn't help but admire the way his new clothes fit perfectly.

"Men aren't beautiful."

"You are. Your new glasses make you look very *GQ*."

Dylan rolled his eyes and opened the car door for her. "Super, just the look I was going for, that of a forty-year-old executive. And I'm a guy. I'm not *beautiful*. Devastatingly, knock-your-panties-off handsome, maybe." He laughed when she groaned.

"No, I just meant you look really nice, in a model sort of way." Jennifer buckled her seatbelt, determined not to let his teasing unnerve her.

"Please stop. This is getting worse."

"Can't we have the top down, Dylan? I love this car."

"Nope. I want us to look perfect when we arrive," he responded.

"Perfect for what?" She looked at him curiously. He always looked perfect.

"It's show time."

Chapter
Seventeen

The modern restaurant overlooking Birmingham provided a spectacular view. As the pink and purple dusk settled into night, lights twinkled in the valley. This was the most expensive place to eat in the city, and Jennifer's knuckles whitened around her purse. She'd lived here most of her life and had never even driven up to see it.

Dylan insisted on opening her car door and held her hand. The simple act made her ridiculously happy.

A bright flash momentarily blinded her, and she blinked with surprise.

"Who did that?" she asked, noticing Dylan's tight-lipped smile.

"Paparazzi," he muttered, steering her into the restaurant. He flashed his beautiful smile at the hostess, but it didn't quite reach his eyes. His demeanor was one of a sleek cat, ready to pounce.

"Good evening, Mr. McAthie. We have your table waiting. Right this way." The hostess returned his smile with a star-struck giggle.

Jennifer scowled and stumbled. Heat flooded her face as people stared.

"You okay?" He steadied her and frowned.

"Heels," she whispered, inhaling the compelling scent she'd forever associate with him.

"Funny, in the movies I've seen nurses walk just fine in heels," he mused, pulling out her chair. "Maybe I should've brought my cane for you to use."

"I can only imagine what kind of movie has a nurse in heels," she replied.

Leaning in, he nuzzled her neck and kissed her cheek. "You're gorgeous," he whispered before sitting across from her.

Startled by his public display of affection, she knocked her silverware to the floor. She bit back her groan. *Why does this always happen to me?* A waiter deftly replaced her fork. She resisted the urge to pick up the ice-cold water glass and place it on her burning cheeks.

The eager waiter flourished her napkin, moving to put it in her lap. She grabbed it from his hand with annoyance, wishing he'd leave her alone.

When she looked up, Dylan sat across from her, biting his lip before a wide grin spread across his face. Jennifer perused the menu, pretending to ignore him. She gasped at the prices.

"Dylan, this is way too *expensive.*"

"I'm pretty sure I can afford it. Don't worry, you won't have to do dishes."

The waiter reappeared, awaiting their order, hands behind his back.

"Diet cola for my beautiful date, and I'll have Glenmorangie ten-year, neat."

"Very good, sir. And an appetizer, perhaps?"

Jennifer shook her head. She didn't know what any of the items on the menu were, and she wasn't going to risk eating something disgusting. Dylan dismissed the waiter with a wave.

She leaned forward again and whispered, "Dylan."

"What's wrong with you?" His blue eyes appeared to dance behind his glasses.

He leaned back and watched her, his head on his fist. His lips curved in a sexy smile.

It should be criminal for a man to be that beautiful. "I don't know what to order. I don't understand the menu."

"Order whatever you want to eat. If you prefer, I can order for you. I'll make sure it's the greasiest, unhealthiest item on the menu, if that would help." He smirked at her glare.

"A lousy cheeseburger would've been fine with me," she grumbled as she went back to trying to make heads or tails out of the menu.

The waiter returned with their drinks and waited for their order.

Jennifer cringed under his haughty look and became even more flustered. "I, um, er…"

"A lousy cheeseburger for the lady, please. Would you like fries with it?"

She nodded, flipping her fork over and over. The waiter gave an appalled sniff, but his face remained impassive.

"And I'll have your pasta puttanesca with eggplant. Thank you."

"Very good, sir." With a nod, the waiter turned on his heels and left.

Dylan leaned forward, took Jennifer's hand, and kissed her knuckles. "Candlelight becomes you. You're the prettiest girl here."

Jennifer opened her mouth to say something and then closed it. *Am I dreaming? Aliens have abducted Dylan and replaced him with an android. It's the only explanation.*

"Dance with me."

She returned from her musings. A small band played in the corner, and a few couples were dancing to an instrumental piece. "I don't dance, Dylan."

"Why not? You know you want to grab my ass."

This was more like the Dylan she knew.

"I don't dance. I have two left feet. Besides, you didn't bring your cane. You know what they say, *Pride goeth before a fall.*"

"Says who?"

"The Bible, silly."

Dylan pulled out his phone and laughed. "I'm using this as blackmail. That's a misquote. Proverbs 16:18 actually reads, 'Pride goeth before destruction, and an haughty spirit before a fall.' I think you owe me a kiss to not tell your dad." He slipped his phone back in his pocket. "Anyway, I'm not asking you to throw down some moves. Just come dance with me."

"No. No dancing. I'm adding that to our prenup." She raised her chin in defiance.

"No dancing is part of our prenup?" He snorted a laugh and had to take in gulps of air to recover.

"Shh, people are watching us." Jennifer stared at the table as their neighbors whispered.

Dylan quit laughing. "Better get used to it."

The waiter brought their meal, and Jennifer timidly asked for ketchup. The poor man's jaw dropped before snapping shut. With a scowl, he returned with the condiment in a bowl. "Anything else, *miss?*"

Jennifer shook her head as Dylan laughed.

"Have some fun and relax, okay?" He smiled from across the table.

She glanced around, and her stomach flipped. People were still watching them.

"Something wrong with the burger?"

"No, it's fine." The ice in her drink clanked with her trembling. At this rate, she'd end up wearing her dinner. She picked up a dry French fry and began to nibble on it. She paused when a couple approached the table from a large dinner party across the room. They appeared close to her age and shifted back and forth on their feet. All eyes from their table focused on them.

"Uh, s-sorry to interrupt. Um, are y-you Dylan McAthie?"

Dylan put down his fork and wiped his mouth. Only a faint look of annoyance played over his face. "Yes, I am."

"I told you it was him!" The boy smiled at his girlfriend, giving her a high five. "Can we get your autograph?"

"Ask him for a p-picture," the girl stammered with wide eyes.

Dylan smiled, autographed a piece of paper with a grand gesture, and patiently posed as Jennifer took pictures with the couple's cell phones. He shook hands with the guy and gave the girl a quick kiss on the cheek. Blushing, she had to have her boyfriend assist her back to their table.

Sitting, Dylan threw back the last of his drink. "Sorry about that. One of the drawbacks of the business—you rarely get to complete a meal uninterrupted." He sighed and pushed his plate away. "You barely touched your food."

"I'm not hungry." As a matter of fact, she felt nauseous.

Dylan motioned for the check. "What's wrong? Don't worry. Everything is being handled."

He flipped open his wallet, and Jennifer gasped when she saw the picture. The room began to swim before her eyes. Trembling, she stood, almost knocking over her chair.

"Jen?"

"I need some air."

Dylan signed the receipt and guided her toward the front door. She tried to pull her hand from his, but he held it firmly. He stopped at the desk and asked the valet to bring his car. Even though it was dark outside, he put on a pair of sunglasses.

Leaning in, he whispered in her ear. "I'm sorry, angel."

Jennifer looked up at him, confused as they stepped out the door. Then she blinked and covered her eyes as flashes blinded her.

Dylan drove like a bat out of hell. He'd put the top down on the car, and the wind whipped around them. He kept glancing in the rearview mirror. After several minutes, he lit a cigarette and eased up on the gas. Jennifer glanced behind her. Thankfully no one followed.

"Where to, milady?"

"I think I want to go home." *I don't know where I want to go.*

The photo of Sara in Dylan's wallet, followed by the unexpected paparazzi, had tilted her world off its axis. She wondered if she was making the biggest mistake of her life. *God, how I wish this was just a nightmare.*

"I'm sorry. I should have filled you in on the plan." He stole a glance at her before returning his eyes to the road.

"The plan? Oh. Never mind." She huffed, annoyed. *Everything reverts to his stupid plan.*

"My people alerted the tabloids that we'd be at the restaurant. Tonight is the beginning of the publicity spin. It is, unfortunately, a necessary evil. Which way do I go from here?" His voice registered no emotion whatsoever.

"Whichever way *your people* tell you, I presume."

Dylan sighed. "I meant which way to your dad's house. I got lost ditching the paparazzi. I haven't lived here since I was a kid."

"I feel lost, too," she murmured.

He sighed and turned on the GPS.

They drove in silence to her father's house. Thank God no one was waiting to jump out of the bushes to take a picture. Before she could open her car door, Dylan was there. The light from the front porch beckoned like a lighthouse.

Closing the door, he held her trapped against the car, and she caught her breath at his very nearness.

"We really didn't talk about our marriage. But I have something for you," he whispered as he kissed her neck. She pushed him away, her body warring with her confused thoughts.

"Stop, Dylan. I…" Words escaped her. "That picture…I can't… do this."

Dylan stopped and turned her face up to him. "Don't worry about the photos. I told you, my people are handling it."

The faltering dam on her emotions burst, and Jennifer covered her face with her hands, sobs engulfing her.

Dylan pulled her into his arms. "What's the matter? Please don't cry." He held her tight, rubbing her back until her sobs subsided. Kissing her temple, he pulled away, cupping her face in his hands. "I know this is scary, but everything will be okay, I promise. Trust me?" He wiped the tears off her cheek with his thumbs.

Trust him? Did she?

"Dylan." She took a deep breath. "I'm not her. I can't take her place. I…"

"Whose place? What are you talking about?"

"S-Sara's. Her picture in your wallet—I know you loved her—"

Dylan took out his wallet and removed the picture. "I forgot it was in there. I'm sorry. She's dead, Jennifer." His voice sounded hollow and distant.

"I know, but, Dylan…" She paused, watching him set the picture on fire and drop it to the driveway. "What are you doing?"

He lit a cigarette as the photo curled and burned. "The day I buried her was the hardest damn day of my life."

"Of course. You loved her—"

"Not that day. I hated her. She was pregnant."

Jennifer gasped. "Pregnant? Oh my God. I'm so sorry. What happened? I didn't know."

"It was an overdose. She was five months pregnant, and the drugs were more important to her than her child, me, or her own goddamned life."

He threw the cigarette down and ran his fingers through his hair, looking lost, alone, and in pain. Jennifer watched, feeling helpless as he paced, his limp suddenly pronounced. She moved toward him, wanting to comfort him, but he held up a hand and shook his head. His throat bobbled, and his shoulders sagged.

"Dylan—"

"Stop. I'm not talking about it."

Jennifer refused to be stopped this time. He was hurting. Wrapping her arms around his neck, she kissed his cheek. His revelation had shocked her, but she didn't know what else to do. Her confusion about their current situation fell away as she comforted him.

"I couldn't save her," he mumbled into her hair. "I couldn't save the baby..." She could feel him struggling to contain his emotions. "And I couldn't save Greg from the damn drugs, either. He couldn't deal with the fame, the pressure. And I didn't see it happening until it was too late. But by God, I'm going to save you."

"It wasn't your fault, Dylan. None of it. Stop blaming yourself. No one else is." She cupped his face and kissed his cheek.

Picking her up, he sat her on the hood of the car. He held her face in his hands. "You're an incredibly sweet girl. I wish there was another way out of this mess. You deserve so much better..."

Jennifer sighed. "I admit, this isn't how I pictured my life. But we made choices, and now we must handle the consequences." She gave a hollow laugh. "The punishment for our crimes?"

His thumb stroked her cheek. "We didn't do anything wrong. Unfortunately, there is no privacy in my world, and you have become collateral damage."

He leaned in closer and smiled. "But I have to say, at this moment the punishment doesn't seem too bad."

One hand traced up her leg, and the other trailed to the back of her neck. His mouth captured hers, gentle but inquisitive. He twisted her hair in his fist as the kiss deepened. A soft whimper escaped from deep within her. He feathered soft kisses across her cheek to her earlobe and down her neck before once again claiming her mouth. Her body didn't want him to stop; her conscience reminded her to be cautious. She still wasn't sure what to make of this latest turn in their relationship.

Dylan pulled away, and a slow smile spread across his face. "Damn," he rasped. "I pray to God your old man is asleep and not getting his shotgun oiled."

She giggled, taking a deep breath to calm the raging desire firing every nerve in her body. He helped her from the hood of the car, and her eyes widened when he dug in his pocket, retrieving a small box.

"Wait. Do you care for me? Even a little? I know this is going to be a fake marriage…"

He frowned. "Of course I care. If I didn't I'd have fed you to the media wolves and not thought twice about it. We'll get married and see where it goes from there. If it doesn't work, we can part as friends." He winked. "Friends with benefits are nice. Let's make this official." He popped the box open and pulled out a ring. "I hope to hell it fits. I guessed at the size."

The ring slid easily on her finger.

Jennifer looked at it, stunned—a dark stone surrounded by diamonds. Just like Dylan asking her father for her hand, an engagement ring had never crossed her mind. Suddenly, the "plan" was very real. Knowing she was falling in love with him made it *surreal*. She wasn't sure about his friends-with-benefits suggestion. She wanted him, but casual sex would sell her heart short. She wasn't willing to throw all her dreams away. The first time should be special, with someone she loved. She'd make sure he understood that when she signed all of his legal paperwork.

Dylan kissed her fingers. "It's an amethyst. It reminded me of your eyes." He leaned into the car and flipped on the radio, turning the volume low. "Dance with me, Jennifer. And you can grab my ass if you want to."

"I don't dance…" Her voice trailed off as he pulled her close. They moved in sync over the charred picture of Sara.

She forgot she didn't dance.

She forgot he didn't love her.

She didn't think at all as he softly sang along with the Righteous Brothers.

Dylan lit a cigarette as he meandered back to the car after another searing goodnight kiss. The more he thought about his future, the less gloomy it seemed. Life with Jennifer could be fun—a new and welcome beginning, for as long as it lasted. He wanted this girl and didn't think he was misreading her signals—she wanted him, too.

Maybe he'd even resurrect his music career. His band was over, but there was nothing preventing him from pursuing the studio work he loved. He could get into production. Glancing at his watch, he heard soft laughter and splashing from Rob and Cat's pool next door. Taking a deep, confidence-bolstering breath, he decided he might as well break the news of his impending nuptials to his family. This way, he could get the damn lecture from Junior over with tonight.

Dylan opened the gate and grinned when he saw Rob and Cat in the water. He threw himself in a chair. "I take it the kids aren't home." He didn't attempt to hide his smirk.

"Oh my God! Dylan!" Cat shrieked, pulling Rob in front of her.

"Dammit, Dylan! What are you doing here? Turn around so we can get some clothes on," his brother growled.

"Why? We've all been skinny dipping before—lots of times." Dylan winked at Cat, hoping to further provoke his brother.

"We were kids, you idiot. Now turn the hell around!" Junior scowled, and Cat hid her face in her husband's shoulder, her arms wrapped around his waist.

"Okay, okay." Dylan chuckled and stood, turning his back, as they rushed out of the pool. Wrapped in a towel, Cat squealed and shot past him into the house. He turned around to face his brother.

Rob wrapped a towel around his waist and crossed his arms. "To what do we owe the pleasure of this uninvited visit?"

"Sarcasm doesn't become you, Junior. Do I need a formal invitation to visit with my family?" Dylan asked with feigned indignation. "Where are the kids? Do they know their parents engage in such scandalous behavior?"

"Shut up, Dylan. The kids are out for the night," Rob snapped as he stormed past him. Laughing, Dylan followed. After a moment Cat came downstairs, drying her hair with a towel, her face almost as pink as her fluffy robe.

"Well? Why are you here? I'd really like to go get dressed." Rob waited with his hands on his hips.

"I, uh…" Dylan stammered. *Damn, Junior looks like Dad.* "Jennifer and I are getting married." The words came out more as a challenge than anything. He pressed his lips together, realizing antagonizing his older brother wouldn't help in *this* situation.

"What?" Cat and Rob asked simultaneously. The shock on their faces would've been funny if Dylan wasn't so damn nervous. Rob swore under his breath.

"Robert, go get dressed. I'll make some coffee," Cat urged as she grabbed Dylan's hand and pulled him toward the kitchen, out of Rob's way.

Rob marched upstairs, cursing. Dylan flinched when the door slammed.

"He took it only slightly better than the good reverend."

"Not funny, Dylan. What are you doing? Have you lost your mind?" Cat flung the coffee into the filter.

Dylan sat on a barstool and perused a plate of chocolate chip cookies. Finding the biggest one buried at the bottom, he snatched it and took a bite. "I'm doing the right thing by everyone involved. Mmmm, these are good."

"Some things never change. You used to steal my mother's cookies." Cat smiled and cocked her head to the side. "Do you love her?"

"Yep, but she wouldn't marry me. Said I was too young."

Cat smacked his arm. "Jennifer, not my mother!"

He squirmed under her stare. "I care a great deal for her. Why else would I be marrying her?"

"That's not enough, Dyl—" She paused as the phone rang. "I hate when Robert's on call. Hopefully he can handle it by phone."

"Cat, I have to do this. Jennifer understands this is to protect all of us. I don't want her or our families harmed by the scandal. I'm trying to spare everyone the negative PR that could come from this mess." He accepted the cup of coffee she handed him and ate another cookie.

"Is it really that bad?" she asked.

"'Fraid so." He took off his glasses and rubbed his brow. Rob slammed another door upstairs, swearing voraciously. Suddenly exhausted, Dylan decided now might not be the time to suffer through Junior's lecture. "Do me a favor?"

"What?"

"Will you try to calm Rob down before I discuss the details with him? I'll see him tomorrow and explain everything, I promise."

Cat bit her lip, looking at the ceiling as something crashed above them. "That might be best."

Dylan grabbed his glasses and stood to leave. He kissed her cheek. "Thanks for the cookies and coffee, and thanks for taking the heat off me with Junior."

"You're welcome."

He swung around when he reached the back door.

"And, Cat?"

"Yes?"

"You look damn fine to be a thirty-one-year-old mother of two. Rob's one lucky man." He winked and hurried out the door as Robert tromped down the stairs. Pausing in the backyard before he left, he peeked in the window.

Cat's eyes lit up as Rob stomped into the kitchen. He couldn't hear what they said, but a tinge of jealousy tweaked his heart when Cat wrapped her arms around his brother's neck and they kissed.

Surprisingly he wasn't jealous because his brother was kissing the girl he'd loved in high school and had hoped to marry. Instead it was the happiness they shared that he found himself longing for. When Cat stepped away and started to untie her robe, Dylan turned to go.

Will I ever find that kind of happiness?

Chapter Eighteen

Seated at the dining table in Dylan's expansive hotel suite, Jennifer ignored the view of the city and stared at the stack of legal papers, numb and confused. The past six weeks had been a rollercoaster of activity and emotions. Her father was resigned to her decision, her friend Vickie ecstatic that she and her daughter were to be in the wedding, and David had avoided her. Dress fittings, caterers, invitations, guest lists, flower choices — the tasks were endless. She'd been in more states, both literally and figuratively, the last few weeks than she'd been in her entire life.

Only three decisions had been left to Dylan's sole discretion: their honeymoon destination, the photographer, and music for the wedding. Dylan had feared she'd choose Wagner's "Bridal Chorus" or Mendelssohn's "Wedding March."

Well, duh, it's a wedding.

At this point, she didn't care about any of it and just wanted it to be over.

She twisted her amethyst-and-diamond engagement ring, struggling to bring her attention back to Jimmy's explanation of the prenuptial agreement. He might as well have been explaining astrophysics for all she understood. Glancing over at Tyrone, she gave him a small smile. An ex-Navy Seal, her bodyguard was her new best friend. He'd permanently joined her side two weeks ago, shortly after an irate fan had accosted her at the grocery store and slapped her for having the nerve to be engaged to Dylan McAthie. Over two hundred pounds of dark, beautiful muscle, Tyrone looked like he ate broken glass for breakfast. Jennifer didn't doubt he was tough, but around her, he was a big teddy bear.

He gave her a brief nod and resumed looking out the window. She guessed he was searching for some unknown threat. Perhaps the paparazzi were scaling the walls, or circling in a helicopter. She wouldn't put anything past them. Her father had been forced to change their phone number, and they now had security to keep people from ringing their doorbell night and day.

The worst incident had occurred one night when she took out the trash and found a man rummaging through their garbage cans. She'd argued with him, and the resulting photo of her with a tangled mop of greasy hair and a zit on her chin, wearing toothpaste-stained pajamas, made the front page of *The National Intruder*. Dylan had teased her, proclaiming it to be his favorite photo of her, even putting it in his wallet where Sara's picture used to be.

He'd been kind and caring through this entire ordeal; whatever she needed, he'd provided. He was even trying to quit smoking. But the one thing she wanted, he didn't give, and she didn't know how to ask. She still had no clue regarding his real feelings. He'd said he cared about her, and in his words, they were a "team." He often copped an "us against the world" attitude, but she couldn't help but wonder about the strength of their alliance.

On the rare occasions they didn't have to make an "appearance" at a public function, they'd order in pizza or Chinese food. Afterward, they'd snuggle and watch TV, and it was the only time Dylan's guard really seemed down. Their talks about his dreams and their future on those evenings gave her a sense of hope.

But those incidents were few and far between, and after the fact she was never sure if they'd been real. Each time she tried to sort it all out, her heart broke a little more.

For the most part, their conversations remained superficial. And they were rarely alone anymore — members of his team wandered in and out of the hotel suite, and escorted them everywhere. She missed the days of being alone at the lake, when things had been uncomplicated and real.

The tapping of a pen on the table brought her attention back to the documents in front of her. She yawned and pinched the bridge of her nose.

"Seriously, Jennifer. Where's your legal counsel? You shouldn't trust me," Jimmy advised, running a hand through his short, copper-colored hair. "Not that I'm trying to screw you over or anything; it just isn't wise." He glanced up when Dylan walked into the room. "Tell her, Dylan. Tell her she needs to have her lawyer look over this stuff."

Dylan took the lollipop out of his mouth and frowned. "Jen, we talked about this. Where's your lawyer?" He sat across from her.

"I trust you. Why don't you trust me?" Peeking at him from under her lashes, she admired her future husband. Dressed in a T-shirt and jeans, he was barefoot. The man even had nice feet. He wore his hair in a ponytail and looked totally hot, even with the glasses he hated so much. She wondered for the umpteenth time why he always looked handsome and put together, whereas she was a frumpy mess. She shoved a curl behind her ear and re-tightened her ponytail.

"What do you mean why don't I trust you?"

"Why do I have to sign this stuff? I told you I don't want your money. And why don't *you* have to sign a prenup and nondisclosure agreement?" She raised an eyebrow.

Dylan's mouth twitched, and his eyes crinkled. Jimmy stopped pacing and stared at her as if she'd just sprouted horns.

Dylan sucked on his Tootsie Pop another moment before asking, "And what exactly would you want in your prenup, baby?"

"Well, I don't know. I mean, I like my car. It isn't the dream machine, but it's mine, and I'd want to keep it."

Dylan grinned and nodded. "Jimmy, make sure I can't take her car from her."

"What?" Jimmy stopped pacing and ran a hand through his hair. With his eyes bugging out, he looked ready to stroke.

"Do it," Dylan ordered.

Jimmy rolled his eyes, but nodded.

"What else, angel?" Dylan leaned forward; his blue eyes danced with merriment.

"Well, my mother's jewelry. You can't have it." The fact that he didn't take her seriously fueled her anger.

"And why would I want it?" Dylan frowned around the sucker.

"I don't know. You could get mad at me and give it to a fangirl or something." Her eyes narrowed. "Quit patronizing me. If it's required that I sign one, you're signing one too."

Dylan threw up his hands in mock surrender and laughed. "Done. Jimmy, draw up an equitable prenup. Anything else?"

"I can't draw up her prenup," Jimmy muttered. "Her legal counsel has to do that."

Jennifer ignored him. "I want you to sign a non-disclosure agreement."

"Fine, but just out of curiosity, why?" Dylan quit laughing when she shot him a dirty look. He stuck the sucker back in his mouth, waiting for her reply.

Jennifer found it quite distracting, watching his mouth work around the candy, and squirmed in her chair. "This marriage is our business and ours alone. When it's over, I don't want you writing some gross tell-all book. What happens while we're together stays between us."

"Hmm, so I can't give an interview about what kind of panties you wear?"

"That won't be an issue. *You* won't be seeing them. This isn't a real marriage."

Jimmy snorted before busying himself with shuffling papers when Dylan glared, and Tyrone's shoulders shook.

Dylan leaned back in his chair, hiding his mouth under his fingers as he pondered. He twirled the lollipop in his other hand. "But I have seen them. You have a preference for pink satin panties and white bras that don't match."

Jennifer blushed, recalling the pink satin panties he'd removed the night he helped her with her bath. "Well, from now on, I'll be sure to wear only plain white cotton panties," she hissed.

"By all means, I wouldn't want to leak *that* to the press." Dylan snickered.

It sent her frayed nerves over the edge. "Stop laughing at me!" She jumped up, banging her fist on the table, tears of rage threatening to spill. "I'm sick of this. I'm sick of all of this. I don't want to do it anymore! I'm tired! I quit! For once you can't fire me, *because*

I quit. Let them print the photos; I don't care! Do you hear me? I don't have to do this!" Her voice rose and cracked under the strain of the past six weeks.

Dylan motioned for Tyrone and Jimmy to leave the room, and waited until the door closed.

He sat on the table, pulling her to him and wrapping his arms around her to stroke her back. "Shh, baby. I know you're tired. Hang in there. You can't quit on me now; it's almost over. We're a team, remember? Take a deep breath, love. We'll finish up with the legal documents, go to the rehearsal this evening, and by tomorrow night, all of this will be over."

Jennifer sucked in a big gulp of air, nodding, drawing a semblance of comfort from his words. After all, being a team was better than adversaries.

She sniffed his shirt. "You smell so much better since you've attempted to quit smoking."

"Attempted?"

"I know you sneak one every now and then. Tyrone told me." Closing her eyes, she held on to him, not wanting to let go. In his arms, she could pretend he loved her.

"Hmmm...maybe I need to look in to *his* non-disclosure agreement," Dylan growled. He pulled her face up to his and smiled. "Let's seal this deal with a kiss. Then you can either sign the papers or do as advised and get a lawyer to look at them first."

"I want to ask you something. Just between us."

"Of course."

She took a deep breath. "What are you expecting after the wedding?"

He frowned. "What are you talking about?"

"Sex, Dylan. I'm talking about sex!"

"I think that's a natural progression after marriage." He smiled and gave her a quick kiss.

"But this isn't a real marriage!"

"Baby, you're stressing too much. We'll take things slow. I won't hurt you, I promise."

Jennifer bit her lip to keep from sighing. It wasn't physical pain she was worried about. It was her heart. She pulled away from him, searching his eyes.

"I'll sign after Jimmy makes the amendments, and I'll find a lawyer, somewhere."

Dylan laughed and kissed her nose. "Fair enough. I'm going to grab a shower. I have a couple of things to do before the rehearsal." He added, with a seductive purr, "Unless you want to join me."

"Oh, much as I'd love to, I have to go get my nails done," she said, trying very hard for nonchalance. "And a Brazilian wax, too." Vickie, her friend since nursing school and matron of honor, had made the appointment for her. She'd nearly fainted when she found out what *Brazilian* meant, but she didn't know how to back out without blowing her cover.

"Pity, it's such a big shower with two showerheads…" His voice trailed off as he sauntered toward the bathroom. He poked his head back out the door and leered at her. "I could really use some help scrubbing my back."

"Want me to call Mrs. J?" She batted her eyelashes in feigned innocence.

"Hell, no," Dylan hollered as he slammed the door. He opened it again. "Did you really say you're getting a Brazilian wax?" His eyes smoldered. "Niiiiiiiiiiiiice." He licked his lips before ducking back into the bathroom.

"You won't be seeing just how nice it is," she shouted back.

The door opened. "Is that a challenge, Miss Adams?"

"It's a promise, Mr. McAthie."

"Spoilsport," he grumbled, closing the door.

As she picked up her purse to leave, Dylan's phone rang. She was going to let it go to voice mail until she saw a photo of a beautiful blonde flash on the screen. "Lust for Loree" was the ringtone. Why was Loree Jamison calling Dylan? Curiosity got the best of her, and Jennifer picked up the phone. Before she could say hello, a breathless voice started talking.

"Dylan, darling, this phone tag is driving me *nuts*. I can't wait to see you in two weeks. I have such big plans; you will absolutely *love* what I have in mind for you. Think flesh next to flesh, screaming *sex, sex, sex*. Maybe we can throw a little kink in there. BDSM is all the rage now, and if you're a good boy I'll even let you smack my ass. If you're not, well, I'll smack *yours*." A sultry laugh followed before the chatter started again. "My mind is just racing with the possibilities. Your hot body next to mine—yummy…Dylan? Are you there?"

Jennifer hung up, stunned. Two weeks? They would just be getting back from their so-called honeymoon in two weeks. A text message popped up on the phone:

Got cut off. Glad your marriage won't change anything.
I have big plans for us. I'm thinking of oiling your abs...
woohoo, so fuckin hot! ttyl and cya in 2wks. xoxoxo

Jennifer deleted the message as she wiped away angry tears. *What a jerk!* No, he was worse than a jerk. He was a dick! She dropped the phone on the sofa, working hard to keep from throwing it. It might be a marriage on paper only, but he could at least give the pretense of being monogamous for her sake, at least for a while. And why bother being so nice if there was already someone else? She heard the water in the shower cut off and knew she either had to pull herself together or leave. She paced, her mind racing over her options.

Dylan walked in, still damp from his shower, one towel around his waist and another drying his hair. Jennifer stopped pacing and stared at the flawless male specimen in front of her. No wonder this Loree wanted his abs oiled.

He flashed a wicked smile. "Still here? Wanna dry my back?"

Jennifer dragged her eyes from the towel around his hips and walked over to him. Wrapping her arms around his damp neck, she looked down, not wanting him to see in her eyes the icy numbness that had settled around her heart.

"I've been thinking over our prenup, and I have two more requests I want in writing, Dylan," she whispered. The pulse in his neck quickened, and she heard him suck in a breath. Keeping her face blank, she looked up into his beautiful eyes. She wrapped a wet lock of his hair around her finger.

Dylan smiled and pulled her closer, his arousal evident beneath the thick towel. "Tell me what you want. I'll give you anything, angel." His voice was hoarse with passion.

"I want your *car*," she whispered as she tugged hard on the lock of hair wrapped around her finger.

"Ow! My what?" Frowning, he pulled back and looked at her, confusion written all over his face. "What's the second thing? My Gibson?" he asked sarcastically.

"No sex." Jennifer slipped away, picked up her purse, and headed to the door. "The dream machine and no sex. Actually, make it three things: I want a separate bedroom. That's my payment for this marriage."

"Payment? My car?" He stood with his hands on his hips, taken aback. "Wait one goddamn minute—no sex? Separate bedrooms?"

"You heard me correctly. Or no marriage." She blew him a kiss and left, nearly collapsing on the other side of his door. Tyrone and Jimmy were in the hall talking, and they stopped to look at her with concern.

"Jennifer, are you all right? You're shaking." Jimmy put a steadying hand on her arm.

"I'm fine," she snapped as she shrugged out of his grasp. She stormed toward the private elevator that would take her to the lobby, with Tyrone on her heels. She punched the door open. As the elevator door closed, she called to Jimmy through clenched teeth. "Make sure you ask him about my additional requirements for the prenup, or I'm not signing."

Dylan sat in the church alone, thinking about his past, anxious about his future. Squirming in his seat, he glanced around the sanctuary. It was beautifully decorated, but the heavy scent of flowers disturbed him. The last two times he'd been in church were for funerals—Greg's, followed much too soon by Sara's. He frowned with distaste at the modern structure, so different from the gothic church he'd attended as a boy. No stone pillars, no heavy scent of wax candles, no incense, and no statues of Mary.

*Hail Mary, full of grace...*As a small boy, he'd thought he was praying to his deceased mother, who'd been named Mary. Rob and Gran told him more than once that he favored his mother. He wished his grandmother were here; she would've loved Jennifer.

Jennifer. Leaning forward, elbows on his knees, he closed his eyes. *Am I doing the right thing?*

Following her outburst yesterday, he didn't know. After she left, he'd realized he'd been so wrapped up in the outward appearance of this engagement, he hadn't put much effort into making her understand he truly cared about her, wanted them to have a chance. Even that wasn't what she deserved, but it was as close to fairy tale as he could get. He'd never thought of himself as a marrying man. His career choice wasn't conducive to long, happy marriages. Being on the road was stressful. His and Sara's stormy relationship had been testament to that. Then again, being on the road was no longer an issue, dammit. A hand squeezed his shoulder.

"You okay?"

Dylan gave his brother a wry smile. "Maybe this wasn't the day to finally quit smoking. Thanks for the patch."

"Not a problem. I was just thinking, I wish you'd been at my wedding. No one knew where you were…" He clasped his hands behind his back as he looked around the church. Dylan glared at him. Rob shrugged. "What?"

"Cut that out. It's really disturbing how much you look like the old man."

Rob sighed. "I'm not our old man. Quit saying that." They watched as the chamber orchestra filed into the church. "Overkill, much?" he asked.

Dylan grinned. "Did you really think I'd settle for one measly organ?"

"Nope."

They sat in silence as florists adjusted flowers and the orchestra tuned their instruments.

Rob chuckled. "Remember the time you nearly set the church on fire knocking over the candle with the processional cross?"

"At least I didn't hit old Sister Bernard with the thurible. That was brilliant." Dylan's voice held genuine admiration.

"It was an accident." Rob laughed. "She was a mean old biddy. Reckon we're still on Father Martin's list of worst altar boys?"

"I should hope so; we worked hard to get there." Dylan tugged at his collar.

"It's almost time." Rob stood. "You sure about this?"

"No, er, I mean yes." Dylan stood as well, refusing to meet his brother's gaze.

"It isn't too late to call off this charade."

Dylan glanced around, tabloid headlines racing through his mind. "Afraid it is. Everything will be fine."

"I mean it, Dylan. Cathy believes Jennifer is truly in love with you. Don't hurt her."

After what she said yesterday? Dylan shot his brother a look and scoffed. "Don't be ridiculous. We both know exactly what we're doing, and everything has been discussed. All papers have been signed with i's dotted and t's crossed. It's merely an unholy alliance."

"Then I feel extremely sorry for both of you." Robert sighed and walked away.

Chapter
Nineteen

The wedding planner shooed the bridal party out to take their places and closed the door. Jennifer let out a slow breath, glad to be alone at last. In the distance, the orchestra played chamber music. Bach, she presumed. Dylan loved Bach. Her hand shook a little as she applied lip gloss. She stared at herself in the mirror. *Is that really me?* She'd been professionally styled, and it was a far cry from her usual casual appearance.

Her hair was swept up from her face and cascaded in artfully arranged curls down her back. Jennifer checked to make sure the small diamond tiara was secure—her something "borrowed." A beautiful piece of jewelry from some ridiculously overpriced store, it had come with its own personal guard who would take it back to the store after the wedding. Dylan had wanted to buy it for her, but she'd refused.

A knock sounded, and in the mirror, she saw her father peek in the door. She nodded for him to enter, giving him a tremulous smile. He motioned for her not to get up and stood behind her, placing both hands on her shoulders. Gazing at her reflection with a sad smile, he leaned over and kissed her cheek.

"You look so much like your mother." His voice cracked with emotion. "Simply beautiful."

Jennifer squeezed her father's hand. "Thank you, Daddy."

"Dylan isn't the man I envisioned you marrying. You know that."

Jennifer nodded, knowing her father loved David like a son.

"Are you one-hundred-percent sure about this, my dear?" He held her gaze in the mirror.

No, far from it. "I love him, Daddy." Her heart broke at the truth in her words.

Giving a small nod, he murmured, "All right, then." He reached for the strand of pearls on the dressing table and fastened them around her neck. "Your something old, your mother's pearls. How she would have loved this moment," he said. "You've always made me proud, Jennifer."

Strains of Pachelbel's "Canon in D" filtered into the room.

A hint of a smile played at the corners of his mouth. "I'm pleasantly surprised by the music."

Jennifer gave a small laugh. "Me, too. Dylan said he didn't have time to get any of the bands you'd hate most. They're all on tour."

Her father chuckled and kissed her on the forehead. "Good."

Jennifer stood and went into her father's arms, hugging him tight. "I love you, Daddy."

"Now, now, no tears. I love you, too." He hugged her back.

She kissed his damp cheek and grabbed some tissues, thankful for waterproof makeup.

The wedding planner bustled into the room. "Are we ready?"

Jennifer gave a timid nod as the knot in her stomach tightened. Her father wrapped her arm around his and gave her hand a squeeze. With her convoluted feelings, the music now sounded like a funeral march.

Taking their places at the back of the church, she and her father watched Cathy and Mary McAthie, in their beautiful ice blue gowns walk down the aisle. Mary turned and gave Jennifer a shy wave. Vickie followed as matron of honor.

Robbie, the ring bearer, complained in *sotto voce* for Vickie's daughter, the flower girl, to "slow down," causing a wave of soft laughter.

Jennifer kept her head lowered, wishing she'd opted for a thick veil instead of the tiara. In appearance, this was the wedding of her dreams. But it was all a staged illusion. If it weren't for the fact that she'd ruin lives, she would've run toward the exit.

A trumpet fanfare signaled the wedding guests to stand. She gripped her father's arm and prayed she wouldn't trip. *When did the aisle to our church get so long?* As her father slowly escorted her, she stole sideways glances. Friends and members of the congregation filled the left side of the church. To the right were A-list celebrities.

She drew a steadying breath before looking toward the altar. Dylan stood with his hands clasped in front of him, a heart-breaking grin on his handsome face. His gray morning suit accented his long legs and broad shoulders. The vest and tie were the color of his blue-silver eyes.

She bit her lip to keep from laughing. He was squinting, too vain to wear his detested glasses. His beautiful, sun-kissed blond hair lay in a neat ponytail, and his jaw bore designer scruff. He refused to shave it completely, saying he had a baby face. Regardless, in no way did he look like the wild, unkempt shell of a man she'd met less than three months ago. He was the prince of her dreams, and this wedding was a fairy tale...but sadly, without the happily ever after.

Dylan's stomach gave its familiar gut-wrenching roll. This was as bad as going on stage. The only thing that saved him from hurling was the knowledge that cameras and cell phones were everywhere, ready to film. As Jennifer's attendants approached, Dylan concentrated on his breathing and kept his smile camera ready. For the hundredth time he wished they'd just eloped and then released the news to the press.

Robbie drew near, tugging on the flower girl's sash, and Dylan grabbed him just as he took a swing. Robbie squirmed and protested with a loud stage whisper, "She went too fast!"

The rings flew off the pillow, but Rob retrieved them and moved Robbie to his side, keeping a firm hand on his shoulder. Jimmy, his best man, chuckled.

Dylan stared down the aisle as the trumpet blare signaled Jennifer's entrance. *I should've worn my glasses.* He squinted, bringing her into focus, and his heart damn near stopped. Eyes downcast, her long dark lashes contrasted with her pale, blushing cheeks. She looked like an angel in her white satin dress covered with antique lace and seed pearls. A small ice blue sash broke the white expanse, and lace three-quarter sleeves covered her arms. At his request, she'd kept her long, silky hair down. She was without a doubt the most beautiful woman he'd ever seen.

In that moment, he realized he was about to take vows to care for this girl forever. This blinding truth damn near buckled his knees.

"You okay?" Rob asked, steadying him.

Jimmy whispered, "No tossing the cookies, cowboy. Cameras are everywhere."

Dylan nodded and stood straight, despite the fact that his world had just teetered off center.

I'm falling in love.

He wanted to rush down the aisle and tell her, but he couldn't risk screwing up everything his team had worked so hard for. But he'd damn sure spend the rest of his life proving it. His grin broadened. She was going to be his *wife*.

Jennifer's father paused before placing her hand in his. Today his only role was father of the bride. His associate pastor would be performing the wedding ceremony. Dylan turned to face his bride. Grasping her shaking hands in his, he gave them a squeeze and kissed her icy fingertips. When she looked up, he saw cold, stark fear in her eyes. For a moment, he was afraid she was going to make a run for it. *Responsibility*. It started now; it started with reassuring her. He nodded toward the choir loft and smiled at his future wife.

Leaning in, he broke protocol by kissing her soft cheek as he whispered, "My gift for you, Lauretta."

Jennifer's eyes sparkled with tears as the beautiful, clear voice of the soprano began to sing "*O Mio Babbino Caro.*"

Instead of happiness, Jennifer felt empty. The wedding had been almost picture perfect, and to her surprise, Dylan had choked up during his vows. He'd even had to pause for a few seconds. He'd probably been afraid of being struck by lightning for lying in church. The knowledge that their union was a sham was almost more than she could bear. This was not at all what she'd dreamed about as a little girl. Forcing another fake smile, she posed for yet another photograph.

She glanced down at the simple platinum band underneath the amethyst-and-diamond ring. *Married. I'm officially Mrs. Strachan Dylan McAthie.*

"Look this way! That's it; now tilt your head to the right. There! Hold! All right, now where is the groom? There he is. Stand with your arms around your beautiful bride." The photographer's soft French accent was commanding.

Dylan stood behind her with his arms wrapped around her waist. The temperature had nothing to do with the heat she felt. Dylan's thumb grazed under her breast as he pulled her even closer, and she inhaled sharply.

For a moment, she thought it was an accidental brush, until she heard the hum in the back of this throat. *What is that about? Seduction 101 Dylan McAthie style?* If she wasn't careful, it would work. She shored her resolve to protect her battered heart.

After a moment, Dylan's eyes narrowed, his stance stiffened, and he cursed under his breath. Concerned, she turned looked around and gasped. Donald Rowe stood next to their photographer, snapping pictures. He lowered his camera and smirked.

"I'm sorry, angel," Dylan whispered. "I'll explain later."

After an excruciating hour of photos, it was time to leave for the reception. Wedding guests were already waiting for them to arrive. Dylan escorted her out of the church, pausing to pose for more photos and navigating through a screaming throng of fans and paparazzi. Would it always be like this? Jostled, blinded, and yelled at?

Donald Rowe approached. "Thanks for the photos, McAthie. Do you have a statement you'd like to make?"

Dylan ignored him as he helped Jennifer into the waiting limousine. He slammed the door shut behind them and knocked on the privacy glass, signaling the driver to go. Leaning back, he rubbed his eyes. Still feeling like his nurse, not his wife, Jennifer automatically took his hand in hers. Confused, stressed, and tired, she stared at her bouquet of white roses and bluebells as she kicked off her heels. Reaching inside his coat pocket, Dylan drew out a flask and offered it to her.

Jennifer pulled away, shaking her head. "You promised Daddy no alcohol."

"I promised your father no alcohol would be served at the reception. We aren't at the reception yet." He took a deep drink and wiped his mouth with the back of his hand. He offered it again. "Sure? I won't tell."

"I'm positive," she snapped.

Dylan capped the flask and put it back in his coat pocket. He picked up her feet and massaged them. "Relax, it's over. Now we can enjoy ourselves. I'm sorry about that asshole, Donald Rowe. It was part of the deal brokered not to publish the other photos. Don't worry, he won't be at the reception."

"You could have told me. I'm tired of you treating me like a child," she grumbled.

His hands continued to work magic on her aching feet. She closed her eyes and sighed, giving in. "I wish I could've worn my tennis shoes. Nurses don't wear heels."

"In my dreams they do. Just what type of stockings are you wearing?" Dylan asked with a soft, wicked laugh.

She sighed, her eyes still closed. "I wish we could skip the reception."

"Me too," Dylan whispered. "Jen, I uh—"

The limousine came to a stop.

Dylan sighed. "Later." He kissed her forehead.

What does he mean by that? Her eyes flew open, and her breathing stuttered. Nervous, she pulled her feet from his hands and adjusted her gown.

The door to the limo opened, and they left its quiet privacy to greet their guests.

Jennifer stood next to him in the receiving line, ramrod straight, barely smiling and looking more like a military general than a beaming bride. Dylan kept a protective hand on her back, wishing there was something he could do to relieve her tension. He should have insisted she take a drink in the limo. She was wound up so tight, he was afraid she was going to unravel at any moment. Yet again he regretted letting Wendy and Jimmy talk them into this huge wedding. It had escalated out of control, and Jennifer was paying the toll. Tonight he'd lay his cards on the table and take the risk, tell her he was falling in love. He needed to convince her to give him a chance, to give *them* a chance.

"Dylan, I'm so happy for you and Jennifer. You two were made for each other." Mrs. Jordan patted his cheek.

"Thank you. Save a dance for me, okay?" He gave her a quick kiss on the cheek.

Cat beamed and gave him a hug. "It was beautiful, Dylan. You look so handsome. Take care of Jennifer. I mean it." She straightened his tie and patted his chest before darting away to yank Robbie away from the poor, tormented flower girl.

Dylan frowned as David Patterson gave Jennifer a hug and whispered in her ear. Jennifer's eyes filled with tears when David moved away without speaking to him. Dylan had a momentary pang of regret and a crapload of jealousy. It was obvious David cared deeply for Jennifer, but did she love him? She'd never said so, but then again, he'd never asked. *Have I ruined her chance of a happy marriage with him?* The thought left him unsettled and irritated. Grabbing Jennifer's hand, he motioned to the dance floor. Alan Mitchell and the band were ready to begin.

"Where are we going?"

"First dance, angel."

Jennifer stopped dead in her tracks. "I don't dance! Daddy doesn't like dancing— 'it leads to lascivious behavior,'" she quoted.

Dylan cupped her chin in his hand and grinned. "I certainly hope so, Mrs. McAthie." He winked and allowed his eyes the luxury of roaming over her body.

Blushing, Jennifer's wide eyes scanned the room. "Please don't do this to me," she begged, attempting to pull away from his hand.

"It's expected. See all the cameras? It'll be fine; just follow my lead."

Jennifer's face lit up with a triumphant smile. "But the prenup—*no dancing!*" She again tried to pull away, but he pulled her back to his chest as the music started.

"Jimmy and I both advised you to read those damn documents. You chose not to. The no-dancing clause isn't in there." He chuckled in her ear. "And neither is the no-sex clause. And you never had a lawyer send anything for me to sign." Slanting his mouth to hers, he kissed her as the music began to play.

Jennifer's heart hammered, and her knees felt weak when his lips left hers. *Dance? How can I dance? I can barely stand after that kiss. Not to mention these stupid shoes.* And ugh, he was right. Where had she been supposed to find a lawyer? Everyone she knew was a friend of her father's, and anyway, the fewer people involved in this mess the better. So she hadn't followed through with getting documents drawn up, and she'd signed his late last night without really reading.

She stole a glance at her father, who stood with his arms crossed, his mouth thinned into a line as he listened to whatever nosy old Mrs. Baxter was saying.

Dylan pulled her to the center of the dance floor. All eyes were on them, and she knew her face must be the color of his car.

Then it dawned on her what he'd actually said. "Sex?" she squeaked in his ear.

He laughed. "Not here, eager beaver."

"That's not what I meant," she hissed.

"We have lots to talk about when we're alone. For now, just relax and follow my lead. I've got you, baby." He held her firmly. "Trust me," he mouthed.

Alan began to sing The Flamingos' "I Only Have Eyes for You."

Dylan whispered, "I thought this was appropriate, considering how we met."

He flashed his famous Dylan McAthie melt-your-heart smile, and her resolve slinked off the dance floor, deserting her in her time of need. Jennifer followed his lead, her heart pounding so fast she couldn't breathe. Despite his slight limp and her awkwardness, they spun around the dance floor. His warm body against hers promised more than a dance, and she understood why her father didn't like dancing.

To her mortification, her palms were sweaty, and she couldn't breathe. Her heart pounded so hard, she was sure he could hear it. Dylan sang along in a seductive voice, and she closed her eyes, feeling light-headed. Pulling away to gain a modicum of self-restraint, she tripped, but he caught her. Dylan looked at her as if he wanted to devour her right there on the dance floor—in front of God and everyone. He removed one arm and twirled her, only to pull her back into his hard, lean body.

"Breathe, Jen. Take a breath or you're going to faint in my arms. And no grabbing my ass in front of your dad."

His breath on her neck fanned the flames of desire. The song ended, and she gave in to his kiss, gripping his arms to stay upright. The applause and cheers brought her back to reality, and she hid her face in Dylan's lapel as he laughed and kissed the top of her head.

Their guests joined them on the dance floor as the band began to play again. This time it was pure rock and roll as Alan belted out "Sweet Child O' Mine." Dylan held her hand up, offering the dance to her father. He frowned, declining.

"Guns N' Roses? Really, Dylan?" Jennifer chided as they went to get something to drink.

"You are *mine*. And I didn't want to disappoint your old man." His smirk was pure Dylan.

A breathless voice called his name. "Dylan! Do you ever return a text or phone call?"

Jennifer's moment of happiness dissolved as a beautiful woman caught hold of her husband's sleeve and kissed his cheek. *Loree Jamison.* Bile burned the back of her throat.

"Dance with me for old time's sake, darling?"

Said the spider to the fly. Ugly jealousy reared its head in the pit of Jennifer's stomach.

"Sure! I'm so glad you made it!" Dropping her hand, Dylan led Loree to the dance floor without a backward glance.

David walked over, looking awestruck. "Wow. Isn't that Loree Jamison, the model?"

"Shut your mouth, David. You'll catch flies," Jennifer snapped. She stormed out of the ballroom and headed to the bathroom. One last glance at the dance floor confirmed her fear. They looked like a Nordic god and goddess together with their blond hair, blue eyes, and perfectly toned bodies. Dylan threw his head back, laughing at something Loree said.

Staggering into the ladies room, she held on to the sink, taking deep breaths to check her convoluted emotions. She gazed at herself in the mirror and sighed at the image. As usual, she looked like a hot mess with her flushed cheeks, mussed hair, and twisted sash.

Attempting to put herself back to right, she stilled when she realized two women were in the stalls.

"Oh my God, can you believe all the celebrities here?"

"I know! Is it bad form to ask for autographs at a wedding?"

"I dunno, probably. Did you see Loree Jamison with Dylan on the dance floor? They look so hot together."

"I can't believe she was invited. You know they have a history. *The National Intruder* used to publish reports about all their wild parties. It's rumored she cheated on her husband with him. Have you seen her kid? Looks just like him…"

Jennifer dashed out of the bathroom as the toilets flushed, not wanting to be caught eavesdropping. She clenched her fists as she slumped against the wall. Miserable and defeated, she just wanted this day to end.

After a moment, though, she straightened her shoulders and plastered a fake smile on her face.

Vickie, her matron of honor, pounced on her and hugged her. "There you are! Oh my God, there are so many stars here! But your husband is by far the sexiest. Are you ready to get out of here and get on with the honeymoon? I think it's time to cut the cake." She grabbed her hand, tugging her.

If she only knew the sorry state of my marriage. Hiding her nervousness, Jennifer returned to the reception.

Chapter
Twenty

"Want me to carry you over the threshold?" Dylan asked.

Jennifer raised her weary eyes to his. "Let's not and say we did."

Laughing, he opened the door. "I've been working out. I wouldn't drop you."

Far from being tired, he felt energized after all the dancing. His new bride, on the other hand, appeared to be wilting and ready to collapse. "Jen, you okay?"

"I'm fine. I just want out of these heels and clothes."

"Ah, well, I want to see you out of those clothes, too. Heels and stockings, however, are optional." He tweaked her nose and laughed.

Jennifer rolled her eyes. "That's not what I meant, and you know it. No sex. The only reason we're sharing this suite is to protect *your* non-existent virtue. Bed or couch? Your choice."

Frowning, he stopped teasing. She swayed, and her breathing seemed erratic.

Cupping her face, he took in her dilated pupils. He could practically smell her fear. "Relax. You know I would never hurt you, right?"

Jennifer closed her eyes. "I-I want to go take a bath, p-please."

Dylan nodded. Her anxiety was contagious. *Maybe I should wait until she's had some rest before talking about the future. Tomorrow, in Key West.*

"Okay. You need to eat something, too. What do you want? I'll order something from room service."

Jennifer shrugged. "Whatever. Just make sure it isn't unpronounceable or fungus."

Dylan grinned. "How about a cheese and fruit tray? Maybe a little champagne, or if you insist, a diet cola?"

"Yes, I'd like that. Champagne is fine." She moved toward the bathroom and stopped. "Um, can you undo the hundred stupid buttons on this dress?" Her voice squeaked an octave higher than normal.

Dylan scooped her luxurious hair over her shoulder. His fingers fumbled a few times, and he found himself growing aroused as her back was slowly exposed. *Damn, she smells so good.* He wanted to kiss her skin after opening each button, but knew he needed to take things slow with his shy bride. A little champagne would help to calm her nerves—his too, if he was totally honest with himself.

Kissing the back of her neck, he held her in his arms for just a moment before giving her a gentle push toward the bathroom. He smiled when he heard her lock the door.

He ordered from room service and kicked off his shoes and socks. Slipping off his tie, he threw it on the bed and shrugged out of his vest and shirt. He could hear the water still running in the bathtub. He knocked on the door. "You okay?"

There was a pause, and the water cut off. "Yes, thank you. I-I'm fine."

"Okay." Tearing the nicotine patch off his arm, he grabbed his lighter and a cigarette from the pack he'd hidden in the bar. Guiltily, he stepped onto the balcony. If he was quick, he might be able to smoke the whole thing.

A few minutes later he was back inside to hear the elevator ding, and room service was delivered. He dug in his pocket for a tip, thanked the delivery boy, and signed an autograph. And still she didn't emerge.

What the hell is taking her so long? The bar beckoned with the promise of liquid courage. Maybe another cigarette? Instead, he paced off his nervousness. The tabloids would have a field day if they knew how damn unsure of himself he was. *Why won't she hurry? I need to talk to her, to tell her how I feel...*

The lock on the bathroom door clicked, and he smiled.

Jennifer crept into the room wrapped up in the big, fluffy white robe provided by the hotel, her wet hair wrapped in a towel. Dylan looked sexy as sin in just his wedding trousers. He also looked guilty about something. The lingering smell of cigarette smoke gave her the answer. Running his fingers through his hair, his eyes roamed over her body with a perplexed frown. Turning her back to him with a smug smile, she undid the towel around her hair to finish drying it. *Not the see-through lingerie you were hoping for?* Did he think she was kidding when she said no sex? She'd show him.

To keep from giggling, she returned to the bathroom, sitting at the vanity table to bring order to her impossible hair.

To her dismay, Dylan followed and took the brush from her hand. Slowly and methodically, he brushed her hair. A dream-like memory of him doing this once before haunted her. His gaze never left hers in the mirror as he detangled her hair, precisely and gently. Pausing with the brush in midair, he leaned over her shoulder, squinting at the mirror.

"What?" Guilt made her flush with unease.

Dylan turned her around on the vanity seat and peered at her, looking perplexed. "Your eyes."

She smirked. "I have two, yes."

"You're squinting. Like me."

"I wear contacts," Jennifer admitted.

"I never realized…"

"I'd put my glasses on, but men don't make passes at girls who wear glasses." *Where did that come from? Dummy, it's as if you want him to make a pass at you.*

"Wanna bet?" He shook his head, chuckling. "I'll be damned. We're more alike than I realized."

"I'm saving for the Lasik eye surgery. That was one of the reasons the salary your brother offered to care for an impossibly noncompliant patient was worth it. Then I wanted to travel."

"I wasn't that bad, and I'll take you anywhere you want. To the moon even." He held out his hand, and Jennifer followed him to the living area. He turned the sound system on to a slow love song.

"Dance, Mrs. McAthie?" he whispered in her ear.

"I don't dance, Mr. McAthie," she murmured, gripping his biceps and looking at the floor.

Dylan ignored her and sang along softly with Etta James as they swayed. She hid her face in his chest, wishing the words were true. When the song ended, he popped the cork on the champagne and poured two glasses. Jennifer looked over the fruit and cheese platter, realizing she was starving despite her nerves. Her mouth went dry as she watched Dylan bite into a chocolate-dipped strawberry and lick his lips.

"Mmmm…good," he hummed. He reached over and popped one in her mouth before leaning back, propping his long legs on the coffee table. He cocked his head to the side as he looked at her. "You've seen mine. I want to see yours." He grinned and rubbed her back.

Jennifer choked on the strawberry. "W-What?" she gasped as she held her robe closed tight.

"Glasses. I want to see your glasses. What did you think I meant?" He pulled one of her curls and laughed. "Jennifer Adams McAthie, get your mind out of the gutter."

"My glasses?" She took a sip of the champagne and gasped. "That tickles. They're just glasses, Dylan." She'd have to go easy on the alcohol.

"Please?" He watched her like a cat with a mouse.

Jennifer rolled her eyes, walked to the desk, and removed the simple, black frames from her purse. She shoved them on her face and stood before him, arms akimbo.

Dylan grinned as he popped a piece of cheese in his mouth. "You look like a school teacher."

"Precisely why I don't wear them."

Dylan stood and stretched, his muscles rippling. Jennifer wasn't sure if it was him or the alcohol making her feel warm and tingly all over. Dylan walked toward her, and she gulped. *Definitely Dylan.*

He nuzzled her neck and whispered, "I will so make a pass at you in those glasses. But right now, I'm going to get a quick shower. Eat something before you get drunk off your ass, angel." He chuckled and swatted her behind as he walked into the bathroom.

"Wash the stench of that cigarette out of your hair, too," Jennifer retorted.

"Will do!"

She sank to the couch, contemplating what was to come next. *My heart will be broken, regardless. I'm in love with a man who already has a rendezvous set up with another woman.* She looked at his crumpled tie and took another sip of the champagne, thinking.

Dylan grinned as he brushed his teeth. Jennifer in glasses had been a surprise. *Damn if that woman doesn't make glasses and a ridiculous fuzzy bathrobe look hot as hell.* He rinsed his mouth and ran his fingers through his damp hair. Not bad, although he'd need to watch what he ate for the next couple of weeks. He'd promised Loree he'd be fit and ready. Snapping the light out, he padded toward the bedroom, a towel wrapped low on his hips. At the doorway, he lingered to admire the sight before him, making sure to pose so the low light defined his muscles.

Still wearing her glasses, Jennifer didn't look up from her phone. *So much for my grand entrance.* Her black satin gown hugged her curves and was cut lower than he'd anticipated for his shy bride. She'd haphazardly pinned up her hair with delightful dark tendrils brushing her neck.

Pulling the glasses off, she asked, "Chopin, Pitbull, your work, or Rob Zombie?"

Dylan raised his eyebrows. "For?"

"Ambience."

"Ah, well, whatever the lady desires…I can accommodate." He winked. "But I thought you said no sex. If you've changed your mind, perhaps something soft and unobtrusive."

"I guess that means no 'Superbeast.'" She placed her glasses and phone on the bedside table. Her trembling hand belied her bravado.

Dylan threw his head back and laughed. "Tell you what, we'll work toward it." He growled, pulling her close. "Now c'mere, Mrs. McAthie. I need to talk to you."

"You're so bossy. Why can't I be in control for a change? I'm tired, and I'm sick of talking," she whispered, pressing her satin-clad body into his as her hands ran through his hair.

"Me bossy? Never! Now shut up and kiss me." *Proceed with caution, virgin ahead. Go slow, go slow, go slow…*

"I have a present for you."

"Angel, you're present enough for me, and I can't wait to unwrap this delightful package." He kissed down her neck to the spaghetti strap on her shoulder and pulled it aside with one finger.

Jennifer cupped his face in her hands and gazed into his eyes. "But, Mr. McAthie, you may need this, for later…" Her eyes were bright with mischief, intriguing him.

Dylan curbed the sigh and pulled in his raging need for this woman. *Patience, patience, patience. She's innocent…*

He moved away, raking a hand through his hair as the soothing sounds of Chopin filled the air. Shifting to ease his discomfort, he waited for the gift she was retrieving from her purse. He was surprised and touched that she'd remembered his birthday with all the crazy wedding planning. And things were going better than he'd expected. Might this actually be a real wedding night?

Jennifer opened his hand and placed a bottle in it. Biting her lip, she appeared to be on the verge of laughter. He looked down, horrified.

"Viagra? Seriously?" He scowled when he read who'd written the prescription. *Rob is a dead man.* He threw the bottle, and it rang as it hit the garbage can. *Shit, what if the tabloids find out about this?*

Jennifer shrugged. "It was a joke because you're *old*. Robert came up with it, and I thought it was funny." She laughed and darted across the room. He captured her, threw her on the bed, and was on top of her before she could catch a breath.

"Do you really think I need it?" He leaned in and nipped her neck.

He pressed his arousal into the apex of her thighs, and she sucked in a ragged breath. She shook her head, closed her eyes, and bit her lip.

"My angel of mercy," he murmured, kissing her eyelids. "My wife." He kissed her soft cheek.

Her eyes snapped open, and she stared at his mouth.

"My sweet temptress." He pressed his lips to hers, teasing her mouth open as his tongue delved deep. He skimmed down the black satin to the hem of her nightgown, and she whimpered, panting, but not with lust. He stilled his hands and brushed kisses across her face.

"Relax, love. Calm down. Breathe for me, baby. We'll only do what you're comfortable with." He slowly inched the gown up to her waist. He kissed down her neck and nipped her hardened nipple through the satin.

She squirmed when he traced his finger up her thigh. Patiently, he took his time, stroking soft circles closer and closer, easing her legs open.

He smiled against her neck. "I'll be damned. You weren't kidding. Niiiiiiiiice." He hummed his approval against her skin. He wanted to bury himself deep within her, but stopped. Her mixed signals were confusing, and he knew it was best to err on the side of caution. Hurting his beautiful bride was not an option. She was his to care for. Forever. He needed to tell her.

"Jen?"

"What?" she managed to squeak. Her heart beat so fast she feared she was having a heart attack. Some heart conditions were genetic after all...

Jennifer gasped when he kissed her *there*. The warmth of his mouth on her almost made the painful waxing worthwhile, even as it threatened to make her lose sight of her goal.

"Shut the hell up, Dylan."

His head shot up, and he peered at her through his bed-mussed hair with a wide grin. "Did you really just say *hell?* Such language, Mrs. McAthie." He chuckled and scooted up the bed. Lying on his side, with his head on his hand, he gazed down at her. Stroking her jaw, he murmured thoughtfully, "Jenny, Jenny, Jenny...you're full of interesting contradictions. What am I going to do with you?"

Now was her opportunity.

She rolled, flipping him on his back, and crawled on top of him. "Let me be in control?" she purred.

He threw his arms wide in surrender. "I'm all yours. Do with me what you will." He gave her his lopsided, adorable grin, and the sight of those two beguiling dimples almost swayed her off course.

How many women have fallen for those dimples! He's a player! Hold steady to the plan.

She sat up and reached behind her, her breasts straining at the gown. He hardened beneath her, and she smiled with triumph. His hands roamed freely, attempting to remove her gown, but she stopped him.

He watched, bemused, as Jennifer wrapped his wedding tie around his wrist, securing it to the bedpost. Her body shimmied against his, and he growled with need. *Shit, this is hot as fuck!*

She used the tie from her robe to secure his left wrist to the other bedpost. His mouth was dry, and his voice ragged when he managed to gasp, "Angel, what's my safe word?"

Her perfect brows knit together, and she paused. "What? What's a safe word?"

Phew. "Never mind." He decided to relax and enjoy whatever she had planned. *I never in a million years thought she'd be this adventurous. I'd still bet my last dollar she's pretty damn innocent.* He tugged on the restraints, realizing they were tight and expertly knotted. "Who taught you to tie knots like this?"

Jennifer smiled and whispered in his ear, "Tyrone—ex-Navy Seal, remember?" Kissing his jaw, she hesitantly moved her lips down his neck to where his pulse pounded. The citrus scent of her hair acted as an aphrodisiac. When she began kissing his chest, her tongue licking at his nipples, he shifted, becoming even more aroused. Closing his eyes, he moaned, wishing he could hold her. But tugging at the restraints proved futile.

"You're so beautiful," she whispered as she pulled his towel off and threw it on the floor.

Why does she sound so sad and detached?

She stood and lifted the gown over her head. Her beauty stunned him.

"You're killing me here," he whispered.

She pulled on a pair of panties and a bra and then stepped into a pair of jeans. He frowned, not understanding.

"Jen?"

She shrugged into a T-shirt and leaned over, kissing his forehead as she retrieved her glasses and phone from the bedside table.

"What the hell are you doing? Where are you going?" He tugged at the restraints.

Jennifer grabbed the keys to his car, then turned and smiled at him. She placed his phone just out of reach on the bed. "When I said no sex, I meant no sex. Thanks for the car. Have fun with your slut in two weeks." Grabbing her purse, she left, slamming the door.

He lay there, stunned, for all of five seconds. *What the hell is she talking about?*

"Come back!" he yelled. Goddammit, his marriage was over and it hadn't even begun. She hadn't let him tell her anything.

And how the fuck am I going to get out of this? His anger skyrocketed as tabloid headlines screamed through his head and he struggled against his restraints.

Chapter
Twenty-One

The phone rang—not an unusual occurrence at two in the morning, but nonetheless annoying. Robert extricated himself from Cathy's arms. "Dr. McAthie."

"Rob? I need you."

Robert sat up, rubbing his eyes. It was hard to hear Dylan, but the panic in his brother's voice registered through his exhaustion. "What's the matter?"

Cathy stirred a bit, and he reached out and smoothed her hair.

"Come to the hotel. They're expecting you at the front desk and will have the pass card ready. Come alone, but hurry!"

"Are you okay? Is Jennifer okay?" Robert held the phone between his ear and neck as he pulled on a pair of jeans.

"Fine, just hurry!" The phone went dead.

"Shit!" Robert stubbed his toe in his rush to pull on a T-shirt and shoved his bare feet into loafers.

Cathy sat up, yawning as she turned on the bedside lamp. "What's going on?"

"Hell if I know. Dylan's in trouble again. Where is my damn stethoscope?"

"On your dresser next to your keys, where you always put it. Robert, what's wrong with Dylan? Is he okay? Is Jennifer okay? Do I need to come with you?" She pushed the covers back.

Robert leaned over and kissed her forehead. "No, stay here with the kids. He wants me to come alone. I don't know what's going on. I'll find out and kill him later." Heart racing, he dashed from the bedroom.

His mind raced through endless scenarios he might find in Dylan's room, none of them good. He drove with his emergency lights flashing, praying he wouldn't be pulled over for speeding. Tires squealing, he pulled into the hotel. Leaving the car running, he motioned to the sleepy attendant and dashed inside.

Robert slowed his pace as he approached the desk, not wanting to draw any unnecessary attention. He calmly showed his ID and was given the key card and directions to the private elevator. Once the elevator door closed, he punched the floor button over and over. The doors opened, and he sprinted toward the room. It took him three tries before he managed to get the door to unlock. A quick survey of the living area revealed nothing out of the ordinary. One lamp was on and an open bottle of champagne sat on the end table. On the coffee table was a picked-over fruit and cheese tray. He breathed a sigh of relief. *Maybe one of them simply has food poisoning.*

"Dylan? Jennifer?" He knocked sharply on the door.

"Come in and, so help me, don't say one goddamned word."

Robert frowned and threw open the door, terrified. He blinked. He rubbed his eyes. And then he laughed.

"Shut the fuck up, Rob," Dylan shouted, rubbing his wrists as Robert closed the pocketknife. He grabbed a pair of jeans, throwing them on commando, and stormed into the living area. His asshole brother trailed behind him, still chuckling. He threw things until he found a cigarette and lit it.

"Let me get this straight. Sweet little Jennifer tied you to the bed with professional-grade knots, taught to her by an ex-Navy Seal, and stole your car?" Rob collapsed on the couch in another fit of laughter. "Damn, she's good. And here I thought writing the script for Viagra was funny as shit—but this takes the cake!"

Dylan backhanded his brother's head. "It's not funny." He paced, smoking like a chimney. What the fuck? Had she been setting him up all along? More than anger, he felt a deep sense of betrayal.

"Are you kidding me? This is the funniest damn thing—" Rob deflected another blow. "What if I hadn't come? What if I'd sent Cathy instead? Or better yet, what if the maid found you?" Rob erupted in another fit of laughter, wiping tears from his eyes. "Oh, man, I should've snapped a picture. Cathy's never going to believe this!" He started hiccupping.

"If you don't stop laughing at me, so help me God I'm going to throw your ass out that goddamn picture window. And if you *ever* tell anyone, including Cat, I'll fuckin' *kill* you. Do you hear me?"

"But I've never s-signed…" Rob sputtered and gasped, still hiccupping "…a…non-dis…closure…agreement." He snickered, but stopped when Dylan came to stand over him with his fist drawn back.

Rob swallowed, biting his lip to keep from laughing. One last hiccup escaped. "How the hell did you get to the phone tied up like that?"

Dylan kicked the cheese tray off the table. "It wasn't easy—stop laughing at me, asshole! She left my cell just out of reach, but after an hour or so, I managed to squirm enough to get to it. So help me, if you don't quit laughing I'm gonna knock the shit out of you. Stop it!" Dylan shook with anger, and his vision tunneled. This was so not okay. He wanted to throttle his *wife* and his *brother.*

"Okay, okay, but why did she do it?" Robert's eyes narrowed. "What did you do to her?"

"Nothing. I didn't do a damn thing to her. And I mean that *quite literally.*" Dylan lit another smoke off the one he was finishing.

"Well, something had to have happened. This is totally out of character for Jennifer." Robert straightened and glowered.

"Dammit, didn't you hear me? *I didn't do anything*. Why do you always think the worst of me?"

"Because you always react irrationally, instead of like a responsible adult. What exactly did she say?"

"She thanked me for the car and told me to have fun with my slut in two weeks. Which doesn't make a damn bit of sense, because I'm working in two weeks." Dylan marched into the bedroom, throwing clothes in a duffle bag. No way he'd reveal the no-sex comment to Junior.

Rob followed him. "Call her. She's probably waiting to hear from you. You two can kiss and make up, then drive on down to Key West. This is probably all just a joke. Relax, have a good laugh, and enjoy your honeymoon. Damn, she got you good, though."

Dylan shrugged into a shirt, paused, and took a draw off the cigarette, wanting to wipe the smirk off Rob's smug face. "Are you kidding me? I'm not calling that little—"

Rob interrupted, pointing his finger. "Don't you *ever* refer to your *wife* in a derogatory manner."

"Stop it, Junior. You're not my father. Quit acting like it."

"Then grow up, Dylan. Call her. She's a kid, and you're thirty damn years old."

Dylan ignored him and dialed a number. "Jimmy! Get your ass over here. I need you to do a clean sweep on this place and check me out. I'm outta here." He paused to listen, then barked, "No. Plans have changed. Cancel Key West, too." Turning the phone off, he grabbed the pack of cigarettes and his guitar. He slung his duffle over his shoulder and shoved past Rob. Jimmy could damn well pack up the rest of his shit.

"Where are you going?"

Dylan stopped dead in his tracks and turned around. Digging in the garbage, he found the bottle of Viagra and threw it at his asshole brother. "Get rid of this. I sure as hell don't need this found by hotel staff."

Rob caught the bottle, shoved it in his jeans pocket, and frowned. "Answer me, Dylan. Where are you going?"

"Probably to hell!" Dylan bolted down the hall and onto the elevator, flipping off his brother as the doors closed.

Jennifer drove to the only place she could think of to avoid the paparazzi. She refused to return to her father's house and hear the lecture. Lucky for her, no one expected the bride to flee on her wedding night, and she was confident she hadn't been followed to Pine Bluff. She turned the car down the long gravel drive just as the rain turned torrential.

Lightning arced through the air, followed by a loud clap of thunder. Scared, she grabbed her suitcase and purse and made a mad dash toward the front porch, sloshing through the mud. Using the hidden key, she slipped into the dark house. The door slammed shut from the force of the strengthening storm. Another clap of thunder had her squeaking like a scared mouse.

Dragging her suitcase to her room, she quickly changed and dove under the covers. A loud crash sounded, and the house plunged into darkness. This had been a huge mistake. There was no cell phone coverage, and she was too terrified to move to use the house phone. Her plan was to stay here for the night and in the morning return and set Dylan free. By that time, she figured he would be mad enough to grant her an annulment. She clearly could not handle herself in a fake marriage.

But this storm wasn't letting up. It had picked up strength as she drove, and she didn't want to risk driving his car—make that *her* car—any more in weather like this. The house shook with the howling wind, and the windows rattled with a deafening boom.

Feeling ridiculous, she tiptoed to her suitcase and unzipped the outside pocket. Grabbing the stuffed rabbit that had been her companion through other miserable moments in her life, she hugged it to her chest as tears fell. What a silly, stupid girl she'd been when she'd first arrived at this house all those months ago. Longing for adventure and excitement, all she'd ended up with was misery and heartache. Another flash of lightning and crack of thunder sent her diving under the covers.

No longer feeling smug about her revenge, she realized she wished Dylan were here. Was she that weak and pathetic? He was a player; she should be glad to be rid of him! The wind whistled around the house, and she covered her face with her pillow, hugging the beloved bunny.

Alone, she began to second-guess her hasty decision. Maybe she should have given him a chance to explain. Had she jumped without thinking? The emotion he'd shown as he recited his vows replayed over and over in her mind. And afterward, at the hotel, he hadn't pushed, he'd been considerate…Had she fallen that hopelessly in love with him? *Yes.*

The storm outside intensified, no less violent than her self-recriminations.

Chapter
Twenty-Two

At seventeen, Dylan had hitchhiked cross-country to California. He'd slept on a park bench, hungry and broke, yet had remained optimistic and full of ambitious dreams. At age thirty, he'd thumbed a ride for a mere seventy-five miles and was wet, miserable, and fuckin' depressed. His only bit of luck was that the truck driver who gave him a lift didn't have a clue who he was. He trudged down the driveway in the pouring rain. His guitar was ruined. Even worse, so were his cigarettes. He really needed a smoke.

He considered himself a pretty good judge of character. But not this damn time. How could he have been so wrong about Jen? *Dumbass, you were wrong about Sara, too.* Ah, there was the answer. *Love.* Love fucked with your mind. Like Scarlett O'Hara shaking her fist and vowing to never be hungry again, he vowed never to love again. He would become the player everyone—his wife included—thought he was. He'd lick his wounds for a few days and head back to California…

Seeing the car parked in front of his house made his heart soar for a brief second before crashing back to Earth. *Sonofabitch!*

Furious, he kicked the tire of his beloved NSX. *She's here.* He stood in the pouring rain, contemplating his next move. Lightning arced across the lake, followed by a deafening crack of thunder. First move was to not get struck and die on his wedding night. He could well imagine the headlines.

He hurried to the front porch, kicking off his soggy shoes and socks. He tried the knob, and the door opened. Part of him wanted to shake Jennifer for being careless enough to leave the door unlocked. Another part of him wanted to shake her to just get some damn answers. How dare she do this to him? He'd never been so humiliated in his life! Maybe it would be best if he didn't wake her. He needed to calm the fuck down first.

As he dropped his wet things on the couch, a sound from her old bedroom made him frown. Another crash of thunder shook the house.

"Oh shit!"

The expletive surprised him. Jennifer rarely cussed. He made his way into the kitchen and found a candle and matches. Sweet, there was a pack of cigarettes, too. Lighting the candle, Dylan hurried to Jen's room where he found her curled up on her bed, sobbing, a stuffed rabbit clutched in her arms.

"Hey, you okay?"

A terrified scream pierced through the rumbling of the storm, and the stuffed rabbit hit him in the face. He damn near dropped the candle.

"What the fuck, Jen?"

"Dylan?"

A bundle of crying angel launched off the bed and torpedoed into his arms, making him stagger backward. He just managed to put the candle down. Her arms wrapped around his neck, and her body shook with sobs.

His anger subsided, and he held her tight, inhaling her sweet, warm scent. "Shh, you're okay."

"The power's out."

He chuckled at her grasp on the obvious and winced at her iron grip on his hair. The only way she could get any closer was if he were buried deep inside of her. His cock twitched to life. She stilled, and her breathing stuttered.

"You're wet," she croaked, loosening the grip on his hair and pulling away. She scrambled into her robe, knotting the belt.

"Uh, yeah. *Someone* stole my car. I had to hitchhike." The room lit up again, and thunder rumbled.

She buried her face in his shirt, and her shoulders shook. Patting her on the back, he murmured, "You're okay; it's just a storm."

"*My* car." The words were muffled by a giggle.

"What?"

"Prenup. The dream machine is *my* car." Another giggle escaped.

"Not funny." He wasn't ready to laugh.

"How did you get loose?"

"Rob." Like a switch had been flicked, his anger returned, and he pulled away. Grabbing the candle, he marched back into the kitchen for a cigarette.

"I was going to come back in the morning," she offered from behind him.

"Before the hotel staff found me?" he snarled, lighting the smoke.

"It's our wedding night. I put the Do Not Disturb sign on the door."

"Well, it didn't fuckin' work, 'cause I'm pretty goddamned disturbed," he shouted.

She crossed her arms, and her chin lifted. "How do you think I felt—the day before our wedding—when I found out you're planning some hot rendezvous with Loree Jamison? I read the text about how glad she was our marriage wasn't going to ruin your *relationship*."

"What the hell are you talking about?"

She lowered her gaze. "I know it was wrong, I shouldn't have answered the phone or deleted the text, but I was under so much stress and…" Her voice trailed off, and she took a deep breath.

"It hurt my feelings," she admitted, looking at the floor. "I knew this wasn't going to be a real marriage, but…I guess I didn't realize you were involved with someone else. I mean, I knew about Sara, but you never mentioned *her*. Did you write the song 'Lust for Loree'?"

"What? I wrote the music, not the lyrics. I'm gonna ask again. What the hell are you talking about? I'm doing an ad campaign in a couple of weeks for her new clothing line…"

Realization hit. At the reception, Loree had mentioned that he never returned her text with ideas for the photo shoot. *Jen was jealous!*

A faint smile teased the corner of his lip. "You mean to say you left me all tied up in knots—*literally*—because you thought Loree and I were going to continue our 'relationship' and it involved sex?"

Jennifer nodded. "Kinky sex. She said so."

"Oh she did, did she?" Dylan shook his head, relief flooding him, and he laughed a deep, gut-shaking laugh. "Did it include some bondage, or did you come up with that all on your own?" He gazed at her, unable to quit chuckling despite his best effort.

"Stop it! Stop laughing at me!" She slapped the counter.

He laughed harder. "The shit you put me through over nothing…" He struggled to contain his amusement. "The phone call and text—*which I never received*—"he looked pointedly at her "—were about the photo shoot we're doing in a couple of weeks."

He decided now was not the time to mention Loree had been his first girlfriend when he moved to California. With her blond hair and blue eyes, she'd reminded him of Cat.

Jennifer sighed and covered her face with her hands, rubbing her eyes. "What are we doing, Dylan? This marriage…it's a joke. I know we did it for good reasons, but I don't think I can handle the lies."

"There are parts of the world that still have arranged marriages." He took a last draw off his cigarette and stubbed it out.

"I hardly think my father would've chosen you."

"True. But that's not my point. Love can grow. I care about you. Those vows I took? I meant them, Jen." He brushed her hair from her face and stared into her eyes. "I want to see where this can go. Do you care about me, even a little? Can you give us a chance? If in a few months it doesn't work, we'll at least know we tried."

Her gaze held his and he held his breath, waiting for her answer.

"Really?"

"Really. You're mine. I want to take care of you. I want to see if we can make this a real marriage."

Tell her you love her, asshole. Past betrayals played through his mind. He kept his mouth shut and waited for Jennifer's answer.

"I, um, I do care about you. But I'm confused, and I'm exhausted…"

He watched as every conflicted emotion played across her face. He held his breath.

Swallowing, she bit her lip and her cheeks grew rosy. "Okay," she whispered.

Jennifer paced back and forth, glancing at the door. What exactly had she just agreed to? Would he make a move to push their relationship forward tonight, or would he go sleep in his old bedroom? If not, would he just walk in the room naked? Picking up the stuffed rabbit, she held it to her chest. The bathroom door opened, and she dove into bed, pulling the covers up to her chin. With a groan, she tossed the stuffed rabbit toward the dresser. She missed and once again hit her husband in the face.

"Uh, is this some sort of routine with you?" He tossed the rabbit in her suitcase.

He had a towel wrapped around his waist. She wanted to stare, but didn't want him to know she was staring. With a groan, she pulled the covers over her head. The bed dipped with his weight, and he snuggled into her, pulling the covers down to below her chin. He brushed her hair away from her face and leaned in to kiss her.

"Are you n-naked?"

"Um, yeah? My clothes are soaked." He sighed. "I'll go to my room." He moved to get up, and a crack of thunder shook the house.

"No!" Jennifer squeaked. "I mean, please don't leave me."

He kissed her forehead. "Are you sure?"

"C-Can you blow the candle out?" she squeaked. This was going to happen.

He paused and smiled. "But I want to see my beautiful wife."

"P-Please?"

He blew the candle out and crawled into bed. "I'm scared, too."

"You are? Why?"

"Where's the tie to your robe?"

Jennifer laughed. "Across the room."

"Good. Now I'm not so scared," he teased, spooning her. He kissed the back of her neck. "Goodnight, Mrs. McAthie."

"Goodnight? Like, sleep goodnight?"

"Yup. I'm old, remember? And I'm exhausted, and so are you. We have all the time in the world for other *good* nights."

"Oh, thank God," she whispered, relaxing.

He chuckled. "Damn, you sure don't help a guy's ego."

"Sorry. I just think we need to talk—"

"Goodnight, Jen," he interrupted.

His breathing became regular, and she realized he'd fallen asleep. She'd put him through hell, and yet he was here and being nice, respectful—dare she think it? *Loving*. Maybe he truly meant what he'd said. Maybe she needed to learn to trust him. The storm continued to rage outside, but the one within her quieted.

She awoke to a minty fresh kiss. She turned her face. "Stop, I haven't brushed my teeth."

"Go brush your teeth," he smiled against her ear.

She scrambled out of bed and decided to take a quick bath, too.

Shyly, she returned to the bedroom wrapped in a towel. Dylan lay on his side, his head propped on his hand. His eyes glimmered with simmering passion, and his grin widened. He held his hand out. Swallowing her fear, she dropped the towel but scrambled under the covers.

He chuckled and gave her a quick kiss. "Now, where were we before you ran out on me?"

"Let me get my robe tie."

Caging her body with his he growled, "No way." He smiled against her lips. "Relax, baby. You sure about this?"

She nodded.

Slowly he explored her mouth, teasing, nipping, and sucking. Still reeling from his kisses, she inhaled sharply as his hand moved up her leg, leaving a trail of fiery need in its path. When his thumb flicked her clitoris, she gasped and bucked. He began kissing his way lightly down her body…

"What are you doing?" she whispered.

"I'm enjoying breakfast."

Oh, dear Lord.

He calmed her with reassuring strokes, taking his time, exploring her uncharted territory with his warm, strong hands. His lips soon followed, and Jennifer panted and shook with an overwhelming need for something more.

"God, you taste good."

"Shut up, Dylan," she gasped out, closing her eyes in anticipation. He stopped and kissed the inside of her thigh. "What?"

"Don't stop, just Shut. The. Hell. Up. And keep doing what you're doing!"

"Did you just say *hell*, Mrs. McAthie? We have all day, bossy."

"I wish we'd done this last night and got it over with. I think we're going backward."

"Got it over with?" He stopped and pulled himself on top of her. "Our whole fuckin' relationship has been backward. Why change anything now?"

Brushing the hair from her face, he gazed into her eyes. "I want to make love to you. But only if you're ready."

"We're married. And apparently, there wasn't a no-sex clause." She picked at the sheets with trembling hands. "Maybe I'll go to law school…"

He laughed softly and stroked her cheek. "If you want to go to law school, that's fine. But let's consider it later, okay? I want you to understand that this marriage is a partnership. It isn't about me and what I want. It's about us."

Heat rose in her cheeks. It was hard to think with his warm body on hers, and his amazing eyes, so full of passion and gazing at her so intently. "Thank you. I've never…"

"I know, baby."

"I don't know what to do…" She meant both the act and her decision.

"Do you trust me?" His thumb stroked her cheek.

"I don't know."

"Fair enough. Let me tell you what I want to do."

She wrinkled her nose, hoping he wouldn't get graphic. "I'm a nurse…" she said with an irritated grumble.

He stopped her protests with a kiss. As if he could read her thoughts, he broke the kiss and softly stroked her cheek. "I want to show you how much you mean to me. I want to pleasure you with my lips." He spread soft kisses across her cheek and whispered in her ear, "With my tongue." He licked the shell of her ear. "And with my hands." He caressed her swollen, aching breasts. "And lastly, with my body." He rocked against her.

She gasped at the sensation, wanting more.

"Forget the legal shit. Forget the reasons we married. We agreed last night to give our relationship a try, right? Let me show you heaven. I'm not a religious man, but your body is my temple. I will honor it as I worship it. This is my vow to you."

Her heart raced as the pieces of her world fell into place. This felt right. She loved Dylan. She belonged with this man. Forever.

"Dylan?"

"Yes?"

"Take me to the moon…"

Chapter
Twenty-Three

Jennifer woke to the sound of rain hitting the old tin roof and the even breathing of her husband, who was *not* snoring for a change. Propping up on her side, she watched him sleep, as she had so many times before, but never so intimately. He lay on his back with one arm thrown over his eyes and one hand rising and falling on his well-defined abdomen. The partially cast-aside covers provided her with a tantalizing view of his sculpted body. Heat crept into her cheeks as she found herself wanting him, yet again. *Will it always be like this?*

"Enjoying the view, Mrs. McAthie?" he asked with a smirk. His husky voice sent shivers down her skin. He hadn't moved the arm over his eyes.

How did he know? "Very much so, Mr. McAthie." Leaning over, she kissed his scruffy jaw as she explored the hills and valleys of his abdomen with curious fingers.

He removed his arm and peeked at her with a wicked grin. "Good Lord, I've created an insatiable sex fiend. Give an old man a break. Didn't we just get to sleep?"

"Just making up for lost time, and we slept a couple of hours." She licked his nipple and with her finger wrote *mine* over his heart. He hummed in the back of his throat, and she grinned as the sheet tented.

Dylan ran his calloused fingers down her back, and heat coursed through her body. Turning on his side to face her, he traced her lower lip, gazing at her sleepily. She nipped his thumb.

"Ow! I may need to change your nickname from angel to tiger." He yawned, pulled her to his chest, and murmured, "Just another half hour."

Jennifer watched him fading back to sleep and sighed dramatically. He opened one eye.

"Maybe I need to get Dr. McAthie to call in a refill on a certain prescription…" The pillow hit her before she knew what had happened, and she squealed with laughter.

"Go make me some coffee, wife."

"Now who's being bossy?" She swung out of bed and winced as muscles she never knew existed made themselves known.

"Are you okay? I'm sorry. Oh shit…" He sat up. "Stay here, I should be waiting on you. You need some ibuprofen or anything?"

Jennifer held his cheek and gave him a kiss. "I'm not a bit sorry. I'm fine." Kissing him again, deeper this time, her tongue teasing his, she smiled against his lips, "More than fine. Now you're mine."

"Always. And you're mine. But I didn't mean to hurt you."

"You didn't hurt me. It's normal. I mean, you knew I was a…" Her voice trailed off.

Dylan got up and grabbed the towel on the floor, wrapping it around his hips and hiding his morning wood.

"Yes, of course. I just hate that you're uncomfortable, that I caused you pain…"

She found his embarrassment out of character and terribly endearing.

Jennifer stood and threw her arms around his neck, kissing his cheek. "For the last time, Dylan, I'm okay! Don't ruin the best day of my life. I can't believe I'm going to say this, but go smoke a cigarette. You need it."

She kissed him hard on the mouth and left the room, humming.

Dylan shook his head. *Damn, the girl can't carry a tune with a bucket.* Finding his jeans, he slipped them on and stepped out on the front porch. With a loud yawn and a stretch, he lit a cigarette and took the first draw deep into his lungs. He couldn't seem to stop grinning.

I'm happy. What the hell have I done to deserve this fuckin' awesome woman?

Lightness filled his soul. The demons of his past withdrew into a dark cavern as hope for the future enveloped him, giving him a sense of peace for the first time in…well, forever. He wanted to have a press conference and let the world know. *Dylan McAthie is a happy man.* He laughed just for the joy of it and stubbed out his cigarette. *Maybe it's time I really quit smoking.*

With a spring in his step, he hurried inside, stopping by the kitchen. Wearing his shirt and ridiculously modest panties, Jen had her back to him. He grimaced and shook his head when she belted out a few lines of a pop song. She added a few awkward dance moves. God love her, his girl didn't have any rhythm, either. None of it mattered. She was his, and she was sexy as hell. Plugged into her phone, she was oblivious to the fact that he was watching. She missed another high note.

Note to self, never put Jen on backup vocals.

Turning around, she grinned and waved as she scoured the cabinets for something edible. Dylan laughed and sauntered to the bathroom. Married life might be a hell of a lot of fun, if his hearing survived.

Jennifer found him moments later, getting ready to shave. He was considering doing away completely with the stubble. He paused when she gave him a pretty pout in the mirror.

"What's the matter?"

"Don't shave."

"Why?" He put the razor down and frowned. Her soft, pale cheek was still pink from their lovemaking a few hours ago.

Jennifer blushed, rubbing a finger up and down the doorframe. "I dunno, maybe 'cos you look more like the bad boy my daddy warned me to stay away from?" She grinned and cast him a flirtatious look, twirling a lock of her unruly hair around her finger and biting her lower lip.

Dylan laughed. "Yeah, but if I shave, I'll look closer to your age. Don't worry. I'm just cleaning up the lines. Run a bath, will you?"

"Why are you always so bossy?" she complained half-heartedly as she filled the tub with bubbles.

He damn near slit his throat watching her in the mirror. She slowly unbuttoned his shirt, watching his reaction. Easing it off one shoulder, she licked her lips, tossed her hair, and winked.

Dylan raised an eyebrow and returned her smile as he finished shaving. He rinsed his face while watching her striptease. Before the shirt dropped, he grabbed her wrists and pulled her close, nuzzling her neck.

"Why, Mrs. McAthie, are you teasing me?" He felt her shiver.

"Most certainly." She ran her hands up his back, pressing her breasts into his naked chest. She tilted her head back and grinned at him. "I wish I still had your neck tie."

"I bet you do." He turned her so her back was against him and wrapped his arms around her waist. Starting at her ear, he kissed his way along her neck. A gentle nip on her shoulder made her knees buckle, and she would have collapsed if he hadn't been holding her. He smiled in triumph.

He fondled her breast, teasing and pulling until her nipple pebbled. Watching her face in the mirror as he seduced her, he growled with need when her skin flushed and her nails dug into his arms. Eyes closed, she moaned, sagging against him as his hand went lower, finding her ready and needy. He grabbed his shirt and tied it to cover her eyes.

"Payback's a bitch." He chuckled.

She struggled for a moment. "Dylan?"

"Breathe, Jennifer. Trust me," he whispered in her ear. Kissing her neck, he continued to run his hands down her body. He lifted her and placed her in the warm, soapy bathtub. She moved to take off her blindfold, but he stopped her. "Don't move. I'll be right back. Trust me."

"Dylan?" She clutched the bathtub, her heart pounding with anticipation. From the kitchen, she heard him opening and closing cabinets. *He left me to go eat?* "There's nothing there, I've already looked. We need to go shopping." The citrus smell of her bubbles tickled her nose, and she reached to tear off the blindfold.

"Tsk, tsk. Naughty girl." Dylan grabbed her hand and kissed it.

Startled, she squealed. He laughed and, scooting her forward, climbed in the tub behind her, sloshing water. Settled, he trailed kisses down her neck, and she sighed contentedly.

The sound of water dripping preceded a warm, soapy bath sponge running up and down her arms. He didn't say a word, letting his touch do the talking. He blew in her ear. Unable to see, her other senses were heightened. It was sinfully erotic. Turning her head, he ran his fingers up and down her throat. She moaned and her toes curled. His arousal pressed into her from behind, and she relished her power as a woman. She jumped when something sticky rubbed up her neck and across her jaw line, teasing her lower lip. When the smell of cinnamon and apple hit her nose, she opened her mouth. Sweet and spicy, she'd never look at apples as mere fruit again. Dylan purred behind her when she sucked the juice off his fingers.

"Where did you find apples?" she croaked.

He chuckled. "I didn't. It's a can of pie filling. Beggars can't be choosers."

Again, she moved to take off her blindfold. And again, he stopped her, laughing at her impatience. The sponge moved over her stomach, and one hand cupped an aching breast, teasing it, pulling on her nipple, sending shockwaves down her body. His warm lips found her neck, and the hand that had cupped her breast moved to push her hair aside. The sponge dipped lower and lower as he continued to fondle her breast and kiss her back. It was sensory overload of the best kind.

Still a bit sore from last night, but enthralled with the new sensations, she squirmed.

He paused. "You okay, baby?"

She nodded and croaked, "Don't stop. For the love of God, don't stop."

He chuckled in her ear. "Your wish is my command."

Slowly, he teased her again and again until she opened her legs, wanting more. He stroked and circled until she panted, begging for release. Jennifer gripped the side of the tub, her head flung back until she screamed his name. Collapsing against her husband, every nerve in her body hummed as she recaptured her breath.

Somewhat embarrassed by her reaction and eager to return the favor, Jennifer pulled off the blindfold and turned around to face Dylan. He leaned back against the tub, his hands behind his neck, a satisfied smirk on his face. He silver-blue eyes sparkled with anticipation. Jennifer straddled his lap, sloshing water as she leaned forward and captured his lips.

"Mine," she whispered as she kissed him again.

"Always," he acquiesced, wrapping one hand in her hair while the other guided her to him. As their flesh melded into one, he whispered again, "Always."

Jennifer drifted awake to the sound of Dylan's snoring. He spooned her from behind, his fingers interlaced with hers. Brushing a kiss across the top of his wedding band, she smiled. His rough fingertips that could play such beautiful music had played her pretty well, too.

"I love you," she whispered, softly. Without waking, he stirred a bit and rolled to his back, throwing one arm over his eyes. Maybe she'd get the courage to tell him again later. Or was it too soon? She peeked at the clock. It was after noon, and still raining. And decisions like this definitely needed coffee.

Jennifer's stomach growled, and she thought about the sorry condition of the refrigerator and pantry. This wasn't Key West, but so far she had no complaints about their honeymoon, despite the rocky start. Eventually she'd give Dylan the satisfaction of telling him he'd been right to leave off the no-sex clause.

Her stomach rumbled. Sadly, she'd have to venture out into the real world for food at some point today. As much as she enjoyed making love with her husband, they couldn't keep going at this pace without sustenance. Gingerly she arose, disentangling her hand from Dylan's, and shrugged into her robe to go in search of caffeine and ibuprofen. She tiptoed, careful not to wake him, knowing full well he wasn't a morning person—no matter what the actual time was.

Passing by the bathroom, she blushed at the mess. Dylan's shirt hung over the side of the tub, and the open can of pie filling sat next to the sink. She added cleaning house to her mental to-do list. Starting the coffee, she realized for the first time that she held a glimmer of hope this marriage could work. She loved Dylan, and he'd said he cared for her and wanted to make this a real marriage. Unbidden, her father's words cast a pall on her happiness.

"Jennifer, it takes more than love to make a relationship work."

She shoved the unwanted thought aside, took her cup of coffee into the living area, and sat down, enjoying the soft sound of the rain on the roof and ticking of the mantel clock. She started scribbling a shopping list. A loud snore drifted from the back of the house. *Add earplugs to the list.* Dylan's phone was on the table, and she decided to drown him out with music. She put the earbuds in and paused. He had one unread message that must have come through before he hit the no service zone.

It was a text from Loree.

Sorry I had to leave the reception early. Caught an early flight home. Meghan misses her daddy. Me being away was too much. We can't wait for you to get here in two weeks. She needs you. Me too. Lots to talk about.

Attached was a photo of a crying, blond-haired, blue-eyed child.

Jennifer felt her breath leave her. Confused, and angry, she let her curiosity overrule Dylan's privacy. She thumbed through his pictures. There were hundreds of them. His screen saver was a picture of her holding Robbie's kitten. She didn't even remember him taking it. Next was the awful picture of her taking out the garbage from *The National Intruder*. There were pictures of Sara and the band. But she paused when she came to a series of pictures that showed Dylan the way she remembered him when she was a little girl.

Except he was naked.

And in bed with Loree.

In some they were kissing. In others, making faces at the camera.

One was captioned: *Young, broke, and stupid.* Which was exactly how she felt.

The next photo broke her heart completely.

Dylan held a newborn baby, kissing the infant's forehead. It was captioned: *My girl.*

There were also videos: The little girl's first steps. Her birthday parties. Dylan singing her to sleep. But the last one shattered her hopes for the future—the child was sobbing and wailing, "I want my daaaaaaddy."

Every nasty rumor that had ever been splashed across the news-stands and on television flashed before her eyes. Her stomach clenched as the enormity of his betrayal overwhelmed her. Rationally, she knew she should talk to him, ask him to explain. But she felt anything but rational, and she wasn't sure she was strong enough to hear it. Didn't this *prove* there was more than business between Dylan and Loree? How could she have fallen for this twice?

"*Dance with me for old time's sake, darling.*"

"*It's rumored she cheated on her husband with him...*"

"*Have you seen her kid? Looks just like him...*"

Chapter
Twenty-Four

Dylan woke with a start when Jennifer slammed her suitcase shut. Dressed in jeans and a T-shirt, she tore around the room in a dither, her hair wet and tangled, and hanging down her back. Finding her glasses on the dresser, she shoved them on her face.

"Where are you going?" He sat up, rubbing his eyes.

"Home."

"You are home. Well, one of them, anyway." He yawned and stretched.

Jennifer grabbed the keys off the dresser. Dylan jumped out of bed with a sick sense of déjà vu. Grabbing his jeans off the floor, he pulled them on in haste, damn near tripping in the process as he followed her to the living room.

"What the hell is going on?" He grabbed her arm.

"Don't touch me. Don't talk to me." Jennifer shrugged out of his grasp. She fled with him fast on her heels.

"Why not? You wanted me touching you just a few hours ago. What the hell is wrong with you?" His heart hammered, and his stomach sank with a sick feeling.

"Shut up, Dylan! Just shut up!" Finding her purse, she grabbed it and dragged her suitcase out the front door, headed toward the car. "I have to get away. I need to think. I can't talk to you right now."

"Wait," he shouted. "Think about what? What the fuck have I done now?"

Sheets of rain pelted them, and a crack of thunder made them both jump.

"Why? Why are you leaving? What happened?" He threw his arms up in total confusion.

She threw the suitcase in the trunk and slammed it shut. "This was all a huge mistake. You are such a liar, and I can't do this. I don't know a thing about you. This isn't a marriage, no matter what you say you want. It's a business agreement, and I quit! I don't understand anything about your life. I don't even know your favorite color." She shoved him, and he stumbled backward, almost losing his balance.

Dylan shook his head. "Don't you dare do this to me!" He ran a shaking hand through his wet hair. She was leaving. Everyone always left him.

She threw herself into the car, but Dylan squatted next to her seat, preventing her from closing the door.

"Please…" He searched her face for a clue. "What has you so upset? Why are you leaving me, baby?" He could fix whatever was wrong if she'd just calm the fuck down.

"I'm not your baby. You already have one of those." Jennifer looked at him, and a tear rolled down her cheek from under her glasses. She shook her head. "Let me go, Dylan. Go back to California. You belong there, not here."

"What the hell are you talking about?" He gripped the door, getting angry now. "I thought we had this shit straightened out. This doesn't make any sense. Grow the fuck up and talk to me." As soon as he said it, he knew he'd made a tactical error.

"There isn't anything to talk about. I wouldn't believe you, any-way. I'm done. I can't do this." She looked straight ahead, refusing to meet his eyes.

"Don't do *this*. Come back inside." He stroked her arm. She pulled away, refusing to look at him.

They sat in a stony silence as the relentless rain continued. After a few minutes, Dylan stood and backed away, holding his hands up in defeat. Jennifer slammed the door and drove down the driveway. Watching her, he kicked a puddle and said, "Your eyes. That's my favorite goddamned color."

Robert was not happy. He was sick and tired of being his younger brother's caretaker, especially when said younger brother didn't seem to give a damn about anyone except himself. The only reason he'd agreed to drive up to Pine Bluff was to put a halt to Cathy's incessant nagging and Jimmy's repeated phone calls. For nearly two weeks, Jennifer had been withdrawn and refused to talk about what happened. Media remained camped out on their street, and he'd had to hire extra security at his office, where she now worked.

He slowed the car and frowned. Paparazzi surrounded the entry to his grandmother's driveway. He angrily showed his ID to get through Dylan's security. With a scowl and a string of oaths he never used in front of his children, Robert drove down the long driveway and parked. He slammed his car door, ready to confront his obnoxious, selfish, asshole brother.

He found Dylan passed out on the screened-in porch, surrounded by cigarette butts and holding an almost-empty fifth of vodka. If he wasn't mistaken, there were a few roaches, too—and not the insect kind. Robert kicked the swing and watched Dylan try three times to stand before falling on his ass. It would've been funny, if he hadn't been so pissed. It was obvious Dylan was tore-up-from-the-floor-up drunk, stoned, or a combination of the two. Robert prayed he wasn't using anything else.

Dylan finally managed to stand and threw his arms wide, one hand holding the vodka bottle. "Junior!" he slurred as he fumbled and lit a cigarette. "Welcome to my humble abode! *Mi casa es su casa*, except not really. What the hell are you doing here?" The cigarette fell from his shit-eating grin and grazed his bare abdomen. He didn't even flinch.

Silently counting to ten, Robert stamped out the cigarette and shoved his fists in his pockets to keep from punching his brother. Wearing nothing but an old of pair pajama pants, Dylan looked as if he hadn't bathed or shaved since Jennifer left. Wrinkling his nose, Robert waved the air.

"Good God, Dylan. You stink like three-day-old garbage."

"Why thank you, that's one of the nicest things you've ever said to me. Want a drink?" Dylan favored him with a stupid grin as he waved the bottle.

"No, ten thirty in the morning's a little early for me. Are you adding alcoholism to your list of accomplishments?" Robert snapped as he surveyed the wreckage.

"Nah." Dylan scratched his belly. "I rather think I perfected that a long time ago. I'm a lost cause, remember?" He took a swig from the bottle and wiped his mouth with the back of his hand, staring at Robert with glassy, bloodshot eyes.

"What the hell are you doing, Dylan?"

"Nuttin', Rob. What the fuck are you doin'?" Dylan turned and stumbled into the house.

Robert shook his head and followed, gasping when he saw the mess. More empty vodka bottles littered the table next to an overflowing ashtray. The house stunk of liquor and stale smoke. Walking into the kitchen, Robert was mildly disturbed to find there were no dishes in the kitchen sink. He started a pot of coffee and looked in the refrigerator.

"When did you last eat?"

"I dunno." Dylan frowned and swayed. "I think maybe whoever the fuck is on duty brought me a pizza…sometime."

Robert shoved Dylan in a chair, took the vodka out of his hand and handed him a cigarette, deciding it was the lesser of two evils. "What happened, Dylan? Eat something." He placed a glass of water and package of crackers on the table.

Dylan stared, the cigarette burning unattended in his fingers, and shook his head, in a stupor.

"What did you do?" Robert sighed and grabbed the cigarette, stubbing it out in the ashtray before the fool burned himself.

Dylan put his head down on his folded arms on the table and took in a long, ragged breath. "What I always do, Rob. I exist. I fuckin' exist."

"Oh, for God's sake. Stop with the melodramatics. What the hell are you talking about?" Robert grabbed Dylan by the hair and shoved him upright. He poured two cups of black coffee, putting one in Dylan's hand.

"Here, drink it."

Dylan put the cup to his lips but put it down again. Intense pain etched his face, which Robert found disturbing. It was a look he'd seen on dying patients—one of giving up.

"It's all my fault," he whispered.

"What Dylan? What's your fault?" *Dammit, I don't have a degree in psychiatry and never wanted one. I don't have the patience for self-pity.*

"She left. I'm a terrible *pershun*," Dylan slurred, rubbing his red, glassy eyes.

Robert silently counted to three to keep from agreeing with him. "Why do you think that? *What happened?*"

"I kill people."

"Dylan, this isn't making a damn bit of sense, and quite frankly, I don't have the time or the patience for this shit. Now tell me what happened, because I swear I'm at the end of my rope. I'd just as soon beat your ass as listen to your whining."

"I-I must've hurt her."

He kills people? "Hurt her how?" Robert held his breath, waiting for the drunken confession, praying he wouldn't have to have his brother arrested.

Dylan swallowed a few times. "I-I didn't mean to..."

"You didn't hit her or anything, right?"

Dylan jumped up, swaying a bit. "Hit her? You think I'm capable of hitting a woman? Fuck you and the horse you rode in on."

"No, but I'm at a loss as to why she left you."

"I thought we'd worked things out. I mean, I found her here, and we talked. We, you know...I was her first...But next thing I know, she's throwing her shit in her suitcase saying she can't live with a liar." He motioned in an expansive, drunken manner and ran his hands through his hair.

"That doesn't make any sense. What did you say to make her think you're a liar?" Robert began to wonder if he was in some sort of parallel universe.

"Gee, Sherlock, if I knew, this wouldn't have happened. Things were going great. I told her I cared and I wanted our marriage to work!" Dylan rubbed his eyes with the heels of his hands.

"Do you?"

"Do I what?" Dylan blinked.

"Care for her."

"Worse. I'm in love with her." Dylan slumped to the floor, wrapped his arms around his legs, and buried his face in his knees. "But I didn't tell her. I couldn't...I'm sick of people leaving me."

Robert ran his fingers through his hair. *McAthie men don't cry.* His father's voice echoed in his ears, and he shoved the thought away. Their father had been a cold, uncaring bastard. He squatted beside his younger brother and patted him on the back.

"Hey, Dylan, it's okay. You'll get this straightened out, buddy."

"Don't hit me," Dylan mumbled, protecting his head.

Robert winced. The motion was reflexive. More than once he'd intervened when his father beat Dylan.

Robert sat next to his brother. "I'm not Dad." He sighed, exhausted.

"I know. Dad hated me. You tolerate me." Dylan hiccupped, his face still buried in his knees.

"I don't tolerate you. Okay, sometimes I tolerate you. But I love you, Dylan. I've always loved you."

"Don't love me, Rob. I don't deserve it. I kill people."

"Why do you keep saying that?"

"Sara, the baby, Greg, Mama…"

"Your ego is astounding. You really think you're that powerful?" Robert scoffed. "You don't kill people. You've lost a lot of people, but you're not responsible."

"That's not what Dad said."

And there it was. The root of Dylan's problems. Robert hung his head and rubbed his eyes. Their mother had died from complications after childbirth. Their sonofabitch father had always blamed Dylan; he'd been a sick man. And Dylan had suffered for it, more than Robert realized. Dylan needed therapy.

But right now, he needed love. Robert pulled his brother close and held him.

After sleeping for a few hours, Dylan woke with a raging headache. He took the ibuprofen and ate the toast Jen had left on the nightstand. *Not Jen. She's gone, dumbass.* The room spun, and he rolled over, holding the pillow over his eyes. Death would be a welcome relief.

He couldn't remember the last time he'd been on a bender this bad. Even his first night back in Pine Bluff had just been one night of excess. When the room quit spinning, he eased up, wishing he had a hair of the dog. Somehow he doubted Rob would agree to the remedy.

A curse from the kitchen brought Dylan out of his room. Holding his aching head, he found Rob scrubbing the oven. The house was spotless. His brother must've been going at it for some time. Staggering, he threw himself in a kitchen chair. The jackhammer in his head was unrelenting, and his mouth tasted like donkey piss. He groaned.

"Did you find the ibuprofen, water, and toast?"

Dylan nodded into his arms without looking up. "Thank you," he mumbled miserably. "Please tell me you're not cooking eggs."

"Nope, but I sure wish I'd thought about it." His asshole brother chuckled as he washed his hands. Rob gave him another glass of water and sat across from him, propping his legs up on another chair. "I plugged your phone in while you were asleep."

"Why bother? No service here. It's why I like it." He rubbed his eyes with his hands, wishing the pounding in his head would ease. Praying he wouldn't vomit, he tossed back the water.

Rob leaned his head against his fist and asked, "Care to explain the text from Loree Jamison?"

Dylan shrugged. "What text? I haven't checked my phone since I got here. How did you get service? Has she changed the date for the photo shoot? Wait just a goddamn minute—why are you even looking at my phone?"

"I think you need to check it out." Rob shoved his phone at him. "And maybe put a password on it if you're not going to be open with your wife."

"Why?" Frowning, Dylan checked his messages.

"Because I'd be willing to bet I'm not the only one who saw this."

Dylan covered his face with his hands. "Oh shit. What's the date?"

"The twenty-first."

"Fuck, I need a ride to the airport."

"The airport? What about Jennifer?"

"I'm supposed to be at a photo shoot tomorrow. I've got to finish up business in California. I can't let Loree down. I'll take care of Jen when I get back, promise."

Robert stood. "You're an ass. Get your own ride to the airport. You don't deserve Jennifer." He left, slamming the door.

Sadly, Dylan agreed.

Chapter
Twenty-Five

Eight days later, Dylan regretted his decision to help his friend for at least the hundredth time. He didn't have the patience for modeling. *Smile. Don't smile. Turn this way. Turn that way.* It was boring as shit, and he was only doing it because he loved Loree.

"Just a little oil. I don't want him looking like he's in a bodybuilding contest," Loree directed.

"C'mon, Loree, oil? How cheesy is that?" he complained, rolling his eyes.

"Hush, I'm in control here." She peered over the French photographer's shoulder into the camera.

Grayson Deschanelle was not only the best in the business, he was a friend and had been his and Jennifer's wedding photographer.

Dylan scowled. He didn't relish *any* woman being in control, and likely never would after Jen's latest stunt. A female assistant came and rubbed a light coat of oil onto his naked torso, her fingers lingering a bit too long for comfort's sake. Dylan shrugged away from her.

"Wow, she's right. It does make your abs look great." The assistant's voice was laced with promises Dylan had no interest in pursuing.

Laughing at the ludicrousness of the situation, he rolled his eyes again and decided to have fun. Preening, he drawled, "Damn, I do look hot!" He flexed his biceps, licked his finger, touched his abs, and made a sizzling sound. "Do I turn you on, Gray?" he taunted. "How about you, Loree? Do you think I'm sexy?"

Grayson shook his head, replying with his soft accent, "You're not at all my type, Dylan. I have a date with twins tonight. Care to join us?"

"No thanks," Dylan responded immediately.

The photographer shrugged. "Now, can we get started, *s'il vous plait?*"

"What about this scar?" Dylan asked, pointing to the small mark left from the chest tube.

"Air brushing. It will take out the lovely zit on my chin, too. And your bloodshot eyes. Really, Dylan. The heroin chic look is dead," Loree fussed.

She'd given him hell over the condition he'd arrived in and had postponed the shoot for a week. It was costing him a helluva lot of money, but was his own damn fault.

Loree stepped in front of him, positioned his hands, and brushed a strand of hair off his face. "Check the lighting and get the fan ready," she instructed her staff.

"Tape on your nipples? Hell, I've seen them before, Loree." Dylan grinned.

"Oh shush, we're working here. And loosen up. You're too stiff, and I don't mean in a good way. I'll put some music on to help."

The light man called, "Okay, we're ready."

Loree nodded and ducked out of the way.

A small fan blew and music blared as Grayson shouted, "Just a hint of a smile!"

As Right Said Fred declared himself too sexy for his shirt, Dylan held the pose.

"Got it," Grayson yelled.

"Ha ha, very funny! I'm not *that* bad," Dylan grumbled, laughing.

Loree waved aside his complaint. "I'm the creative genius here. Sex sells, baby. I had to get you in the right frame of mind. Would you prefer 'I'm Sexy and I Know It'?"

"Stop!" He laughed so hard the makeup artist ran forward to retouch his face.

Loree walked back on set and unbuttoned his jeans. "Ms. Jamison, are you trying to get in my pants?"

"Been there, done that, never going back. Now, hook your thumbs in your pockets." She ran her fingers through his hair and waited as the lighting was checked.

"Great!" She punched the remote for the music.

Dylan laughed again as Carly Simon's voice rang out. "Stop, you're killing me here—and wasting time, which is money! *My* money since I'm backing this adventure. You know that damn overpriced Grayson Deschanelle doesn't work cheap."

Grayson chuckled and nodded as he began to shoot.

Loree laughed. "Okay, some folks just can't take a joke."

"Last one, Dylan. This time it will be the two of us. You standing behind me, your arm will cover my breasts, and my jeans will be the center of attention. I want you to be whispering in my ear."

Dylan nodded and did as he was told, whispering, "When do we get to eat?"

"Eat? I'm a model; I don't eat," she replied, sucking in her cheeks and laughing.

"The hell you say? You eat like a damn horse."

"Okay, but work first! Now quit messing around. Remember, time is money! We'll go out tonight to celebrate wrapping this up."

Jennifer sat at the McAthies' kitchen table, stirring her coffee for the umpteenth time and grateful Cathy wasn't talking about *the situation*. She was quite enjoying her pity-party. She'd deleted all texts from Dylan without reading them and ignored his repeated phone calls. Swallowing her pride, she'd returned home to her father's I-told-you-so looks and gentle homilies on consequences for poor choices.

The press hounded her daily, wanting a statement. Thankfully, Tyrone had deflected them. He kept assuring her it would die down soon. Unable to afford his services on her nursing salary, she'd tearfully tried to dismiss him. But he remained, steadfast and true—after admitting Dylan still paid his wages. She assumed his job wasn't so much to protect her from the press as to make sure she upheld her non-disclosure agreement.

"Eat, Jennifer. You're much too thin." Cathy sat down with a cup of coffee and pushed a plate of goodies toward her.

Jennifer took a bite of an unwanted pastry to appease her. She didn't have an appetite, and her clothes now hung on her. Robert strolled into the kitchen, his golf bag on his shoulder.

"Morning, Jennifer." He patted the top of her head before leaning over and giving his wife a kiss on the forehead. Jennifer bit her lip and looked away. *Why can't Dylan be more like Robert?*

"I'll be home this afternoon. Jerry and I plan to eat a late lunch at the country club. We're going to try and get nine holes in if one of us doesn't get paged."

"Okay, be careful." Cathy smiled at her husband as he left. Then she turned her attention back to Jennifer.

"You say Dylan's tried to call and text but you haven't answered? Why? He's an ass, but it sounds like he's trying to reach you. And he's still paying Tyrone and depositing money in your account? If you ask me, you should spend every dime and not think twice about it."

Jennifer shrugged. "I have nothing to say to him. I don't know who deposits the money, him or one of his employees. I don't want his money. I never did. I don't even want his car anymore. It's parked in the garage. I can't bear to drive it."

"Jennifer, the fact remains, you're his wife. Robert and I never agreed with this crazy plan, but now that you've gone through with it, you two must communicate or you'll never make it work. I think of you as a younger sister, so I'm going to give you some sisterly advice. You need to talk to him. Perhaps he's coming around and growing up."

Jennifer shook her head. "I think we're too far gone for talking."

Cathy sighed. "Do you love him?"

"I thought I did, but now I don't know." She shrugged. "Maybe you're right. We're going to have to talk at some point. I guess he's not the only one who needs to grow up."

"Mama! Jennifer!" Mary screamed from the den.

They ran to see what was wrong. Jennifer gasped. On the television, looming larger than life, was a photo of Dylan and Loree. Both were bare from the waist up, although Dylan's arm was positioned to cover Loree's breasts. He appeared to be whispering in her ear, and she was smiling.

Cathy and Jennifer sank into the couch as the anchor of the entertainment program said, "It seems all is not well in the McAthie marriage. As you may recall, Dylan McAthie, former lead guitarist for Crucified, Dead and Buried married his private-duty nurse in a lavish wedding after a whirlwind courtship. However, the couple has not been seen together since the wedding. Jennifer Adams McAthie resides with her father in Alabama. Meanwhile, Dylan has been seen around L.A. with model Loree Jamison. Loree's husband, Greg Jamison, former lead singer of Crucified, Dead and Buried died tragically of a drug overdose after the breakup of the band. Prior to his death, rumors of infidelity circulated but were never confirmed. This exclusive video is from the photo shoot for the model's new clothing line, Jamison Jeans. McAthie and Jamison have not commented on their relationship, but their representatives maintain it is merely professional."

The male anchor turned to his co-host and smirked. "I'd like to have a *professional* relationship like *that*."

She nodded. "We'll let the audience decide after seeing this video. Personally, I think the wedding was just a publicity stunt. These two seem awfully *close*."

"It's obviously a setup. I, uh, wouldn't worry about it." Cathy patted her back.

Mesmerized, Jennifer couldn't stop watching Dylan. It felt surreal. He appeared to whisper in Loree's ear. She laughed, covered her breasts, and ducked out of the picture. Dylan stood alone, staring straight into the camera, a hint of a smile on his face. He tossed his hair back and stood with his thumbs locked in the waist of his tight, unbuttoned jeans.

The image faded as the anchor went on to the next story. A tear slipped down her cheek.

Dylan wasn't wearing his wedding ring.

Dylan held the little girl's hand tight, but decided it best to hoist her on to his hip before she got crushed in the crowd. She wrapped her arms around his neck and hid her face from the paparazzi's flashes. He'd worn sunglasses precisely for this reason. They ran the gauntlet and finally made it into the restaurant.

"Okay, baby, you're okay," he murmured into her ear. Meghan peeked at him with a grin, then gave him a resounding kiss on the cheek.

"Yet another female swooning at your feet, Dylan?" Loree sighed as she took Meghan from his arms, buckling her in the booster seat.

He shrugged. "What can I say? She had my heart the first time she wrapped her hand around my finger." He fondly patted his goddaughter's blond curls and tweaked her nose. Meghan gazed at him with naked adoration.

Loree snorted. "You spoil her rotten!" She smiled widely as Jimmy joined them at the table.

"Loree, lovely as always," he murmured, kissing her cheek.

"Thank you. I know," Loree replied with a wink.

"Damn, Loree, was the doorway to this place big enough? It must have been hard to get you and Dylan's inflated egos in here," Jimmy teased.

"I resemble that remark." Dylan laughed.

They ordered their meal and popped champagne to toast Loree's new clothing line.

During the meal, Dylan noticed Jimmy was unusually quiet. When Loree excused herself to go to the ladies room, Dylan asked, "What's up, Jimmy?"

He shrugged. "I've got a lot on my plate right now. The jerk I work for is a problem, and some personal issues."

"Oh really? The jerk you work for has always been a problem, so it must be the personal issues that have you upset. Is it Loree?"

Jimmy turned as red as his hair and skirted the issue. "Have you spoken to Tyrone?"

Dylan knew then he wasn't going to like the turn the conversation was about to take.

"He checks in daily. Why?" He swirled the champagne in his glass.

"Someone at the photo shoot taped some of the session, and it was on one of the trash tabloid TV shows today. They want to know why you and your lovely wife don't reside in the same state, much less the same household. Everyone is buzzing about your relationship with Loree."

Dylan shrugged, refusing to meet Jimmy's eyes. "It isn't any of their damn business. It never has been, never will be."

"Look, I don't know what happened between you and Jennifer, but by staying apart, you're feeding into the media frenzy that always seems to follow you. Go home, Dylan. Go home to your wife. Tyrone says they're hounding the hell out of her, and from what I hear, she isn't handling any of this well. Have you even called her?"

"What goes on between me and my *wife* is our business," Dylan snapped. "Not the press's, and not yours."

Loree returned to the table as dance music started. Meghan clapped her hands and cheered, "Dance, dance!" The tension at the table lightened as Jimmy swept her out of the booster seat and twirled her around the dance floor. Loree smiled, and her face lit up as she watched Jimmy with her daughter.

"He's crazy about you and Meghan," Dylan commented.

Loree nodded and blushed. Dylan smiled, genuinely happy for his two friends.

"Jimmy has really been there for us since Greg died." Tears pooled in her eyes. "We...I mean, I...just want to take things slow."

Dylan smiled as he leaned in and kissed her cheek, speaking into her ear to be heard over the music. "Jimmy's a good man. Believe me, I know it's been tough. But it's okay to move on with your life. It's all good, Loree." She nodded and smiled, then gave Dylan a quick, chaste kiss on the lips.

She laughed and wiped her lipstick off his mouth. "Thank you, Dylan."

"Now, come on and dance with me," Dylan coaxed, pulling Loree to the dance floor. When the song switched to a slow tune, he switched partners with Jimmy.

Meghan laughed. "You're like Prince Charming, Uncle Dylan."

"Nah, I'm the ugly frog..." He frowned, reaching for the memory skirting the back of his brain. He loved his goddaughter, but he dreamed of dancing with a dark-haired girl with violet-blue eyes.

Dylan sat on the porch just off his bedroom, listening to the waves as they hit the shore. He'd bought this house for the view of the ocean, but he was rarely around long enough to enjoy it. The place had never felt like home. He took a draw off his cigarette and rubbed his brow. He'd royally fucked things up with Jennifer and didn't know how to begin to fix them, or if he should try any more. He'd quit calling after a week of her ignoring him. In his heart, he knew this wasn't something that would be solved in a phone call anyway. They needed to sit down together and figure shit out.

Blowing a smoke ring, he gazed at the moon. Dancing with Meghan in his arms had rekindled his longing for a family. Looking through his pictures earlier, he'd realized he no longer thought of Sara with anger, just a deep sense of sadness over a wasted life.

It was his wife who haunted his dreams and every waking moment. It was her picture he stared at when he couldn't sleep. Over and over, he replayed in his mind the twenty-four hours after his wedding night. Her rejection had hurt more than he would've thought possible. And foolishly, he'd put his pride and sense of duty to Loree over his marriage.

Picking up his phone, he gazed at Jennifer's picture again. It was a beautiful candid shot of her holding Robbie's favorite kitten. Curls escaped her ponytail, and her eyes sparkled as she smiled. Sitting with the phone pressed against this forehead, he considered calling her. But fear of rejection won, and he threw the phone down. Instead, he grabbed his keys and did what he always did. He ran.

Jennifer checked her reflection in the rearview mirror and pushed the curls back into her ponytail. She should've covered the circles under her eyes with makeup. *Oh well, it isn't like Daddy hasn't seen me like this. And what's one more unflattering photo for* The National Intruder? Glancing in the rearview mirror, she saw her shadow, Tyrone, pull up behind her in the dream machine. He'd offered to drive, but she'd declined. She should've known he'd follow her.

Stepping out of the car with her purse and the picnic basket, she gave a small wave to the always-patient Tyrone. He nodded. The church was dark and quiet until she rounded the corner toward her father's office. Mrs. Beal, the church secretary, was not at her desk. A piercing, frantic shriek from her father's office made Jennifer's blood run cold. She took off running.

She found Mrs. Baxter screaming and shaking her father, who was slumped over his desk.

Jennifer threw her purse and picnic basket down and went to her father. Her heart slammed in her chest, her mind in shock. Tugging him to the floor, she checked for a pulse and respirations as her training took over.

"Call 9-1-1!" She began chest compressions.

Mrs. Baxter stood frozen, crying and wringing her hands.

"Call 9-1-1 now!" Jennifer ordered as she continued doing CPR, tears streaming down her face.

A sobbing Mrs. Baxter nodded and finally called 9-1-1. She heard the sirens as Tyrone barreled through the door, dropped to his knees, and took over the compressions.

Jennifer collapsed on the floor, exhausted and shaking. The paramedics arrived behind him and quickly took over.

Mrs. Baxter wept, repeating over and over, "I'm so sorry, I'm so sorry."

Tyrone swept up the spilled contents of Jennifer's purse and escorted her to Dylan's car as the ambulance drove off. Her father had never regained consciousness. Shock took over, and she shook uncontrollably.

"Everything's going to be okay, Mrs. McAthie."

"Th-Thank you." She choked on her silent sobs. She was a nurse; she knew things were not good with her father.

Jennifer sat in the waiting area of the emergency room, her face in her hands, rocking. She couldn't cry. She couldn't pray. She couldn't think. She couldn't do anything but sit and wait. Tyrone rubbed her back as he sat beside her.

"Jennifer? Any news?" Cathy rushed in and sank into the chair next to her.

"No, they're still working with him." She sat up and opened her purse to get Cathy a tissue, but pulled out a copy of *The National Intruder* with a puzzled look on her face. "Where did this come from?" she demanded.

Tyrone looked over, and his eyes widened. "I guess I must have picked it up off Pastor Adams's desk when I was gathering your things. I—I'm sorry." He looked away, shaking his head.

Jennifer stared at the cover photo of her husband kissing Loree Jamison. "McAthie Marriage on the Rocks," read the headline. A damn of fury broke, and unmitigated anger fired through every fiber of her being. *Daddy saw this?*

"Dear God." Cathy's mouth dropped. "Don't even read it. Not now. That damn fool."

Robert walked in, motioning them toward a private room. Jennifer's heart sank, and an overwhelming sense of dread snaked through her body. She shook so hard she dropped her purse, and Tyrone retrieved it for her. Grateful for his strength, she held on to him until he guided her to a chair in the consultation room.

"Thank you," she whispered.

Tyrone patted her back before leaving the room, his kind face lined with sadness.

Cathy sat next to her, gripping the arm of the chair. Robert closed the door, stooped down in front of her, and held her hand in his. "I'm sorry, Jennifer." His eyes filled with tears.

Jennifer shook her head. "No, please, no," she whimpered. *He can't be gone. He's all I've got. He's my rock. He's my only family. Please, God, not my daddy.*

"We tried everything. He never responded." Robert's voice was soft, full of compassion. Beside her, Cathy wept.

A roaring filled her ears, and she remained rooted to the chair as her world fell apart once again.

Chapter
Twenty-Six

Dylan cursed as he tried to make some semblance of a knot in his tie, failing miserably. Failure seemed to be his gift of late. Yanking it off, he stuffed it in the pocket of his navy blue sport coat. Irritated, he popped a breath mint in his mouth to hide his cigarette breath. He glanced at his watch.

"Step on it. I'll pay the damn ticket if needed," he instructed the driver.

He rubbed his forehead, regretting the past forty-eight hours. He'd driven up the coast to do some serious soul searching, leaving his phone at home. After spending the night alone on the beach under the stars, he'd come to the painful conclusion that it was time to grow up and face the consequences of his poor choices. He was in love with his wife and didn't want to lose her. It was time to put Jennifer first, if she'd take him back.

It took him four hours to drive back to his home in Corona del Mar. There were more paparazzi swarming the front of his gated mansion than usual, which was annoying as hell. In his customary greeting, he'd flipped them off.

Jimmy's SUV had been parked in the driveway, which wasn't out of the ordinary, but Jimmy threw open the front door as Dylan stepped out of the car, which was.

"Goddammit, Dylan, where the hell have you been, and where is your fuckin' cell phone?"

"Nice to see you, too. I drove up the coast. What's going on? What's with the excessive douchebags hanging by the front gate?"

"You don't know?" Jimmy had shook his head. "Jennifer's father is dead!"

So here he was, late for his father-in-law's viewing because he'd been out of touch — ironically, making the decision to come home to his wife.

Why does this shit always happen to me?

The limousine pulled up in front of the funeral home. Throngs of visitors and paparazzi surged. He put on his prescription sunglasses, even though it was dusk, before stepping out of the limo. Ignoring the reporters' requests for a statement, he made his way into the funeral home, grateful for Tyrone's help in getting through the throng. Disregarding the open-mouthed, shocked stares of visitors, he searched for his wife.

Jennifer stood beside her father's coffin, her hands clasped. She counted the five buttons on her blue dress for at least the fiftieth time. David and the dreadful Mrs. Baxter stood beside her as countless friends and members of the congregation came to speak to her in hushed tones, extending their condolences. Digging her nails in to her hands, she concentrated on not screaming.

Truly, she was going to lose it if one more person commented, "It looks just like Pastor Adams. So peaceful."

A hint of a smile played across her lips at the bizarre thought that popped in her head. She pictured herself running through the funeral home screaming, "*Hey, everybody! Guess what, that dead body doesn't look a thing like my daddy! It looks like a stupid dead body with a tacky pink light shining on it.*" Just watching Mrs. Baxter faint would be worth it.

"Jennifer."

David's whisper and nudge brought her back to the present. Mrs. Beal was recounting, for the sixth time, how much she'd enjoyed working for Pastor Adams. Jennifer patted her parchment-thin hand

and nodded, thanking her. She swayed, feeling dizzy. David took her by the elbow, making excuses to the people waiting to see her.

"Give us a moment. She needs to sit down," he told them as he guided her away from the mourners.

In a trance-like state, Jennifer followed David into a small private room. He pulled her into his arms and held her tight. "You're okay."

Why do people say that? I'm not okay. My father is dead. But David meant well, and having him here for support did help. Jennifer nodded and closed her eyes.

"Why are your hands always on *my* wife?"

Startled by the sound of Dylan's voice, Jennifer pulled away from David. Her husband stood leaning in the doorway. His silver-blue eyes looked as lethal as his voice sounded. Holding his sport coat over his shoulder, he appeared tan and fit in his crisp white shirt and tailored gray pants. His sunglasses were perched on his head.

Of course he looks well; he's been in California, probably tanning naked with Loree Jamison and doing God knows what else.

David kept one arm draped around her shoulder. "Because *you* are never here for her." His voice dripped with loathing.

Dylan pushed away from the door, tossing his jacket on the chair. "I'm here now; you can leave."

"That's up to Jennifer." David's voice was low, but firm.

It was like being at a ping-pong game, and she was the battered ball. The picture of Dylan kissing Loree flashed unpleasantly in her mind.

"I'm not doing this now. I'm leaving," she announced.

The last thing she wanted to do was deal with Dylan here. Her father was likely dead because of him and his indiscretions. She had nothing to say. Jennifer pressed David's hand gratefully and headed out the door. Dylan grabbed her arm.

"Jen?"

She shrugged out of his grasp without looking at him, squared her shoulders, and strode into the foyer packed with people paying their respects. The size of the crowd took her aback and made it difficult to walk. Jennifer stopped as an older man grabbed her hand to extend his sympathy. She nodded, keeping a thin smile on her lips, and not hearing a word he said, as she wished she was a hundred miles away. A warm, familiar hand came to rest on her lower back. Jennifer turned and faced her spouse, shaking with anger.

"Don't touch me," she warned, for his ears only. She wanted to beat him with her fists and make him hurt as much as he had hurt her. At the same time, she longed to melt in his arms and beg him to help her. Furious with herself, she shrugged away from him. How could she betray her father's memory like this?

Again, Dylan grabbed her arm, turning her to face him. "Jennifer—" Without thinking, she slapped him so hard his head reeled back. The room went silent as all eyes turned toward them.

"What was that for?" he asked, his eyes wide as he rubbed the red handprint on his cheek.

"You know perfectly well what that was for," she hissed, attempting to free herself from his grasp.

Dylan pulled her close, speaking low in her ear, "Calm down. You're making a scene. Get a grip, angel. We'll talk later; not *here*, okay?"

Jennifer shoved him away so hard her hair fell loose. Her chest heaved with her angry breaths. "I'm making a scene? You show up at my father's funeral from God knows where, and you dare to say *I'm* making a scene? *Go to hell, Dylan!*"

Dylan's eyes darted around the silent room, and Jennifer finally became aware of the curious stares. She lifted her chin and silently dared anyone to say anything. Without another word, she returned to her father's coffin.

Mrs. Baxter followed close on her heels. "*Oh, my!* I know it isn't right to condone divorce, but in this case, I don't know anyone in this church who would find fault with you, my dear. Have you read the things they say about him? I was going to show your dear father that *horrible* picture on the cover of *The National Intruder*, but I never got the chance. I found the poor man slumped over his desk.

"You're young and impressionable, and I'm sure that dreadful man swept you off your feet, but, Jennifer, he is *not* husband material. Now, take that nice David Patterson. We all assumed you two would marry, even if he is a Methodist…" Her voice droned on as Jennifer sank into a wingback chair, feeling sick. *Daddy never saw the article?* Covering her face with her hands, she rocked, confused and drained.

"Come with me. I'm going to take you home. Excuse us."

Jennifer looked up into the kind face of Mrs. Jordan and gave an almost imperceptible nod as the shock of the past few days numbed her reactions. She followed her in slow motion out to the car, thanking Tyrone as he closed the door behind her. Shutting her eyes, she prayed for the day to end.

Back at her father's home, Tyrone helped her from the car, despite her weak protests.

"You go get some rest, Mrs. McAthie," he told her. "Mrs. Jordan is getting you some tea. I'll be outside, and I'll make sure no one disturbs you."

Jennifer squeezed his hand. "Please, call me Jennifer. You're a good friend. Thank you for everything you've done for me and Daddy…" Her voice trailed off as she controlled her emotions. She was afraid if she ever started crying, she'd never stop.

"Aw, don't mention it. I'd do anything for you." He gave her hand a pat and left.

She wandered down the hall to her father's study. Frazzled and exhausted, she sank into his oversized leather desk chair and closed her eyes. In this room, she could still smell her father's aftershave and almost believe this was all just a horrible nightmare.

Laying her head on her father's well-worn Bible, she tried to pray, but couldn't find the words, her heart too heavy with grief. The door to the study opened, and she heard the clink of the china teacup on the desk.

"Thank you, Mrs. Jordan. I think I'd just like to be alone now," she said without opening her eyes. She felt a comforting hand brush the back of her hair.

"That's the last thing you need right now."

"Dylan." Jennifer sat up, burying her face in her hands. "What are you doing here? Where's Mrs. Jordan? Please, just go away and leave me alone."

"Mrs. J went back to Rob and Cat's. It's just you and me." He knelt beside her chair. "I'm truly sorry about your dad. I got here as fast as I could. I was out of town…but I'm here for you now. What can I do to help?" His voice was soft and soothing.

She wanted his arms around her, but her distrust overrode all other feelings.

Jennifer leaned back in her father's chair, crossing her arms. "The only thing I want from you is a divorce."

Dylan shook his head, his gaze never wavering from hers. "No."

"What?" She sprang to her feet.

Dylan stood. "No. No divorce."

"Why? Afraid the bad publicity might ruin your relationship with Loree Jamison?" she spat, shoving her hair behind her ear.

"What? No." Dylan drew his brows together. "Tonight isn't the time to discuss our marriage. You're in no condition to make any major decisions. You need to eat something, get a bath, go to bed, and have a good cry."

"Don't you *dare* tell me what I need—" her voice lowered and cracked "—You're not my father. You're not even close to being like my father. Daddy was a good man, an honest man, a *moral* man…" She looked down and rubbed a hand over her father's Bible, holding back the tears. She took a deep breath, pulling in the last ounce of strength she had in reserve. "On one thing we can agree: I can't do this right now. I'm too tired to argue with you. I'm going to bed."

"Good girl." Dylan nodded and stepped aside to let her pass by him.

"Stop being a condescending ass, Dylan. Where will you be?"

A hint of a smile played at the corner of his mouth. "According to my wife, in hell."

An hour later, Dylan knocked, but there was no answer. Opening the door, he peeked in and found Jennifer in her robe, slumped over her dressing table. She'd buried her face in her arms, her wet hair hanging down her back.

"Jennifer?"

"Go away."

Picking up her brush, he began untangling her hair. He was pleasantly surprised when she didn't protest. He frowned as his hand brushed against her backbone. She was much too thin.

"You should eat something. Rob's got a mild sedative for you if you need it."

"No, thank you," she whispered.

Dylan put the brush down and turned back the covers on her bed. Her room looked exactly the way he'd pictured it: pale blue walls, white crown molding, furnished with antiques, and neat as a pin. He was kind of glad he'd left his tie downstairs in his coat pocket when he saw the four-poster mahogany bed.

"Bedtime." He grasped her hand, pulling her up and slipping off her robe. Wearing a long, thin, white cotton gown, she looked like a broken angel with her riot of damp curls and bare feet. She moved as if in a stupor and didn't protest as he tucked her in bed, placing a chaste kiss on her forehead.

Jennifer sniffed and wrinkled her nose at the acrid smell of smoke. Dylan sat in her window seat, the ember of his cigarette burning bright in the dark room. Her dreams mixed with reality.

"You're going to die from those one of these days," she murmured with a yawn. For some odd reason, it comforted her having him here. At the sound of her voice, he jumped, and she snickered.

"Shit, you scared me!" Dylan stubbed the cigarette out and slid the window shut. He sat on the bed beside her and brushed the hair out of her face. "You need anything?"

"I don't know." She caught his hand in hers. "Why are you here?" Stroking his hand with her thumb, she paused when she discovered his wedding band.

"Go back to sleep, baby," he coaxed, kissing her cheek. "Want me to sing to you?"

"You have on your wedding band?" She almost forgot she was mad at him. "Were you saying goodnight to the moon?" she whispered.

"Of course I'm wearing my wedding band. What did you say about the moon?"

Too weary to respond, but not wanting to be alone, Jennifer shook her head and rolled over, still holding his hand. The bed dipped, but he remained on top of the covers and spooned her back.

Softly, he sang the old lullaby, "I See the Moon."

With her thumb, she rubbed his wedding band, and her eyes drifted shut.

Chapter
Twenty-Seven

"Dylan." Jennifer nudged him.

"Hmmm?"

"I can't move."

"Payback's a bitch." Not fully awake, he shifted, pinning her even more. A soft snore escaped his parted lips.

Jennifer rolled her eyes in exasperation. Dylan lay on top of the covers with an arm and a leg thrown over her, trapping her in a cocoon. He'd snored for the last hour, and she needed to use the bathroom. She pushed hard against him, loosening the cover and falling out of bed in the process. The loud *thud* finally woke Dylan.

"Whatcha doin' down there?" he asked with a sleepy grin.

Jennifer glowered. "You seem to have a talent for sneaking into my bed."

"Hmm, you never seem to remember, either. One of us has a problem."

She stormed into the bathroom, slamming the door shut and locking it. She hid until she heard him tromp downstairs.

After a quick shower, she threw on a pair of jeans and a T-shirt, yanking her hair into a ponytail. She slipped on her glasses and steeled herself to confront Dylan.

He stood in the kitchen's open backdoor, stretching and yawning. The muscles of his broad, tan shoulders and contoured back rippled. His worn, torn jeans fit snugly on his lean hips and long legs. He took a draw off his cigarette and ran his other hand through his bed-rumpled hair. No matter her feelings toward him personally, he was a perfect physical example of the male species. Jennifer stared at him with quiet appreciation as a woman, not an angry wife.

Why does he always have this effect on me—even when I'm so mad I could spit nails? No man has a right to be this attractive, especially when he's just rolled out of bed.

When he realized she was behind him, Dylan jumped and cast a guilty look at the cigarette before throwing it out and closing the kitchen door.

"Go put some clothes on, Dylan." Jennifer poured a cup of coffee. The sight of his mouth-watering muscles was not helping her warring emotions.

Dylan looked down and back at her, his brows knitting together. "I'm dressed." He scratched his bare stomach, yawned, and stretched again. "I've been dressed. I even slept dressed."

"I meant go put a shirt on," she retorted as she over-sugared her coffee, trying to ignore him.

"What's for breakfast?"

"Breakfast? I no longer work for you, and I'm not preparing your breakfast like I'm your little wife."

"Uh, well, if you want to argue about it, technically you never did work for *me*, and legally you *are* still my little wife." Smirking, he poured himself a cup of coffee. "I merely meant you need to eat. You're too thin, baby."

"I'm not your baby, and my weight is of no concern to you. Besides, you seem to have a thing for model-thin women. And don't get me started on babies." Jennifer wearily sank into a chair and removed her glasses, rubbing her eyes. "I can't do this."

Dylan kissed the top of her head before sitting beside her, his face serious. "Then don't. Just get through today. We have plenty of time for us."

Jennifer looked at him pointedly and blew out an exasperated breath. "There is no *us*, Dylan. I'm begging you; just end this farce of a marriage. Daddy's gone. I don't care about the photos anymore."

She took a sip of her coffee. "Look, you're a rich musician god with millions of adoring fans. You've traveled the world, seen more and done more than I can even imagine with your glamorous lifestyle. Until I met you, I'd never been outside of Alabama. I'm nobody, just a preacher's kid struggling to pay off my student loan and car."

Bitterness laced her next words. "Look at us—we don't even look like we belong together. You're devastatingly handsome, and I'm just plain old me. I don't belong in your world, and I can't compete. I'm no model—" Jennifer paused as she noticed Dylan's mouth curved into his mega-watt, lopsided grin. "What's so funny?"

"*You* are. You don't really know anything about me, do you?"

"I-I, well…" she stammered, confused by his laughter.

"Let me tell you about my glamorous life. I've been so damn broke I picked up an apple core off the street and ate it. I've been homeless. You think I just flit around playing guitar without a care in the world? Do you know how difficult it is to make it in this industry? And how hard we struggled to not be one-hit wonders? When we toured, we were gone eight to ten months a year. Traveling like that is grueling. It's a job and a lot of hard work.

"We didn't sightsee; the only thing we saw was the inside of a damn bus, or an airplane, a hotel room, and the arena where we played. The days were long and tiring, sometimes sixteen to eighteen hours. I admit we used to let off steam and party too much—mainly because we were so fuckin' tired and bored. You can't stop once you've made it either, or the fans will move on to the next new act. I've performed with the flu and a temp so high I was dizzy with dehydration. We performed when we weren't even speaking to each other, when we hated each other's guts. It didn't matter, because *the show must go on*. You can't disappoint the fans."

Dylan leaned his head into his hand, covering his eyes, and sighed. "I don't even know if I have a career to go back to because I've been out of circulation so damn long. My home in Corona del Mar? It doesn't even feel like home. Stuff is still packed in boxes. People whose names I don't know live there, either working for me or sponging off me.

"As for models? I don't care for them—too damn skinny and too much ego. It doesn't leave any room for mine." He flashed a self-deprecating smile and winked.

"Oh, really?" Her voice dripped with sarcasm.

Dylan paused, took a sip of his coffee, and held her gaze with his own. "You've been skirting an issue ever since I arrived. Instead of this passive-aggressive shit, just lay your cards on the damn table."

Passive-aggressive shit? Jennifer stalked to the kitchen counter and rummaged in her purse, pulling out *The National Intruder* Tyrone had found on her father's desk. In frustration, she took the paper and hit Dylan with it before throwing it on the table. She stood with her hands on her hips and waited for an explanation.

Glancing at the tabloid trash, he stood and faced Jennifer. His eyes narrowed, glittering with silver shards. Fury stamped his face. She backed up a step.

"I'm not going to tell you this again. Don't *ever* raise a hand in anger to me. I have never been physical with you, and I expect the same respect. As for this crap—" He motioned furiously at the tabloid and pointed his index finger at her. "I would think *you* of all people should know not to believe this sensationalist *bullshit.*"

Stamping her foot in frustration, she shouted, "I don't care what the stupid magazine says. I saw the text message. Not to mention the pictures and video of you and Loree plastered all over social media and television. I guess your 'job' explains why you and a half-naked, gorgeous model are all over each other. But please tell me, why were you two photographed at a restaurant kissing? And when were you going to mention you had a daughter?" She looked away, not wanting him to see how hurt she was. "You told me you wanted our relationship to work, but you have this whole other life. One I'm not part of, nor do I want to be. Call me a spoiled only child. *I don't share!*"

"A daughter?" Dylan cocked his head to the side, rubbing the back of his neck. This wasn't going at all like he'd planned. She refused to look at him.

"I saw the pictures and videos on your phone," Jennifer spat, refusing to look at him. She crossed her arms and stared out the window.

He pulled his phone out and began scrolling through his pictures. Understanding dawned and he hesitated, weighing his words. She was an emotional wreck, he didn't want to make things worse than they already were.

"Please sit down, and let's talk things over like reasonable adults." *What the fuck? Did that just come out of my mouth? I sound like Rob. Crap, I'm getting old.* He sat and pulled her into his lap. She tried to hop off, but he wrapped his arms around her.

"No. You're not running away again until we talk. Don't make me get my tie out," he threatened with a grin. She stopped struggling.

"I wish you'd look at me, but at least hear me out. I'm a dick. I've handled everything wrong from the very beginning. Loree is my friend and business partner. Her daughter, Meghan, is my goddaughter. I know I've mentioned her before. I'm like an uncle to that baby." He scrolled through the pictures and showed them to her.

"Look, this is Meghan the day she was born. I'd never held a baby before. She was so tiny! And here she had colic. She'd cried for hours until I sang her to sleep. I laughed and told Greg I was gonna take over as lead singer."

He chuckled. "Oh, and that's her second birthday party. I bought her a rabbit and the damn thing got loose in the house. Seventeen toddlers and a scared rabbit. It was chaos. Loree has forbidden me from buying anything else that breathes. She has a third birthday coming up. Hmm, do fish breathe?"

He thumbed through more and sighed. "And this video? She wasn't crying over *me*. She was crying for Greg. It's been tough on her, losing her dad. He had his problems, and he turned into a real bastard—addiction does that to a person. But he was a good dad."

He put the phone down and rubbed her back.

"Jimmy and I have both stepped up to be positive male influences in Meghan's life. I'm also backing Jamison Jeans financially, and to save money, we decided to do the modeling for this first round of publicity shots for her new campaign. There isn't anything inappropriate going on between me and Loree."

Jennifer sat glaring, her arms crossed. "I saw the photo of you two in bed on your phone," she snapped.

"I'm sorry. Did you happen to notice how youthful I looked? Those are old photos. Loree was my first girlfriend when I moved to California. Truthfully, I got with her because she reminded me of Cat, who at the time was my unrequited love. Or as much love as a selfish, seventeen-year-old can have. Loree and I lasted a month, remained friends, and I introduced her to Greg. Do I have a past?

Yes. Do you want a cataloged inventory of every woman I've ever been with? I could try, but it wouldn't mean anything. None of them meant anything, except Sara."

"But…the photo of you and Loree kissing. And you didn't have on your wedding ring in the photo shoot." Jennifer's brows knit together as she twirled her own wedding band.

"You're right, I took my wedding band off for the photo shoot, but it was in my pocket and went back on after we were done. It's an advertising thing. As for the photo on the cover of *The National Intruder,* Loree had just confirmed my suspicions that she and Jimmy are exploring their feelings for one another and getting close. I didn't think anything of it. It was a peck. That's it. She's an old friend. We were out celebrating, wrapping up the campaign for Jamison Jeans. Jimmy was there, too."

"Did she have to be half-naked in the other photos?"

"It's an ad campaign. As she told me, 'Sex sells, baby.' It isn't the first time I've seen her topless. Hell, she's a model; everyone's seen her practically naked. Sara and I vacationed a few summers ago with Greg and Loree in St. Tropez. Most of the women were topless, so nudity is no big deal to her."

"It's a big deal to *me,*" she fumed.

"I know it is." He stroked her hair and kissed her forehead. "We're going to talk and get all of this straightened out. I want you to understand everything, and I have a helluva lot more to say. But not now. Not when you're dealing with more important things. It can wait. But know this: I'm not leaving, ever again."

She sighed and squirmed. "You're right, I guess. I don't know; I'm too tired to think."

"Jennifer." His voice was low and raspy. He loved her pouty lower lip and wanted to suck on it.

"Y-Yes?"

"Don't squirm unless you want me to make a pass at you in those sexy glasses."

Jennifer scrambled out of his lap and stared down at him, hands on her hips. "Is that all you think about?"

Dylan looked up at her wryly. "I'm like a man dying of hunger with an all-you-can-eat buffet in front of me. What do you think?" He stood and opened the refrigerator. "I'm joking. Relax."

"What are you doing?"

"I'm interrupting my apology to make breakfast. We can talk more about this later. Since you refuse to cook, I will. You need to eat. You have a long day ahead of you."

Her demeanor crumpled, and she blinked back tears. Dylan picked her up, placing her on the counter next to the stove. Stroking her cheek, he kissed her forehead. "You supervise. It's been a long time since I've done this. How do you want your eggs, boss?"

Jennifer gave him a small smile. "Runny with super-greasy, undercooked bacon, please."

Dylan grinned, shaking his head, relieved to see a bit of humor. "I believe that would be the Mrs. J Special. Scrambled it is, with toast, no bacon. But I bet you have a tater tot casserole squirreled away in your refrigerator from some nice church lady." He grinned when she groaned, wrinkling her nose.

He quickly whipped up some breakfast and handed Jen her plate, leaving her sitting on the counter. Standing next to her as he ate, he watched her shove the food around the plate, never taking a bite.

"Eat, baby." He kept his voice soft, but firm.

"I can't," she confessed. "I can't swallow…This lump in my throat… I just can't. I don't know what to do. I just…" She put the plate down and hopped off the counter.

Dylan pulled her close, holding her tight. His fingers played with the curls of her ponytail. "I understand. You're hurting. You're going to hurt for some time. It's like a hole in your heart, but it will get smaller eventually." She kept her eyes downcast, her dark lashes in stark contrast to her pale cheeks.

"Thank you for not saying everything is going to be okay. I'm sick of hearing that. I just want to be alone for a bit. Please?"

"I don't want to leave you alone, but I understand." He remembered needing time to process his own grief. "I'm going to go see Cat and Rob. I'll be back soon."

Jennifer nodded, looking lost and despondent. Dylan patted her cheek, dreading the moment when she'd realize he was all she had left.

He hoped he'd be enough.

Chapter
Twenty-Eight

Jennifer tried for the fifth time to fasten her mother's pearls, unable to stop her fingers from trembling. Flinging the necklace down on her dressing table, she covered her face with her hands. *I can't do this.*

She'd tried to rest, but her mind worked overtime, mulling over everything Dylan had said. And everything he hadn't. Like *I love you.* Her father's funeral was in an hour, and she was thinking about the man who had abandoned her. *No, you left him*, her conscience chided.

Dylan said he had explanations. But would they be enough to make this a real marriage? Her father hadn't liked Dylan, but he hadn't had a chance to get to know him…And he'd brought her up to not be a quitter. And to forgive.

Her thoughts were interrupted by a knock on the door.

"Come in."

"Are you ready?"

Jennifer looked in the mirror and spun around in her seat. "What have you done?"

Blushing, Dylan ran a hand through his short hair, causing a lock to fall over his forehead, giving him a rakish look. "I, well, your father never liked…" He shrugged. His tie was loose around his crisp, white shirt, and he stuffed his hands in the pockets of tailored black pants, looking at the floor. After a moment, he peered at her over the rim of his glasses.

"*You cut your hair.*" She voiced the obvious, astonished. Not that it was a bad shock—quite the opposite. His new look was one of casual elegance; he could easily play James Bond. "You look wonderful," she said with a soft smile.

Dylan grinned and shoved his glasses up his nose. "Do we look like we go together now?"

Jennifer nodded as she stared at their reflection in the mirror. She wore her hair in a simple chignon with a few wispy curls around her face. Her black dress was a bit too big due to her recent weight loss, but there had been no time to shop for a new one. No amount of makeup would cover the circles under her eyes, so she wore very little. But, yes, they did look like they belonged together. She found the thought both unsettling and strangely encouraging.

Picking up the pearls, she tried again to fasten them. Dylan took them from her shaking hands and fastened them for her. It was a mere brush of his fingers that flickered across her neck, but it sent a jolt of electricity into the pit of her stomach. Her gaze held Dylan's in the mirror. A slight hint of a seductive smile crossed his lips before he backed away. Her cheeks flushed.

Dylan motioned to his tie. "Please?"

"I used to do this for Daddy." She tied his tie and straightened his collar. *He still smells like sex and sin.* Quickly putting a safe distance between them, she slipped into her black pumps.

"Do you have a hat?" Dylan asked, peering out the window.

"No, of course not. Daddy didn't like affectation at funerals. He said it showed poor taste." She patted her hair again and ran a sheer pink gloss over her lips.

"Um, well, wear your sunglasses." He picked up her old stuffed rabbit and smiled before placing him on her bookshelf.

Sunglasses? The weather forecast was for rain: perfect to match her mood. She peered out the window. Seeing the paparazzi waiting at the end of her driveway, her shoulders slumped in despair.

"Why? Why can't they leave us alone?"

Dylan shrugged apologetically. "Because you're my wife."

Jennifer and Dylan made their way from the gravesite to the limousine. The associate pastor's message and David's eulogy had been moving and memorable, or so people were saying. She hadn't paid attention. She'd been too afraid her emotions would overwhelm and consume her. Maintaining dignity for her father's sake was her utmost priority. David walked on her left side, speaking to her in a reassuring tone. Again, she didn't dare to truly listen as she struggled to keep her feelings in check.

To her right was her husband, who had surprised her at the end of the service with a beautiful *a capella* rendition of her father's favorite hymn, "Amazing Grace." She'd been surprised he knew all the words. Dylan was silent now, but the tension between him and David was palpable as he lit a cigarette, snapping the lighter closed. She tucked her arm in Dylan's, aware the paparazzi were watching.

She leaned in and whispered, "Please take me home." Dylan nodded and hugged her shoulders as he guided her to the waiting limousine, ignoring the cameras and shouting.

Dylan resisted the urge to flip off both the cameramen and David Patterson and helped Jennifer into the limousine. Once in the limo, he unknotted his tie, unbuttoned his collar, and popped a breath mint in his mouth. He offered one to Jennifer who declined. He was thankful the windows were tinted as the paparazzi continued to take pictures. David crossed his arms and glared as they pulled away. It was the highlight of Dylan's day.

"I wish we didn't have to face any more people," Jennifer whispered as she removed her sunglasses and closed her eyes. "If one more person tells me Daddy looked like he was sleeping, I'm going to go postal."

"We can go home, if you'd like."

Jennifer looked at him, her eyes weary. "I thought that's where we were going, home." She rubbed her brow and sighed. "I guess it won't be my home much longer. The church owns it."

"We have a home in Pine Bluff. We can go and get away from everything. Just tell me, and I'll have the limo take us straight there. Or I can take you to California. Anywhere you want to go, I'll make it happen."

"I have responsibilities here, Dylan. My father's church expects me to be there this afternoon, and I have a job to go back to next week. It's okay; we can stop pretending this is a real marriage. Just have Jimmy draw up the divorce papers, and I'll sign. I don't want anything, not even your car. I'll find someplace to live. I can make it alone—I mean, on my own…"

The limousine pulled into her driveway. She buried her face in his shoulder. "Please tell me there are no cameras."

Dylan peered out of the window and gave her a kiss on top of her head. "No, thank God. You're not alone. You have me, and I'm not going anywhere. Look, we're not talking about our marriage now. Your only job right now is to get through this day. And I'm here to help. Afterward, we'll go away."

"I don't know."

"Look, I'll even book a suite with separate bedrooms. You know the ladies auxiliary is going to be all over you like mother hens. You're not going to get a moment of peace and quiet…"

Proving his point, Mrs. Baxter and Mrs. Beal met Jennifer at the car. Jerking the door open, they walked her into the house, leaving Dylan standing alone in the driveway. He shook his head in defeat. Those two old buzzards were scarier than the damn paparazzi and the nuns from parochial school. He bummed another cigarette from Tyrone—who didn't smoke, but kept them knowing he couldn't quit—and tousled Robbie's hair as the rest of his family and Mrs. Jordan walked across the yard from Rob and Cat's.

"How's Jennifer holding up?" Rob asked. He snatched the cigarette out of his mouth, stepped on it, and offered him a lousy piece of gum.

Dylan rolled his eyes and accepted the gum. "Fine. Just dandy. She buried her father today. How the hell do you think she is?" His irritation increased when David Patterson pulled into the driveway. He shoved the gum in his mouth.

"Now, boys, this isn't the place to fuss," Mrs. Jordan admonished with a look that said she wasn't above administering punishment if needed.

Dylan shoved his clenched fists in his pockets, fuming as David walked into Jennifer's house.

"Jealous?" Cat whispered with a smug smile. Dylan scowled and stormed after David, ignoring the knowing laughs of his family.

He found Jennifer in the living room talking to the two old bats. The expression on her face resembled the pictures of martyred saints the nuns used to hand out in grammar school.

"It was a beautiful service, and your dear father looked so peaceful. It looked like he was sleeping," Mrs. Baxter said, patting Jennifer's hand.

Dylan saw Jennifer's eyes narrow and her lips tighten into a thin line.

Throwing an arm around her shoulder, he faced the old harpies. "I totally disagree. I didn't think it looked like your dad at all." Pausing, he looked down at his startled bride. "Any time *I* ever saw your old man, he had steam coming out of his ears!" Giving her a mischievous wink and a kiss on the forehead, he left the room.

Jennifer bit her lip to keep from laughing while Mrs. Baxter's three chins quivered with outrage. Mrs. Beal slipped away.

"Jennifer Adams, I don't know what you see in that young man. I would have given him a piece of my mind, but I didn't want to look a gift horse in the mouth!" She sputtered with righteous indignation. "I'm on the building committee, and the more-than-generous donation he made in your father's name for the new soup kitchen was a blessing, but it does not excuse poor manners. I never…"

Speechless, Jennifer watched the old biddy hurry out of the room on her way to spread gossip. It was her mission in life, after all. She turned when she felt a gentle hand on her shoulder and found David standing there, his face full of concern.

"How are you?" He kissed her cheek and drew her in for a hug.

"I'm surviving. Thank you for being here and for your help with the service. It was perfect. You've always been my anchor." She accepted his familiar, friendly hug.

"It's time to pull anchor and set sail." Dylan's voice was soft, but dangerous, and his words gave pause to conversations around them.

Jennifer pulled away from David and wearily looked at her angry husband. *Not again.* This was the last straw. Dylan glared at David. David glared at Dylan. She'd had enough. She turned to Tyrone. "Please have everyone leave. I'm done."

Tyrone nodded and efficiently cleared the house. Jennifer pressed her hands to her eyes, wishing she could magically disappear, too.

Jennifer had refused see Dylan the afternoon of the funeral, claiming she needed time alone. He'd promptly relied on his old coping skill, alcohol. That was his first mistake. Uber and taxi services didn't give a rat's ass that he was Dylan McAthie when he didn't have his credit card and ran out of cash. He'd called his brother when the bouncer threatened to have him arrested if he didn't leave. That was his second mistake. Rob tried to take him straight to rehab. He refused. That was his third mistake. Now he was going to have to face Cat's wrath. He just prayed Mrs. J wasn't going to be there too.

Nauseated, Dylan kept one arm over his eyes and wondered if Rob was driving at a snail's pace on purpose. Without a doubt, the dickhead was intentionally hitting every bump in the road. His head pounded in time with the blaring bass. The bastard could at least have the decency to not play heavy metal. *Please, God, get me out of this car and I'll never drink again…for at least a month.*

"If you puke in my car, you'll buy me a new one. I don't appreciate being hauled out of bed at six in the morning on my one damn day off!"

Dylan flipped Rob off and concentrated on not puking. The damn asshole would probably soak him for a Lamborghini. Rob pulled into the garage and slammed his car door, more than likely a passive-aggressive payback for the obscene gesture.

Walking into the kitchen, Dylan's stomach revolted at the smell of eggs, and he dashed for the bathroom.

Okay, I promise I won't drink for two months.

Feeling wretched, he looked up and found Robbie watching him with the same intense blue eyes as his father. Great, a fuckin' audience. He flushed the toilet.

"Gross." Robbie's nose wrinkled.

"Let it be a lesson, kid. Don't ever drink." Dylan stood and washed his hands and face. He muttered his thanks when Robbie handed him a new toothbrush and toothpaste.

"Daddy says you're a dumbass," Robbie stated matter-of-factly.

"He might be right," Dylan admitted.

"Mama says you're just stupid and need to grow up. And Grandma says you're gonna turn out to be a no-good drunk like Leroy Tyler if you don't get your act together."

Dylan put a hand on his hip and looked down at his nephew, not hiding his annoyance. "Any other words of wisdom or observations you'd care to impart?"

Robbie nodded, warming to his subject. "I think you need to go next door. I saw Jennifer crying when she took out the garbage last night. Daddy says she looks like S-H-I-T."

"Your father should be fuckin' ashamed using language like that," Dylan muttered, shooing him out the door so he could shower.

After a four-hour nap, Dylan slowly made his way to Jen's front door, trying his damnedest not to jar his aching head.

"What are you doing here?" David marched up the lawn, looking not at all like a Sunday school teacher.

Fuck. "Look, Deacon, I'm not leaving. You can't make me leave. She's *my* wife. This isn't any of your damn business, so just shut up and go back to your Bible study." Faking bravado, Dylan leaned against Jennifer's front door, giving David an arrogant smirk, hoping like hell he could bluff him. He wasn't a fool; he knew David could, and would, beat the shit out of him if push came to shove.

Part of him felt sorry for the guy. It was obvious he loved Jennifer. But it didn't negate the fact that David's concern for Jennifer pissed him off to no end. The door swung open, and he fell on his ass at her feet. He could only imagine the headline. *Aged musician Dylan McAthie breaks hip.*

Seeing his opportunity, he scooted on his aching butt into the house and looked up at Jennifer with a pained smile. "See? I'm falling at your feet, begging for mercy."

Behind Jennifer, Tyrone hid his grin behind his hand.

Dylan glared. *Just who the hell still pays his salary? Traitor.*

"Oh, for heaven's sake, get up off the floor, Dylan." Jennifer rolled her eyes and sighed. Turning to David and Tyrone, she ordered, "I've got this handled. You two can leave."

Neither moved until her mouth narrowed into a thin line. Dylan watched with fascination as the two men cowed to her command.

Damn, she's feisty.

She shut the door and turned to face him.

"Give me a hand, angel?" Dylan held his hand out with a hopeful grin.

Jennifer clapped slowly for a few seconds before stepping over him and retreating to her father's study. Dylan struggled to his feet, cursing under his breath. He found her sitting in her father's chair, her arms crossed and not speaking.

Dylan slumped in the chair opposite the desk. "This is the thing, Jennifer. I'm not leaving, and you're not leaving, until we talk."

"I'm sick and tired of you making all the decisions." She jumped up and slammed her hands on the desk. The sound reverberated in the silent room, and a picture of her as a young child with her parents toppled. With a shaking hand, she righted it, rubbing her index finger over the glass with a sad sigh.

Shit, she's so damn fragile. And again, he was fucking things up. Easing around the desk, he leaned against it and faced her. She wrinkled her nose.

"You've been drinking and smoking."

"Yes."

"Is this a problem? Alcohol?"

"It's proven to be a poor coping mechanism, that's for damn sure. I have an appointment next week with a therapist. I'm a fucked-up bastard, but I'm willing to work hard and change. For me. For you. For us. I'll even become a teetotaler if necessary. How are you holding up?"

She shrugged.

He stroked her hair. "I wish there was something I could do. I'd do anything to lessen this pain. Anything."

He eyed her for a moment and took a deep breath. "I want to come clean and tell you everything." He sighed. "I don't talk about shit. I never have. It's why therapy has never worked for me. But

I want us to work. So here it goes—no more secrets. The tabloid rumors about Loree cheating on Greg with me are so far from the truth it isn't even funny. But Loree and I made a pact: our personal lives would remain personal. We never talk to the media about that stuff. Ever.

"The fact is, Greg cheated on her. With Sara. To be honest, I don't even know whose baby Sara was carrying. But damn how I wanted him. It was a boy…"

"Oh my God. I'm so sorry." Tears glimmered in Jennifer's eyes, and she wrapped her arms around him and tucked her head under his chin.

"Loree and I have a history. I'm not denying that. But like I told you, it hasn't been anything but friendship for more than twelve years. Meghan is Greg's daughter. Loree even had a paternity test done to prove it to him. They were separated and about to divorce when he overdosed. By this time, Sara was pregnant, and we were trying to work our own shit out. She was in treatment, but she loved her drugs more than me, herself, or her baby."

Jennifer pulled away, putting some distance between them. His heart sank at the sad look on her face.

"Here's the thing I can't quite grasp. You say you and Loree are just friends. But even though this was a marriage of inconvenience, I'm your *wife*. And you put her before *me*." She took in a deep breath. "Do you know how that made me feel? I know you say all this tabloid, social media mess is fake news. But it doesn't lessen the pain when you think the man you lov—er, never mind…It hurt my feelings. Deeply."

Did she almost say she loved me? It gave him hope and courage to continue, and he took hold of her hands. "I love *you*. I love you so damn much I can't think. I'm not worthy of your love, and God knows you have no reason to believe me, but I do. I'm thirty god-damned years old, and I've been running since I was seventeen." He pulled her closer, holding her face, searching her eyes.

"I was wrong to put my friendship and business ahead of you. Terribly wrong. And believe me, if I could re-do all of this, I'd fucking go back to the lake house and start over. I'd date you properly, and I'd be totally honest with you. I'd even get down on bended knee and ask you to marry me.

"I'm tired of superficial relationships. I went to California to run away from home. I ran from California to come back home. *To you.* I don't know how this happened, but I can't imagine my life without you. I love you, Jennifer. I'm asking you to please forgive me and let me start over." He hung his head and swallowed. He looked back up at her. "But I'm thirty. You're only nineteen. You have years of living to do. So, I love you enough to let you go, if that's truly what you want."

She stared at him. "I'm almost twenty. You love me?"

He smiled sadly. "Cross my heart and hope to die."

"You already tried that; don't tempt fate." She interlaced her fingers with his. "Despite what you think, thirty isn't old. Besides, Daddy always said I'm an old soul. I think it's part of being smart."

Dylan laughed. "My family has told me repeatedly that I need to grow up and that I'm pretty damn stupid. Maybe we can meet halfway?"

His heart grabbed the sliver of hope her laughter offered.

He pressed further. "Marrying you was the biggest mistake of my life and the best thing I ever did. Jennifer, you saved me. You believed in me when I didn't believe in myself. Hell, you put up with my bullshit and even liked me when I hated myself."

Her eyes filled with tears.

When her lower lip quivered, he leaned forward and kissed her. With a gentle hand, he pushed a curl behind her ear, his finger lingering on her jaw.

"Hear me out, angel. I'm laying this all on the table. I love you with every ounce of my being. You are the music of my soul, my heart, and the love of my life. I am everything with you and nothing without you. I'm sorry I ran to California and my commitment to Loree instead of staying to make things clear to you. That won't happen again. I want more than a partnership. I want to be your everything. Your husband, your lover, and, if we're lucky, someday the father to your children. I want to start over and show you just how damn much I adore and cherish you. Is there at least a little part of you that could possibly love me in return? I'm asking you to give me a chance to say goodnight to the moon with you, every night, for the rest of our lives." He held his breath, praying she would say yes.

Covering her mouth, she gasped. "You remember?"

When he nodded, she threw herself into his arms, hugging his neck. Her tears fell, soaking the front of his shirt. Picking her up, he twirled her around, laughing and kissing her damp face.

"Finally. The stuffed rabbit you threw at me triggered the memory. Then seeing it on your shelf sealed it."

"You really love me?"

"I do. Do you love me?"

"I do." She sighed. "How did we get so messed up? I agree, I wish we could go back in time—to the lake house, before all of this. Maybe if we'd let our relationship progress naturally we'd stand a chance..."

"I'm a savvy businessman, if nothing else. And I think our odds are pretty damn good." He kissed the top of her head.

She nodded and smiled. "I've been an awfully silly girl. I'm sorry I didn't let you explain. And I had no business going through your phone. I'm no better than nosy old Mrs. Baxter."

He chuckled. "You're a lot cuter than that old battle-ax. And I'll never lock you out of my secrets again. Just next time, ask me, okay? No more running. I'm getting too old to catch you." He pinched her nose, and she laughed.

"No more running," she promised.

"Through a series of weird, cosmic, careless actions, I met you when you were a little girl, we ended up married, and then we fell in love, which is all pretty bassackward. So, Mrs. McAthie, I'm proposing a strange solution." He put her back on her feet and smiled, waiting for her reaction.

Jennifer pulled away and looked up at him suspiciously. "What?"

"Let's start over and date." He grinned down at her.

She gave a most unladylike snort. "Date? Haven't we already put the cart before the horse?"

"We've only been out twice. Once you ended up under the influence of a spiked drink and in bed with me. The second time I rather nonchalantly shoved an engagement ring on your finger after being media blitzed by the paparazzi. I think I owe you a courtship so we can get to know one another."

"Courtship? You want to court me now? Why can't we just go to bed?"

He threw his head back, laughing. *God, how I love this woman.*

Dylan loves me! Jennifer gripped his arms, afraid she'd collapse into a puddle of happiness at his feet if she let go. *Dylan remembered the night he found me saying goodnight to the moon…*

"Jennifer? You with me?" His soft voice brought her back to the present, and she looked up at him.

"I was thinking about the moon. I think I've loved you for a very long time," she whispered. "Even longer than I despised you." It seemed strange to be sad about her father and so incredibly happy that Dylan loved her. This emotional pendulum was taking its toll. *Am I dreaming?*

He grinned. "I was saying, starting tomorrow, we're dating. After a few dates, maybe I'll convince you to come away with me. I'm a fast mover."

She giggled. "Better make it a short courtship. I go back to work next week."

"Call in. I know your boss is an ass, but surely you can fake being sick or something."

"No, I can't do that. Dr. McAthie has been good to me."

"I think you could call him Robert."

"I *do* call him Robert, but not at *work*."

"We have a week to figure things out. Actually, we have the rest of our lives. I'll see you tomorrow." He brushed his lips across her wedding band.

"Where are you going?" she asked, still feeling stunned and afraid of losing him again.

"I'm going next door so my older brother can finish ranting and raving about my stupidity and the dangers of alcoholism. My life story will be used as a learning lesson for Mary and Robbie. I hope Cat pops popcorn for the show; it ought to be a doozy."

"You're not staying here?" Blushing, she twisted her wedding band, looking at the floor.

"Not tonight, angel. As cliché as it sounds, I have a raging head-ache." He gave her a self-deprecating smile. "I'm afraid you'd have to get Rob to call in that refill of Viagra, because quite frankly, I'm too damn hung over to be of any use to anyone. I am in desperate need of more sleep." He grinned. "And I have a courtship to plan, maybe a rocket ship to buy." He gave her a tender kiss. "Tomorrow, for dinner. We'll celebrate your birthday."

"You remembered my birthday?" Jennifer gazed into his bloodshot eyes and had to admit he did look bad. "I want to celebrate alone. I don't want cameras. Come here. I'll cook."

"Of course I remembered your birthday. My assistant sent me a text and reminded me. You? Cook?" he teased.

"Careful, or I'll make eggs."

He shook his head and chuckled. "Anything but eggs."

"What kind of cake? I owe you a birthday cake; our wedding cake shouldn't count."

His eyebrows rose. "You knew it was my birthday when you were so mean to me?"

She ran a finger up and down the doorjamb. "The prescription was Robert's idea."

"And tying me up?"

"Mine. Are you saying that's a hard limit?" She peeked up at him and bit her lip to keep from laughing.

"Can I get back to you on that one? Or can we negotiate? Maybe you could wear stockings, heels, and your nurse hat when you do it?" He grinned.

She felt the heat rise in her cheeks but smiled. "I think that could be arranged. My cap's upstairs. Sure you want to sleep next door?" she purred.

"Brat. Positive. Like I said, I'm afraid I'd be useless tonight. Besides, I have plans to make. See you tomorrow night." Dylan blew her a kiss as he left, closing the door behind him.

She looked up when the door opened again.

"But remember, you have a non-disclosure agreement. I'll deny it if it's leaked to the media that I am anything less than a high-performance sex god." With a wink, he ducked back out of the door, and Jennifer collapsed on the stairs, laughing and crying at the same time.

Chapter
Twenty-Nine

Jennifer wrapped a loose curl around her finger as she looked at the dining room table. Everything was perfect. Her mother's china and silver were arranged on a white damask tablecloth, accented with white candles. It was probably an invitation for disaster to use the white linens.

Planning what to cook for an ovo-lacto vegetarian had been harder than she anticipated. She finally decided on spaghetti, salad, and rolls, ruling out garlic bread. Dylan would *not* be going back to Robert and Cathy's tonight if she had anything to do with it. Alone in her bed last night, she'd realized she needed him as much as he needed her. When she thought about her future, she couldn't imagine him not in it. They had a long way to go and issues to sort through, but life was too short not to go after what you want. And she wanted her husband. She wanted love. She wanted a family.

After arranging the blue hydrangeas, she placed the chocolate-dipped strawberries on Dylan's chocolate birthday cake. She smiled. It was rich and decadent: like him. If she played her cards right, she would be his real dessert. She'd even bought new sexy underwear that was, at this minute, crawling up her butt. No doubt sadistic men had invented thongs.

The doorbell rang as she sat on the stairs attempting to buckle her new strappy, high-heeled sandals. *Add stilettos to the list of things invented by sadistic men.* She stood and ran her hands over her fuchsia dress, as nervous as a teen on her first date. Opening the door with one shoe still in her hand, she gazed appreciatively at Dylan in his crisp white shirt and black jeans. His hair was a bit tousled, as if he'd just raked his hand through it. The man was so far beyond beautiful, mere words were inadequate to describe him. He was something to be experienced, in an intimate, personal way. She drank in his appearance. *This god is mine?* Her smile widened to a grin. *This god is mine!*

"You look good enough to eat," she blurted.

His eyebrows lifted over his glasses, and he flashed a wicked, sexy smile. "Sounds like a plan to me."

Stunned, she blocked the doorway as his words sunk in.

"Uh, may I come in?"

"Oh, yes! I'm sorry!" Hobbling in one shoe, she stood to the side and shut the door, feeling incredibly awkward. "Would you like something to drink?"

"Scotch?"

"N-No, I meant a glass of tea or something—I don't have any alcohol. I'm not old enough, and Daddy doesn't drink." She blinked back tears. Her father would never again forbid her to do anything.

Dylan caressed her cheek with his thumb. "I'm teasing. Maybe in a minute." He circled her and gave a low whistle of approval. "You take my breath away, angel."

She nodded, still unable to find her voice. He kissed her forehead and her breathing hitched.

Looking down at her one bare foot, he chuckled. "Is it midnight, Cinderella?"

Jennifer groaned at her awkwardness. Dylan knelt to help her put on her shoe. She ran her hand through his hair. "Are you my prince?"

The warmth of his hand on her foot sent shockwaves straight up her leg. He kissed her ankle. "Nah. I'm the frog, remember?" He struggled to clasp the strap. "These damn things are as tricky as bra hooks."

"Forget it. Nurses don't wear heels," she muttered, kicking off the shoe and unbuckling the other. She cast a shyly seductive look toward her husband. "I don't want to end up in the ER with a broken ankle. I have better plans for this evening."

Dylan laughed and smacked her bottom. "I'm good with that."

After the dinner dishes were cleared, Jennifer brought in the birthday cake with two lit candles. Together, they blew them out, and he kissed her, tasting chocolate.

"What did you wish for? And you're busted, I taste fudge icing," Dylan whispered, nipping her lower lip.

"You." She smiled against his lips. "I confess. I couldn't help it, I ran a finger along the edge of the plate when I was in the kitchen."

He laughed. "Sneaky. You stole my wish. I wished for *you*. Dinner was delicious." He popped a chocolate-covered strawberry in his mouth instead of his customary after-dinner cigarette. Jen leaned over and cut the cake, exposing a tantalizing amount of cleavage. He shifted to ease the discomfort in his jeans. *Slow down, hoss.* He wanted her right now on the dining room table, covered in chocolate icing.

Jennifer licked icing off her index finger. The candlelight brought out the beauty of her skin, and desire filled her expressive eyes. Her lips curved. It was the mysterious smile of a woman fully aware of her goddess-like power. With difficulty, he managed to swallow the last bite of strawberry and shifted yet again.

"Open your present, Jen." He stopped fantasizing about licking chocolate icing off her breasts and shoved the package toward her.

Jennifer carefully examined the gift, shaking it before untying the ribbon. Dylan drummed his fingers on the table as she took a fingernail and undid the tape with slow precision. Rolling his eyes, he swore it would be her next birthday before she ever unwrapped the gift.

"Hurry up, woman!"

Jennifer laughed. "I like to take my time and savor the anticipation." Her eyes widened, and she gasped in delight when she opened the box to see a new phone, a piece of paper, another wrapped present, and a Tiffany's jewelry box.

Jennifer examined the piece of paper first. It was an appointment for Lasik eye surgery. She gasped. "No more glasses?" She threw herself in Dylan's lap and gave him a kiss and a hug before turning her attention to the new phone, glancing through the playlists he'd loaded.

"I'll add the ones from your old phone, too. And you can password protect it," he teased. Wrapping his arms around her waist, he peered over her shoulder. The feel of her warm body, the smell of her skin, and the sound of her voice as she *oohed* and *ahhed* over the different songs made him feel happy, complete. He'd uploaded the entire Crucified, Dead and Buried catalog. One playlist called "Wedding" contained the music from their ceremony and reception. She scrolled to the playlist he'd titled "Dylan" and giggled at some of the songs: "Fooled Around and Fell in Love" by Elvin Bishop, "All Tied Up" by Robin Thicke, and "Do You Wanna Dance" by The Beach Boys.

"I love the phone. Thank you," she exclaimed, kissing his cheek.

His arousal became downright painful when she wiggled against him in excitement.

She opened the sloppily wrapped present next and gasped at the first-edition copy of *Goodnight Moon*.

"This was my favorite book growing up. My parents used to read this to me."

She tucked her head under his chin and wept into his chest. He held her, acknowledging her grief. He wished he could take her pain away, but that was something she'd have to work out on her own, over time. All he could do was be here. And be here, he would. He'd never leave her again.

She wiped her tears and smiled. "You're an incredibly thoughtful man. Thank you. This book has special meaning to me."

Foreheads touching, he kissed her tenderly. "Someday we'll read it to our children."

"Devilish blond-haired, blue-eyed little boys?"

"I was thinking more like dark-haired, angelic girls."

"You do realize they grow up and fall in love with devilish boys, don't you?" she teased.

He chuckled. "Remind me to donate to a nunnery." He handed her the last present.

Biting her lip, she carefully undid the white bow on the aqua box.

"Tiffany's," she whispered, lifting the lid reverently.

He chuckled and mentally thanked Cat for the tip.

Jennifer pulled out the dainty chain with a moon charm, her eyes sparkling as she laughed. "Perfect!"

"Yes, you are." He held her in his lap.

"Silly, I meant the book and necklace. I l-love you so much," she admitted shyly. "I think part of me always has."

"Geez, I'm not gonna say the same. That would put me in the creep department. My reputation isn't that great to begin with."

They laughed. She removed his glasses and placed them on the table. He closed his eyes and she pressed soft butterfly kisses on his eyelids. She smelled of citrus and sweetness. The unique scent was like a siren song, enticing and dangerous, and happiness infused his soul in the perfection of this moment.

"Would you like your present now?" she asked softly, running her thumb across his lower lip.

"I'm holding it."

"No, a real present, silly."

"You got me a present?" He couldn't remember the last time he'd been this excited over the prospect of a birthday gift. The smile on her face lifted his heart as she hopped off his lap. She returned with a neatly wrapped present.

She sat watching him as he tore into the gift. He felt like a five-year-old on Christmas morning. When he pulled out the blue-and-silver-striped silk tie with directions on how to tie different naval knots pinned to it, he burst out laughing. "Uh, is this for me or you?"

"I guess for whoever can tie a knot fastest. But let me remind you, I've spent lots of time with Tyrone lately." She gave him a naughty grin, full of wicked promise.

Puzzled, he looked at the small jewelry box and opened it. Putting his glasses back on, he read aloud the inscription on the small, simple gold medal. "*I shall love mine yet; and take him with me: he's in my soul. Emily Brontë.*" On the back of the medal, their intertwined initials were engraved, along with their wedding date. Dylan didn't speak for a moment, embarrassed that her gift had moved him this much.

He swallowed three times and finally asked in a quiet voice, "Will you put it on the chain for me?"

"I know Cathy and Heathcliff didn't have a traditional happy ending, but their love was so powerful it defied the grave. I just wanted to do a little something special. One of my happiest memories is reading that book to you." She stood behind him and unclasped his St. Jude medal. "Dylan, you're *not* a lost cause. I know this medal is special to you…" Her voice trailed off.

"Replace it with my new one, please." He took the St. Jude medal and placed it on his key ring as she fastened his new gift around his neck.

"Do you like it?" she asked with a slight hitch in her voice as she stood behind him.

"No. I love it. I love you so damn much."

"I have one more present." Her voice was husky as she nibbled on his ear.

"Yeah?" His voice cracked as her lips moved down his neck, making his skin tingle with need.

"Me."

"You're making this hard…"

"That's the point." She waggled her brows.

"I thought we were going to take things slow." He pulled her into his lap, pushing a loose curl behind her ear. His eyes locked with hers.

"Slow, fast—I don't care, as long as you take me," she whispered with a smile against his lips.

"Here or upstairs?" he whispered. He pulled one strap of her dress down her shoulder with his teeth as he stood, holding her.

"Both?"

"Excellent." With great care, he laid her back on the dining room table, noting her flushed skin and hard nipples under her fuchsia dress. Her hair fanned out on the table, and she chewed on her lower lip in anticipation. Although she was stunning by candlelight, he leaned forward and blew out the tiny flames. He was going to worship at the altar of his wife tonight, and he didn't relish a repeat of his altar boy experience.

"Come with me to the moon, Jennifer."

"I'll go anywhere with you. You're mine."

"Always."

The End

The series will continue with David Patterson's story in
The Redemption of Emma Devine

Acknowledgments

This book has been a labor of love, but without the encouragement of Jill Odom, Carrie M. and Vickie W., it would have remained stuffed under the bed in a cardboard box. Thank you for believing in me.

Jessica Royer Ocken, you took my dream and helped me make it a reality. I love working with you and the fact you believe in me has kept me going. I'm still a little star-struck that you took me on! You are quite simply, the best.

Shannon Lumetta, your graphic skills are amazing. Thank you!! This cover rocks it!

Coreen Montagna you make all my books as beautiful on the inside as they are on the outside. I couldn't do it without you.

To my family who doesn't see me for days on end when I'm in the writing cave, thank you for putting up with me and my craziness. Especially my husband, who never knows if I'm talking about "real" people or "make believe" people, but has learned to smile and say, "Yes, dear."

To my Cain Raisers. You are my tribe, my chosen book family and your love and support keep me going. Your reviews, shares and daily "atta girls" never fail to put a smile on my face. I write for you.

And to those core, supportive authors, my O sis and SLOBS. Chin up. We've got this!

To the bloggers who took a chance on an unknown author and have supported me, I can't thank you enough for your honest reviews. You inspire me to write and I've learned from all of you.

About the Author

During the day, Nancee works as a counselor/nurse in the field of addiction to support her coffee and reading habit. Nights are spent writing paranormal and contemporary romances with a serrated edge. Authors are her rock stars, and she's been known to stalk a few for an autograph, but not in a scary, Stephen King way. Her husband swears her To-Be-Read list on her e-reader qualifies her as a certifiable book hoarder. Always looking to try something new, she dreams of being an extra in a Bollywood film, or a tattoo artist. (Her lack of rhythm and artistic ability may put a damper on both of these dreams.)

Website: nanceecain.com
Blog: nanceecain.com/blog
Goodreads: goodreads.com/Nancee_Cain
Facebook: facebook.com/NanceeCainAuthor
Reader's Group (Cain Raisers): facebook.com/groups/Cain.Raisers
Twitter: twitter.com/Nancee_Cain
Pinterest: pinterest.com/nanceecain
Instagram: instagram.com/nanceecain
BookBub: bookbub.com/authors/nancee-cain
Newsletter: eepurl.com/bhFMtX
YouTube Channel: bit.ly/2xsU6Ad
Spotify Playlists: open.spotify.com/user/12184539074

Books by Nancee Cain:

Paranormal Romance (Angels)
Saving Evangeline
Tempting Jo
Loving Lili (novella)

Contemporary Romance (Pine Bluff Novels)
The Resurrection of Dylan McAthie
The Redemption of Emma Devine
The Rehabilitation of Angel Sinclair
The Redirection of Damien Sinclair
The Reinvention of Jinx Howell
The Reintroduction of Sammie Morgan
The Realization of Grayson Deschanelle

Contemporary Romances

pine▮bluff

Although each of the titles in this series can be read as standalone stories, this is the preferred reading order:

The Resurrection of Dylan McAthie
A Pine Bluff Novel

Maybe You Can Go Home Again

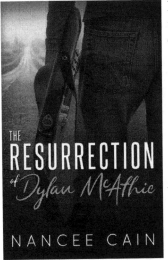

Hounded by paparazzi, Dylan McAthie—the former lead guitarist for Crucified, Dead and Buried—craves quiet anonymity to regroup and sort out his life. An accident leaves him dependent on the family he once ran from, with no choice but to return to the small town of Pine Bluff, Alabama.

Hired by Dylan's estranged brother, private-duty nurse Jennifer Adams remembers the charming boy Dylan was before fame and misfortune. And she notices he's developed a knack for blaming everyone else for his problems, rather than bothering with introspection. She's not having it.

Despite their clashes, as her patient heals, the chemistry between them grows undeniable—until scandal finds Dylan again, threatening to destroy the progress he's made and the couple's growing respect and affection. Can Dylan fix what fame has so easily broken? Or will his public resurrection mean the death of any relationship with Jennifer?

The Redemption of Emma Devine
A Pine Bluff Novel

A Little Shake-Up in Life Can Be Devine

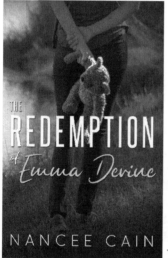

Emma Devine is on the run and fighting to survive. Her tortured past makes trust difficult, especially where men are concerned. But she has no choice other than accepting the help of the man who catches her shoplifting on Christmas Eve.

When not stopping shoplifters, David Patterson leads a quiet life in Pine Bluff, Alabama, working as a high school teacher. His random act of Christmas kindness brings unexpected joy to his life, as he finds himself drawn to the mysterious Emma. When she leaves, his world is turned upside down, and his dreams are changed forever.

Four years later, Emma returns in search of long-overdue redemption. But despite an undeniable attraction between the two, trust is an even greater issue now—for both of them. Can they find their way to a place of understanding? Or have yesterday's mistakes destroyed their chance for a future together?

The Rehabilitation of Angel Sinclair
A Pine Bluff Novel

Love — the Hardest Addiction to Kick

Angel Sinclair arrives in Pine Bluff, Alabama, determined to make amends for his past and move on. But that changes after a chance encounter with a beautiful inn owner, and instead he finds himself pursuing two things that haven't been in his life for years: love and trust.

Still reeling from a bitter divorce, Maggie Robertson wants to focus on making her business a success. Getting involved with anyone in this gossipy little town is the farthest thing from her mind...until she finds herself tempted by a younger man.

Neither Angel nor Maggie can ignore the sizzling heat between them. But Angel's secretive nature soon fills Maggie with doubts about the man she's allowed into her heart.

Was she wrong to believe love could conquer all? Is their age difference an obstacle they can't overcome?

The Redirection of Damien Sinclair
A Pine Bluff Novel

Sometimes You Get What You Need

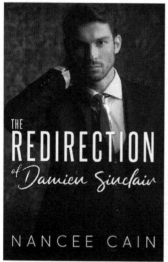

Acclaimed divorce attorney Damien Sinclair has witnessed more than his share of love's ugly aftermath. He keeps things black and white, preventing anyone from getting too close. But his illusion of control fades when an attempt on his life leaves him struggling with PTSD.

Enter Damien's childhood friend, the free-spirited Harley Taylor. Shrugging off the awkwardness of their teenaged fling and her broken heart, she appoints herself his caregiver. The man needs to learn not to take himself so seriously, and she's hellbent on snapping him out of his brooding funk.

After a decade apart, Harley and Damien find their attraction is stronger than ever. Could Harley's sunny disposition be the bright spot Damien needs in his life? Or will their differences overshadow any hopes of a future together?

The Reinvention of Jinx Howell
A Pine Bluff Novel

Can Love Unmask Their True Selves?

Hiding behind her wigs and heavy makeup, Jinx Howell masks her insecurities—which even she doesn't understand—with bravado, slashing through life with reckless abandon. Lonely, but unwilling to get close to anyone, she finds the ideal solution: a hook-up with the campus's most notorious heartbreaker.

In similar fashion, Mark "Two-Time" MacGregor protects his heart and keeps himself unencumbered through a string of one-night stands. A chance meeting with the edgy Jinx in a dark alley seems like destiny. She claims to want sex with no ties, making her perfect. *Like attracts like.* But this girl with a switchblade has more hang-ups than he does, which is a hell of a lot.

When tragedy strikes, Mark's hit-and-run lifestyle takes a backseat to his need to protect the broken girl whose secrets are unraveling. Along the way, both of them will find their truths unmasked. Can they forge a real relationship, or will they give up on their romance as jinxed?

The Reintroduction of Sammie Morgan
A Pine Bluff Novel

Can Life Get Any Crazier?

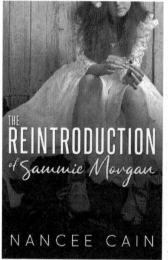

Still reeling from the tragic deaths of his wife and daughter, Matt Tyler trudges through life, caring for his young son, managing his cantankerous father, and working as much as he can. Despite his best efforts, bills are piling up and his vindictive in-laws seem determined to take Luke away from him.

Things change when he stumbles upon Sammie Morgan—with a car that won't run and her mother's ashes in the backseat. Best friends growing up, Matt and Sammie have spent years apart following very different paths. Now they've both run out of options. Without a dime in her pocket, Sammie has nowhere to go. And Matt lacks the stable home life he needs to fight his former in-laws.

Their hasty solution? A marriage of convenience.

But how convenient will this reintroduction be if it means Matt and Sammie have to relive the most painful parts of their past?

The Realization of Grayson Deschanelle
A Pine Bluff Novel

Sex, No Strings Attached

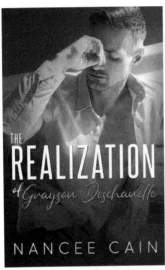

Despite a high-profile clientele, fashion photographer Grayson Deschanelle prefers being behind the lens, away from public scrutiny. After his movie star girlfriend dumps him, he flees to his stepbrother's remote cabin to hide from the paparazzi.

Caught by surprise, Grayson finds Lissy much different than the girl he's known for years. She's no longer a child — though her teenaged crush is still very much intact. Snowed in with her, he tries to fight his growing attraction. But being with Lissy brings what his life is lacking into sharp focus.

The ice melts, and they return home. When their families discover their secret, Grayson must decide what kind of life he truly wants — and whether he'll fight to keep Lissy by his side.

Paranormal Angel Romances

Although each of the titles in this series can be read as standalone stories, this is the preferred reading order:

Saving Evangeline

Tempting Jo

Loving Lili (novella)

Saving Evangeline

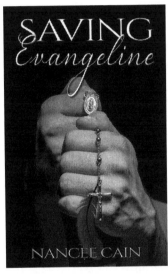

Evangeline is the town pariah. Everyone knows she's crazy and was responsible for the death of her last boyfriend. Even her mother left her and moved cross-country. Lonely and desperate, Evie decides to end her life.

Rogue angel Remiel longs to return to Earth, but there's just one problem. He tends to invite trouble and hasn't been allowed back since Woodstock. The Boss sends him to save Evangeline, but there's a catch: he can't reveal his angelic nature, and he must complete the task as *Father* Remiel Blackson.

Forced together on a cross-country trip, a forbidden romance ignites and love unfolds. A host of heavenly messengers tries to intervene, but Remiel and Evangeline are headed on a collision course to disaster. Will his love save her, or will they both be lost forever?

Tempting Jo

Forbidden love is hell…

Confident and quirky, Jo Sanford thinks her boss is God's gift to women — and she couldn't be further from the truth. Devilishly handsome, Luc DeVille will stop at nothing to lure his administrative assistant right into his arms — and bed.

Over Rafe Goodman's dead body…

Rafe, Jo's best friend, refuses to sit by and watch as Luc tries to win the heart of the woman he's always protected. After all, Rafe is her guardian angel. Suddenly, Jo's caught in the middle of a battle between good and evil. But the closer she gets to the fire, the hotter it burns. Now, Jo's going to learn that when love battles lust, Heaven and Hell collide.

Loving Lili (novella)

Their lovemaking is hot and dirty. Their break ups are nasty and epic.

Tired of taking the blame for every wicked thing that happens on Earth, fallen angel Luc DeVille decides to write a tell-all-book exposing The Boss.

Sharing a long and passionate history, Luc is shocked when Lili Nix arrives to interview for the job as editor. Immediately the verbal sparring begins, but the sexual chemistry remains combustible. Fascinated by this heavenly creature, Luc changes his game plan. After all, she's the only angel who has ever held his attention and understood his intentions.

Being in this world, but not of this world, is a lonely business. Can two lost angels connect and make it last this time?